254

STANLEY PIGGOTT
BOX 295, R. 1
BENTON HARBOR, MICH.

THOSE OTHER PEOPLE

The French Market sounded like a flock of parrots

THOSE
OTHER
PEOPLE

by
Mary King O'Donnell

Drawings by F. Strobel

HOUGHTON MIFFLIN COMPANY, BOSTON · 1946

The characters in this book are
fictitious; any resemblance to real
persons is wholly accidental and
unintentional.

For E. P. O'Donnell

THOSE OTHER PEOPLE

1

---

4 a.m. — 9 a.m.

IT WAS EARLY MORNING. A small wind off the river wandered through the narrow French Quarter streets and along the alleyways between the houses. Banana leaves rustled; a curtain moved; a shirtsleeve twitched on a clothesline. Along St. Philip Street a few shutters creaked on worn hinges—shutters closed through the day to keep out the burning heat of New Orleans pavements in June, but set open at night to welcome any wind. Waked by a creaking shutter, old Mrs. Peralta felt the wind. She sighed gratefully, turned her wet pillow, patted the lottery tickets that lay under it, said a prayer for good luck on the lottery today, and fell asleep again.

IN THE ADJOINING ROOM, Leah Webster snapped off her electric fan. Through the open French doors of her bedroom she saw a patch of star-filled sky above the low peak of the Tarantinos' roof next door. She could not see the clock on the dresser, but the stars sagged with the mellow ripeness of early morning. The sound of a creaking shutter came to her thinned through unimaginable distance. It came, she thought, from the stars that slanted over the Tarantinos' roof—a plaintive whining of heavenly machinery in labor to produce another day.

Leah was perhaps too sensible of her cosmic unimportance. For forty years she had been waiting for something to happen to her, and nothing important had happened. Every morning she woke wondering if today she would accomplish anything worthy of the vast mechanics of returning daylight, and was afraid she wouldn't, and so went to sleep again. But not this morning. The gesture of turning off the fan had been automatic, and up until now she had been half asleep. Suddenly, as the memory of forty years of purposeless awakenings threatened to engulf her, she knew that she was through with waiting for things to happen to her; that she could not wait for Joe to come back. Today, she meant to look for him. At this revelation of a purpose of which she had been unaware until an instant ago, her heart beat hard and fast.

Over by the docks a switch engine coupled onto a string of freight cars. The crash traveled from car to car down the line.

Two courtyards away, a cat paused in his stealthy glide toward a wall, and looked up as the wind shifted the banana leaves over his head. A little farther on, he leaped into the air as a stronger current whirled the blades of a small tin windmill fixed to the low branch of an oleander tree. Notched ears flattened, the cat streaked for a hole in the wall. A soft bump, a scraping sound unheard in the sleepy mumbling and stirring of the garden behind him, and he was through the hole and had emerged into another courtyard.

A dog growled. Disdainfully, for the dog was old and incapable of speed, the cat continued on his way and passed through another hole into another courtyard. This courtyard—Leah's—was bare except for a dusty fig tree in one corner. The cat sat down and scraped the brickdust from his flanks with a quick careful tongue.

Leah sat up in bed. Through the wall, in the other half of the double house where Maudie, her young sister, slept with her husband, Victor Peralta, she thought she heard love-making. And now that she was wide awake, she heard, in the next room, Victor's mother snoring in the way old women snore who try so earnestly all day long not to make a nuisance of themselves they carry the thought with them even into sleep.

Another crash, less violent than the first, traveled the length of the freight train. The wheels ground on the rails and began to move forward. The bell clanged; the engine panted; the whistle blew. The wheels turned faster. The train rolled out of hearing.

Leah lay down again. From far away, on Royal Street, came the muted tapping of a night watchman's stick against a mellow wall. The sound changed, doubled, and became rhythmic. It was coming closer. It was made by a horse's iron-shod hoofs on the hard street. Since that summer night a year ago, when the blind woman had spoken to her on the street, Leah had suspected that wherever other people might find love or compassion or kindness, she herself would never discover it anywhere but on the street. And now there was nowhere to look for Joe but on the streets, for she did not know where he was staying, or even know the name of his ship, or the line he shipped for. She could not even be sure that he was still in the city. Maybe she was too late. Maybe Joe's ship had left the dock while she was still asleep, and was even now pointed down the river to the Gulf, while she lay in her bed but a few blocks away.

She turned on her side and listened intently. She did not know what she expected to hear: a blast from a tugboat, a throbbing propeller? But this time she heard nothing at all but a mouse rustling the loose papers in the fireplace. Last night she had tossed an apple core behind the screen.

She waited, while urgency to be up and searching, and anger at what her brother, Merlin, had already said about her picking up a seaman in a bar, and astonished at her own boldness, and then the anger and urgency again, pinned her uncomfortably to the hot sheet.

The brickdust cleaned from his flanks, the cat in Leah's courtyard stood up and called. And waited. And called again.

Lonely, defiant, insolent—Leah heard the voice as an immediate and wordless challenge. Without waiting to think any longer, she got out of bed, went into the bathroom, and turned on the light.

The bright square of the window flashed on the courtyard wall. Gray cat, green fig tree, snatched from secrecy and darkness, were caught and framed in yellow light. The cat stood still; his eyes gleamed. Across the bright square of the window reached a hand and bare forearm. The cat crouched closer to the tree. His body bunched and quivered. He leaped away. The courtyard was empty again.

Closing the door of the medicine cabinet which Maudie had left open the night before, Leah looked at herself in the mirror and found that she was smiling. The smile was not becoming. She straightened her mouth, but the eyes in the mirror were still ironic as she thought:

'If that cat hadn't called in the courtyard, you'd still be in bed, and might have stayed there all day.'

This was true. Early rising was not a habit of Leah's. But the cat was a frequent visitor to her courtyard; and, from experience, she knew that she would not have been allowed to return to sleep, where she might have found Joe with no effort and no embarrassment; that ultimately, she would have been forced to get up anyhow, to chase the cat away. Getting up was the difficult, the decisive action. Once on her feet, Leah knew what she had to do.

Decisive action was no more a habit of Leah's than early rising. Perhaps the most decisive act of her life, until this morning, had been the returning of that empty beer bottle which had fallen off Joe's table, and the words with which she had returned it—shameless words. Later, she knew she need not have been so explicit.

'Will you buy me a drink?'

'Sit down, honey. What'll you have?'

Somebody to forgive my peculiarities; somebody to love me
when they laugh at me; somebody like you, she thought. 'A
beer,' she said.

But tonic as the single act had been, it had not been enough
to break the habit of years of equivocation—hence Leah's indecision about getting up. Something had been needed to prod her,
and the lonely voice in the courtyard had served this purpose as
well as any.

As Leah pulled her nightgown over her head, and washed in
cool water from the basin, she thought wryly that because a cat
had called in her courtyard her life might be changed. A life that
could be changed by such a trivial happening seemed of little consequence to her; and indeed, she felt very thin and small and of
no consequence to anybody as she paused, both hands submerged
and groping for the soap, to stare at a crack in the plaster and
comfort herself with the thought that Robert Bruce's life had
been changed by a spider; and to conclude that what had been
the matter with her all along, no doubt, was that she had expected
so much of life she had been afraid.

But Joe was all she wanted now, and if he were still in the city
she meant to find him. If he were not in the city—but she refused
to think of this.

She dressed hurriedly, not wanting to look at herself again in
the mirror even to put on powder and lipstick; managing this
part of her toilet in a way she had long ago learned of seeing and
not seeing at the same time a blur of black and white and red
which was her face. A sense of adventure gripped her. For the
first time in her life, she was leaving in secrecy the place where
she had slept. Nobody knew that she was leaving; nobody knew
where she was going, or why. No apologies or explanations were
necessary. It was wonderful. As she slid the bolt on the alley door,
she laughed to herself. She felt as free and stealthy as a cat. But

she was not at all like a cat compared with Maudie, she reassured herself. Lazy, selfish, sunning her legs all summer in the court-yard—Maudie was a real cat. But Victor wasn't aware of it. Victor Peralta, on the WPA Writers' Project, seemed aware of little except legend.

With her hand on the iron thumb-latch, Leah looked behind her down the alley—a last look at the mossy bricks, red patched with green in the light from the street lamp. This place had been her home for eight years, and she wanted to remember it. She felt as if she were going on a long, dangerous journey today, and might never come back. As she looked, the alley lengthened and twisted into a labyrinth of all the back ways of her own mind, and she stood still, listening.

But nothing was following her. The fern that trembled on the wall had probably been brushed by her own shoulder in passing, or by the wind. She stepped out on the sidewalk, and closed the door.

In her blue linen suit, bareheaded, carrying her hat in her hand, she passed the Tarantinos' house. And now she was passing her brother's house with its fresh white walls and clean, green shutters—the only well-kept house on the block. Here, she felt a need to walk softly, but her foot had already struck the tin lid of the garbage can. It made a loud grating noise on the sidewalk, and she quickened her steps.

At this hour of the morning, the old Quarter was as silent as a swamp, and as rich with hidden life. Under the steep slope of the roofs, behind the brick walls of the houses set flush with the side-walk, lay hot, sprawled sleepers who would soon wake up and stretch, slide into their clothes, and emerge into the sunlight. In an hour or so, St. Philip Street would be noisy with scampering children and all the busy traffic of the day; but now it was empty of any human shape except her own.

St. Philip Street was outside the popular lanes of tourist traffic; and its people, with the exception of Leah, kept respectable

'At this hour of the morning, the old Quarter was
as silent as a swamp'

hours. The French Market Coffee Stand on Decatur Street, however, stayed open all night; and it was toward this favorite place of rendezvous that Leah was heading. Yesterday morning, at just about this time, Joe had taken her to the French Market for coffee and doughnuts. If he were still in the city, she might find him there.

She crossed Bourbon and Royal Streets. On two houses in two blocks, she saw Merlin Webster's black-and-white business signs: *House for Sale* . . . *Apartment for Rent* . . . Once, when Merlin had been telling her of some miserable little house he had picked up at a bargain and sold at a profit, she had surprised both of them by saying:

'I doubt if the Lord intended the world to be a real estate business. I don't want to buy the world or sell it, either. I just want to live in it.'

Merlin had been more than surprised; he had been shocked and hurt. He had been angry, too. 'Where d'you think I get the money I've been supporting you with?' he had demanded. 'If you don't like the way I earn my money, earn some of your own!'

Well, she was earning her own money again, though you got little enough as cashier in a neighborhood movie, and such a job might be said to have social disadvantages. Merlin's wife had hardly spoken to her since.

The sky was turning gray. The stars were gone. Doors and windows gaped wide to the pale, cool morning. High and low and various-shaped against the sky, colored like time, and bound together by their balconies, the old houses inhaled and exhaled quietly. A smell of human sleep flowed from them; a smell of dusty rugs and wicker furniture and ash trays. From the gutters rose a smell of uncollected garbage . . . a smell of urine in a shop doorway . . . and here and there, the swift sweet scent of night-blooming jasmine leaped over a courtyard wall.

'Clean out the sewers,' Joe had said to his companion, just before his lively elbow had swept the empty beer bottle to the floor.

'Clean out the world's sewers, and then talk to me about people's souls. I doubt if we have to talk so much about them then. Clean out the sewers, and the souls will take care of themselves. No worry, no bother—am I right? My God, it isn't healthy!'

But she was not the only early riser, Leah saw. Ahead of her a door opened, and a bar of light shot across the sidewalk. Through it a man backed, buttoning his shirt.

'I'm going!' he shouted. 'I'm going now! Don't try to stop me!'

'Who's tryin to stop you?' A woman rushed through the door barefooted, in her nightgown. She reached for the man. He warded her off. A small boy danced around them in pajamas.

The group was too absorbed to notice Leah. As she passed, she glimpsed two more children sitting up in bed. One was crying. The other had its finger in its mouth.

'Because it won't do no good!' shouted the man. 'I'm fed up! I'm through. I've had enough. This time, I'm going. Don't try to stop me!'

'Who's tryin to stop you?'

'You are!'

'Oh no, I'm not!'

'Oh yes, you are!'

'All right!' shouted the woman. 'All right! But lissen to this, Thomas Ferrabee, and what I'm sayin now, I'm sayin before God an your children as witness. If you go, don't come back. If you go, don't never come back. Don't dare!'

'Gimme my hat.'

'Give you nothin!'

'Rudy, run get papa's hat for him . . .'

In the next block, a man passed Leah walking swiftly, swearing under his breath. He was in his shirtsleeves. He wore a hat crammed over his ears. He must be Thomas Ferrabee, she thought, as he turned a corner. Men like Thomas Ferrabee were always appearing and disappearing around the corners of the world.

She crossed Decatur Street and opened the door of the Coffee Shop. Her eyes, circling the mirrored room, picked up a tipsy couple in evening clothes who were shaking the powdered sugar, meant for the doughnuts, in each other's hair; a tourist asking in an injured voice if he couldn't have real, pure coffee instead of this chicory substitute; a bored policeman; an Italian laborer frowning at a comic book; two pimpled boys in striped T-shirts; and her own strange face. Her hand went to her face. She had forgotten her glasses. Joe was not here.

Near the door, a table was vacant. Leah sat down. The waiter came with coffee stains on his white apron, and bloodshot, sleepy eyes. Leah was a frequent visitor to the Coffee Shop; she knew the waiters by sight, and they knew her. Perhaps they also knew Joe.

'Do you remember the man who was with me yesterday morning?' Leah said.

'Nah, Miss.' The waiter shook his head. 'So many comin an goin.'

'I thought you might know him.'

'What's his name, eh? What's he look like?'

'Joe,' she said, and paused. She did not know his last name. How could she describe him? . . . A man who can level this city to its sewer pipes, and put it together again in five minutes much better than you've done in two hundred years? But the waiter might think she exaggerated. . . . A grown man who gets so excited about living, he stutters? But that sounded silly. . . . A very ugly, a very gentle, a very funny man? It was impossible to describe him.

The waiter yawned and wiped the table with a corner of his apron. 'Yessum?' he prompted.

'A seaman,' Leah said. 'A middle-aged man. He has red hair. He was probably wearing dungarees. Has he been by here this morning?'

'Nome,' said the waiter.

'Coffee and doughnuts,' Leah said.

As she stirred the hot cup of chicory coffee, she wondered where next to look.

WHEN LEAH'S FOOT struck the lid of the garbage can before his house, Merlin Webster had sat up in bed abruptly, pulling the sheet off his wife, Marie.

'It's early yet,' she said. She rearranged the sheet, and cleared her throat a time or two. 'Lie down,' she said. 'It's early yet.'

Braced on his hands, Merlin continued to look questioningly at the solid bulk of wardrobe and dresser black against the pale plaster walls, as if he were not quite sure where he found himself. The ceiling seemed uncomfortably close.

'What are you listening for?' Marie said. 'Did you hear something?'

'No,' said Merlin. He had the mirror lined up now, a watery pool bisected by the thin spindle of the fourposter bed. In the dim light, his eyes followed the post upward until they arrived at the canopy over his head. Marie had put up the canopy only a few days before; he had not yet grown used to it. 'No,' he said, rubbing the back of his head, 'I didn't hear anything.' Above the canopy was the high, beamed ceiling. He breathed more freely. 'I was dreaming about Leah,' he said. Above the ceiling was the spacious attic, and above that, the sky. Merlin lay down again. 'Do we have to sleep under this tester?' he said. 'I felt like I was smothering.'

Leah again, Marie thought. Merlin was always worrying about Leah. If Leah were worth worrying about, it would be a different matter. Marie looked up at the canopy. 'You'll get used to it,' she said. 'It's really much more hygienic. It keeps the dust from these old ceilings from falling on the bed.' She thought he had dropped asleep again, but presently he spoke.

'I wonder what's got into Leah,' he said. 'It isn't like her to do such a thing.'

'Stop worrying about Leah. If she wants to spend her Saturday nights with strange men, I don't see what you can do about it. She isn't a young girl. You've already done everything for her a brother could be expected to do.'

'I can't help but feel I've failed her, somehow.'

'Nonsense!'

'I should have reasoned with her more. I shouldn't have lost my temper.'

'Leah's so perverse. If you hadn't pushed her, she'd probably have married Preston Dillon. By this time you should have found out that the only way to make Leah do something is to insist on exactly the opposite. She's so perverse.'

They had been over all this the night before. They had gone to sleep talking about it: How Maudie and Victor had dropped into the St. Regis after a movie and seen Leah sitting alone at the bar; and how, before they could speak to her, before she was even aware of their presence, Maudie said, they had seen her approach this man, who was obviously a stranger, and speak to him; how the man had bought her a drink; and the two had left the St. Regis together; and Leah had not come home that night. They had reviewed Merlin's talk with Leah on Sunday; and now, Monday morning, they were back on the same subject.

At first they spoke hesitantly, each breaking a long silence which followed the other's words. But both voices were loud and worried in the quiet house. Although the two lay side by side and a whisper would have carried between them, for years they had shouted at each other on first waking in the morning. As two strayed members of a picnic party grope toward each other through underbrush, over roots, past vines, around tree-trunks, guided by sound of voice alone until they meet on the same path, so husband and wife stumbled toward each other from the distances of sleep. Once met, they usually disagreed.

'I told her she must have been drunk to do such a thing,' Merlin said.

'You should have ignored the whole matter.'

'And when I said that such hurry was bad taste, to say the least, she said the strangest thing. She said, "I've been hurrying all my life, and now there isn't time to hurry." . . . What did she mean?'

'Leah is so vague. Always making something complex out of something simple. Always trying to explain what she means, when it's clear she can't mean anything at all. She ought to see a psychiatrist. She's really quite pathetic.'

'But why . . . ?'

'Oh, nonsense . . . !'

THE MORNING DUET of her parents' voices was familiar to Georgiana Webster, who slept directly above them in the airy attic bedroom. Every morning for as long as she could remember, the sound had waked her. Usually, she fell asleep again until breakfast; but this morning she was not sleepy. Daylight was growing in the room. School was out. The long summer vacation stretched ahead. Georgie lay still and listened to the voices, seeking a clue to the day, to the summer; a sign she could read; a path she could walk. But although she could hear the voices rising and falling, questioning, answering each other, she could distinguish only a word now and then—nothing that made any sense. Georgie, at eight, was often puzzled.

The first few days after school let out, she always felt this way. In a world grown suddenly so large and beautiful—so full of things to see, things to do; so full of hours in which to see and do them—she was lost, and could do nothing at all but tread on her mother's heels, a tremulous dogged shadow, persistent with questions.

'Mama, are we going to Florida again this summer?'

'Wait and see what daddy says.'

'If we go, can Lucille go with us?'

'We'll see. But Lucille will have to mind me better than she did last summer.'

'If Lucille can't go, I think I'd rather stay here.'

'You'll go where mama and daddy go. And that's settled.'

'Mama, can I take dancing lessons? Miss Hiss says my co-ordination is bad, and I ought to take dancing this summer.'

'We'll see about it.'

Georgie Webster was not pretty. She was overgrown and awkward. Her feet were big, her eyes slanted, her nose turned up, and her lips were thin. Her only beauty was her hair, long and thick and yellow, which she wore in two heavy braids down her back. She was a sober child, a responsible one, good in all her lessons, and very gentle with younger children. She had a touching dignity.

Now, flushed with sleep and sunburn, she lay on her back and wondered about many things. It was daylight now; it was a quarter of six o'clock, for the bell began to ring—the St. Louis Cathedral bell, tolling for early Mass.

Georgie counted the strokes of the bell, and lost count. Through her open attic window she heard shutters close, a front door slam, and footsteps pass along the sidewalk. Old Mrs. Peralta was going to church. Presently, she heard other footsteps, and faintly, in the distance, other bells. Church bells all over the city and across the river in Algiers were ringing Catholic people out of bed to come to church and pray.

'I wonder who rings the bells?' she thought.

How beautiful it must be to ring a big bell like the St. Louis Cathedral bell in the morning, and bring all the people to church. Catholic churches were prettier than Baptist churches. Once, she and her friend, Lucille Budd, had gone with Lizzie Cansino to St. Peter and Paul's; but her mother had told her not to go again.

Baptists went to the Baptist church, her mother said; and Baptists went to church on Sunday, God's day of rest. Baptist bells rang only on Sundays, but Catholic bells rang every day. Who rings them? Georgie wondered, and lay very still, a little awed and frightened, for it had occurred to her that maybe God, with a great soft hand from heaven, was rocking the bells.

Did she dare ask, or would they laugh at her?

'But why . . . ?' her father said, downstairs.

'Oh, nonsense . . . !' said her mother.

Georgie wondered a great deal about Catholics and Baptists. Nearly all the people who lived on her block were Catholics. Mrs. Tarantino was a Catholic, and went to church every morning. Mr. Tarantino was a Catholic, but he didn't go to church. Mrs. Peralta, Uncle Victor's mother, was also a Catholic, and went to church every morning like Mrs. Tarantino except when her feet hurt too much, and then she soaked them in a tub of warm water and Epsom Salts and said her prayers on her rosary, so it was almost like going to church anyhow. And the Gomezes were Catholics. She didn't know about Dan and Iris Clark. They were colored people.

It was funny living in the same block with colored people, Georgie thought, still listening to the bells. The only children on the block besides Frankie and Leander Gomez were colored; and you couldn't play with colored children. You couldn't even play with Frankie and Leander because their father was a Filipino, and nobody knew what nationality their mother was. They lived in Clark's apartment house. And you couldn't go to school with the other kids in the Quarter; you had to go uptown to school with children of your own social class. Georgie was glad that Lucille was her own class. Lucille's father was a doctor. The Budds lived uptown, on Prytania Street. She wished that she could live next door to Lucille, but she couldn't.

Once, she had overheard her mother say to Lucille's mother that it was a good thing to own at least one of those beautiful old Vieux Carré houses, because more and more uptown people were moving into the Quarter, and property values were going up. Besides, a person could make some handy pin-money if he remodeled those picturesque little slave houses that stood in nearly everybody's courtyard, and rented them out as apartments. She was doing that very thing with the slave house in her own garden. Of course, it was small and crude, and had been built originally for colored servants, but it could be fixed up quite comfortably. Merlin had said that she could keep the rent.

Georgie jumped out of bed and ripped off her pajamas. She had just remembered that people were coming to live in the Webster courtyard apartment today. As she struggled with the buttons of her playsuit, she heard Frankie and Leander Gomez already out on their balcony, clattering across the loose planks on their one roller-skate. The Tarantino shutters banged shut, and the door slammed. Mrs. Tarantino was late for church. In Clark's courtyard, somebody was stepping on the starter of a car. The starter buzzed, but the engine didn't catch.

'Which one a you boys taken mah pliers?' Clark called.

'Frankie done it!' shouted Leander. 'I seen im!'

'Ah swedda Gawd . . . !'

Another day! Georgie could not wait to buckle her sandals, but raced downstairs with the straps flapping loose and tripping her up as she ran, and the sound of the Cathedral bell swinging slower, more faintly across the morning, until, as she reached the bottom of the stairs, it was only an echo, and like an echo in answer, 'I wonder who rings the bell?' she thought, before she pushed open the door into the garden.

IN THE MEANTIME, Leah had drunk three cups of coffee and left the Coffee Shop. The sense of adventure she had felt on first getting up was gone now, and she was troubled and nervous.

The task she had set for herself seemed not only impossible but foolish. How could a woman like herself ever hope to find a nameless seaman on shore leave in a city like New Orleans? What would she say to him if she did find him? But to turn back now would be to give up hope that anything existed for her outside the narrow lives of her family and the people she had always known. Joe had given her a glimpse of something else; and the very act of looking for him, even if she didn't find him, seemed worth while. Because she felt the morning so large, and a man without a last name so small and difficult to find, and because she must begin somewhere, Leah walked in the direction Joe had taken yesterday morning. She walked down Decatur Street toward Esplanade Avenue.

'I'll be seeing you,' Joe had said, before he walked away. But he had not meant it; and remembering, too late, that he had gone without leaving a thread in her hands by which she might follow him later, or pull him back, 'Joe,' she called, 'wait a minute!' But he was already too far away to hear; and so she had turned in the opposite direction and walked home.

If Joe had gone through any door along this street yesterday morning, she did not know which door. She looked at all the doors on both sides of the street. She tried a few of them, and found them locked.

In every city, she told herself, is one door if you can find it; and beside this door is a mail box in which you are accustomed to discover friendly letters, for everybody understands you and likes you, and sometimes you laugh together about the sad, foolish things you used to do. For instance, that hot June day you went looking for Joe, and didn't know his last name, and finally found him—where? Where do you find anybody? Leah wondered. On a page, in a looking-glass, in an empty beer bottle? . . . A door to close on the day's casual encounters and open on quiet conversations with somebody fond of you, in loving tolerance of your gradual idiosyncrasies as you grow older. How sweet, she thought, to be loved for one's faults as well as for one's virtues—and which are the faults, and which the virtues? One never really knows, until somebody else tells one. As for herself, nobody but her brother had ever bothered to tell her about her faults, and nobody at all about her virtues. She suspected she had a few virtues, but was not quite sure.

Decatur was a street of many bars and small gray eating places and a few hotels—a street of Italian grocery stores with their good smells of cheese and smoked herring and mushrooms; of grain and seed stores, with fat sleepy cats dozing away the afternoons in sunny windows, prowling at night for mice; of hardware stores; ropes and nets and tackle and pirogue poles and hip-boots; guns and shells and muskrat traps and decoy ducks—and, up until well past midnight, a busy, colorful street swarming with seamen, truck-drivers, farmers, fishermen, prostitutes, produce men, and tourists, and noisy with juke-box music. But it was empty and quiet now, except for a beggar woman feeling around in a garbage can that hadn't been emptied the night before; and one lone man with his hat crammed over his ears. Could the man be Thomas Ferrabee, looking at crab nets in the hardware store window?

'Got any hairpins, dearie?' said the beggar woman to Leah. 'White hairpins?' She wore a black shawl around her shoulders; but her head was uncovered, and her abundant hair shone milky white under the street lamp. When she smiled, she had no teeth. She was well known around the French Market, where they called her 'Mea Culpa,' half in pity, half in derision at the heavy load of sin she professed to carry. The Negro helpers made it a polite 'Miss Culpa.' She smiled ingratiatingly at Leah, and repeated her question.

'No hairpins,' said Leah. 'Only bobby pins.'

'White hairpins is so hard to find. Dammit to hell.'

At Esplanade Avenue, Leah turned right and walked toward

the docks and the river. She crossed the railroad track and climbed the incline of the levee.

The river was gray in the dawn, swift and high in its June rise. A freighter was coming in to dock a little way up the river from where she stood; and, for an instant, seeing it caught in the cross-swing of the current, the tugboat nuzzling its bow, Leah thought it might be Joe's ship leaving, and her heart jumped into her mouth. But it was merely coming in, and so had no meaning for her. A man was dumping garbage over the side and a few early gulls were diving for breakfast. Other ships were tied up along the riverfront, but she couldn't reach them. She had forgotten that the docks had recently been fenced off.

Leah walked back through the Farmers' Market. Trucks were coming into the long shelter; and produce men and street peddlers with head baskets and pushcarts were bargaining for their loads. Leah wove through the crowd, and emerged at the back door of Batistella's Restaurant. She opened the screen and searched the room with her eyes. The men looked up. One of them was Thomas Ferrabee, eating red beans and rice for breakfast—or was it? The men looked down and went on eating. Joe was not here.

As long as she had made up her mind to look for him, Leah thought, she had better begin at the beginning; she had better go talk to the woman who ran the rooming-house where Joe had taken her Saturday night. What was the woman's name? Joe had called her something like 'Neeley.' Yes, that was it. He had said that he always dropped by to see Neeley when he got in town. He hadn't taken a room with Neeley this time; but the two had seemed good friends. Neeley, then, was the person to see, the one person she knew who might be able to tell her something about Joe. But Neeley, who lived on Royal Street, wouldn't be up for hours yet. She would have to eat breakfast, and then wait for Neeley to get up.

As Leah walked through St. Anthony's Alley, beside the gray

bulk of the Cathedral, she passed Father Vela just coming out of the Parish House door with his hand on the collar of Tony, the German shepherd watchdog.

'Good morning, Father,' Leah said, as she passed.

'Eh? Oh. Good morning.'

FATHER VELA crossed the alley and unchained the gate of St. Anthony's garden behind the Cathedral. Inside the gate he released the eager dog to run, and himself paced slowly, with bowed head, under the oak trees.

Father Vela was a small round man with kindly eyes, gray pendulous cheeks, and a pointed nose. Quite a bit of white sock showed between his black trousers and his black shoes, and the back of his coat was wrinkled and shiny; its pockets bulged. Young Father Poole was saying Mass this morning, and he need not have come out so early except for Tony.

Tony slept in the vestibule of the Parish House. In spite of his size and strength, he was quite young and awkward and in need of discipline. Nobody paid much attention to him but Father Vela, who, deep in his devotions a quarter of an hour before, had heard the dog's toenails clicking on the hard floor as he moved restlessly back and forth in the vestibule; and, finally, the toenails scratching the inside of the oaken door, and the urgent whine. For Father Vela, the night had been hot and sleepless with the old struggle, and peace not won. He had come out willingly into the pale, cool dawn.

From habit, he glanced up at the dim face of the Cathedral clock and saw that it was five-thirty. But he need not have looked at the clock to tell the time, he thought. The sparrows would have told him. Every morning at this time they woke in the oaks and the magnolia and chattered and fussed for a few minutes— thousands of them from the cacophonic medley of their voices —before leaving the night shelter of the Cathedral garden to look for crumbs in Jackson Square. They were leaving now. The small gray-brown bodies hurtled through the oak leaves above Father Vela's head. Tony began to bark.

'Stop it, Tony,' said Father Vela abstractedly, pacing back and forth under the oak trees, pausing now and then to look up into the soft gloom of spreading branches.

Father Vela was a student of poetry, a lover of the lines by which men give their souls to paper as wholly as in last confession. For whatever poets may say, he thought, they do not lie; and their words through the ages adumbrate man's soul with all its passion, its wild seeking, and its angry laughter—and, too, he thought, pacing with measured tread under the oaks—the clear tranquillity of final knowing, the harvest of God's goodness reaffirmed, the peace, the quiet glory.

Last night in a friend's library, he had happened on a volume of Sidney Lanier's poems. Yes, he knew the older Southern poets. Long ago in his youth, he had read Lanier. Live oaks and wide sea marshes, and the strong tide flooding in. What was the name of the poem? Ah, yes, *The Marshes of Glynn*. As he thumbed the book to find the poem, the thin pages, long immured behind glass on the bookcase shelf, had released to his nostrils the sweet, musty, timeless odor of the marsh itself.

> Gloom of the live oaks, beautiful-braided and woven
> With intricate shade of the vines that myriad-cloven
> Clamber the forks of the multiform boughs . . .

he quoted softly to himself, remembering, as he walked in the cool morning under the oaks.

Out over Father Vela's head plunged the first resonant note of the Cathedral bell, calling for early Mass.

For some time he had been aware of footsteps in the alleys on both sides of the garden, of passing shadows in the dawn: the laborers, the servants, the sleepless, always the first to rise—they would always rise and pass under the summoning voice of the bell. He had also been aware of Tony's mad race around the inside of the garden fence, and of his hoarse barking. But the sounds of life, of awakening day, did not disturb Father Vela. He was alone.

> Beautiful glooms, soft dusks in the noonday fire,
> Wildwood privacies, closets of lone desire . . .

He turned at the central flower-bed, and paced back toward the oaks.

> Cells for the passionate pleasure of prayer
> For the soul that grieves . . .

He joined his hands behind his back. His eyes were on the ground.

> Cool for the dutiful weighing of ill with good . . .

And now, seeking a still deeper solitude, he moved toward the only thick cover in the garden, the clump of banana trees in the far corner of the iron fence.

He stepped into the concealing greenness. The great round stalks with their broad silky leaves closed about him and climbed above his head. He stood still. The breeze lifted and turned the leaves with a faint swishing sound. The softly stirring greenness brushed Father Vela with memories of tall marsh grass and early morning birds when once, the boy who had been himself, his ears still ringing with Easter bells in the little church at Golden Meadow, had stolen away from his people to the hillock in the marsh to be alone with what he had discovered. That morning, he had resolved to become a priest.

Father Vela stood very still among the banana leaves, and looked up into the sky. The sky was pink with sunrise. White gulls wheeled and circled in the pure morning air above the old, sinful city.

> As the marsh hen builds her nest on the watery sod,
> Behold, I shall build me a nest on the greatness of God!

Truly a time of peace, the early morning. A newborn day, tender and virginal and exalted, and free from stain. God's goodness re-affirmed, the soul victorious over all the dark evil which night could send against it, the quiet glory. White gulls wheeled in majestic freedom, upheld by loving hands.

> I shall fly in the greatness of God as the marsh hen flies
> In the freedom that fills all the space 'twixt the earth
> and the skies!

But two soft early morning voices began to talk at Father Vela's elbow, just outside the fence.

'Good mawnin, Mis' Robido. How you feelin dis mawnin?'

'Feelin fine, Mis' Clark, essep misery in de bone. Hit sho layin off to rain. How you feelin?'

'Feelin fine.'

'Dat's good. Long as hit don rain, ah feels okay fa a ole lady.'

'Why, Mis' Robido, you ain ole! Say, how all y'all's folks?'

'Dey fine.'

'Dat's good.'

'How all y'all's folks, Mis' Clark? How yo maw and paw? How Dan?'

'Feelin fine, essep Dan got a risin in his ear, and worryin bout dat boy, Cooter. He in jail.'

'Dat's Mis' Bilbo's granson, en't?'

'Cooter nevah rob no grocery sto. Mis' Bilbo tan de hide off'n him ef he so much as peek at a stray nail in de street.'

'Sho. Cooter a good boy, ah heah.'

'Dan say dis mawnin, mebbe Mr. Webster kin do somepun. He ain lak to ask hisseff, accounta rent troubles. He say, could you?'

'Who? Dat prissy hatchet-face ah wuks fo? Huhn! All Mista Websta evah study bout is chokin a dollah to death.'

There was a long pause. The banana leaves sighed. Mrs. Clark spoke.

'How Mis' Lou takin her trouble dat lib nex do to y'all?'

'She gittin a dee-voce, she say, soon as she run down de yalla gal responsible.'

'Tchk, tchk, tchk. Ain it a shame? How Jawn restin sense it happen?'

'Ressin good as a niggah kin res, wid a cotton hook in his behine.'

'Hyah, hyah, hyah!' Both voices laughed softly.

Father Vela stepped out of the banana trees. 'Good morning, Iris!' he said sternly. 'Good morning, Orena!'

The women gave him a startled greeting, and hurried away toward the Cathedral—Orena, black and truculent and broad-beamed, in a pink straw hat; Iris, stooped and sallow, with hurt eyes hidden behind bifocal glasses.

Father Vela resumed his pacing. He felt a little tired. The bell was swinging slower now; its voice was barely audible. It sounded as if it had grown tired of repeating what it had clearly proclaimed so many times before.

Tony still raced around the garden, barking loudly at nothing in particular. His red tongue dripped between his strong white teeth. Such wild and prolonged expenditure of energy toward no purpose, Father Vela found a little irritating. 'Stop it, Tony!' he said. 'Stop that noise!'

More footsteps were coming along St. Anthony's Alley— a late sleeper, a bed-lover, a laggard toward worship. The footsteps neared Father Vela. They faltered, stopped, and came on again. Father Vela turned with words of rebuke on his tongue, but did not speak them, for the woman was Mrs. Tarantino, and one of her eyes was discolored with a bad bruise.

'Good morning, Mrs. Tarantino,' he said kindly.

The woman covered her eye with her hand, and ducked her head. One quick shamed glance, a mumbled greeting, and she, too, hurried into the Cathedral.

Father Vela looked after her with worried eyes. Mrs. Tarantino was one of the shyest persons he had ever known, and one of the most scrupulous in church attendance. For such a shy, conscientious woman she seemed to get herself in a lot of trouble. For years, she had been coming regularly to confession; but in spite of prayer and penance she was getting no better. If anything, she was getting worse. It was partly Bruno's fault, no doubt. Rumor said that Bruno Tarantino had in his possession books of which the Church did not approve—a library of the pernicious little Haldeman-Julius blue books on Science and Philosophy and What Every Man Should Know. Bruno was definitely not a good influence; he was not a good Catholic. Look at the way he had beaten Mrs. Tarantino this morning—or had he? Who else but a good woman's husband would dare lay hands on her? But Mrs. Tarantino, in confession, had never mentioned a beating from Bruno.

No, thought Father Vela sadly, peace was not yet. The struggle went on, the ageless struggle between good and evil in the human soul, in Mrs. Tarantino's soul. He must struggle with her toward victory. Peace was not yet.

Tony was swinging around the garden on a dead run. He leaped the dahlia bed and broke off a flower. He whizzed into the banana trees, rolled out of them scratching and scrambling, and was off again around the garden.

'Tony!' called Father Vela. 'Heel!'

Tony surged toward him and braked to an abrupt halt ten feet away. Head cocked, tail wagging, tongue laughing, he looked at Father Vela and waited.

'Good boy, Tony. Heel, Tony, heel!'

The dog pounced playfully, and shot off in a mad leaning circle around and around the priest.

A little discipline was needed. Father Vela stepped to a pomegranate bush and broke off a limber switch. He cracked the switch against his leg. 'Heel!' he said again, sternly. 'Tony, heel!'

Tony saw the switch and stopped running. When Father Vela came toward him, he dropped to his stomach, put his head between his paws, and whuffed apologetically. As Father Vela came closer, switch in hand, Tony rolled over on his back and looked beseeching.

No, thought Father Vela, a little discipline is needed. No, he thought, bringing down the switch on Tony's curling flank, Bruno Tarantino is not a good Catholic. He never comes to church.

MRS. TARANTINO'S HUSBAND, Bruno, was a large handsome man who built skiffs in a shed at the rear of his courtyard on St. Philip Street. The shed roof was shaded by a tall oleander tree which dropped pink petals all summer long in the sawdust and shavings about the door. Bruno did not make much of a living building skiffs, but for the past decade he had declined any other occupation.

Once, he had worked in a macaroni factory on Chartres Street. He had married Mrs. Tarantino, reared five daughters, married off four of them, and turned gray during the time he worked here. He had seen much trouble in his life. The day after the fifth and youngest daughter ran away to Mobile with a young Irish brakeman—as if he had not had trouble enough already— a large crate of macaroni slipped from a stack piled ready for shipment and fell on his head, and he was taken to the hospital unconscious.

As consciousness began to return to him, but before it had quite returned, it had seemed to him that the nuns tending the ward, their feet lost from sight in the voluminous black cloth of their habits, swooped and coasted by him on roller-skates, and continued dreamily, through the window, two stories above the street.

Listening in a fever for the sound of their bodies striking the pavement below, for the cries of pity and horror and alarm one would expect to accompany such a tragedy, he had been surprised to hear nothing; and had reasoned that they must have struck an awning to arrest their fall. Some time later, as the sisters continued to coast through the window, and none of them, so far as he could determine, had yet fallen, he concluded that his reasoning had been wrong, and that through the ward window they had continued in swift yet stately procession into heaven.

The idea tickled Bruno, and he woke laughing. Nuns coasting into heaven on roller-skates! He could not shake off the comical fancy. Thereafter, it became impossible for him to attend church, for no matter how hard he tried to keep a sober face at sight of a nun, he could not do so, but broke into loud chuckles and clasped his sides and shook until Mrs. Tarantino had to lead him outside.

Bruno's stay in the hospital changed him in other ways also. With no explanation to Mrs. Tarantino other than that he wouldn't be living always, and might as well do as he liked while he was, he quit his job at the macaroni factory, roofed a corner of his courtyard into a workshop, and began making excellent skiffs which were much in demand by duck-hunters and fishermen in the wide marshes and shallow waters surrounding the city. It was at this time that Bruno began to collect Haldeman-Julius blue books. He also collected a supply of liquor, mostly red wine and beer. Since prohibition had not yet been repealed, the liquor was bootleg obtained through Bruno's Cousin Julius, who had good connections with a hi-jacker at East Pointe-à-la-Hache on the Mississippi River below New Orleans.

Bruno had enjoyed a period of considerable affluence through skiff-building, for nearly every member of the State Conservation Department had bought skiffs for private use with public funds; and, through Cousin Julius, who also had good political connections, Bruno had been the favored craftsman. This good fortune, while seeing the Tarantinos comfortably through the depression, had ended recently upon Federal investigation, a delayed auditing of the Conservation Department records, and the subsequent jailing of Bruno's best customers and Cousin Julius. Bruno himself had been summoned to court for questioning; and for a time it looked as if he, too, might go to jail. Finally released, he returned to skiff-building, more convinced than ever that the only possible way for a man to be happy was to mind his own business and read books—which he proceeded to do. Reading books did not make him happy; it made him think, which made him unhappy; but he kept on reading. Defending his right to mind his own business, he got into several fist fights with his friends, thrashed them thoroughly, and missed them painfully when they stopped coming around. But he continued to mind his own business. He did not make so much money at skiff-building as before, but he made enough to live. Merlin Webster owned most of the houses on the block, but not Bruno's. Bruno owned his own house, a sturdy story-and-a-half red brick reinforced with cypress timbers, and paid rent to nobody. It was Bruno's reiterated opinion that everybody worried too much.

WHEN THE CATHEDRAL BELL called Mrs. Tarantino to Mass on this June morning, Bruno had resumed work on a skiff in his courtyard shed. For two hours he had worked steadily under the hanging-light globe without even noticing that the sun had risen, or, presently, that sunlight lay across his feet. Dan Clark, his colored neighbor, coming in to borrow a pair of pliers at eight o'clock, had turned off the light. Clark now leaned against the icebox, pitching and catching the pliers nervously, a worried frown on his face. Bruno had been talking about a man named Machiavelli, whom Clark did not know. Besides, he could not hear very well this morning. A wad of oil-soaked cotton plugged his right ear.

The workshop was hot and strongly scented with pungent odors of tar and turpentine and fresh paint. An orderly array of well-sharpened, well-oiled tools hung along the walls. Flies buzzed in and out of the streak of sunlight.

'Machiavelli,' said Bruno, while his broad thumb slid along the trail his plane had just smoothed on the skiff's gunwale— 'Machiavelli was a Italian that lived in Florence in the fifteenth century. Famous man, like Huey Long. Liar. No good. Machiavelli an Huey Long, they mighta been bruddas.'

'Is dat a fack?'

'No scruples,' said Bruno. 'Mussolini—worse.'

'Ain it de truf? Dat boy doin plenny hollerin off galleries dese days.' Clark's black mechanic's cap was pushed to the back of his head, and the front of his blue cotton pull-over was stretched in long damp scallops from mopping his sweaty face. He lifted the lid of the icebox, and peered inside. 'Mr. Tarantino,' he said. 'Yo ice is bout gone.'

'Hava bottla beer before she gets hot,' said Bruno.

'Hit's too early.'

Bruno moved around the skiff trestles toward the icebox. He was wearing a vest, but it was unbuttoned. His shirt, with sleeves cut off at the shoulder, was also unbuttoned and open to his belt. The curly gray hair on his chest was peppered with sawdust. He moved slowly, now and then stooping to sight along the gentle curve of the boat from stern to bow, or to press a large hand lovingly over the smooth cypress wood. 'She'sa good boat,' he said with satisfaction.

'Sho is, Mr. Tarantino.' Clark frowned into the sunlight, and pitched and caught the pliers.

The entrance to Clark's apartment house and his Body and

Fender Works was on the next street; but the rear wall of his courtyard was also the rear wall of Bruno's courtyard, and so, in spite of the wall between them, the two men worked but a few feet apart. Their friendship was still tentative, retarded by ancient fears and prejudices and also by the opposition of their wives. As a matter of fact, they had no idea of becoming friends; they merely liked each other's company. Several months before, Bruno had backed his truck into a fireplug and bent the rear axle; and Clark had refused money for repairs on the grounds that they were neighbors. Bruno had paid off with a bottle of beer. Half a dozen times since then, Clark had dropped around by Bruno's workshop to borrow some tool, or to drink a beer on a hot day. In return, he hammered out the fenders on Bruno's old truck.

'Mussolini and Machiavelli,' said Bruno, 'they mighta been bruddas. All the time fool the poor people, and lie like hell. No good.'

'Dat is sho de truf, Mr. Tarantino.'

The iceman was in the next block. They could hear his voice, and the popping motor of his truck. *Ice! Ice! Ice!* The voice was one of controlled rage. The same iceman had served the block for years. People listened for his coming, and were fond of him because he came when they expected him and could always make change. But he was always angry. Nobody knew why. Nobody would ever really know. The truck stopped. Doors opened. Women called, 'Ten pounds!' and 'Twenty pounds!' and 'Fifty pounds!' and 'Lissen, you! Gimme a nickel wort' dis mawnin!'

'He's gotta grouch on the whole world!' Bruno said.

'He worried, lak evahbody,' said Clark.

'Hell,' said Bruno. 'He'sa iceman. People gotta buy ice. He was born. He sell ice an make a living. Some day, he die. What t'hell he got to worry about?'

'Pro-gress an Frigidaires, mebbe,' said Clark. He looked at

the other man understandingly. He knew that Bruno worried more than most men; that he was looking for answers he hadn't found in the little blue books hidden in his tool chest. Bruno might conceal his worry from others, but Clark knew and sympathized. 'Mr. Tarantino,' he said, 'hit ain dat easy. Take me. Mah wife want a garden. Ah promus her a garden when she marry me, an five yeahs pass, an she gittin hellbent to hab it. Now, ah gotta use dat co'tyard to park mah cars in, Mr. Tarantino, cause dat's mah bidness, an ain no room fo flower-beds. But mah wife smell Mrs. Webster's flowers nex do, an nilly go wile. Dat's one worry.'

'Girls gotta be girls.'

'Den Mrs. Gomez. She come up to me settin on de steps Saddy night an say, "Clark, how kin ah make mah ole man stop hittin de bottle and stay home nights?" So ah set. An ah study.'

'Man, you crazy!' said Bruno. 'A man gotta mind his own business.'

'Mebbe,' said Clark. 'But ah owes Mr. Webster lease money fum las month, an cain pay hit till ah gits mah rent money fum Mrs. Gomez, an mah rightful rent money sparkplug some kinda fancy job fo Mr. Gomez, an Mrs. Gomez git so mad she bus dishes an keep me an Iris awake. Iris gittin awful sour wid no garden, an Mrs. Gomez bussin dishes. Furthermo, dem Gomez kids swipe mah tools. Huccum ah ain got no pliers dis mawnin, is Frankie taken em.'

'Throw em out,' said Bruno.

Clark shook his head. He couldn't do it; they owed him money. And something else was on his mind. He turned the wad of cotton in his ear, and cleared his throat. 'Mr. Tarantino,' he said, 'Clara Bilbo come by yestiddy.'

'Yeah?'

'De po-leece run her granson in jail fo robbin dat grocery sto on Dauphine Street, which he nevah done, an beatin him up wid a rubbah hose, she say.'

'Yeah?'

'Mr. Tarantino, you got influence . . . ?'

'Not any more,' said Bruno. 'I minda my own business.'

The ice truck stopped before the Tarantino courtyard gate, and the iceman entered the workshop with fifty pounds wrapped in newspapers. 'Hello, Mussolini,' he said to Bruno, and dropped the ice in the box. The piece was too large. He took the pick from his belt and began to chip. Slivers of ice rained around him and melted on the warm bricks. Some of the slivers hit Clark's chest. He watched them melt. The iceman stabbed angrily with his pick. When the ice slid into the box, he slammed the door and stalked to his truck.

Bruno shrugged his shoulders, kicked the newspapers into the courtyard, and went back to work. 'Nobody can make me mad, because I minda my own business,' he said. 'Everything, she's fine. Everything, she's okay.'

Clark faded silently through the sunlight across the courtyard. Mrs. Tarantino's dog began to bark. Mrs. Tarantino, long returned from morning Mass, came through the kitchen door with a basket of wet clothes to hang on the line.

WHEN BRUNO STOPPED going to church and to confession, Mrs. Tarantino blamed herself. Bruno's sins did not appear to bother Bruno, but they bothered Mrs. Tarantino. She bore them alone for several years, but the weight was too much. After all, hadn't marriage made her one with Bruno? This being so, his sins were her sins, and there was nothing for her to do but to confess them, as well as she was able, along with her own.

A devoted mother, Mrs. Tarantino had lived through her children. She was painfully shy. Her face bore a disfiguring birthmark, a harelip which had never been corrected and which she had allowed to inhibit her life in a manner disproportionate to its importance. It was not nearly so bad as she imagined. Her daughters had grown used to it, and Bruno had forgotten it; but

Mrs. Tarantino appeared in public as little as she was able. She went scarcely anywhere but to Mass and to the corner grocery. Although she knew the names and faces of her neighbors, her shyness had kept her from entering into their lives. She lived behind her courtyard walls, and the walls were high. Sometimes, several days would pass without Mrs. Tarantino seeing a soul except Bruno, and, perhaps, the angry iceman. When her five daughters married and moved to other cities, her life became so empty and uneventful she felt tired all the time. She felt so tired she neglected her washing, and Bruno was often without clean underclothes or socks. And then she was no longer tired. This change came about through Bruno.

Before Bruno roofed the end of his courtyard into a workshop, Mrs. Tarantino's clothesline had run from a corner of the house to a pole in the middle of the yard. After Bruno took up skiff-building, however, and began to run his truck in and out of the narrow courtyard to bring in lumber and haul away the finished boats, he had found his wife's clothesline in the way and had moved it to the only available space, the shed roof. Mrs. Tarantino had then discovered her neighbors in her own way, and was no longer tired.

From the shed roof she could look down into Merlin Webster's courtyard on one side, the courtyard of the Webster sisters on the other side, and into Dan Clark's busy courtyard at the rear—and this, from an eminence so high she was seldom noticed or called upon to speak. Something was always happening; and very little happened without Mrs. Tarantino's knowledge. What she did not see or hear for herself, she gathered from the clotheslines, the bedding hung to sun on the balconies, the cooking smells; from the silence, the smoke of the old houses themselves; from the very air, hot and sweet with flowers from April to November, and warm and bright enough, even in winter, for many good washing days. Or she got it from her dog.

Her dog was quite old, a small white woolly dog with a docked tail and a black patch over one eye. His name was Rocco. Living so long with Mrs. Tarantino, Rocco had learned to lie quietly on his stomach in a hole scratched out between the oleander roots, with wistful eyes glued to a hole in the wall. Often, Mrs. Tarantino at the kitchen window or passing through the courtyard on business other than washing, seeing the dog's ears prick questioningly, his short tail jerk, his dusty pelt ripple with excitement, would sweep up a dishtowel, wet it, wring it, and climb the stairs to the shed roof. Sometimes she would see her neighbors doing strange and interesting things in their courtyards, and would be well repaid for her effort. Or she might see only a cat.

Bruno always had clean clothes after Mrs. Tarantino discovered her neighbors. If she felt lonely, she washed three or four times a day, even if it were only to rinse out the dishtowels or the washrags, or maybe a handkerchief or a piece of crocheted lace to hang on the line.

Her brown arms lifted, her hands busy with pins, her shy face hidden under a wide straw hat, Mrs. Tarantino became such a familiar figure to her neighbors that, after a while, if any of them did happen to glance up and see her on the shed roof, they took no notice. Perhaps, because she never spoke, they forgot that she had eyes and ears. She had become as much a part of the landscape as the top branches of the pink oleander, with whose color her faded print dresses merged in summer until she was almost invisible anyhow.

Mrs. Tarantino had been confessing her husband's sins for several years when she began to include some of her neighbors' sins also. Nothing, of course, but venial sins—the little things that made life interesting. She began timidly, taking one or two at a time. Mrs. Gomez came first.

From the shed roof, Mrs. Tarantino had a clear, close view of the second-floor balcony of the Gomez rear apartment and of the two small boys who played there. They were round, brown, mischievous little boys, only two or three years old when they had first moved in. Their seal-smooth heads were always peeping between the rusty iron tulips of the balcony railing. She took them at once to her heart. 'Hi!' they called to her at first; but when she did not answer, they soon forgot her. They never seemed to stop running; and neither did Mrs. Gomez, a thin dark young woman in bright slacks, with a carrying voice forever breathless as she sped from one end of her small living quarters to the other in pursuit of something she never caught, calling:

'You, Frankie! You, Leander! Stop hittin each udda an stay off duh rotten ironwork or you'll fall, an stop spittin on duh cars, or by God, I'll tell yo papa . . . !'

'Frankie, where are you . . . ?

'Leander, where are you . . . ?

'Y'all better answer mama!'

Mrs. Tarantino did not approve of Mrs. Gomez' language.

A sound of running feet on the balcony . . . a scuffle . . . a sharp slap . . . then Mrs. Gomez' voice . . . Mrs. Tarantino would hurry to the shed roof.

'I'll slam duh hell outa botha youse, you wake up mama when she's takin her nap, an goin to the Lone Ranger too, an all dat in your nice new suits, an she can't even take a nap you two gotta be on topa each udda . . . you say Frankie, he bit you? . . . Huh, Leander, did Frankie bite you? . . . So! Well! Come here by mama, Frankie!'

Frankie would be caught and held until Leander, a size smaller, could find a spot quiet enough on his brother's squirming body to sink his white teeth. A short, angry yell would explode on the hot air, and in a few minutes the two would be laughing and playing again.

From behind the oleander tree on the shed roof, Mrs. Tarantino saw and heard everything. She winced at the bad word, and made a mental note.

The Clarks committed no visible sins except the obvious one of being Negroes. Mrs. Tarantino resented Dan Clark, not only for this, but also because she felt he shared Bruno's taciturn company in such a way as to make it seem less taciturn. Iris Clark kept herself pretty much to herself. Judging from her kitchen smells and her clothesline, she was a good cook and housekeeper. She tried to grow anything that would grow in a cracked pot, but she didn't have much luck. Dan was always backing his cars over her flowers and drenching them with crankcase oil.

Mr. Gomez worked on the banana wharves, and was said to commit adultery every Saturday night—a sin which Mrs. Tarantino refused to include in her confession. As he went to work early in the morning and came home late at night, she seldom saw him. She knew him chiefly by his clothes on Mrs. Gomez' line. His clothes, she thought, looked evil.

The Webster sisters had moved into the house on Mrs. Tarantino's left during the depression, eight years before. Since the house belonged to their brother, the real estate man whose white business placards could be seen on so many houses in the Quarter, they were not obliged to pay rent. This was a good thing, Mrs. Tarantino learned, because Maudie, the younger sister, couldn't hold a job; and Leah had lost hers, and couldn't find another. Up until last year, when Maudie had married Victor Peralta, and Leah had finally got a job as a theater cashier, their brother had supported them both.

Then, as now, their courtyard was bare of flowers. Often, brown paper bags of garbage lay around on the bricks at the back door for a week at a time; flies came; rain fell; the bags split open, and finally had to be removed with a shovel. The sisters had quarreled about this, as they did about everything. It was usually Maudie's fault.

Leah would come into the courtyard and find her lazy sister sunning herself in the canvas deck chair, with sun-goggles on her eyes, and a magazine on her lap.

'It's your garbage,' Leah would say. 'Get the shovel and scrape it out. It smells to high heaven.'

'What's the hurry, honey? I don't smell anything. But I'll take it out in a minute.'

'You lazy parasite.'

'I don't see you rushin off to work at ninety miles an hour either, honey.'

Maudie still sat around the courtyard sunning herself all summer; but, although bare, the courtyard was clean now. Victor Peralta carried out the garbage every evening. He was a nice man. Often, he made love to his pretty, lazy wife in the courtyard. His mother, old Mrs. Peralta, could seldom be seen from the shed roof, because she sat all day on her front doorstep watching the street. Once, during the past year, Mrs. Peralta had walked with Mrs. Tarantino to church; but they had never become friends. Mrs. Peralta had spoken of her aching feet, which reminded Mrs. Tarantino of her own affliction; and thereafter she had avoided her neighbor—waiting until Mrs. Peralta was well on her way to the Cathedral before she herself ventured out.

Leah Webster liked to walk up and down her courtyard drinking cigarette smoke. Mrs. Tarantino wondered what heavy sin lay on Leah's mind to make her so unhappy; and thought, whatever it was, that it should be confessed. But she did not know what it was, and she could not find out. She did not like Leah Webster.

Neither did she like Mrs. Merlin Webster; but she liked very much to look down into her courtyard. Honeysuckle, clematis, and coral vines tangled with moonflowers on the walls. From the center of the green lawn rose an oleander tree, a large white one which Mrs. Tarantino liked much better than the pink one in her own yard. She wanted some of its flowers for the Blessed Mother, but had been too shy to ask. In the flower-beds, in season, grew roses, lilies, violets, phlox, petunias, poppies—more

flowers than Mrs. Tarantino could begin to name. And nailed
to the low branch of the oleander tree was a small tin windmill
which Mr. Webster had bought for his daughter when they had
first moved into the house, two years later than Maudie and
Leah. The red-and-white paint had worn off the windmill, and
now it rattled instead of whirring. Mrs. Webster wanted it taken
down, but Georgie had cried, and Mr. Webster had said that it
should remain.

Mrs. Tarantino thought Georgie Webster a strange child.
Once, she had spent two hours creeping slowly around the garden on hands and knees in the gathering dusk, her eyes intent
on something Mrs. Tarantino couldn't see. What had the child
lost? What was she looking for? Mrs. Tarantino climbed the
stairs to the shed roof several times in an effort to solve the mystery.

Dark came. Lights were lit in the Webster house. Mrs. Webster called, 'Georgie, it's bedtime! Come take your bath!'

No answer from Georgie. Her mother came to the door.

'For Heaven's sake, why are you creeping around like that?'

'I'm following a snail,' Georgie said. 'He's been everywhere.
I want to see where he goes.'

Another time, the Websters were eating dinner in their garden while Mrs. Tarantino was taking in her wash.

'Ah,' said Mr. Webster, rubbing his hands together. 'Turtle
soup.'

'I bought a live turtle at the French Market this morning,'
Mrs. Webster said. 'Georgie helped me pick it out. The butcher
killed it, and cut it up for us . . . I thought it was time Georgie
learned about marketing.'

'A very good idea,' said Mr. Webster. 'I like turtle soup.'

'I don't,' said Georgie. 'It had yellow eyes. Very yellow eyes.
It looked at me very hard. I expect it didn't want to die.'

'Eat it.'

When dinner was over, Mrs. Tarantino heard Georgie talking to herself in the dark courtyard. The words were worse than Mrs. Gomez used. Hearing them, Mrs. Tarantino crossed herself twice with a shocked forefinger.

Since Bruno was too busy building skiffs and minding his own business to be interested in anything she saw or heard, there was nobody to tell but Father Vela. And so, her shy face screened in the confessional, Mrs. Tarantino blurted out such sins of vanity, gluttony, sloth, and blasphemy that Father Vela was hard put to understand.

But there was one sin of Bruno's which Mrs. Tarantino could never bring herself, from loyalty, to confess. Sometimes, Bruno beat her.

He had done it again, this hot June morning.

And now, Mrs. Tarantino, back from morning Mass and busy at her washtub, could hear her husband talking with Dan Clark in the workshop as calmly as if nothing had happened.

Mrs. Tarantino listened for a minute, her hands immersed in soapsuds; and then she dried her hands on her apron, and stood on tiptoe before Bruno's shaving mirror to examine her black eye. It wasn't a bad black eye; she had had worse ones. Taking a nickel from her purse, she dropped it in the juke-box Bruno had given her for a thirty-fifth anniversary present. While the music played, she peeped from behind the curtain to see if Bruno were in any way touched or softened.

> Good-bye, little darlin', I'll miss you,
> When from you I'm far away . . .

But Bruno wouldn't look toward the house. He was hard, Bruno was—a fearless, godless man who laughed at nuns and had almost been to jail.

Out by the courtyard wall, Rocco broke into a paroxysm of barking.

For the past month, both Mrs. Tarantino and Rocco had been busy, for Mrs. Webster had been remodeling her slave quarters into a small two-story apartment. A few days ago it had been finished and furnished. Mrs. Tarantino was eager for a sight of the new tenants. Perhaps they had come this morning.

Her wash was not finished, but she couldn't wait. Catching up the basket half-filled with wet clothes, she stepped into the courtyard. Clark passed her silently, with his head down.

'Madonna mia, you gotta nosey dog,' Bruno said.

'Nobody can steal nothing in this house with such a good watchdog,' Mrs. Tarantino replied, with more spirit than usual. 'Down, Rocco!' she said sternly to the dog. Paying no more attention to Bruno, she climbed the stairs to the shed roof.

She pinned up one of Bruno's striped shirts, a pair of long underdrawers, and one of her own aprons; and then, screened by the swaying, dripping clothes, she looked into the courtyard below.

SHE SAW ONLY THE WEBSTERS—nobody new.

Mr. and Mrs. Webster stood in front of the new courtyard apartment. Georgie was jumping up and down on the flagstoned walk, her braids spanking her bare back. 'The Tuttles are coming!' she said, excitedly. 'The Tuttles are coming!'

Mr. Webster wore his hat and coat. He must be nearly ready to leave for his office. One neat, brown-and-white shoe was braced on the red-brick doorstep of the little house. Resting his weight on the other foot, Mr. Webster lounged forward with an elbow on his bent knee and his chin in the palm of his hand. He was smoking his after-breakfast cigarette. Smoke drifted across the courtyard. Mrs. Webster, eyes squinting in the bright sunlight, looked at Mr. Webster's shoe.

'The Tuttles are coming, huh, mama? When?'

'Confound it,' said Mr. Webster. 'Why wasn't my paper delivered this morning?'

'I don't know,' said Mrs. Webster.

'Why?' said Mr. Webster. 'Why? I like to read my paper before I go to work. I pay for a morning paper. Why shouldn't I get it?'

'I don't know,' said Mrs. Webster. 'I'm sure it was an oversight.'

'I don't pay for oversights.'

There was a brief silence. Mrs. Tarantino pinned another shirt on the line.

'I think you should have told the Tuttles this apartment was fifty a month,' said Mr. Webster. 'They've got four rooms and a bath, all modern conveniences upstairs and down, everything new and clean. And they've got two fireplaces, and a balcony, and the garden besides.'

'I don't know,' said Mrs. Webster. 'I think forty is enough. After all, they're friends of the Budds, and they're young, just starting out. This is Mr. Tuttle's first position. From what I hear, Tulane instructors don't get too much salary. And they have a baby, too, you know.'

'When will they get here, mama?' Georgie began to jump up and down again. 'How old is the baby? Will Mrs. Tuttle let me play with him?'

'When do they get here?' said Mr. Webster, looking at his wrist watch.

'Some time this afternoon, I think. Driving down, it's hard to say, but they planned on this afternoon. They sent that wire the other day, you remember—the day they left Princeton. They said they'd wire again if they were delayed.'

'They'll pay for their own utilities, of course?' said Mr. Webster. 'You made that clear?'

'Of course.'

'What's the baby's name, mama? What's his name, huh? What's his name?'

'Confound it,' said Mr. Webster, 'I don't think I'm going to like strangers living in our courtyard. Why didn't they stay in New Jersey where they belonged?'

'Well,' said Mrs. Webster, 'it seems Mr. Tuttle is writing his doctor's thesis on something about the niggers in the South, and then he got this job teaching sociology in Tulane Summer School . . . From what Helen says,' she added, 'they're lovely people.'

Mr. Webster snorted. 'What would he know about Southern niggers? Doctor's thesis, eh? Probably a lot of communistic nonsense. Let these Northerners have the problem in their laps for a while. They'd find it educational, all right. He'll find out.'

'Yes, I expect he will,' said Mrs. Webster. 'But Mr. Tuttle comes from the right sort of background, and I doubt if he's a communist. His father was one of the best brain specialists in the country.'

'Mama?' said Georgie, tugging at her mother's dress. 'Mama, will—'

Mrs. Webster removed her daughter's hand from her skirt. 'Georgie,' she said, 'you're getting too big a girl to hang onto mother every minute, and do stop jumping up and down in this heat. Run get some of that sun-tan lotion in the bathroom. Rub it all over your face and arms.'

Georgie went in the house. Mr. Webster looked at his wrist watch, and stared moodily at the grass.

'I wouldn't worry any more about Leah,' said Mrs. Webster, in a guarded voice. 'She's old enough to take care of herself.'

Mr. Webster looked up sharply. 'I wasn't even thinking about her!' he said.

Georgie came out with a bottle of sun-tan lotion. 'I rubbed my face and hands,' she said, 'but I can't reach my back. Daddy, will you rub my back?'

She squatted on the grass. Mr. Webster took the bottle, poured lotion in his hand, and began to rub his daughter's bare, pink back. 'D'you think she ought to stay out in the sun like this, Marie?' he said. 'Her skin is awfully tender. These play-suits don't give much protection.'

Mrs. Webster, searching for bugs on the petunias, replied, 'The sun is good for her, if she doesn't stay out too long at first.'

'Don't stay out too long, sugarpie,' said Mr. Webster.

'All right,' Georgie answered. 'Daddy?'

'What?'

'Who rings the Cathedral bell?'

'Why, I don't know,' said Mr. Webster. 'The priest, I suppose. I don't believe I ever heard who rang it.'

(Mrs. Tarantino, on the shed roof, nearly answered the question herself; but clapped a hand on her mouth in time.)

'Maybe God—'

(Mrs. Tarantino shook her head violently.)

'Dear,' called Mrs. Webster from across the courtyard, 'd'you want the car this morning?'

'No,' said Mr. Webster. 'I feel like walking. The walk will do me good.'

'That's fine. I can use the car this morning. Georgie and I are going to the French Market.'

Mr. and Mrs. Webster went in the house, leaving Georgie alone in the courtyard. She drifted aimlessly for a few minutes, and coming to rest under the oleander tree, looked up at the little tin windmill.

Mrs. Tarantino also looked at the windmill, and saw it trying to face the uncertain breeze that eddied down the alley and over the courtyard wall. It whirled and faltered; felt this way and that; stopped completely; then sprang into busy motion again as the breeze pounced on it from a new direction.

But a street peddler was coming. Mrs. Tarantino heard him chanting his morning song. 'I got tomatoes, ripe red tomatoes . . . I got squash, nice summer squash . . . I got green beans, I got cucumbers . . . ripe red tomatoes . . . I got squash!'

With a last puzzled look at Georgie and the windmill, Mrs. Tarantino descended from the shed roof to complete her morning marketing. Now, she wouldn't even have to visit the grocery store. She could make her purchases at her own door.

Alone in the hot fragrance of the garden, Georgie looked at the windmill. Her lifted face was grave and watchful.

BUT HE HAD BEEN THINKING about Leah, after all.

As Merlin Webster fished the car keys from his pocket, handed them to his wife, kissed her cheek, and closed the door, he was debating with himself whether or not to have another talk with his sister before he went to work.

He looked toward Leah's house and saw old Mrs. Peralta sitting on the doorstep as usual, watching people pass. She smiled and bobbed her head at him. Congratulating himself that she was merely the mother of his brother-in-law and no blood kin, Merlin replied with a brief salute.

He hesitated on the sunny sidewalk. Leah was probably still in bed. She didn't have to appear at her disgraceful job until four o'clock in the afternoon, and since she didn't get off until nearly midnight, she was no doubt sleeping late. Leah had always liked to sleep late. He would not disturb her now; but later in the morning he would telephone her, and perhaps the two of them could have luncheon together.

Merlin looked again at his wrist watch, and stepped off briskly into the morning. He turned the corner at Bourbon Street, and walked uptown toward his office and his day's work; but he was not thinking about work this morning; he was recalling his conversation with Leah the day before.

'Maybe it was wrong of me to ask that man for a drink,' she had said. 'Maybe it was stupid. All right. I'm not ashamed to be wrong any more, and I'm not afraid to be stupid. So far as my making a fool of myself is concerned, I don't believe that's anything new.'

'Did you have to spend the night with him?'

'I don't see that it matters to you—but we only talked.'

'Do you expect me to believe that?'

'No.'

'Don't you care what your friends will say?'

'Certainly.'

'Then, why . . . ?'

'But not much.'

'What about Preston Dillon? He wanted to marry you, didn't he?'

'Oh, Preston. He asked me several times, but only when I happened to be wearing that long green dress, and he couldn't see my legs. I couldn't help but notice it after a while. I couldn't wear that dress the rest of my life, could I?'

'This is no time to be funny. Maybe you don't realize, but this is pretty difficult for me. I want you to be happy, Leah. You had a hard time of it when you were a girl—going to business school, working in an office, keeping house for Maudie and me all at the same time—and when you lost your job, I was more than glad to take care of you as well as Maudie. I wanted to give you a rest, help you meet the right sort of people, have a good time. I still do. You know you don't have to work. I want you to be happy, Leah, and I can't stand by and say nothing while you make a fool of yourself. You can't afford to throw yourself away on such people as this man you met last night. From what Maudie says, he was just a common sailor. You've always trusted my judgment about people. Why won't you listen to me now?'

'You treat me as if I were Maudie's age! Don't you feel a little ridiculous? Besides, I'll probably never see the man again. But I wish I could.'

'Do you actually imagine yourself in love with him?'

'Oh, I don't know. I suppose you could call it that.'

'Does he love you? Did he ask you to marry him?'

'Good Heavens, I met him only yesterday!' She had begun to laugh . . .

A postman was approaching Merlin along the sidewalk, a small blue-gray man the color of ashes, with dark sweat circles under his arms and a heavy mail bag slung by a strap over his shoulder. Merlin knew him by sight; this particular postman delivered his own mail on St. Philip Street. He thought to stop and inquire about letters; but somebody else was ahead of him. For several blocks, Merlin had been aware of the figure walking ahead of him. The man's back, as stiff as the black umbrella he carried with the handle crooked over his arm, was unremarkable when studied in detail; but its general conformation, along with its shadow on the sidewalk, had thrown a shadow over Merlin's thoughts. When the man halted the postman and Merlin saw his face, this shadow sharpened into animosity. The man looked like Adolf Hitler.

'Do you have any messages for me this morning?' The voice was austere and reedy, distinctly unpleasant.

'I'll see, Mr. Graber.' The postman eased the mail bag in front of him, drew out a bundle of letters, and began to shuffle through them. Aware of Merlin's nearing footsteps, the man pivoted his body. His eyes brushed Merlin in a glance of pompous contempt. Merlin passed, without stopping to inquire about his own mail.

'No letters, Mr. Graber,' said the postman.

Merlin looked over his shoulder. The resemblance to Hitler was no coincidence; it had been deliberately achieved. Why else the dyed mustache and the hair combed over the forehead? Except for the red bow tie, which Merlin could not remember having seen publicized as part of Hitler's sartorial equipment, and the black umbrella of a type usually associated with Mr. Chamberlain, there was a striking resemblance.

Merlin laughed shortly, and dismissed the man as a crackpot. He had been thinking about Leah. He had asked her if the seaman had mentioned marriage.

'Good Heavens,' she had said, 'I met him only yesterday!' And she had begun to laugh.

'I don't see anything funny.'

'But it's all so terribly funny, such a tempest in a teapot! Maybe I'm laughing because just thinking about Joe makes me want to laugh. Everything seems simple when I think about Joe. I feel good. I feel happy. I want to laugh.'

'You could have waited.'

'I've been waiting all my life, and nothing ever happened to me. Nothing I wanted to happen. I don't see much sense to the way most people live their lives. Look at the way mama and papa lived. Twenty years paying for that old house on Galvez Street, and as soon as they got it paid for, they died.'

'That house gave me my start in the real estate business.'

'It doesn't matter. Can't you see? Their lives went into that house. It was all they lived for. They were looking for the rabbit in the wrong brushpile. So are you. So was I, until Saturday night. All of us poking in an old brushpile, so dignified and bloodthirsty, and the rabbit we're looking for isn't there at all. He's behind a tree, simply splitting his sides. By the time we discover he isn't where we think he is, he's clean over the horizon —too far away for us ever to catch. And it's too late. . . . Life could be such fun, Merlin. Just being alive could be such fun. Can't you see what I mean?'

'All I can see is that you must have been drunk Saturday night, or else you need a psychiatrist, like Marie said.'

At this point, Merlin nearly spoke to a woman coming out of a Pet Shop, thinking she was Marie, until he realized that Marie could not possibly have had time to dress, drive uptown, park the car, buy a canary, and emerge from the shop with the cage in her hand; and had never cared for canaries, anyhow; and, besides, had been going to the French Market. The woman with the canary had only resembled Marie.

It was strange, he thought, how almost every woman of her age in the city seemed to resemble Marie; and that sometimes, if he happened to think of her during the day, he had trouble recalling her face. But Marie and Leah must be about the same age; and Leah did not look like anybody but herself. He had always been proud of the way Leah looked. Men had always noticed Leah. The trouble had been that Leah hadn't paid much attention to men until this seaman came along.

Merlin had arrived at Canal Street. At a sidewalk stand he bought a morning paper.

MR. GRABER, walking slowly, planning his day's work, was also nearing Canal Street. Mr. Graber had been one of those who materialize on park pathways and in public gathering places at the beginning of warm weather, pushing an iced container of Eskimo pies. Already of oblique intellect and peculiar social habits, from reading a copy of *Mein Kampf* which had inadvertently fallen into his hands, he had suffered a nervous breakdown. Afterwards, he had imagined himself the author of the book. A nephew, also in the Eskimo pie business, now supported Mr. Graber and left him free to follow his career. Once, when the two had been having a meal of Hamburger steak, French fried potatoes, and coffee, the nephew had been surprised into wondering how consumption of the same food could result in such pleasant sensations in himself and such rage in his uncle. But the cause of Mr. Graber's rage had not been food. As he was mopping up his gravy, he had suddenly noticed that the waiter was a Jew, and had smashed his coffee cup.

Mr. Graber had a mission, but he wasn't talking about it. Not yet. Now, the important thing was action. Keep on the move.

Infiltrate the city. Discover weak points, and mark them for those who would enter when the time came. That stupid clerk in the white linen suit, who had passed him while he stood talking with the postman, was unfit to survive. When the time came, he would not survive. . . . Neither would this Negro child survive, he thought, striking with his umbrella at the dog the child was dragging behind her. The puppy had bolted sideways, tangling its yellow lead-string around Mr. Graber's legs. He struck again with his furled umbrella. The puppy cringed and yelped. The child dodged around Mr. Graber, untangling the string, and hurried away in the crowd.

'Dogs!' said Mr. Graber, his eyes flashing over the crowd. 'Stupid, cringing dogs!'

But he did not trust the United States mail. He hooked the umbrella over his arm. Fingering the cards and the chalk in his pocket, he moved toward Canal Street. He did not need the United States mail. He was strong and agile enough to carry his own messages for the time being. Some day, and soon now, his day would come. The clouds were gathering.

THE WIND HELPED MERLIN WEBSTER to open his newspaper. He scanned the front page.

Hitler's storm troopers were shooting university students in Prague. The King and Queen of England were at Hyde Park, and the King had eaten a hot-dog at Eleanor Roosevelt's picnic. Federal Investigator O. John Rogge had succeeded in indicting three more prominent New Orleans citizens—technically for mail fraud; in reality, for swindling the State University out of seventy-five thousand dollars.

Merlin glanced at the faces around him. They looked the same as always. Nobody seemed to be troubled, or even very interested in what was happening.

In his modest real estate business, Merlin Webster had been guilty of no misdemeanor in which the law itself would not uphold him; but lately his face wore an expression of nervous apprehension on opening the morning newspaper. Since Mr. Rogge had arrived in town, a man hardly knew what to expect. Even the innocent protested their honesty too elaborately to their friends, and felt foolish about it afterwards. Merlin himself had been guilty of such protestations; and when he stepped into an elevator and saw the heavy doors slide shut, his mind sometimes played uncomfortable tricks, for several of his acquaintances were behind much heavier doors in the Federal Penitentiary at Atlanta.

Since Roosevelt had been occupying the White House, life had changed. Nothing was stable. Look at the dust belt. Whole farms had blown away. Look at the taxes. High taxes on real estate. Building impossible except with Government aid; and everybody working for WPA. It was almost a relief to speculate on the clouds gathering over Europe. Europe was far away.

'What dey gunna steal next?' said the newsboy. 'What gunna happen next?'

'Maybe it'll rain,' said Merlin facetiously. He was looking at the weather report. A cloudy afternoon with possible thundershowers was predicted. It would be a welcome relief from the heat.

With the newspaper folded crisply under his arm, Merlin stepped toward the curb. A puppy was crying behind him. He glanced over his shoulder. A Negro child was dragging a mongrel puppy along the hot pavement by a yellow string around its neck. The sound it made was excruciating. Still looking over his shoulder, Merlin stepped off the curb into the street.

A traffic whistle blew indignantly. Brakes squealed. Tires skidded. Merlin leaped from the path of a truck trying to make the intersection before the light changed.

His newspaper lay in the street, crumpled and marked with tire treads. He bent to pick it up.

THOMAS FERRABEE, in the speeding truck, was oblivious of the fact that he had nearly run over a man. His action with the brakes had been purely automatic. A block away by this time, with narrowed eyes and jutting jaw, he was talking to himself.

'I give it to her straight,' he said. 'I let her have it right between the eyes. . . . "I'm going," I said, "and don't you try to stop me!" . . . She didn't think I had it in me, but I showed her. . . . Man, did I rock her on her heels! . . . "I'm through," I said. "I'm finished—get me? . . . I'm fed up for the last time—get me? I'm pulling out of this crazy-house!" . . . and man, I went!'

THERE HAD BEEN NO TIME to be afraid, Merlin thought, as he continued across the street to neutral ground, and waited for a streetcar to stop, the people to crowd off and on, and the car to move again—and yet, this very minute, he might have been lying in a pool of blood in the street, while these same people, these students and nurses and vacuous, perambulatory housewives whose blank faces now gazed placidly past him through the windows of the car, might have been pushing and crowding around him.

'Call the ambulance!'

'Don't lift him!'

'Stand back and give him air!'

He had seen it happen so many times, himself one of the crowd come running at the sound of a crash and the smell of blood— blood so privately, neatly channeled in the veins a minute before, then suddenly so public on the street's hot grainy asphalt, like a love-letter brutally torn from its envelope and laid open for the cruel world to read.

Merlin's stomach contracted in a hard, cold knot. His knees trembled. The palms of his hands were damp with cold sweat. He drew a deep breath.

JESSE McPHAIL, the traffic policeman, spat his whistle from his mouth and rocked from heel to toe under his green umbrella in the middle of Canal Street. Let it pass, he thought. The man ogling the little colored girl had made neutral ground safely, after all. The man driving the Bruce's Juices delivery truck should have been given a ticket on general principles. But let it pass.

What a town for traffic! he thought. The Canal Street lights held so long that cars jumped them; and half the time pedestrians didn't even bother to look at them, but poured across the street wherever they saw an opening. People were always getting spattered around. It wasn't his fault. He didn't like blood. He did his best, but he couldn't be eyes for everybody.

Just look at them, he thought, watching the slow crowds swim toward and past him now that the car had moved. Nine-o'clock office workers, sleep-walkers too fresh out of bed, although the sun was high and the reflected heat off the pavement had been burning his own face for an hour—too fresh out of bed, most of them, to know whether they were coming or going.

Because he had been seeing them at this crossing for quite a while now: the same faces at the same time every morning, until they had become familiar to him (here, glimpsing in the crowd the man at whom he had whistled, and counting him familiar, too, his freshly shaven face a little pale because of his narrow escape, McPhail nodded sternly and made a brief gesture with his hand which the man ignored or did not see, and, lowering his head, hurried on); and because he often understood more than he could have explained, it seemed briefly to Jesse McPhail, under his green umbrella, that there was something terrible about these people all wearing the same face at ten minutes to nine in the morning; as if they weren't alive; as if something had wound up their bodies, pushed them through their doors, pointed them toward the business district, and here they came—the distance between house and office nonexistent in their minds, or a dreamy no-man's land they crossed by luck or habit or instinct, he didn't know which. And they wouldn't be alive again until they sat down at their desks.

'Like a bunch of zombies,' he said to himself.

Jesse McPhail, with a ruddy skin, a good digestion, and a fishing trip planned for the week-end, felt happy this morning, and looked about him for a happy face. 'Hi, spider legs,' he said to the brightest thing he had seen this morning—a little colored girl in a purple blouse and a floppy, red straw hat. She was carrying a puppy in her arms. The puppy was licking her face. She stopped laughing and looked up, startled. 'Hi, spider legs,' said McPhail, grinning. 'Wanta sell that pup?'

'Nawsa.' She walked a few steps, looked behind her, and began to run. Her white tennis shoes were very white and flat at the ends of her thin black legs, like something out of a Walt Disney cartoon.

Looking at them, McPhail thought of other black legs running, and saw blood appear on them. Lichte, on the homicide squad, had told him only last night that they had caught the nigger boy who had robbed the grocery on Dauphine Street, and had worked him over to make him talk.

No, thought McPhail, blowing his whistle again. Traffic might be tough, but he'd rather be on traffic than on the homicide squad. He didn't like beating up people. He didn't like blood.

Frowning, he glanced across the street after the man who had begun this train of thought in his mind. There he was, in his white linen suit, just climbing the opposite curb with legs that looked a little wobbly. Another sleep-walker saved for his desk.

McPhail looked down at his feet, and began to swear. Right in front of him, somebody had chalked a swastika on the pavement. Some fool kid, some practical joker, had been trying to pull his leg. McPhail glared about him. But, at the moment, nobody was anywhere near him but a dignified elderly gentleman wearing a sporty, red bow tie, and carrying a black umbrella. He was just boarding a streetcar. McPhail smudged out the swastika with his foot.

HOW FRESH AND FRAIL the morning was, Merlin Webster thought. The curb gained, he leaned against a light standard, for his heart was still pounding and his legs were unsteady. He took the newspaper from his pocket and spread it open; but the print was blurred by tire treads, and the wind ruffled the torn sheets until they hissed at him. He folded the paper and restored it to his pocket.

How fresh and frail, he thought, remembering, surprisingly, his own garden as it had appeared to him from his bathroom door at seven o'clock: still cool in the shadow of the house; still wet and crisp with dew; the moonflowers still wide on the walls; the oleander so heavy with bloom its branches bent with white weight toward the ground; the first fluted bud of the scarlet hibiscus just beginning to uncurl—so easily snapped at the stem and falling, falling into blackness.

Man cometh up as a flower, he thought, moving away from the light standard, walking another block along Canal Street, then turning up Baronne . . . *Man cometh up as a flower, and is cut down* . . . getting farther away from the garden with every step he took as strength returned to his legs; attaching himself more firmly to the hot June morning with each deep breath he drew of the coffee-scented air.

For now he was aware of it—the smell of roasting coffee. The wind that fluttered the women's light summer dresses was also spilling the benignant smell of roasting coffee liberally over the business district. Merlin Webster, who dealt in the solid and not so solid structures men build on solid ground, breathed deep of the coffee-scented air laden with memories and certainties of his childhood, and looked with guarded, wistful eyes at the women inside their summer dresses. These things, at least, had not changed.

Gratitude was due somewhere, for something. For the women, for the coffee, for the garden still safe inside its walls, for the blood still neatly, privately channeled under his white linen suit?

When he saw the blind woman singing with her guitar, his hand, already in his pocket, came out with a crumpled bill. His fingers opened above the cigar box the woman wore slung on a string around her neck. The bill fell into the box without a sound. Merlin Webster walked on.

Ten steps, and he stopped. His hand plunged into his pocket and came out with several crumpled bills. Checking them hurriedly, he confirmed his fear. He moved forward again, hesitated, then turned and walked back toward the blind woman. He had given her a ten-dollar bill instead of a one.

Yes, there was his ten-dollar bill in the cigar box, in plain sight, within easy reach of his hand. Its fall had been noiseless; the woman, unknowing, had not yet gathered it in. If he could retrieve it, he could make change. Merlin's hand moved upward . . .

'Good morning, Mr. Webster.'

A hand in a lace glove tossed a coin into the cigar box. A girl's face flashed at Merlin—white teeth and red lipstick.

Merlin's hand jerked to his hat brim. Blood rushed to his face.

Had she seen? Did she suspect—the young stenographer who worked across the hall from his office, now hurrying away up the street with swaying hips?

She could have seen nothing, Merlin reassured himself. He stopped under a bank awning and lit a cigarette with shaking hands. How could she have seen anything? He had merely been lifting his hand to his hat. His hand had gone in a straight line from his side to his hat brim. Any impulse outward, toward the cigar box, had been stopped by the girl's voice somewhere along his arm, between his mind and his hand. What he had been about to do could have been detected only by a mind-reader. The act was safe in his mind. No mind-readers were on the street this morning. The act was not even in his mind. Ten dollars was a large amount to give a beggar woman when you were sober, but let her keep it. What a windfall it would be to her! She would probably spend it to get drunk, but the blind had few pleasures. Money given to the blind was well given, and, however spent, would be well spent.

The wind sucked down the street. Above Merlin's head the bank awning popped with a startled sound. Merlin jumped, and walked on toward his office.

His stenographer was there before him. 'Good morning,' he said, hanging up his hat. 'I almost didn't get here this morning.' He paused for her question, settling his tie.

'Why, what happened?'

'A truck nearly ran me down on Canal Street.'

'You ought to be more careful!'

The voice was worried, as he had known it would be. He felt better. He shrugged his shoulders and laughed. He lounged to the window with his hands in his pockets and looked out over the roofs to the river's bright arm that curved around the city.

The Mississippi River. He had picked this office because it afforded such a fine view of the river and the shipping. But why did sight of the river in the morning fill him so often with vague dread, like a dark dream half-remembered? It was only a great muddy river, sliding forever past the city while people slept. Merlin Webster tried to remember something he had forgotten, and could not remember. The wind flapped the flag on the Dixie Brewery, and dropped it limply against its pole. Behind him, Merlin felt his stenographer's concern.

'Well,' he said jokingly, turning away from the window and seating himself at his desk, 'let's see if we can make some money this morning. I just lost ten bucks.'

'What a shame!'

'I didn't exactly lose it.' He was filling his fountain pen now. His hands were steady and his voice casual. 'You know that blind woman that plays a guitar in front of the Jesuit Church on Baronne Street?'

'Why, yes,' she answered. 'I've seen that woman. I've been seeing her for years.'

She was standing beside him, large and docile, with dexterous fingers, and a mind almost as shrewd as his when it came to the real estate business. His friends had been trying for years to entice her away with offers of higher salary, but she had not gone. She was devoted to him. Her name was Amelia Decker. Nearly everybody called her Decker.

When anybody looked closely at Decker—which Merlin had long ago ceased to do—he could nearly always detect a safety-pin somewhere about her: securing a shoulder-strap, the hem of a skirt, peeping out from under a belt fastening. This morning it was in plain sight, holding a sprig of sweet olive at the place on her blouse where the third button should have been.

'Decker,' he said, wiping the point of his pen very carefully on a blotter, 'I reckon I'm just a soft-hearted fool, but I gave that woman ten dollars this morning.'

Her capable fingers caressed the small flower on her dress as she gazed at her employer's thin, sandy profile. 'That was like you,' she said.

Smiling, he glanced up at her, and saw her eyes. She smiled back at him.

Saved from the street, from the river, from darkness; healed and forgiven and comforted for the moment—and not even knowing why—he began to open his morning mail.

HEARING THE FALL of the coin in her box, the coin which had followed Merlin Webster's bill, and, more than hearing, feeling its fall, for the thin cedar wood of the cigar box always vibrated against her breast with the dropping and rolling of a coin, the blind woman reached into the box with a brown, stubby hand, and found the bill. She dropped the coin in her pocket. The bill she stuffed quickly in the bosom of her cotton dress.

She had had no time to feel of the bill and so determine its value; but even from such hurried passage through her fingers, she was pretty sure that it was more than a one-dollar bill. Of course, it might be only a two, but two-dollar bills were scarce; and, besides, did not feel as this one felt. Then it would have to be a five. Last Christmas Eve, a woman had given her a five-dollar bill. Generosity beyond this, the blind woman could not imagine.

She did not stop playing; she did not even stop singing; but the shape of an idea began to steal upon her. It did not seem to be born of her own mind at all, but to be creeping upon her from the outside, stalking her from the jungle of street sounds; from the hiss of shoe leather on concrete, the wallowing rumble of streetcars, the squawking of horns, the squeal of brakes suddenly stepped on, the shrill birdlike *peep pee-eep!* of the traffic police-man's whistle on Canal Street.

She stiffened her mind against the idea. She sang louder. Around herself, with voice and humming strings, she threw up a barricade. But the idea kept coming closer. She left her place against the church wall and moved some thirty feet to stand under the awning in front of the bank. It was cooler here, but the shade was unquiet and she could not stay.

Slowly, sliding her feet a few inches at a time, as if she were wading into water whose depth she could not immediately judge, she moved out from the wall and into the stream of sidewalk traffic. She was jostled a little, but she was too sturdy to be knocked off her course. After she had taken a few steps, the stream split around her and went by on both sides.

Back and forth she walked along the block—a broad, powerful woman who would have been handsome, with her black hair, her even white teeth, and her plump brown face, if her eyelids had not been seared shut and sunken deep in their sockets. As it was, her face did not have the blank look of most blind people, but was carried forward on her neck with curiosity and aggressiveness. Her upper lip was outlined with a faint black mustache.

Her name was Dora Klopstock. A jealous husband, worker in a small Mississippi mill town in the pine woods, had thrown acid on her face and gone to jail for it. He was still there. She had a son named Corey, a child now four years old. Friends had been keeping him for the past three years. She could not remember his face; she had not even had him close to her until five months ago when, feeling curious about him, and thinking, too, that his presence on the street with her might touch more pockets, she had mailed the five-dollar Christmas Eve bill and asked that Corey be put on the bus and sent to her.

Small, frightened, hating, he had come. He cringed away from the hands that felt over his face, his thin little arms and legs. He would not eat, and grew thinner. He was used to the woods; the city terrified him; but his hatred and terror of the city were not so great as his hatred and terror of the rough brown woman who could not tell night from day.

He would not stand beside her on the street, but time after

time ran away from her. He would not answer when she called. She found him only by sound of his breathing; by the smell of his clothes; by knowledge of his hiding places; by some instinct which led her always in the end to where he shivered under a table or against a wall.

'Lissen, Corey,' she would say, taking a firm grip on his small hand. 'Lissen, son, I want you to learn your way around.'

'I wanna go home! I wanna go home!'

'Now, lissen, son . . .'

At first, because he was so small and frightened and got lost so easily, she often forgot that he was not blind like herself. She was proud of her hard-won knowledge of a dark world; she wanted to pass this knowledge on to her son. And then she would remember that he was not blind, that he had no need for her knowledge, and would have nothing to say. For her, the city was laid out in a familiar pattern of tilt and texture, of heat and cold, of sound and echo—but this was not true for Corey who had eyes, but was too young to read the street signs. She had grown to love him, but she could not teach him to read; she could not teach him anything. Today, she had left him huddled on the bed.

She would have to send him back to Mississippi.

In the middle of the sidewalk, with people all around her but too far away to help, with her fingers busily plucking the steel strings of her guitar, and her mouth open, singing—the idea had caught up with her.

She would have to send Corey back to Mississippi with the money in her dress. Five dollars would pay the bus fare. She would never see him again.

Her hand swept down across the strings—a hard blow, a vibrant discord. She silenced the vibration with another blow from the flat of her hand, and picked up the tune again. She had not once stopped singing.

Hearing the tune, a man waiting for a break in traffic to cross the street, tapped a foot in lazy three-four time. In a near-by

Shoe-Shine Parlor a colored boy, giving the final fillip to a pair of brown oxfords, wielded his cloth in unconscious rhythm. The pliant notes curled along the street and climbed above the head of the slow-moving singer, above the unknowing heads of the crowd, above the roofs, and faded in the bright hot morning among the piling clouds.

> I'll never see no movin' pictures no more—
> Oh La-w-d! I'll never see—
> Dum diddy dum dum—
> Dum diddy dum dum.

A few coins dropped into the box. The bank clock chimed the quarter hour.

2

IN THE SHOE–SHINE PARLOR, the boy finished polishing the brown oxfords, straightened his back, and stood to one side. The man's face was hidden behind a newspaper; he did not notice that his shoes were done.

'All set, suh,' said the boy.

The man lowered the paper and climbed down from the chair. He was short and slender, with a broad brown face deeply creased by lines where lines seldom come on a human face. The general effect was comical, and people usually smiled when they saw him the first time. His keen eyes guarded his face carefully. His hair was red. On one cheekbone was a patch of iodine-stained gauze held in place by adhesive tape. He looked as if he had been in a fight. The shine boy grinned.

The man felt in his pocket and tossed something to the boy. The boy caught the object and looked at it, perplexed. It was a small tin box of Bayer's Aspirin. 'Keep it,' said the man. 'You can have this, too, if you want it.' He flipped a coin on top of the box and went out of the door, fingering his cheekbone.

As he passed the blind woman, he rid himself of another coin. He crossed Canal Street and presently turned down Royal. A short distance along the block, he stopped in a news store.

'Got a Sunday *New York Times?*' he said.

'No, sir, they don't come in till Wednesday.'

'What day is this?'

'Monday,' said the clerk. 'If you'll leave your name, I'll save you a copy when they come in Wednesday.'

'I won't be here Wednesday,' said the man, and was going out of the shop when somebody said, 'Hello, Joe. Get yourself fixed up all right?'

The voice belonged to Coffee, the captain of Joe's ship. 'Hello, Coffee,' he said. 'Yeah. I got fixed up.'

The captain came from the back of the shop and the two men stood in the doorway. 'That was a nasty cut under your eye,' the captain said. 'I think you ought to let a doctor take a stitch in it.'

'It's all right.'

'Just what happened, anyhow? After you changed your clothes this morning, you got away so fast I didn't have a chance to ask you.'

'Nothing worth telling,' said Joe. 'Nothing you can do anything about.'

'Go on. What happened? When you get a 'phone call to get your First Engineer out of jail at four o'clock in the morning, you like to know how he got there in the first place.'

'Well, it was this way,' said Joe. 'I was walking along Burgundy Street yesterday afternoon when a squad car pulled up ahead of me, and four cops jumped out and grabbed a colored kid playin' mumblety-peg on the sidewalk. The kid had a knife in his hand, and they scared him. What would you expect? He took a poke at one of the cops, wriggled loose, and started to get the hell out of there. They hollered, but he wouldn't stop, so a couple of them hauled out their guns and started shooting at his legs. They stopped him all right, but the kid still had a lot of fight left in him, so one of the cops started slinging his gun-butt. That's where I came in. I should have had more sense. No use arguing with cops, the cards are all against you, but I had to stick my neck out. All I said was, "Hell, give the kid a chance," and one of them hauled off and socked me and laid me out flat. So they took us both to the can, and that's about all. Except they worked the kid over—something about some petty thefts in grocery stores—and he made such a racket I couldn't sleep. So I finally bribed a flunkey to 'phone you to get me out.'

'No good,' said the captain, shaking his head. 'No good interfering with the law, Joe. You ought to know it by this time.'

'I can't seem to learn,' said Joe. 'I wonder if I ever will.'

'You're lucky you got off so easy this time—aiding a man to resist arrest. You get in too many fights, Joe. You ought to settle down. When I was your age, I had a wife and four kids. Ever think of getting married?'

'Who, me?' Joe shoved his hat to the back of his head and laughed out loud. 'The thought never entered my mind. I get in enough trouble as it is.'

The captain smiled. 'What are you doing today?'

'I thought I'd walk around awhile and clear my head. Maybe take in a show this afternoon.'

'I'm having lunch with the Port Captain. Want to come along?'

'No, thanks,' said Joe.

'Well, stay out of trouble. We're shoving off at six in the morning. I don't want to ship a new First Engineer at the last minute. See you on deck tonight.'

'Okay,' said Joe, and went on down the street toward the French Market for coffee and doughnuts. As he passed Neeley's rooming-house he thought to ring the bell, and changed his mind. Neeley was an old acquaintance, but she would be grouchy if he woke her. Her coffee was no good, anyhow.

The sight of Neeley's house, however, reminded him of Leah Webster. Saturday night, not knowing what else to do with Leah, he had brought her to visit Neeley. Now, as he walked down Royal Street Monday morning, he tried to remember her face. He had some difficulty at first; but presently, from the lacy balconies; from the clutter of antiques in shop windows; from the glimpse of cool, sprinkled patios through courtyard doors; from the sharp black shadows on the sidewalk—the features, forgotten for twenty-four hours, reassembled themselves. It was a secret kind of face, like a young girl's, he thought; and it had a way of looking tight and rather grim until she laughed. When she laughed, her face was beautiful, he thought with surprise. It had been easy to make her laugh; it had been fun. She had been so pleased to be able to laugh. If she had said anything, he had forgotten.

She was not at all the sort of woman he had first thought her when she had asked him to buy her a drink. Skinny legs, and funny little shoes. And nice eyes. Blue, and deep-set, and maybe a little too close together—but nice eyes.

Once, during the night, he had seen her open her purse and take out her glasses. She put them back hurriedly when she saw him watching. Yes, she had said something. He remembered it now. As she returned the glasses to her purse, she had laughed in an embarrassed way and said, 'We deteriorate rapidly, don't we? . . . but I really don't need them except when I read.'

And once, crossing a street, she had stumbled, and he had waited to see if she would grab his arm. But she hadn't. Independent as a hog on ice, or trying to be. After she had picked him up, she had been scared half to death; and he had tried to make things easy for her. The next morning, he had bought some drinks for a WPA kid on the Painters' Project; and then he had ditched the kid, and found himself a girl.

The French Market Coffee Shop was empty except for a couple of waiters who disappeared into the kitchen after Joe was served.

Joe drank his chicory coffee and ate his doughnuts thoughtfully. He was a gregarious man, and liked to talk. He felt a little lonely. When he had finished his coffee, he sauntered through the long central promenade of the Farmers' Market and looked at the truckloads of vegetables backed in between the columns: white turnips, yellow carrots, dark red beets, great crisp heads of cabbage, early corn, cucumbers, long green pods of okra, bunches of curly parsley and wild anise. Some of the trucks had evidently arrived the previous night, and the drivers had slept in them on blankets. One small Negro boy still sprawled in the back of a truck, oblivious of the noise and movement going on around him: the babble of Cajin, Italian, Negro, English, French; the shouts, the bargaining, the laughter.

Like most men who have spent long years at sea, Joe carried in the back of his mind the idea of some day owning a farm, an area of solid, unshifting element enclosed by stable boundaries and recorded in his own name. Probably, like most of these men, he would do nothing about it, for the thing he wanted was not the thing he loved. When he was long at sea, he thought vaguely about the farm; but after two days on shore, he thought about the sea as a man thinks about liquor or women—that is, he did not think about it at all—he felt about it, and set events in motion to obtain it. And so, since the age of seventeen, Joe had gone to sea. But still, the idea of a farm remained in the back of his mind. It was a good idea. He liked to talk with farmers and pick up what knowledge he could.

But they were too busy to talk with him. Rather disconsolately, he wandered on. Soon, he found himself at the end of the Market, looking up at the back porch and windows of the Federal Detention House which fronted on Esplanade Avenue. Some of the prisoners were walking back and forth on the upstairs gallery. Some stared through the heavy mesh wire, out over the high wall, at the street.

A brown girl in a pert red dress walked down the street. Instantly, the air was full of whistles and ribald invitations. The girl tossed her head, and walked with self-conscious, mincing steps.

Poor dopes, Joe thought. What a place to put a jail! The busy market, where free men came and went all day and half the night with all the rich produce of the countryside; the river, the railroad tracks, the sight and sound of ships and trains—all methods of escape were just beyond the walls. And women passed constantly, just out of reach. He knew how they felt. It was one thing to take away a man's liberty when he had forfeited it; and another thing to dangle food in front of a starving man. But circumstance, no doubt, demanded such an arrangement. The structure, he had heard, had been a Federal Mint before the Civil War. Now it was another kind of mint. An ironic juxtaposition, arranged by circumstance.

The whistling stopped as the girl turned a corner. That girl he had found yesterday had also worn a red dress, Joe remembered. Maybe she was the same girl. She had walked the same way. The only thing good about that girl had been that she hadn't rolled him, and he still had money in his pockets.

Jingling his loose change, Joe walked back through the Market. If he had been with Leah, he thought, it certainly wouldn't have been the way it had been. How would it have been? . . . By God, maybe he'd been a fool. Leah must have liked his looks a hell of a lot, and he had done nothing about it. All women were more or less crazy. Even the quietest ones among them, the ones like Leah, would sometimes do things a man would have too much fear, or pride, or plain common sense to attempt. It must have cost a person like Leah Webster a great deal to walk up to him in that barroom and ask him for a drink. She had wanted more for her money than an all-night conversation and a cup of coffee. . . . So he had merely talked to her, had he? Merely talked to her all night. What a fool he had been, Joe thought. He talked too much.

He stopped to look at a Diesel yard engine pulling a string of aluminum-painted tank cars with 'Black Strap Molasses' in large black letters on their sides; and fell into immediate conversation with the young driver of a shrimp truck, about Diesel engines and reciprocating turbines, and the different types of trawl boats used in the Gulf off Biloxi and Port Eads and Grand Isle. But the conversation was interrupted before it was well begun. Two girls in summer finery, with sandaled feet and bright, bare legs, hailed the truck-driver. ''Allo, Manuel! When you git in town, you?'

With a polite flash of white teeth and black eyes, Joe was dismissed. He shrugged his shoulders and moved away. Presently, he found himself walking past the retail booths of the French Market and looking, not at the produce, but at the women doing their morning marketing. It was a rich sight for a lonely man.

Joe leaned against a column in front of the Mexican Shop, and watched. All kinds of women, all shapes, all sizes, all colors— all chattering. The place sounded like a flock of parrots stirred up in the jungle back of Porto Barrios.

Among the pottery jugs, serapes, huaraches, straw mats and straw hats of the Mexican Shop was one lone grass skirt dangling from a nail on a central pillar, its long brown fibers quivering delicately in the breeze. Joe was looking at the skirt, his fancy momentarily occupied with a possible wearer, when something caught his attention. A funny little fat girl in a blue playsuit, consisting of pants and straps, had wandered out of the crowd of women and brought up in front of the grass skirt.

Joe smiled. A little female creature all intact and complete, he thought. All the knowledge, all the tricks, were inside her somewhere—just give her time. What was in her mind at this minute, no doubt, was a picture of herself as a movie actress in a grass skirt. Poor little kid. With a face like hers, she'd better stop thinking about movie actresses and begin studying. 'Pretty is as pretty does'—wasn't that what mothers told their homely daughters? What a cheat! All females should be beautiful from the cradle up. And what on earth was her mother thinking about, to let her run around in such tight pants? Her frame was certainly unprepossessing.

But the anatomy of the young female after puberty, he thought, often displayed an instinctive but none the less amazing ability to go in at the right places and out at the right places to attract the male. No doubt the kid would manage to lose that stomach and grow up to her big feet, some day. And what would she remember of this morning when she was grown?

Would she remember that the sun, blazing on the khaki-colored awning, colored the light in the Mexican Shop a warm, golden brown? Would she remember the shapes, the sounds, the smells of Decatur Street, the smell of leather and grass in the shop? Would she remember any of the faces? For instance, the face of that colored chauffeur as he lifted a basket of peaches into the back of a car—his incorruptible dignity as he took a peach from the top of the basket, peeled it with his fingernail, and ate it slowly under the awning while shade and sunlight rippled over him? Would she remember the face of that old woman in the black shawl, with the dirty hands and the pretty white hair, who had just picked up a hairpin from the gutter, and now approached a colored man weighing a heap of red tomatoes? . . . 'Heah come po Mis' Culpa. Kin she have a soup-bunch?' said the colored helper to the owner of the stall. . . . Would the fat little girl, when she was grown, remember a man in a gray suit and shiny brown shoes, who leaned against the pillar under the awning and looked at her? Had she even seen him? She had not once taken her eyes off that grass skirt.

No, Joe thought, she would remember nothing from the working, bubbling ferment of this June morning but a grass skirt hanging from a nail. She would remember the skirt as something she had wanted desperately, and had not possessed.

All at once he wanted her to have the grass skirt, and wanted to be remembered as the one from this morning who had given it to her: remembered with gratitude and a faint warm stir of kindly thought some day years hence. For is this not a kind of immortality—to be remembered by a living human creature as

Joe leaned against a column ...

the one who had one day given her the thing she wanted with all her heart, and could not have had unless?

Jingling the loose silver in his pocket, Joe left the pillar and approached the child. 'Hello,' he said.

'Hello,' she answered, smiling up at him.

'Like that skirt?'

'Oh, very much. It's beautiful.'

'Like to try it on?'

'Oh, no. No, thank you.' The child flushed, and backed away.

'Leetle gal like pretty skirt?' said the shopkeeper, a dark polite little Mexican.

'Yes. I do. I like it very much.'

'What's your name?' said Joe. 'I bet I can guess. I bet your name is Dorothy? No? Then it's Catherine . . . no? Betty?'

'It's Georgie,' she answered, scared and giggling. 'But my mama . . . my mama said never talk to strange men . . . I think I better go find her . . . I think . . . I better . . .'

'Georgie, come here this minute!'

The child ran. The shopkeeper shrugged his shoulders and lit a cigarette. Joe looked in the direction from which the voice had come, and saw a pale green turban crowning an expression of outraged loathing. A plump, protecting arm circled Georgie's shoulders and guided her into a car pulled up at the curb.

As the car drove away, the green turban was lowered to the child's ear; and the mouth beneath the turban was plainly imparting knowledge every little girl should know about strange men who offer to buy her presents.

'BUT HOW CAN YOU TELL which is nice people?' said Georgie.

Marie Webster, unloading her packages on the kitchen table, giving directions to the colored cook who was too illiterate to trust with the marketing, wondered how one was able to tell a child the difference between really nice people and people who were not nice.

There were so many signs to recognize; so many words, like passwords, by which nice people knew their equals and let themselves be known. The right magazines, the right books, the right clothes, and the right way of wearing them, as if they didn't matter. The right kind of houses; the right kind of friends, and knowing how to amuse them; and knowing how to keep one's communication lines open only in the right direction. Like a foreign language, the process took years to learn if one had not been exposed to it in childhood. If one had been exposed to it in childhood, however, one knew it quite simply and naturally. This was the way she wanted Georgie to know. She would give her very life, she thought, to spare Georgie such groping as she had experienced while learning how to tell nice people from people who were not really nice. But Georgie must be answered; and so she said, quite simply, 'Mother's and daddy's friends are nice people.'

'Oh,' said Georgie. 'The Budds. They *are* nice, aren't they?'

'Very, very nice . . . Orena, be sure to slice the lemon thin, and cut the radishes like I showed you. Remember?'

'Yas'm,' said the cook.

'Are the Tuttles nice people like the Budds?' Georgie asked.

'Of course they are.'

'Is Miss Decker nice?'

Foreseeing that this inventory might spread to include certain relatives—for instance, old Mrs. Peralta on her doorstep, Marie changed the subject.

'Speaking of Miss Decker,' she said, 'I've just remembered that tomorrow is her birthday. Don't you think it would be nice if you came shopping with me and helped pick out a present for her?' Marie smiled at her daughter. Georgie had grown tremendously in the past few months, and Marie was suddenly aware of the growth. Maybe that awful man in the Market had seen too much skin. 'I think you'd better put on a dress, honey,' she added. 'It would look nicer.'

'These pants are cool,' Georgie said.

'But aren't they a little too tight to be comfortable?'

'Nome,' said Georgie, hitching a strap off her shoulder to ease the pull.

'I think they are. Run upstairs and put on a dress, and as soon as mama makes a list, we'll go shopping, shall we? And maybe have luncheon in town, and see a movie?'

Georgie left the kitchen. Marie turned to Orena, the cook.

'How is Clara Bilbo these days?' she said.

'She fine. She worryin bout her granson. Cooter en jail. Dat boy nevah rob no grocery sto, Mrs. Webster. Dat boy don belong to be en jail. Cudden Mr. Webster witness to de jedge dat Cooter a good boy?'

Marie looked at her fingernails. Such requests were common. They were something of a nuisance. 'I'm sure Clara tried to raise her grandson properly,' she said, 'but young boys Cooter's age very often get out of hand. If he's not guilty, they'll turn him loose. If he is guilty, he ought to take his punishment like a man.'

'Cooter jes a boy, Mrs. Webster.'

'I'm awfully sorry, but I don't see how Mr. Webster can do anything about it.'

'Yas'm.'

'Does Clara like her new job?'

'Yas'm.'

'Now she's getting so old, I thought it would be easier for her to have a job where she could sit down all day instead of standing over a stove. I was so glad I could help her find one.'

'Yas'm.'

'I hear she sells more pralines than any other Mammy in the Quarter. Clara's a hard worker. She's a fine old woman.'

'Yas'm,' said Orena, chopping red onions in very small pieces on the meat board. 'Clara a fine woman, an raise her fambly raight.'

Marie went into the living-room. It was a charming room, high-ceilinged, gracious and cool. The soft colors of the chintz curtains were repeated in the garden beyond in bolder, brighter tones. The waxed floor and the brown satin skin of the antique furniture gleamed from polishing. Everything in the room was just right. 'Keep to the period,' Helen Budd had said. And she had kept to the period.

But was it the right period?

Such doubts were foolish. Of course, it was the right period. She had Helen Budd to substantiate her. But there was old Mrs. Laurent, Preston Dillon's aunt. Mrs. Laurent had asked to see the lovely house she had heard so much about; but when she had seen it, she hadn't said that she liked it. She had said nothing at all except, 'Who is that curious, comfortable old woman sitting on her doorstep next door? I'd like to know her.' . . . Mrs. Laurent was so old and wealthy she could afford to be eccentric. She had a vocabulary like a fishwife; but it was smart to be eccentric when one was as old as Mrs. Laurent. Maybe she would try being eccentric herself, Marie thought, when she was that old. In the meantime, one must bring up one's child in the best way one knew.

How would the Tuttles like the house?

Marie was always nervous when strangers saw her house for the first time. It was necessary to explain to them, particularly if they came from out of town and did not understand the social eccentricities of the French Quarter, why one lived in the same block with colored people and the Tarantinos. And there was a right way and a wrong way to explain.

Would the Tuttles like the way she had furnished their apartment?

Marie went over the appointments of the renovated slave house: the new Frigidaire, the old brass andirons, the copper woodbox for the fireplace, the fourposter bed. Good Heavens, she had forgotten to provide a crib for the Tuttle baby!

She drew a sheet of notepaper from a drawer, and made a neat list.

> present for Decker—gloves?
> Tuttle crib
> head hdkf Orena—blue
>   "   "   Clara—red
> Crescent Beauty Shop—3 pm
> Leah?

Before adding Leah's name to the list, she deliberated for several minutes. But it was wrong to feel antagonistic toward unhappy, muddled Leah. People like Leah could hardly be held accountable for their actions; they were more to be pitied than blamed. It would be much more generous to surprise Leah with a little gift—a book, perhaps. If she could succeed in winning Leah's confidence, she might be able to persuade her to see a psychiatrist. And so she added Leah's name.

While her mother was making her shopping list, Georgie had come downstairs to talk with Orena in the kitchen.

'Orena,' she said, 'do Catholics and Baptists live in the same Heaven when they die?'

'Don bodda me. Ah'm busy.'

'But do they, Orena, do they?'

'All de good an chosen gon live en peace an hominy. De Lawd promus us dat. All de mean an unchosen gon fry en tormention en de bad place. De Lawd promus us dat, also.'

Onions sizzled in the skillet. Orena stirred them with a long fork. Georgie backed away from the stove.

'Will colored people and white people live in the same block?'

'Ain no street blocks en Hebben. Hit's all de Lawd's house.'

'But they got to be blocks, Orena. The Bible says the streets are paved with gold. If they got streets, they got to have blocks, don't they?'

'Hit's de Lawd's big house.'

'God is everywhere, huh, Orena?'

'Praise His name.'

'He can do anything He wants to, can't He?'

'Praise His name. Amen. Ah reckon.'

'He could ring all the bells in the world if He wanted to, couldn't He, Orena?'

'Whut you drivin at?'

'Who rings—?'

The kitchen door opened on Mrs. Webster dressed for a day of downtown shopping. 'Orena,' she said, 'if Mr. and Mrs. Tuttle come while I'm away, you'll have to take care of them. Think you can manage?'

'Yas'm.'

'The key to their apartment is in the front door. Fix them a drink, if they want it, and remember to tell them they're having dinner with us tonight. Dinner is at seven. We'll probably be home long before then, but don't forget. Is everything clear?'

'Yas'm,' said Orena. 'Hit's all quite cleah.'

ON ROYAL STREET, across from the Civil Courts Building, Leah Webster pressed the front-door buzzer of Neeley's rooming-house. Since breakfast, she had been walking nervously about the Quarter looking in antique shop windows, watching faces, passing the time until Neeley, who kept late hours, should be awake. Neeley, whom she had met only once, was the one person she knew who might be able to tell her something about Joe. But Neeley didn't answer the door. Surely, thought Leah, the woman should be up by now. It was nearly ten o'clock.

She buzzed the bell again and again, and was about to turn away when a sleepy voice called, 'Who is it? . . . who is it? Dammit, push the door open before you run my battery down!'

Leah took her thumb off the buzzer and shoved at the door. It stuck for an instant, then creaked open, and she found herself in a hall she remembered. At the end of the hall, on the landing above her, a woman's head peered over the bannister. 'Hello,' Leah said.

'Who is it?'

'Leah Webster. I was passing by, and thought I'd drop in for a minute.'

'Oh.' There was a pause. 'Well, I'm not dressed for company, but come on up if you want to.'

After this ungracious invitation, the head disappeared. Leah climbed the stairs. When she reached the top, nobody was visible. 'Where are you?' she called.

'In here,' Neeley answered. 'Come on in.'

Leah opened a door which seemed to be the right one, and caught Neeley in the act of powdering her face. Both women looked at each other in silent embarrassment. Neeley was still wearing her nightgown. Her eyes were swelled from sleep, and one cheek was creased by the pillow. The bell had evidently waked her.

'I'm so sorry,' Leah said. 'I thought you'd be up.'

'Sit down,' said Neeley, straightening the rumpled bed. 'Sit down somewhere. I should've been up an hour ago, only I didn't get much sleep last night.' She seized a pillow and shook it into shape. 'The noise here last night!' she burst out. 'Radios, radios. Birthday party in one room. Poker game in another. Somebody called the police and complained, and I never had the police in my house till last night . . . Like some coffee?'

'I'd love it,' Leah lied, 'but I think I ought to go away and let you sleep.'

'I couldn't sleep now.' Neeley picked up her clothes from a chair, an aluminum cooking pot from a small gas stove in a corner of the room, and went out the door.

Leah looked around the room. Joe had brought her here

Saturday night, after they had left the St. Regis. She could still feel his presence and hear his voice. He had said things to make her laugh, and had watched her to see that she laughed. She had laughed a great deal that night.

Neeley returned from the bathroom and set the pot of water on the stove. 'How's Joe?' she said, as she lit the fire.

'I haven't seen him since Saturday night.' Leah was nervous. It was going to be difficult to admit to another woman that she was looking for a man who had not disclosed his last name.

'I was asleep when you left,' Neeley said. 'I didn't hear you go.'

'I know,' said Leah. 'It was a shame to keep you up so late.'

'Where did you go when you left here?'

Leah had been prepared for some kind of interrogation. She controlled her annoyance and answered, 'To the French Market for coffee.'

'That doesn't sound like Joe,' said Neeley, lifting an eyebrow. 'Got a cigarette on you?'

Leah offered her a silver case. Neeley's eyebrow lifted higher. 'Well equipped, aren't you?' she drawled.

'I don't know what you mean.'

Neeley sauntered to the stove and poured the boiling water into a drip coffee pot. Turning, she looked at Leah deliberately, from head to toe. 'Listen, honey,' she said. 'I'll give you some good advice. Lay off Joe. You won't get anywhere with him. Not with those mockingbird legs.'

Leah bit her lip at the insult and kept her temper with an effort. Neeley sounded as if she, too, might be interested in Joe. Evidently they had known each other for some time. Joe's manner with Neeley had been that of a casual friend—but how did Neeley feel? Perhaps, thought Leah, she had walked into a situation she couldn't handle. Getting information out of Neeley looked as if it might be something of a job.

'I know my legs are too thin,' she said, 'but they get me where I'm going . . . or do they? Sometimes, I wonder.'

'What do you know about that?' said Neeley, nonplussed at such an amiable reply.

'I'm used to people making fun of my legs.'

'Now, honey, they aren't so bad. I've seen lots worse.'

'Where I work, everybody makes fun of my legs. I don't really mind.'

'You mean *you* have a job?'

'Of course I have.'

'Where on earth do you work?'

'In a neighborhood movie. In the ticket window. From four till midnight, except Saturday nights.'

'Here,' said Neeley abruptly. 'Your coffee's ready.' She brought a cup to Leah and sat on the bed beside her. 'I hope you aren't mad at me,' she said. 'Joe's a good friend of mine, and I thought you were just out for what you could get. When a girl works hard for her living like I do, it burns you up the way some people get it easy. But you never can tell about people. I bet you couldn't tell about me, either. I bet you'd never guess I'm an artist. My studio is upstairs. Want to see some pictures?' Neeley made a motion to rise, and sat down again. 'No,' she said. 'Not right now. If I go out of this door again, somebody'll hear me and come say he can't pay his rent. I couldn't stand it, not this morning. But honest,' she said, 'I apologize. You don't look like a working girl. How was I to know?'

'It's all right,' Leah said. 'You don't need to apologize.'

'Honey, I didn't mean it. I didn't get a good look at you the other night, but now I can see you, I'd know in a minute you weren't anything of the sort. Life is certainly funny.'

'It certainly is,' agreed Leah, beginning to feel that she was getting somewhere. Neeley's antagonism had evidently been for other reasons than jealousy about Joe.

'Look at me,' said Neeley, growing confidential. 'I'm a young woman yet, and I'd still look pretty good if I could afford some decent clothes. But life certainly handed me a dirty deal. The way it was, my husband lost his money in slot-machines. You wouldn't believe it, honey, but the man went simply mad over slot-machines. It got to where he wouldn't even stop playing to eat, hardly, and then he ran out on me, and all the clothes I used to have—where are they? My fur coat—where is it? In the pawnshop. My evening gowns—where are they? In the goddam pawnshop. I have to run a rooming-house to earn my living, and they won't let me sleep . . . But tell me, honey, what's the matter with you? You look worried. Is anything wrong?'

'Oh, no,' Leah said.

'Come on, spill it. You've been biting your fingernails ever since you came in. What's the trouble?'

'To tell you the truth, I'm looking for Joe. I thought you might be able to help me.'

'Why, I don't know where he is. He isn't here. Didn't he tell you where he was staying?'

'He didn't tell me anything about himself. I don't even know his last name. After we had coffee, he told me good-bye and walked away.'

'He's probably staying on board his ship,' said Neeley. 'Why don't you look there?'

'I don't know the name of his ship.'

'He certainly kept himself anonymous,' said Neeley, 'but that's the way Joe is. He's awful close-mouthed for such a talker. What's the idea trying to find him? He borrow money from you?'

'I'm in love with him.'

'My God!' Neeley leaned forward and looked at Leah incredulously. 'It's not that I can't imagine you being impressed with Joe,' she said, after a minute of embarrassing scrutiny. 'There's something about the man, all right, though he don't appeal to me that way. But I understood him to say he'd just met you . . . are you sure you two didn't go anywhere but the French Market for coffee when you left here Saturday night?'

'Certainly not,' said Leah. 'There wasn't anywhere else to go that time in the morning.'

'My God!' Neeley repeated. 'I've heard about love at first sight, but it never happened that way with me. Give me another cigarette, will you?'

She smoked in silence for several minutes. A passing streetcar set the old house to vibrating. Leah's empty coffee cup chattered in its saucer. She set it on the floor and gripped her fingernails into her palms. Time was passing.

'Listen,' said Neeley. 'This is a personal question and you don't have to answer it if you don't want to, but are you a virgin?'

Leah, caught off guard, felt her face coloring. 'It's not my fault,' she said defensively.

'Think of that,' Neeley breathed.

'I never loved anybody in my life till Saturday night,' said Leah, speaking desperately now, laying all her cards on the table. 'Now I'm in love with a man I know almost nothing about. I don't know his last name, or the name of his ship, or how long he'll be here, or anything about him except that he's a seaman. He talked about everything but himself. He liked me, Neeley, I know he did. But he didn't know it. You know how men are.'

'Sure,' said Neeley. 'I know.'

'Maybe I'd meet him again some day, and maybe not. I don't want to wait. I don't know what I'd say to him if I saw him, but I've got to see him, if it's possible. I know I must sound completely crazy to you, but you don't know what it means to me.'

'I can guess,' said Neeley. 'Take it easy, honey. You've been frank with me, and I'll be frank with you. I wasn't going to tell you, but I guess you've got a right to know. Not that I know much. But I'll tell you what I do know.' She poured another cup of coffee. 'In the first place,' she said, resetting herself comfortably on the bed, 'his last name is Onion.'

'Onion?'

'That's right. Funny, isn't it? He thinks it's a lot funnier than it is. He never tells anybody, if he can help it. I found out by accident.'

'So that's why he didn't tell me when I asked him. There's nothing wrong with Onion for a name. Have you known him long?'

'A couple of years, off and on. The first time I saw him, he'd just made town for Mardi Gras two years ago, and wanted a room. I had a room, but I was saving it for my niece and her husband from Dallas, but I said he could have it for fifty dollars, not dreaming he'd take it. But he took it. He peeled off fifty dollars and walked right in, and my niece and her husband had to sleep with me, and the inconvenience was more than fifty dollars' worth, let me tell you. Joe never used that room except to sleep a couple of hours, and I never saw him again till a year later, when his ship docked here again. That time, he borrowed five dollars. But he paid it back. Next time, I borrowed twenty from him, because I don't own this house, honey, I just rent it out, and some heel ran away without paying his room rent, and I had to make it good.'

'But Joe—'

'Oh, he pays his debts as far as I know, and he's single—I happen to know that much—and he's an interesting talker. But honey, he's just a screwball sailor! You're way out of his class.'

'Is he still in town? Do you know the name of his ship?'

'Take it easy, honey. I don't know the name of his ship. He never said, and I never asked him. But come to think of it, I believe he did say he was leaving Tuesday, so that means he's still in town.'

'I haven't much time,' Leah said. 'I have to go to work at four o'clock. Do you know what line he ships for?'

'It's not United Fruit,' said Neeley. 'I know that much. It

could be any of the others. If he ever said, I forgot. But you've been absolutely frank with me, and I appreciate it. I wasn't going to tell you this, but Joe came back here Sunday morning after you and him left, and woke me up, and talked for two hours about how lonesome he gets, and how he keeps looking for the right girl. Could that mean something?' she said helpfully. 'It certainly sounded funny, coming from Joe.'

'Did he really say that?'

'Let me finish. He said something else. He said, "What the hell can a man do about that situation but go and get drunk?" And I said, "Don't ask me, Joe."'

'What did he do then?'

'I don't know. But he had money, and from the look in his eye when he left, I wouldn't be surprised if he's in jail somewhere.'

'Do you have a telephone?'

Neeley sighed. 'Not any more. These bums around here ran up a seventy-dollar long-distance bill on me, and I had it taken out, but there's one in the restaurant on the corner. If you can't locate him in jail anywhere, you might try the Union hiring hall. I doubt if they'd tell you anything if they knew, but you might try.'

'Thank you, thank you with all my heart!' Leah snatched up her hat. The screen door slammed.

'Honey, see if there's any mail in my box!' Neeley called. But Leah did not hear.

MR. GRABER, dismounting from a bus at the entrance to City Park, saw another ash-colored postman with dark circles under his arms. He was crossing the bridge over Bayou St. John at the end of Esplanade Avenue, a short distance away. Mr. Graber waved his umbrella. The postman came toward him in the hot sun. Mr. Graber waited. 'Do you have any message for me this morning?' he inquired.

The postman looked him over. He was a young postman, new on his job, and he had been having difficulties. He had dropped an important letter addressed to Mrs. Bourgeois into the mail box of Mrs. Boudreaux, who lived next door. The resentment of both women had been shrill and voluble. The mistake had been happening with inexcusable regularity over a period of years, they said. What was wrong with his eyes? He might have replied that he was hot and tired, that his feet burned, that he needed new glasses and couldn't afford them, that he was worried because his oldest son, age eleven years, still wet his bed every night—but what would all this matter to Mrs. Bourgeois and Mrs. Boudreaux? Nothing. And so he had suggested flippantly that the two of them swap houses in order that the mistake need not occur again. They had resented his remark even more than his mistake. They intended to report him to the proper authorities. The postman did not know precisely what would happen under the circumstances, and, for the moment, did not care. He had finished his route; his mail bag was empty. He had been about to catch the bus back to town when Mr. Graber accosted him. The bus would wait for a few minutes; and he might as well have a little fun. He looked at Mr. Graber with cynical eyes. This man, he thought, was obviously a nut.

'What's ya name, bud?' he said.

Mr. Graber sucked in his jowls at the familiar tone. But it would be well to establish another residence and confound his pursuers. Postmen were not to be trusted; but, on occasion, they could be used. He conquered his repulsion.

'Sylvanus P. Graber,' he replied—although this, of course, was not his real name.

'Where ya live?'

Mr. Graber had his answer ready. He had snatched a number off an Esplanade Avenue residence in passing. He gave it.

The postman whistled. It was the number of Mrs. Bourgeois' house or Mrs. Boudreaux's—which? The two numbers had clasped hands in his mind, and were doing a whirling dervish dance. In the hot sun, with the bus about to leave, he could not disengage them. But it was very funny. It would be very funny, indeed, if the old nut really did live in one of the two houses— possibly the uncle of Mrs. Bourgeois, or the skeleton in Mrs. Boudreaux's closet. The postman winked at Mr. Graber, and assumed a sly, knowing expression. A flicker of alarm crossed Mr. Graber's face.

'Sure,' said the postman, from the side of his mouth. 'Sure, bud, I got a message for you.' He took an envelope from his shirt pocket, placed it in Mr. Graber's hand, and bolted into the bus.

Mr. Graber glanced at the empty envelope bearing the return address of a Personal Finance Company, and dropped it. He danced up and down on it, grinding his teeth. 'Dog!' he shouted at the tail of the retreating bus.

But he recovered himself quickly, for he looked up and saw General P. G. T. Beauregard on his bronze horse at the Park entrance. General Beauregard was the picture of calm authority and quiet dignity. Mr. Graber had great respect for the military. He mopped his sweating face, adjusted his bow tie, and unfurled his umbrella. Under its sedate shade he strolled up the avenue toward the Delgado Art Museum. The sycamore leaves were crisped by the sun; the grass on the golf course looked wilted. There was not a breath of wind. The heat was oppressive.

The Museum was closed. He had forgotten that it closed on Monday. He wanted to look again at Houdon's reproduction of 'Diana,' and Rude's 'Hebe and the Eagle of Jupiter.' He wanted to rest a trembling finger on a place on the cool bronze no man should touch.

Munching a candy bar, he wandered among the trees, along the flower-bordered walks. He made his mark on a picnic bench.

At ten o'clock on a Monday, he was alone; but the place was dirty. Lovers had been here; he saw the signs. Somewhere above him in an oak tree a locust whirred into sound from the silence. Mr. Graber clutched his chalk in his pocket, as if he had been observed. The invisible insect lifted and lowered its voice a few times under the heat and stopped, apparently unable to continue. Somewhere under the burning leaves its life kept hidden.

A dark, shy bird flitted through the branches. Mr. Graber, looking for the rose garden, followed in the way it had gone. But he lost it among the cypresses—a cuckoo, a raincrow, a silent flitting shadow among the gray buttressed trunks of the cypresses. From a distance, with parched, solitary voice, it begged for rain.

On the goddess in the rose garden, Mr. Graber left his mark.

MAUDIE PERALTA opened her front door and yawned at hot St. Philip Street. A gray tomcat with battle-scarred ears plodded past her, close to the wall, and crept under Bruno Tarantino's truck parked in front of his house. The shadow of the lamp post lay short on the sidewalk.

It was eleven o'clock, and Maudie had just waked up. Her green eyes were clear; her skin warmly tanned. She was considerably younger than Merlin and Leah. She wore blue shorts with a white stripe down the leg, and a red bandana tied around her breast.

'I thought I heard the postman,' she said to her mother-in-law, who was sitting on the doorstep in the sun.

Mrs. Peralta looked up and smiled, and gathered her long black skirt about her knees to make room for Maudie.

'The sun is good,' she said. 'Will you sit down?'

Maudie leaned through the door and looked in the mail box. It was empty. 'The postman,' she said. 'Has he come yet?'

Leah and Neeley

'Yes,' said Mrs. Peralta. 'There was no mail.'

Inside the house the telephone rang. Maudie moved in a leisurely way to answer it. Merlin was on the line, asking for Leah. 'Wait a minute,' Maudie said . . . 'Leah!' she called over her shoulder, 'Leah, telephone!' . . . There was no reply from her sister's room. 'Hold on a minute,' Maudie said. 'I'll go wake her up.'

In a minute she returned. 'Merlin, she's not here . . . No, I don't know when she left. No, thanks, I don't feel like having lunch with you today. I just woke up, and it's too hot to dress. Why don't you ask Victor? . . . 'Bye.'

Maudie hung up the telephone and scraped a long fingernail back and forth on the rough fabric of the chair arm, wondering where Leah had gone so early, wondering about Leah and the seaman. 'Nuts,' she said finally, and went into the bedroom. Here, she paused only long enough to pluck a magazine from the floor and continued on to the kitchen.

The house was old. Maudie didn't like it, and didn't pay much attention to the way it looked. She would have liked an up-to-date apartment with a tiled bathroom and lavender shower curtains. She would have liked a Buick sport coupé, a mink coat, a yacht. But her husband was on WPA, and so she read stories about women who were lucky enough to own yachts and mink coats, and managed to keep fairly well contented so long as the day was sunny.

The kitchen was clean and quiet. Victor and his mother had eaten long ago, and old Mrs. Peralta had washed up. Maudie poured cornflakes and milk in a bowl, and ate standing up at the sink. As she ate, she read. The meal and the story finished, she went into Leah's room to look for a cigarette.

This snooping in Leah's room was a habit of Maudie's begun in childhood. Maudie had been quite small when her parents had died; and Leah and Merlin had been more like mother and father to her than sister and brother. She still regarded their property as her own.

Leah had not closed her shutters when she left. Sunlight blazed on the floor and the unmade bed. A partly used package of cigarettes lay on the dresser beside Leah's glasses. Poor old absent-minded Leah had forgotten her glasses again. Maudie lit a cigarette, and put the rest in the pocket of her shorts. Before the open wardrobe, like footprints left by Leah's feet, lay a pair of small straw slippers, pigeon-toed. Maudie nuzzled them with her bare foot. Leah was a funny old thing, she thought, always upset and fussing about something. Lately, she had done some really weird things. She had turned down Preston Dillon—as if a woman could pick and choose at Leah's age. She had taken a job as cashier in a neighborhood movie when she didn't need to work. She had picked up a seaman in a bar. Watching Leah pick up that ugly little man in oily dungarees had been awfully funny. She had related the incident to Merlin as a joke, with no idea that he would be so disturbed.

Maudie stood before the wardrobe and looked enviously at her sister's smart dresses, too small for her to wear. Yawning, she stretched out on the bed and picked up a book. It was *The Theory of the Leisure Class*, by a man named Veblen. It looked terribly stuffy. Maudie dropped the book and rubbed the soles of her feet against the sun-warmed mattress.

A mouse rustled the loose papers in the fireplace. Maudie bounded across the room and jerked the screen aside. The surprised mouse hurdled her feet and disappeared down a hole gnawed in the wainscoting in the corner of the room. Maudie looked in the fireplace. The mouse had evidently been trying to get at an apple core wrapped in a piece of white notepaper. The paper looked quite fresh and bore several lines of Leah's sprawled handwriting. Maudie picked it up and smoothed it out. It was an unfinished letter.

'Dear Joe,' Leah had written at the top of the sheet. The following lines were undecipherable; but, farther down, Maudie made out several words. '. . . my life . . . simple . . . what would you say if . . .'

Maudie crumpled the paper and tossed it in the fireplace. Bored with Leah's room, she returned to her own bedroom for her sun-goggles and another magazine and stepped into the sunny courtyard. Dragging her deck chair under the fig tree, so that her head was in the shade and her legs in the sun, she began to read.

A street peddler passed, chanting his wares; a hammer beat in Clark's courtyard; a saw rasped in the Tarantino work shop; doors slammed; voices called. But the busy sounds of the block sank into Maudie like rainwater into sand. Lost in her story, she turned page after page. When a cloud moved over the sun, however, she looked up, annoyed.

Immediately, she became aware of a rich smell of simmering onions and garlic and tomato paste, a smell of frying meat from the Tarantino kitchen. She tried to read, but the smells grew stronger and more appetizing; and her eyes shifted from her story to an advertisement: a picture of a luncheon table laid with two plates. Each plate held a golden-brown lamb chop, a spoonful of green peas topped with a square of melting butter, and a dab of yellow carrots. Maudie's mouth began to water. She stood up abruptly and strode toward the kitchen.

The icebox held nothing but a couple of eggs, an avocado, and a wrinkled bowl of mushroom soup. Maudie chose the avocado. She sliced it, shook salt and olive oil and vinegar into one of the halves, and was about to carry it into the courtyard to eat when it occurred to her that her mother-in-law might have been mistaken about the postman. Maybe, by now, the mail had come. Again, she opened the front door onto the hot, bright street. The metal mailbox burned her fingers. It was still empty.

MRS. PERALTA was still sitting in the sun. This time she did not hear the door open behind her or hear the squeak of the mail box lid as Maudie lifted it to look inside. Nor did she hear the door close as Maudie went away. She was watching something across the street.

On the sidewalk, in front of the Cansino Fruit and Vegetable Stand, a small coffee-colored boy with curly hair was struggling to move a stack of large green watermelons out of the sunlight into the shade. Some of the melons were almost as big as the boy. He stooped and clasped, and lifted and shuffled, bent double with the weight. His ragged knickerbockers, too heavy for such hot weather, sagged to his ankles. Mrs. Cansino stood in the doorway with a fly-swatter, and urged him on.

'Hurry up and move em clean outa da sun, boy! Closer by da wall, over here in da shade. How many times I gotta tell you, keep dem watermelon outa da sun or dey git hot, an dey arready so ripe? An pull up yo pants or you gonna lose em, an den where you be?' Laughing heartily, Mrs. Cansino popped a fly on the doorframe, and went inside the store.

'Workin de pants off you, son?' inquired a young Negro in a pink shirt, who leaned against the iron post of the grocery porch, drinking a bottle of Pepsi-Cola.

The boy did not reply. He rested the melon on the sidewalk and tugged at his belt. He picked up the melon again. Shuffling and straddling, he deposited it in the shade. He picked up another melon and moved it.

'But he is so little!' Mrs. Peralta made a comforting sound in her throat. She was so old that her mind often wandered. It seemed to her that the small coffee-colored boy was her son, Victor, and that he was working too hard. When she had come out early in the morning, she had seen him carrying the melons from the store to the sidewalk; and now that the shade had changed, he was moving them again.

'The poor little one,' she said. Shaking her head, she wondered why her husband, who had been dead for twenty years, did not return and take the child fishing as he had promised. Then she remembered that she had pressed Victor's tie for him this morning and picked a thread from the cuff of his coat before he went out of the door. People were always going through doors. Sometimes, they didn't come back.

But the Cansino awning rippled in the heat waves, and beneath it the soft, bright colors of fruits and vegetables rippled and curled before Mrs. Peralta's old eyes like water, like the river passing—and the boy across the street was not her son. He had moved the watermelons. Now he was moving the crates of peaches and plums and pineapples. Now he was climbing on a box to steal a banana from the ripe yellow stalk that swung from a hook under the awning—stripping it, stuffing it quickly in his cheek, throwing the yellow skin in the gutter. It flew through the sunlight and sprawled like a star. The young Negro man in the pink shirt had bought a watermelon. He was splitting it open with his clasp-knife. Squatted on his haunches on the sidewalk, he was cutting the red heart out of the green skin, lifting the heart on the point of his knife in the sunlight. Aloft on the knife blade, the red heart quivered and blazed.

It was as red as Jesus' heart in the Holy Pictures, thought Mrs. Peralta. She loved color. Looking at the colors under the Cansino awning made her feel almost as if she were in church. Beautiful, soft, bright colors of Holiness rippled under the Cansino awning; and the banana stalk swung like a bell.

Mrs. Peralta stood up slowly from the doorstep and crept across the sidewalk. She had just seen a sun-faded lottery ticket lying in the gutter. Supporting herself with a hand on the lamp post, she leaned down, picked up the ticket, and held it close to her eyes. Ten . . . seventeen . . . thirty-nine . . . twenty-seven.

Every day, Victor gave Mrs. Peralta money to buy lottery tickets at the Cansino Stand. She had bought them as usual the night before; and now they were tucked safely under her pillow. Maybe tonight she would win. But maybe the numbers on the old ticket might mean a sign for tomorrow.

Mrs. Peralta studied the numbers. They didn't look lucky. The ticket was days old, dirty and torn. She opened her fingers and let it fall again to the gutter. Seated once more on her doorstep, she smoothed her skirt and spread her hands to the sun.

A little colored girl came along the sidewalk sucking a frozen raspberry popsicle, trailing a broomstick behind her. She walked on the sides of her feet; her bare, black toes curled away from the hot pavement. She stopped in front of Mrs. Peralta, and looked at the old woman with wide, wondering eyes.

Big and black and no-shape, with mottled hands attached to the skirt, and a white head at the end of it—what was this? It had eyes.

Mrs. Peralta smiled. Her eyes disappeared in brown wrinkles as her mouth slid up. The little girl watched with grave wonder. As the mouth slid down, the eyes reappeared.

Soberly, the two regarded each other.

The popsicle began to melt in the sun. A red stream meandered down the small black forearm. It tickled.

The child withdrew her eyes from the old woman and considered what was happening to her. She lowered her head and thrust out her tongue to clean her arm and stop the tickling.

'Nuh-uh-uh!' said Mrs. Peralta sharply.

At the familiar tone of reprimand, the child looked up questioningly, and looked down again, pondering what to do. Both hands were occupied. She started to lay the broomstick on the sidewalk, and changed her mind. Then she started to lay the popsicle on the sidewalk, and changed her mind again. She looked up, perplexed and undecided. Her face began to wrinkle, her mouth to open, the tears to come.

Mrs. Peralta called the child to her, lifted a fold of the short dress, and wiped the small hand and forearm clean. The child

*Across the street, a colored man squatted beside
the watermelon*

backed away and resumed her interrupted course along the sidewalk, the gray seat of her drawers wrinkling between her legs,
her toes curling away from the hot pavement, the broomstick
bumping behind her.

Mrs. Peralta wiggled her own toes inside her soft shoes, and
sat still again, soaking in the sun.

On summer days when the sun shone, she sat nearly all day
on her doorstep. She could have taken the sun in the courtyard,
as Maudie did, but she preferred the doorstep where she could
watch people pass.

Her room had been Leah's living-room before Maudie married Victor, and the Peraltas came to live in the house on St.
Philip Street. The room was crowded with things which she
had saved. She could not bear to throw anything away, nor to
see anybody else throw anything away. Waste was sinful; a use
could be found for everything if you waited long enough. This
old coat of Victor's could be cut up to make pieces for a patch-
work quilt. These spools, threaded on a string, would gladden
some child's heart. These odd lengths of wool could be used for
featherstitching the quilt; and, in the meantime, were soft and
pretty to handle. This perfume bottle of Leah's, although empty
of perfume, was still full of a sweet smell. Even this old piece of
flannel petticoat could be used for something. She knew that she
would find a use for it some day.

No closets were built in the old French Quarter houses; everybody used wardrobes. But no wardrobe had ever been provided
for Mrs. Peralta. Her dresses depended limply from a nail, one
on top of another. When the load became too bulky, the whole
collection would fall, to be picked up one by one from the floor,
smoothed, and replaced gently on the same nail.

Mrs. Peralta did not mind. She was a simple and serene old
woman with a fine disregard for the superfluous niceties of living and an ability to make herself at home wherever life set her
down. She had never felt so much at home anywhere as she felt

in the St. Philip Street house. Her feeling had less to do with the people who lived beside her in the house than with the house itself—the sturdy slate roof; the brick walls weathered the color of roses; the strong iron hooks that latched the heavy storm shutters; the solid, cypress planks—with the memories of living its square shape enclosed as her own flesh enclosed a mute knowledge of pain and happiness and long dull hours of pleasant breathing, perhaps not even her own, merely heard or read about long ago in another language, another country, but become so deeply a part of her, who now knew no great difference in time past and present, that even her own life, her own pain, had become impersonal. She was nearly as mute as the house; but, in her own way, she felt they knew each other.

She moved through the house in soft black shoes which made no sound except a patient whisper on the floor. Her feet hurt a great deal.

Now, the sun was beginning to make her feet swell inside her shoes. Mrs. Peralta leaned over to loosen the laces and saw a brown spot on the sidewalk. It looked like a penny, but probably it wasn't. Probably it was just a piece of chewing gum. Still, you never could tell. It would do no harm to make sure. It would do nobody the least bit of harm in the world if she picked up a lost penny from the sidewalk and hid it safely in her pocket. It might be a good thing if she picked up the penny. It might be a lucky thing. *Lucky penny. Lucky penny.* Mrs. Peralta grabbed for the spot and eased back on the doorstep with a sigh. It was only chewing gum, after all. But it might have been a penny, and she had been wise to look.

Across the street, the colored man in the pink shirt still squatted beside the watermelon. He had eaten the heart, and now he was scraping the last of the pink meat away from the rind. The last bite poised on his knife blade and disappeared in his mouth. He stretched his neck, spat a spray of brown seeds into the gutter, and remained motionless on his haunches, his narrowed eyes searching the sky.

A towering cone of dark blue cloud had slipped over the southern horizon in the past hour, and had nearly reached the sun. Heat lightning played through it from base to bright crown. The distant sound of thunder came again.

The man stood up and wiped his knife blade on his leg. He shoved the rind into the gutter with his foot, put the knife in his pocket, and walked away.

Mrs. Peralta did not hear the thunder, but she saw the cloud. She saw the man walk away. Her eyes followed him until he disappeared around the corner and fled back, frightened, to the Cansino Fruit and Vegetable Stand. The small coffee-colored boy with curly hair had just leaped through the door and was running after the man. The man was gone, the sun was gone, and the boy was leaving, too. 'Victor!' called Mrs. Peralta. 'Where are you going?'

The boy was only going to a grocery store in the next block to buy a poor-boy sandwich with the dime he had earned; but Mrs. Peralta did not know this. People were always going through doors. Sometimes, they didn't come back.

When he had gone, Mrs. Peralta missed him. 'My little son,' she said. 'Come back . . . come back.'

VICTOR PERALTA was going nowhere but to lunch with his brother-in-law, and he was not very happy about it. Merlin always made him feel that the Webster family could have got along better without him.

Half an hour before, Merlin had telephoned the uptown office of the WPA Writers' Project, and proposed that Victor meet him for luncheon at Morrison's Cafeteria at twelve o'clock. Victor, unable to refuse, had spent the intervening time unhappily recalling previous luncheons with Merlin—particularly, the last time, when their conversation had turned unexpectedly on the Magnolia Federal Housing Project for colored people. Victor had said that he thought it a good idea.

'Oh, you do, do you?' said Merlin bitterly. 'I think it's on a par with the rest of this New Deal claptrap—pampering the poor, encouraging indigence, giving our darkies a false sense of their importance. We've always taken care of them, haven't we? They know they can come to us if they're hungry. We don't let them starve.'

'I believe I read somewhere that some of them did starve,' Victor said mildly.

'Any man who starves, deserves to starve. This country can't run on WPA. There's always a way for an enterprising man to earn a living.'

Now, as Victor looked worriedly at the clock, he thought it was probably natural for Merlin to feel the way he did about Federal Housing. Some of his colored tenants had already moved into the Project, and some of those who remained were demanding lower rents and better plumbing.

It was seven minutes of twelve. As Victor put on his hat and coat, a peal of thunder caused him to hurry to the window and consult the sky. A head of dark cloud was reaching for the sun. As he watched, two great jaws opened, closed, and the sun was gone. Resenting the interruption of the luncheon date and the necessity of his own nature to acquiesce under pressure in all except extremely important matters, Victor looked at his umbrella, left in the office since the last rain. Should he take it, or should he not?

'The devil with the umbrella,' he thought recklessly, as he closed the office door behind him. 'The devil with it anyhow,' he thought, as he elbowed himself into the crowded elevator. 'I don't care if I do get wet,' he thought, as he stepped out on the street.

IN WINTER, Victor wore a dark gray suit, rather short and tight in the trousers; and, when the weather called for it, a belted brown overcoat with a dim yellow plaid. But all summer long he wore blue-and-white striped seersuckers. He owned three seersucker suits, identically alike as to cloth and cut. With them, he always wore white shirts. He owned four of these, also identically alike. Perhaps half the men in the city dressed themselves in like summer fashion; but Victor made up for the general anonymity of his appearance by wearing ties in Paisley patterns, usually red or yellow. Many another man followed the same custom—but Victor's ties were unmistakably his own. He had delicate bones, transparent skin, and long, curly eyelashes. His favorite subject in grade school had been history, and the only two passions of his life, until he met Maudie Webster, had been long-distance running and a profound, incalculable hatred for Napoleon Bonaparte.

'You shouldn't hate Napoleon like that so much,' Maudie had said one day, shortly after their first meeting, when they were still becoming acquainted with each other. 'Napoleon was a famous man.'

'I don't care how famous he was. He was wicked.'

'You shouldn't talk like that.'

'Besides, he made me lose a good job.'

'Poor Napoleon's been dead for years!'

' "The evil that men do lives after them," ' quoted Victor. 'I was a waiter at Broussard's Restaurant. You've seen at Broussard's where they have a statue of Napoleon in the patio?'

'Yeah,' said Maudie.

'And every time they serve café brûlot, they turn out the lights and ignite the brandy, and all the waiters got to face Napoleon and stand at attention?'

'Oh, yeah,' said Maudie. 'I think it's a lovely custom. It makes me want to cry.'

'Not me,' said Victor. 'I hated Napoleon from the time I first read about him in school. To salute him would have been against my deepest principles. I refused.'

'I don't know what you're talking about, but you talk mighty big for a man on relief.'

'And why am I on relief?' demanded Victor hotly. 'Because I refused to pay a scoundrel the honor of standing at attention when they served café brûlot. It's an outrage!'

'You better stop talking about famous men that way. Napoleon was a hero, and he died in exile.'

'He should have been shot,' said Victor. 'Just because he died in exile doesn't make him a hero. Listen, Maudie, just because a man is famous doesn't mean he's a good man and everybody ought to salute his statue.'

'No-o-o,' said Maudie. 'I guess not. But Napoleon—'

'Napoleon was like the German Kaiser, Maudie, and you know all the destruction he caused in the world, all those beautiful churches and libraries he blew up. Men like that have absolutely no respect for historical treasures.'

'Maybe you're right.'

'Napoleon is just business in New Orleans, anyhow, because he almost came here, and tourists like to say they saw the house where he almost lived.'

'Well, I never thought about it that way before. But I was just wondering, honey. What did you do when you had to serve café brûlot your own self?'

'I tried to prevent my customers from ordering it, but if they insisted, I went ahead and served it. What else could I do? When another waiter served it—that was a different matter. Then, I usually stepped behind a bush and looked the other way. One night, the head-waiter saw me.'

'What did he do to you, huh?'

'He set out to ruin me. He joggled my elbow. He stuck out his foot and tripped me up. Once, when the lights went out for Napoleon, he pinched me, and I dropped a salad in a lady's lap.'

'He must of loved Napoleon,' Maudie giggled.

'He didn't give a hoot for Napoleon,' said Victor. 'He just resented my principles. I guess he didn't like me. Why should he resent my principles, Maudie? But for some reason, he just didn't like me. My nerves got so jangled I had to quit.'

'For a crazy little ole statue in yellow pants, you quit a good job!'

'Don't tease me, Maudie. It was more than a statue in yellow pants. It was a principle. I lost my job for a principle. Napoleon was a tyrant. This is a democracy. I refuse to bow to even the symbol of a tyrant. Let the democratic government uphold me!'

'Gee,' said Maudie. She was impressed. She stole a sidelong look at him, and clasped his arm. 'Victor,' she said, 'I think it's absolutely wonderful the way you have principles and stand up for them. I think it's beautiful!'

'When I get on WPA, will you marry me, Maudie?'

'All right,' she said. 'We might as well.'

Maudie's interest in abstract principles did not last very long. As soon as she was married, she relaxed even deeper into the comfortable business which had occupied her since childhood— that of thinking and doing as little as possible. Maudie may have liked the idea of yachts and mink coats, but since the hope of getting them was as far away as heaven, and it was not Maudie's way to disturb her comfort by reaching for anything that far away, she very practically contented herself with what pleasures lay at hand.

What plaintive cunning in Victor's mind translated his wife's unscrupulous laziness into the deep serenity he saw in her, nobody would ever know. Because she was never sufficiently interested in any subject to argue with him, or enough concerned about his comings and goings to question or quarrel, he thought she resembled his mother, whose silent devotion had surrounded his life with a patient, warming glow. Perhaps, through faulty rea-

soning, Victor had arrived at the right conclusion after all.
Whatever else Maudie may or may not have been, she was warm.

They had met at the annual Jackson Day Marathon Race. It
had been cold and damp that January day. Victor had been one
of the long-distance runners undertaking the course from Spanish Fort on Lake Pontchartrain to the Cabildo, opposite St. Louis
Cathedral, in memory of the dash of the Spanish Fort garrison
to aid General Andrew Jackson in the Battle of New Orleans.
Already defeated, for the winner had come in ten minutes before, Victor had turned into Pirate's Alley on the last lap of the
race. Head down, arms pumping, thin trunks plastered to sweaty
legs, completely exhausted but doggedly intent on finishing
without glory, he had stumbled on an uneven paving block and
fallen at the feet of a spectator—Maudie's feet.

'P-pardon me!' he gasped.

'My goodness!' said Maudie. 'Are you hurt? Gosh, you look
pooped!' She helped him to his feet. He ran on down the alley;
but he looked back.

'I'm not tired,' he panted over his shoulder. 'N-not now!'

After the ceremony in Jackson Square, he had looked for her
and found her. Maudie had looked very warm and bright in the
cold drizzle of that January day; but she knew almost nothing of
the city's historic past. She had asked him what on earth all those
men were doing, running eight miles, half-naked, on such a chilly
day? Were they trying to catch pneumonia? They were com-
memorating the past, Victor said. He proceeded to instruct her
in legendry. Victor knew almost everything there was to know
about the city's legends. From his school days on, he had written
little poems about the Duelling Oaks, the cypress swamps, and
Jean LaFitte's pirates. All of them ran something like this:

> 'Sieur Henri smote the table,
> And swore a good round oath.
> 'We'll meet tonight at moonrise!'
> 'Sieur George was nothing loath.

The waiter's job at Broussard's Restaurant had been merely a stop-gap. Victor had always intended to become a writer. WPA had opened a way for him to do everything he ever wanted to do. WPA had even made it possible for him to marry Maudie.

He had done much research work for the City Guide Book the previous year; and he had come to love the reverent hush of libraries and museums and the smell of courthouse records. In fact, anything made venerable by passing time awoke in him a feeling of tenderness. That this wealth of feeling was directed toward inanimate objects instead of toward people had long been a subject of argument between Victor and his friend, Lucien Taylor, on the Painters' Project.

'But the people, my God, the people!' Lucien would say, gritting his teeth. 'You don't have to do anything about them. Just look at them!'

'Buildings last longer,' Victor would reply.

'But please, please tell me what's the good of buildings without people? Don't you like people?'

'Oh, people are all right.'

But, except for Maudie, he liked houses much better than people. They seemed more real to him. He loved the old house on St. Philip Street, and was glad that Merlin had not renovated it as he had his own residence; and was glad, too, that Maudie did not want to change it.

A house did not need to be famous for Victor to know about it. Passing a house unmarked in any way, unnoted by any of the city's historians, a little house gently burning away in the soft weather, with slates awry, sills eaten by termites, paint curling and flaking on its shutters, he would be apt to say:

'This house was built by Pierre Lechaise, a free Negro from Haiti in 1798. As you can see, he built it well. Look at those thick walls. Where the plaster has come off, you can see they're reinforced with cypress timbers. There's planks in that floor over two feet wide, cut from virgin cypress. Look at that overhanging roof, pitched steep to slice the rain. Look at that iron-work. After he died, he left the house to his eldest son, who was also named Pierre. Now, the son, Pierre, had a beautiful wife named Elvira with loose morals. Elvira got in trouble and disappeared, and Pierre sold the house and went to find her. He sold it to Dominic Peregrine, another free Negro, in 1815, and it stayed in Dominic's family for three generations.'

'What happened to Elvira?' the listener might inquire. 'Did Pierre ever find her?'

'It isn't in the records,' Victor would reply noncommittally.

He would point to a garage with its gas pumps, its Coca-Cola box, its smell of grease and oil, and say:

'Once a beautiful garden grew here, and in the garden was a great cypress tree, left standing when they cut down the forest and drained the swamp to build the city . . . this entire city, you know, was once a pestilential swamp. . . . But the tree was killed by lightning in 1837, and when the tree died, the garden died, nothing would grow there. And when the garden died, the house died—or so they say. One day, the house just sighed and tumbled down, and for years it was a place of death, and nobody would live here. Then a man named Samuel Barbee from the North, who didn't believe the legend, bought the lot and built another house. Samuel had a pretty daughter named Jennie. The house burned in 1880. One of Jennie's jealous suitors burned it. What a shame!'

'What happened to Jennie when the house burned?'

'Oh, Jennie was inside.'

VICTOR, on his way to meet Merlin Webster for luncheon, looked up at the clouds and hurried. Maybe he would have been wiser to have brought his umbrella, after all. Maybe he should go back and get it. He paused, undecided, on the sidewalk, while his innate caution battled with the new feeling of recklessness which possessed him. In the end, recklessness won, and he resumed his way toward the cafeteria. Strangely, he found himself remembering Leah's face on Saturday night, when she had looked at the man in oily dungarees. Victor had seen Leah's face many times before; it was a nice face; he liked it; but he had thought it a completely unremarkable face until Saturday night. Seeing it then had been like seeing a moonflower tightly curled one instant and wide open the next; or like actually witnessing the instant the street lamps came on at dusk. He did not approve of Leah's subsequent actions. No woman, no matter what the reason, should approach a strange man in a barroom. He suspected that Merlin wished to question him about this incident, and although he did not himself approve of Leah's conduct, he considered it her own business. Then what was there left to tell Merlin, except that something wonderful had happened to Leah's face?

Victor clapped his hand to his hat, almost dislodged from his head by the wind of a truck's passing. Without slowing down or sounding its horn, a Bruce's Juices delivery truck had careened out of a side street and turned onto the main traffic artery on two wheels. Victor, just crossing the street, had been missed by inches. Good Heavens, he thought, I might have been killed!

THOMAS FERRABEE, driver of the truck, had again escaped the crime of manslaughter by his near victim's swift and instinctive reaction toward self-preservation. He had just seen a girl coming out of a drugstore; he was still thinking about her.

'What a doll!' thought Thomas Ferrabee. 'What a doll! . . . Jeez, what legs, what hips, what apples! . . . That's the kind of a doll a guy like me could use for a wife insteada what I got . . . and oh, boy, what's wrong with a little look-see tonight?'

He had been a faithful husband for ten years, and he hadn't been appreciated. So she thought he didn't have it in him, did she? Well, he'd show her! He had already left home, hadn't he? She had told him never to dare show his face again, hadn't she? All right.

'All right for you,' he thought. 'I'm gonna get me a doll tonight, and have me some fun, for a change.'

BUT I WASN'T KILLED . . . I'm still alive, thought Victor Peralta. What a miracle! This, of course, was what had happened to Leah's face: it had suddenly discovered itself alive. Continuing on his way miraculously intact and alive, Victor thought that if the subject of Leah came up during luncheon, he would shield her by denying any knowledge of what had happened in the bar.

Merlin was waiting inside the air-cooled cafeteria. He looked at Victor's tie, and shut his eyes.

'Am I late?' Victor asked.

'Not very.' Merlin dropped his cigarette and stepped on it. He took Victor's arm. 'Come on,' he said. 'Let's eat.'

WHAT HAD SEEMED A SIMPLE THING this morning— a brotherly desire to protect a favorite sister—seemed not so simple now, in the cold room floating with odors of food and noisy with babbling voices and the clatter of cutlery. And Victor looked pale and stupid, with his curls plastered to his forehead like a Sicilian organ-grinder, no better addition to the Webster family than the seaman himself would be, and so nobody to consult for an opinion, nobody to bother about in any event. Merlin decided not to mention Leah.

'How is your mother standing the heat?' he said to Victor. At the same time he bowed to a woman of his acquaintance who was dining at the next table on a cottage cheese and pineapple salad laid out on a lettuce leaf. She was a very handsome woman; she looked like a Queen, Merlin thought. He thought of the Queen of England, whose picture he had seen smiling at the King's hot-dog in the morning paper. From the King, it was but an inch to abdicated Edward and Wallis Simpson. This reminded him of a joke.

'Mother—' began Victor.

But Merlin was already launched on his story. When he had finished, Victor tried to think of a story to tell in return. He began one and lost the point. He groped for it frantically, fumbled it, and dropped it with a chicken bone on his plate. A wave of frustration, of burning irritation, swept over him. He spooned five loads of sugar into his tea, and stirred recklessly. Another story came to him.

'I heard something very funny at the office the other day,' he said. 'There's a fellow on the Project they couldn't keep busy, so they put him to translating Maya hieroglyphics. Of course he didn't know a word of the language, very few persons do, but they gave him a code, or index, or something, and he worked like a dog for six weeks and finally translated two sentences. One sentence was, "Shame, shame, an unmarried woman with seven children!"'

Merlin did not laugh.

' "Horse manure is worthless," ' Victor finished lamely. 'That was the other sentence.'

Merlin ground away on a tough piece of steak, carefully unamused.

Mistake, mistake! thought Victor. Lifting his iced-tea glass, he drank hurriedly. He swallowed a mint leaf and choked behind his napkin. Such jokes should never be told out of school; only another WPAer was capable of appreciating them.

'That's what I mean,' said Merlin, 'about government spending. Taxing the people to unearth such shameless and uninformed nonsense, written, no doubt, by the village idiot nobody knows how many thousands of years ago, and no possible use to humanity now.'

'It's funny,' said Victor. 'Don't you think it's funny?'

'Funny? I should say so. The whole damnable idea is a monstrous joke on the taxpayers.'

'Anyway, the man got paid for it so he was able to eat,' Victor said, and bowed before the deluge Merlin loosed.

'Pioneer spirit . . . great expansion . . . limitless possibilities . . . ounce of pride . . . government stranglehold . . . nincompoop braintrusters . . . people's money . . . balance the budget . . . public debt . . . the nation's needs . . . business a chance . . .'

Once, when Merlin paused for breath, Victor tried to change the subject. 'I was walking along Tchoupitoulas Street the other day,' he said, 'and I saw the most fascinating vista. It really gave you a feel of the city as it must have been in the old days, when the river was crowded with sailing vessels. And—'

'And if Roosevelt would take his foot off the neck of business,' said Merlin, 'the port would be that busy again. Now, don't mistake me. I'm not definitely against the Administration. Not yet.'

Looking through the window past Merlin's ear, Victor saw that the day was growing steadily darker. He had never bothered about politics; he had never even bothered to vote. In Louisiana, under Huey Long whose henchmen regularly stuffed the ballot boxes, voting hadn't been much use. All that was correct and secure in his living had come from the past. Where now was the romantic past? Gone like the graceful sailing ships that had swarmed like birds on the river. Gone to the bottom, gone up in smoke, gone to the ends of the world where their skeletons lay on lonely beaches and sand blew through their ribs. Today was today, immediate and irritating. Today it was going to rain, and he had no umbrella.

But what Merlin was saying wasn't true. It couldn't possibly be true, for his very ear against the window looked vain and misinformed. Victor wished that he knew more about current events so that he could refute Merlin. Before eating another luncheon with his brother-in-law, he resolved to arm himself with the facts, as, trying to save the last tatters of his self-respect, he reached for both checks.

Merlin reached for the checks at the same time. After a polite flurry, he carried them off to the cashier.

As the two men stepped from the cafeteria, they looked up at the sky. The clouds were the color of dirty denim. Flags strained from their poles straight out and awnings crackled. The freshening wind smelled of rain. Others around them looked at the sky. Footsteps quickened along the sidewalks. Thunder slammed a door above their heads.

'Roosevelt . . .' said Merlin, cupping a lighted match to his cigarette. 'Roosevelt . . .' A puff of wind blew out his match. Dropping the dead stick, he fumbled in his pocket for another. He stepped to the wall to strike it, and found himself confronting his own image in a sidewalk mirror: mouth twisted about the cigarette and half open to speak, hands lifted as if in supplication, shoulders hunched against the wind.

In the instant of time it took him to recognize the green attenuated apparition attached to humanity and the beautiful commonplaceness of breakfast dishes and child-rearing and letters dictated to a stenographer by nothing, it seemed, but the yellow tie around its neck—and how could he ever have bought such a tie, much less worn it? for it looked in the strange light like a yellow rope halter and the distorted face above it dead by hanging, and so it was too late, and he did not belong with humanity now, and was completely lost—and the instant of time it took him to strike the match against the wall, and the flame to catch the cigarette, and the smoke to be inhaled and exhaled, Merlin's mind was completely and unequivocally made up about Roosevelt. 'Roosevelt,' he said, wheeling to face his brother-in-law, 'Roosevelt is ruining this country!'

'You're crazy!' said Victor angrily. 'He's doing nothing of the sort!'

'Damn right, he is!'

They glared at each other; and then, each uneasy and troubled, each anxious to reassure himself through the other that the world was just as it had always been—the buildings the same, the signs the same, the hour to be taken in their stride—they fell into step and walked together for two blocks.

'I turn off here,' said Merlin. 'Coming my way?'

'I'm not working at the office this afternoon. I have to check on some notes in the Quarter.'

Their hands met and dropped. Both looked again at the sky.

'By cracky!' Merlin said. 'The bottom's going to fall out in about two minutes. I'll just about make it to the office.'

He hurried away. Victor had walked half a block when the wind swooped on him, swirling grit and dust into his eyes. He grabbed for his hat, and hung on to it. Heavy, intermittent drops of rain spattered the sidewalk for a minute, and then the sky opened.

All over the city rain crashed down on the roofs; drainpipes went crazy; gutters boiled. Children ran into houses. Cats ran under houses. House windows came down. Car windows went up. Pigeons flapped to overhanging eaves. Tumbling trees poured back and forth into each other like green liquor. Frantic hands snatched clothes off clotheslines. Hands were clapped over ears as thunder cracked and slammed at roof level; and candles were lit; and prayers were said for protection against lightning.

Victor, walking with his head down, looked up just in time to avoid collision with a blind woman scuttling along the sidewalk. They passed. The blind woman groped her way up the steps of the Jesuit Church. Victor did not take shelter. In half a minute he was drenched, but he did not notice. He was deep in thought. He was thinking about his umbrella and the feeling of recklessness with which he had discarded it at the office door; and, for some reason, he was thinking again of Leah's face. On the rainy sidewalk he saw it again as he had seen it Saturday night. Suddenly, Victor looked up from the sidewalk and blinked his eyes at the rain.

'I really don't care if I do get wet,' he said aloud, surprised.

Thunder slammed another door over his head.

'By cracky,' he said. 'I don't give a damn!'

3

THE BLIND WOMAN felt her way into the damp vestibule of
the Jesuit Church and leaned against a wall. She wiped the rain
from her guitar. All around her, she heard the sound of others
taking shelter as the surprised one-o'clock traffic of the sidewalk
dodged through the church door and beat the rain from their
clothes. Their voices were small as the squeaking of mice under
the great ceiling of thunder. They were no friends of hers. They
had given her money to send her son away. She would never
see him again; she would never forgive them. 'Run,' she thought.
'Run and be soaked and be damned, you bastards! Rain down
your collars, spatter your stockings, bust all your paper bags!'

As if to answer her, the rain fell harder—a hot, violent assault.
More people ran in the church door. It was a cloudburst. Nobody remained unaware of it. For a few minutes the sight and
sound and smell of rain governed the city like great fear or hope.

Tires skidded, horns blew, traffic crawled. Jesse McPhail appeared in rubber boots and hooded slicker on Canal Street, and
blew his traffic whistle until his cheeks turned purple . . .

Bareheaded and coatless, Neeley had gone to a delicatessen
several blocks from her Royal Street rooming-house to buy her
lunch. She was bringing home a macaroni salad and a pound of
cold, boiled shrimp when the rain caught her. No shelter was

116

near. She ran. The paper bag burst, and a shrimp slid down the
front of her dress. Looking over her shoulder, she saw a long trail
of pink, curled shrimp behind her on the sidewalk—the better
part of her meal. As she ran, a truck cut in beside a streetcar,
splashed through a puddle close to the curb, and muddied her
stockings. It was a Bruce's Juices delivery truck. Thomas Ferrabee, still at large, had splashed Neeley's last pair of clean stockings. She did not know Thomas Ferrabee, but she felt she knew
his type; and she insulted it capably but almost mournfully as,
feeling herself doomed to a life of semi-starvation and endless
stocking-washing, she ran toward home . . .

On a cot in the Parish Jail, a Negro boy named Cooter licked
his dry lips and listened to the splashing patter of rain falling on
concrete. He wondered what they had done with the clasp-
knife his girl had given him for a birthday present, and wished
that he had it in his hands again . . .

Joe Onion pushed through a swing door on Decatur Street
and slung his leg over a stool. He wiped his hat brim, and the
inside of his collar. 'Boilermaker,' he said to the bartender.

Farther along the bar, two boys from the same ship as Joe
looked up at the sound of his voice.

'Hi, Joe. We thought we was getting on dry land for a few
days.'

'What'll you drink? . . .'

In a room on South Claiborne Street, the blind woman's four-
year-old son, Corey, crawled under the bed, and cried, and
thought about the pine woods. When he heard footsteps in the
hall, he stopped crying and remained as still as a young, frightened quail. But the door did not open; instead, a white triangle
appeared beneath it—a letter or postcard. The footsteps went
away. Corey stole from under the bed and picked up the card. It
was one of Mr. Graber's anonymous calling cards: *Down with
the Jews! They are to blame for all your troubles!* and Mr.
Graber was now flitting along the filthy hall with his umbrella

hooked over his arm, congratulating himself on another convert. . . . But Corey could not read. Taking the card into bed with him for company, he thought of rain falling in the pine woods; and would have run away, but was afraid of lightning . . .

From her open doorway on St. Philip Street, old Mrs. Peralta, unafraid of lightning, watched the raindrops batter a pasteboard box dropped by some passing truck in the middle of the street. It seemed to her like an old friend being punished, and she hobbled out in the street, picked up the box, and carried it to shelter. She would have saved the sun-faded lottery ticket, even if it didn't look lucky, but it slipped through her fingers in the running gutter, and disappeared down a drain . . .

Maudie Peralta, chased from the courtyard, lay down on her bed and fell asleep at once . . .

In the next block, Dan Clark was eating dinner. When the rain began, he jumped up from the table and ran out into the courtyard to crank up car windows. The windows of a Chevrolet sedan were stuck and wouldn't close, so he started the engine, and backed the car under the shelter of the second-floor balcony . . .

His dinner just finished, Bruno Tarantino lolled in his chair, popping his suspenders and picking his teeth. Mrs. Tarantino was grabbing clothes from the line on the shed roof. Her mouth was full of clothespins. At the sound of a crash on the Gomez balcony, she looked over her shoulder and screamed . . .

Father Vela, at the Parish House window, was watching the thirsty soil of St. Anthony's garden drink the rain when his telephone bell pealed urgently . . .

THE RAIN SLACKENED for a minute; then the long, straight-falling lines melted into a solid sheet of water that roared on roof and pavement and rebounded in spray from the steps of the Jesuit Church on Baronne Street. The blind woman moved backward as the spray drenched her legs.

A nun paced from the body of the church into the vestibule. From the black cave of her veil her white face gleamed wonderingly at the liquid sky and the misty street. A cool draft swung a fold of her habit against the blind woman's wrist.

'Pray for me, sister,' the blind woman said.

Rain drove through the open doorway across the tiled floor. Somebody closed the door. Somebody opened it. Two old women crept into the church to warm themselves with a sight of the altar.

Leah Webster watched them go; and watched a pretty girl in the green uniform of a cafeteria waitress spread a handkerchief on her head and follow them. A man, who had been watching the girl, removed his hat and walked admiringly behind her. With his hat off, Leah recognized the man. He was Mr. Papadakis who lived across the street from her and called a respectful greeting from his doorstep every night when she came home from work. Presently the girl reappeared, to lean in the doorway and watch the rain. Mr. Papadakis followed admiringly. When, aware of his intent gaze, the girl turned her head, Mr. Papadakis spoke.

Leah shut her eyes. She had not yet found Joe. After many telephone calls, she had learned that he shipped for Lykes Brothers out of New York City; and she had learned the name of his ship. Calling the ship, she had finally discovered that he was not on board. Before she could inquire when he was due back, she was disconnected. She could not get the ship again. Joe was in town—but where, she did not know. She was as far from finding him as she had been in the morning. The rain had caught her crossing Canal Street on her way to luncheon. She had dodged along under awnings until she reached the church door; and the rain coming then in a deluge, she had gone inside.

'Pray for me, sister,' said the blind woman again.

Leah looked behind her. She thought the voice familiar. She thought it had spoken to her one night from a dark doorway, a summer ago.

She could not find a job. She had tried for a long while without success. Merlin might have helped her, but from fear and distaste of the argument which would surely follow his knowledge that she wished to work again, she had not asked his help. Once, she had been a very good secretary; but in seven years of idleness she had forgotten her typing and shorthand. People had been polite; the employment agency had sent her out for half a dozen trials; her old employer had taken her telephone number and promised to call. But he had not called. She had found no job. She was not sleeping well; and when she did sleep, she had bad dreams. She had been idle too long; her life seemed to be disintegrating around her like a broken bottle around a cork. She got a prescription for sleeping tablets, and took three or four of them every night. She felt that she was losing her mind.

She remembered the day she had first felt this. She had been walking through the hot sunlight of St. Philip Street, when suddenly it seemed to her that eyes watched from behind every shutter, every lamp post, from the ironwork of every balcony. The air was on fire with waiting. Not a leaf moved over a courtyard wall. Nothing moved. People passed her, but they were not moving. She heard the gritty sound of her own footsteps on the pavement; but she was not moving, either; she was still, bound by unfathomable stillness of time, lost in a leaf, in a brick, in the sun in an empty beer bottle—waiting.

There had been a time in Leah's life when people had been a source of ironic amusement to her. Shortly after she lost her job in the depression and delivered all economic worries into Merlin's hands, a lonely contentment, a kind of Olympian objectivity, had cushioned her nights and days. People who worked for their living were fools, and she laughed at them. During this time she had formed a habit, while walking along a street, of seeing only one feature of her fellow citizens at a time. For instance, one day the street would be thronged with disembodied feet, those pale servants of a million cross-purposes encased in leather; while another day the street would be a-flutter with nothing but hands. On still another day it might be only eyes she remarked, or ears, or mouths, or noses. A street thronged with nothing but noses was a sight to see. She had found the game amusing.

But this summer afternoon, a year ago, when she fancied the city full of eyes that watched her and waited, the little game begun as a private joke to pass the time had lost all semblance of fantasy. It had become real. It was horrible. And the employment agency had just telephoned her to go to an office and take a competitive test for a secretarial position.

When the test was over, Leah walked out in the hall and pressed the elevator button. While she waited, she looked at her fingers—the fingers that had sped so many swift shorthand notes across so many tablets in the past. They had been very clumsy today. She had not been able to read back a word of the test dictation given her. She would not get the job.

The elevator slid to a stop before her, and she entered. She was the only passenger. She turned her back on the operator. It was not that she felt like crying; it was simply that the muscles of her face, particularly around her mouth, seemed out of control. Her flesh felt curiously tired and unwilling to obey her.

She walked through the lobby, pulling on her gloves. As she stepped through the door onto the sidewalk, she saw with surprise that it was dark; the test had taken some time. The street lights seemed blurred. Her glasses must be wet. Fumbling in her purse for a handkerchief to wipe her glasses, she found the bottle of sleeping tablets which, for some reason she did not bother to understand, she always kept with her. Enough tablets remained in the bottle for a week of oblivious nights. Why not take them all at once?

Leah began to walk swiftly. Home was not far, only about eight blocks. In fifteen minutes she would be home; in half an hour she would be asleep. She walked so fast, she was almost running. She could not stop crying. People looked at her curiously.

She was merely going home, she told herself; and when she reached home she would do nothing she had not done every night of her life. She was merely going home and to sleep. She had lost nothing, she told herself; and yet, from the sharp sound of her heels on the pavement, the narrow street cried out with loss.

A shadow in a doorway stirred and spoke. 'What's the matter, honey? Did you lose your job?'

The voice fell quick and kind on Leah's ears, a warm, impulsive voice—in its very sound a kind of tough defiance of hard pavements and lost ways. Leah caught her breath. Who had spoken to her? A beggar? A prostitute? Nobody like that had ever spoken to her before. But neither had this voice spoken to her, for this woman could not know Leah Webster. The friendly voice had been for a passing sound of grief in a street at night—one nameless human being to another, just as nameless.

Leah retraced her steps and saw a broad face lifted toward a street lamp. The face was blind.

Leah leaned toward the woman. Pity, gratitude, love—there were no words for what she felt. She could not speak. She touched the sturdy shoulder in a quick, awkward caress and walked away. Behind her, she heard the blind woman cough and stumble to her feet. Leah slept well and comforted that night. The next day she found the cashier job in the neighborhood movie. A year later she remembered as she waited, rain-bound, in the Jesuit Church.

The air in the vestibule smelled of wet fabrics and incense. People sniffed and coughed. Behind Leah the blind woman coughed.

More people ran in the door

'Pray for me, sister,' she said again, unaware, in her misery, that the nun had gone. The most profound debts often remain unacknowledged because they cannot be paid. What the blind woman had given her, Leah thought, could not be repaid with words. Upon the frail clumsy body with its sealed lips, then, fell the task of shaping a movement.

Under the circumstances only one movement was possible. At some expense to the good nature of the person wedged against her, Leah twisted herself about and threw a silver dollar into the cigar box.

'Thank you,' the blind woman said to nobody in particular.

'THANK YOU,' said Merlin Webster, accepting change for a package of cigarettes from the pretty blond at the tobacco counter.

He had reached his office building before the storm broke; his white linen suit was only lightly spattered. The lobby was crowded with people off the streets, and others who worked in the building, halted by the downpour on their way to lunch. The vicious stabs of lightning, the uncontrolled attacks of thunder, but principally the interruption to their daily schedule, provoked some irritation and nervousness in the crowd. There was much craning of heads and consulting of watches. The propinquity of so many restless people made Merlin uncomfortable; he felt as if he were smothering. He was elbowing his way toward the elevators when a tentative voice said, 'Webster.' He turned quickly. Preston Dillon leaned against the coffee bar with his hands in his coat pockets. He was biting the inside of his cheek.

'Well, Dillon,' said Merlin to the man he had hoped to secure for a brother-in-law. 'Quite a storm, isn't it? Looks like a cloudburst. I made it back from lunch just in time. Had your lunch yet?'

'What?' said Dillon. He was a large man with heavy shoulders and thin, well-draped legs. His skin was pink and clear. The top of his head was bald, but the neat fence of hair surrounding the bald spot was thick and golden-brown. Except for a deep groove on either side of his mouth, his face was without lines. Dillon had a habit of twisting his mouth in order to nibble the lining of one cheek, then shifting it slowly to taste the other side. The facial expression thus evoked might be considered either judicious or nervous, according to the state of mind of the observer. He was one of the city's most eligible bachelors; and his tentative preoccupation with Leah Webster over a period of years had caused amused consternation among his friends.

'Had your lunch yet?' Merlin repeated, raising his voice.

'What?' said Dillon, shifting his mouth. 'Oh. Yes. Wonderful lunch. I ate an hour ago.'

In spite of the cool air, his tonsured head was wet with perspiration. He was deathly afraid of lightning. He was ashamed of his fear, and had tried long and hard to overcome it; but he simply could not bear to be alone in a thunderstorm; he wanted as many people around him as possible. When the storm began, he had quit his office and come downstairs to the lobby. He looked gratefully at Merlin. He would have preferred Merlin's silent presence in this crisis, but words were indicated—both to conceal his own confusion and to let Merlin know that, in spite of the difference in their economic and social positions, he felt friendly toward him. Being well-liked by everybody, even taxi-drivers and telephone repairmen, was necessary to Preston Dillon's peace of mind.

Now, he spoke of the subject uppermost in a mind which was not at all peaceful. 'See the headlines this morning?' he said.

The question was foolish; nobody in New Orleans missed a headline these days, but Merlin understood and sympathized with Dillon. Since the arrival of Federal Investigator O. John Rogge, Dillon might well have cause for nervousness. Merlin did not know too much about Dillon's brokerage business; but it was 'big business,' and to qualify under this label probably meant at least a modicum of discreet corruption. Merlin did not condemn this; as a matter of fact, he had envied Preston Dillon and his friends until the Federal Government had grown curious about them. In his mind, he had identified himself with them; he, too, was 'big business,' or one day would be: it was only a matter of time. His political opinions had been shaped by this reasoning. Particularly, had Merlin's thoughts identified him with Preston Dillon. He admired the younger man. Dillon's presence at a dinner table made Merlin sit up straighter, cut his meat in smaller pieces, and abjure the creamier foods. Through Dillon's interest in Leah, he had hoped some day for a more intimate identification; and, incidentally, a cut on some of the mobile cash which, according to Rogge, had been changing hands with such easy dexterity that no canceled checks or paper memoranda were left to hint of its disposal. These hopes were finished now.

'Yes,' said Merlin sadly. 'I saw the headlines.' He moved away. Dillon detained him. 'Have a cup of coffee with me?'

'Thanks a lot,' said Merlin, 'but I just had coffee with lunch.'

'How is Leah these days?'

'Splendid,' said Merlin, edging away.

Ordinarily, he would have liked very much to chat with Dillon in the lobby; but now he wanted to get away as quickly as possible. There was no longer any hope of securing the man as a brother-in-law. Leah's Saturday night alliance with the seaman had canceled that prospect. Confronting Dillon, Merlin felt ashamed of Leah. Too, he could not be sure that Dillon was not marked down on Rogge's books for investigation; for the present it would be better not to appear on too intimate terms with him. Most important of all, the crowd made him so nervous he could scarcely contain himself; and Dillon's mouth-twisting only added to his nervousness. Pleading urgent business, he excused himself and fled to the elevator. He hated elevators; but his office was on the twelfth floor, too far to reach by the stairs.

His office door was locked. He took out his key and opened it. Decker had not come back from lunch; evidently she had been caught somewhere by the rain.

The overcast sky made the room quite dark. Merlin turned on the ceiling light and took stock of his face in the mirror over the washbasin. He half-expected to see the same green apparition the sidewalk mirror had disclosed to him—but nothing was wrong with his face; nothing wrong with his tie.

He rubbed his hands together. The dampness of his linen coat in the air-conditioned room had set him to shivering. The wall thermometer read seventy-two, while outside, before the rain began, the temperature must have been around ninety. A change of almost twenty degrees between office and street was too much. He thought to call the building manager and complain, but instead decided to open the window and flood the room with warmer air.

As the window came up, the roar of rain and the multitudinous sounds of rain-hampered traffic entered the room. The air was cool, but warmer than the room air, and fragrant with the smell of hot, rainwashed pavements. The city was veiled in rain. The flag on the Dixie Brewery hung limp from its mast; nobody had bothered to take it down.

In a building across the street a stenographer opened her window for the same reason that Merlin had opened his. Seeing him, she smiled and waved her hand. But he did not see her; he was looking at the river. Beyond the low gray line of the Toulouse Street Wharf, the river ran smooth and swollen, a flat, yellowish-gray. It was full of treacherous currents.

Leaning in the window, Merlin found himself recalling the morning's incident with the blind woman. He felt uncomfortable. Why had he bothered to mention this matter to Decker? Because he wanted reassurance? But he had done nothing for which he need feel ashamed. Even if he had meant to give the blind woman one dollar instead of ten dollars, his motive had been charitable; and whatever his intentions had been, he had actually given the woman ten of his hard-earned dollars. Last night the bill had reposed in his pocket; today it was in the blind woman's pocket for no services rendered. He, and nobody else, had been the instrument effecting this generous change. The woman had the money in her possession—a simple, unarguable fact. What did it matter how a person obtained money, so long as he had it in his possession? . . .

But such reasoning was not entirely correct, he thought, drumming his fingers on the windowsill as he stared at the river through the rain. A stickup man might obtain money by robbing a bank and become, quite obviously, a felon guilty of a punishable crime. And a man might be considered guilty of a punishable crime for much less obvious ways of obtaining money than by robbing a bank with a gun. The Federal Government certainly seemed to think so.

Merlin dismissed the whole subject as absurd. It would make a good story to tell on himself: his generous impulse, his chagrin, his good-humored resignation. Yes, it would make a good story, and the joke would be on him. But not really. He would see to that. He knew how to tell a story.

What a stupid story-teller Victor Peralta was, Merlin thought —always losing the point at the critical moment and begging you with his eyes to find him funny anyhow. WPA jokes! The city was as full of them as it was full of Government money. Mending the streets and improving the public buildings was one thing. The Magnolia Housing Project was quite another. Only yesterday another of his colored tenants on Orleans Avenue had moved across the street into the Project.

Merlin smiled to himself. The stenographer in the window thought that he was smiling at her, and she nodded her head and waved her hand again. But he had not seen her.

Since Victor Peralta liked Roosevelt's ideas so much, he thought, why not let him help make up the deficit? After all, Victor and Leah were both paying the same amount of rent; and, at the same time, Victor's mother was occupying one of Leah's rooms. It wasn't fair to Leah that Victor shouldn't pay—say, five dollars a month more?

While he was on the subject of housing—Dan Clark was behind in collecting rents for the apartment house on Dumaine Street. Clark had been in charge of that property for three years, and he hadn't once caught up; always stalling, always making excuses for not handing over the rent when it was due. In the meantime, taxes had to be paid. Clark's lease would expire in a few months; it would not be renewed. It had been a mistake to lease to a nigger; the only advantage had been that a nigger couldn't insist on repairs. The old building was in bad need of repairs, and something would have to be done about it if he got a white man to manage it. With improvements, of course, the taxes would be raised; but he could raise the rent to take care of taxes and still make a neat profit. The building should be jacked up and new underpinning set in. A new plaster job on all the walls. Three or four new bathrooms. The sagging balconies ripped off and replaced with new planking and new ironwork. A new roof. An over-all paint job.

Again, as it had happened to him this morning before the rain began, Merlin tried to remember something he had forgotten; or something, perhaps, that he had only dreamed. The rain seemed to draw a closing circle about the uncaptured thought.

A raindrop slid down the outside of the windowpane. Merlin traced its course with a finger on the inside of the glass. This had been a habit of Leah's when she was a girl. Every time it rained she stood at a window and watched the drops melt and merge into each other, as if the loss of one raindrop were important to her.

Merlin put his hand in his pocket. He had remembered his

uncle's strawberry field at Hammond, with the packing shed at one end; and, far away across the pale sandy land, the dark pine trees.

At this far end of the field, just before you came to the pine trees, ran a dry gully choked with underbrush and blackjack oak, a good cover for playing Indians, a good place to hide. He and Leah had found it when they were children. One day they had worked with the strawberry pickers. He remembered the pale hot earth; the dark leaves; the smell of ripe strawberries in the sun; the sun burning his back through his thin shirt; Leah's face burned brown from days in the sun; the tight pointed buttocks of the pickers as they bent over—the lazy rise to full height to stretch back and legs.

At about two o'clock in the afternoon, a cloud came over the sun. The pickers stopped talking and worked faster. The field became gray and silent. Birds fled into the underbrush. When the rain came on a sweep of wind, the pickers ran for the shed; but he and Leah were closer to the pine trees. They ran for the gully, and tumbled face downward in the soft dead leaves at the bottom. The thick green leaves above them shut out most of the rain.

The raindrop Merlin had been tracing with his finger on the windowpane had merged with another drop. Clouds gathered; rain fell; a small rivulet trickled down a mountainside where timber had been cut and joined other rivulets to make a stream. The stream grew to a creek and joined another creek roaring down through the scarred mountainside in the rain. Thousands of creeks swept into a river and the river swelled into a larger river. The Mississippi rose against its levees. Men worked by torchlight, but the levees broke. Flood water spread over the land sweeping everything before it: trees, houses, livestock, lives—the lives of many people . . . Leah . . . himself. He saw her face like a desperate swimmer sweep past him out of sight. Nobody remained alive to save, except himself.

Merlin closed the window.

The stenographer across the street took it as an insult. She had waved three times at the man's calm, pleasant face; and not only had he not returned the wave—he had slammed his window shut. She had meant no harm. She had merely felt friendly because of the rain. Now she was hurt. Pouting, she slammed her own window.

Merlin sat down at his desk just as Decker came in the door. She looked as if she had been running. Her face was red. 'Goodness,' she panted, 'it's hot in here!'

'I opened the window for a minute,' Merlin said. 'By the way, did you happen to see that documentary film about flood control when it was here several years ago?'

'You mean "The River," by Pare Lorenz?'

'That's right.'

'Yes, I saw it. Why?'

'Oh, nothing,' said Merlin. 'This gully-washer of a rain made me think of it, I guess. . . . Bring your book, Decker, we have some letters to get out.'

A long sizzling streak of lightning blistered the cornice of a school somewhere in the city and a few bricks toppled into an empty playground. Decker's pencil jerked and came to a standstill on her tablet. But Merlin Webster's voice continued without interruption. The pencil scurried to catch the voice.

THE BRICKS SMASHED NOTHING but a verbena bed, but everybody in the vicinity was sure somebody had been hurt. Victor Peralta, skipping nimbly over the puddles on the uneven sidewalk of Burgundy Street, going home to change his clothes, flinched into a doorway. The bricks had fallen at no great distance from him, and for an instant the wet air was electric with danger. But through the doorway issued a warm, calm cloud of steam and the reassuring odor of cleaning fluid, and a pressing-iron in a black hand thumped the bosom of a white shirt rhyth-mically.

Victor watched the hand while his heart, under his own white shirt, quite soaked now, and sticking to his skin, readjusted its timing to endure the future; and, for some reason, felt unac-countably light as he walked on, now splashing noisily through the puddles without attempting to leap them, even swaggering a bit when he saw himself observed by some timid idler in a doorway. The rain drummed on his stiff straw hat.

He took off his hat and examined it. It would never be the same after such a wetting. He sailed it into the street. The rain was cool on his bare head. He doubled his hand into an unac-customed fist and feinted a blow at a lamp post as he passed. He puffed out his cheeks and blew the rain from the tip of his nose, and laughed to himself at the WPA joke he had tried to tell Merlin. Having no other audience to enjoy it with him, he waggled his finger at a mother cat nursing her brood in a covered alleyway. 'Shame, shame, an unmarried woman with seven children!' he chided.

A Negro woman leaning in her window saw the man talking and laughing to himself in the rain and thought him crazy, and laughed at him. He laughed back at her. Time was long, and the rain was sweet. Nobody needed an umbrella.

Victor was enjoying himself immensely. Any minute, he might be struck by lightning and would see no more of this misty street with its lamp posts; its bright storm shutters; its roofs that sloped in long lovely lines both front and back to split the rain; its fat, generous chimneys—smell no more of its rich smells, loosened now by the rain and set traveling on the damp air. In fact, at any minute, he might belong to the past.

Never, until now, had Victor Peralta belonged so much to the present. This day, this hour, this minute, possessed him as com-pletely as the warm rain which ignored no part of his body. Any minute, the lightning might strike him. Any minute, a brick might fall on his head. This would be fate, and he could not prevent it; but while he was still alive, he turned his head quickly from side to side in order to miss nothing: all sights, all sounds, all smells of the present to record forever.

He did not miss the two oblivious ones on the bed. The window was open, the shutters partly open, and the rag of a curtain was no shield. Long and loose and black in the gloom, locked in each other's arms, they lay under their sloping roof in the rain. On Burgundy Street there was always time for love.

There would be time, thought Victor, now seeing Maudie's face on the rainy sidewalk instead of Leah's. There would be plenty of time. No WPA inspector would come around to check his time on such a rainy afternoon.

A white bone lay on the sidewalk, a round bone shaped like a ring. Some child had probably been teething on it; or it had been a plaything for a dog. Kicking the bone ahead of him, Victor pursed his lips and tried to whistle; but his mouth was too wet to make a sound, and so he whistled a tune with his breath through his teeth. He sped the bone into the gutter with a final well-aimed blow of his wet shoe, and looked up to see a little eddy of people under a porch on the corner. All heads were craning in one direction, like turkeys in a coop. A window went up across the street.

'Whut happen, huhn?' called a colored woman. 'Whut goin on?'

'Dey all goin in Dan Clark's place,' somebody answered.

The woman withdrew her head from the window and appeared in the door. Pausing only long enough to unfurl a large black umbrella, she disappeared around the corner. A child of indeterminate sex, in khaki shorts, ran behind her.

Victor turned the corner. The woman and child were entering Dan Clark's courtyard. Victor followed them.

A dozen or so people stood among the parked cars at the end

of the courtyard. The roar of rain on brick and tin was deafen-
ing. Thunder rolled across the sky. The faces looked up,
and looked down again. Victor looked up. Leander's scared face
peeped through the broken iron railing of the Gomez balcony.
Victor looked down. Frankie lay on the courtyard bricks, with
a roller-skate still strapped to his left foot. His brown face was
pale and his eyes were closed. The colored woman was holding
her black umbrella over his head. Bruno Tarantino was holding
Mrs. Gomez and staring at the roller-skate.

Mrs. Tarantino took her eyes off her husband and saw Victor.
She had forgotten her shyness. 'I seen it happen!' she said excitedly. 'I seen it first! I already called Father Vela.'

'Git a doctor,' said Clark. 'Oh Gawd, somebody wid a phone
git a doctor.'

'Did you call an ambulance?' Victor saw many faces he knew.
The shining eyes and open mouths of the children were gleeful
with horror. The faces of the adults—all except Mrs. Tarantino
—were fixed and vacant, almost dreamy as they made slow motions with their hands to brush rain from their eyes, or shift an
umbrella or a sodden newspaper over their heads. The act had
been accomplished; they had come too late; they could not have
prevented it anyhow. Up in the sky, somewhere behind the
thunder, God's hand had slipped and a life had fallen. It was
God's business. They were not to blame.

'I already called a ambulance,' said Mrs. Tarantino. 'I was
up on my shed roof to take in the wash when it commence to
rain, and the porch planks was wet, it must of been, and Frankie
skidded and went right through the rail. I seen him fall. I already
called a ambulance.'

A broken drainpipe directed a thick stream of water to the
fender of a car below the balcony. The water splashed. Frankie,
beside the car, fluttered his eyelids, moved his left leg, and sighed
as if he were tired. The wheels of the roller-skate spun slowly,
and stopped. Bruno Tarantino wiped rain from his eyes.

'Git a doctor quick,' said Clark. 'He look bad.'

'He's all wet,' Mrs. Gomez whispered.

'Call for duh pries' to come,' somebody said.

'I already called him,' said Mrs. Tarantino.

'She already called him,' somebody else explained. 'He's on his way.'

'When Frankie fell off duh balcony, Clark went an run a car over him,' somebody volunteered.

'Soona it happen to me,' said Clark. 'Ah nevah seen de boy fall. Soona it happen to me dan Frankie.' He stooped over the boy to take him in his arms, but Bruno caught him back. Bent by the weight of tragedy that had fallen into his courtyard, Clark looked from one face to another. Rain beat on his bare, shaved skull.

'What happened?' said Victor.

'Hit starts rainin, see? Ah'm eatin mah dinnah. Ah runs out to crank up de windas on dat Chevvylay see-dan, but dey stuck. Ah jumps in de car an backs hit unda de gallery. Ah nevah seen Frankie bus' dat railin, an couldna stop nohow. Ah gotta risin en mah ear, an nevah heard nuttin tell Mrs. Gomez holla.'

'It ain't your fault,' said Bruno Tarantino.

'Jesus hep us, co'se not,' said the colored woman who held the umbrella.

'Ah wuddna hurt Frankie fo all de worl',' said Clark.

'Co'se not!' said Orena, the Webster cook.

'All the same, he went an backed his car on topa him!'

'You shut up,' said Bruno.

'I think I better hol duh umbrella,' said Mrs. Gomez. Bruno tried to restrain her; but she kneeled, and the colored woman put the umbrella in her hands. The umbrella quivered steadily. Rain spilled off it into Mrs. Gomez' shoe.

Victor unstrapped the skate from Frankie's foot. Mrs. Tarantino tugged at his sleeve. 'I seen it happen!' she said. 'I was taking in my wash because it look like rain any minute, when

Frankie lay on the courtyard bricks

it commence to rain, an I had my mouth fulla clothespins—two, three—I dunno how many—'

'You already said enough,' said Bruno.

'When I heard a big, big noise, a crash, like,' Mrs. Tarantino continued, 'and seem like everything happen at once. But I called the pries' first, and then I called a ambulance, and that was right, wasn't it, Mr. Peralta? Because I seen it happen first.'

'Gawd knows ah wuddna hurt im,' said Clark.

Iris Clark clung to her kitchen door. Behind the thick bifocal glasses her hurt eyes flinched from face to face. 'Hit's true,' she said. 'Hit's true what Dan say.'

'Sho hit's true,' said Orena.

'Anybody kin see dis house rotten, an de railin bus',' said another colored woman. 'Who own dis house, ennyway?'

'Mr. Webster own it,' said Orena.

'Luvva Gawd. Dis house been condemn sense 1933 when de inspector come around. Peoples oughtn't hatta live in sech places.'

A white woman who lived at the end of the block had been listening. She spoke up. 'Clark don't like those kids,' she said in a loud voice to her companion. 'I hear him yelling at them every day. Only this morning, you could hear him yelling all over the block because Frankie taken his pliers.'

'Sangue de la Madonna,' said Bruno Tarantino.

'Niggers and dagoes,' said the woman, smiling in a pained, frightened way. 'They take up for each other.'

'You shut up!' said Mrs. Tarantino shrilly. 'We good Americans as you!'

The Negroes said nothing, but moved closer together. Orena moved close to Iris and put her arm around her. Bruno scowled at the two would-be trouble-makers. They left the courtyard hurriedly.

When Orena moved, Victor saw his mother sitting on the running-board of a car with her head in her hands. He went to her and touched her shoulder. 'Mother,' he said, 'what are you doing out in the rain?' He removed his wet coat and put it over her head and shoulders like a shawl. Through the dangling arms of the coat, she looked up at him, unbelieving.

'Victor, Victor,' she said. 'I thought you were dead.'

'Go home, mother. I'll be along pretty soon.'

'You're wet,' she said, feeling of him. 'You're wet to the bone. Go home and change your clothes before you catch cold.'

'In a little while, mother. Maybe I can help here. But you go home right away. You shouldn't be out in this rain.'

With the coat over her head, Mrs. Peralta waddled obediently away.

The long wail of the ambulance siren cut through the noise of the rain. 'Somebody step on de tiger's tail,' chuckled the child in khaki shorts.

His mother slapped him. 'Hush up! How you feel if it was you?'

The siren screamed higher and closer. Father Vela entered the courtyard gate under a black umbrella. As he approached the group at the end of the courtyard, he looked searchingly into their faces. Some of them were his parishioners. What had they been up to now? They dropped their eyes and bowed their heads as if they were guilty of something.

'It's Frankie Gomez, Father,' said Mrs. Tarantino. 'He fell.'

'Ah nevah seen im,' said Clark. 'Hit starts rainin, see? Ah'm eatin mah dinnah. Ah jumps up . . .'

Father Vela kneeled beside Mrs. Gomez and began to pray. Hats were removed; hands made the sign of the cross. The ambulance stopped at the courtyard gate. Its noise had called out everybody for several blocks, and the sidewalk milled with people. The interne pushed through them and kneeled beside the priest. A brief examination and he motioned to the men with the stretcher.

Father Vela helped Mrs. Gomez to her feet and walked beside her.

'Where dey takin him?' she said.

'Not a sparrow falls but He knows.'

'But he fell,' said Mrs. Gomez in a puzzled voice.

'We mustn't question,' said Father Vela. 'I'll go with you to the hospital.'

The ambulance drove away. Clark and Iris went into their kitchen and closed the door. Orena tapped on the door. It opened a crack and closed behind her. Children pointed their fingers at the spot where Frankie had fallen and jabbered excitedly among themselves. Their parents reflected for a few minutes, then remembered unfinished business and gathered the children and went home. Victor threw the roller-skate in the back seat of the Chevrolet sedan. Leander's scared face still peeped through the hole in the balcony railing. His mother had forgotten him, but Mrs. Tarantino was looking up at him with hungry eyes.

'Bambino,' she said, 'come home with Mrs. Tarantino till your mama gets back.'

Leander shook his head.

'I bake you a cake . . . big chocolate cake . . . mm-m-m!' she coaxed.

Leander backed away from the railing and ran into the house.

'I'll get him,' Victor said.

He found the stairway and climbed to the second floor. Leander was hidden behind a long roller-towel in the kitchen. Victor brought him down and put him in Mrs. Tarantino's arms. Victor and Bruno knew each other slightly. As they walked home, they fell into conversation.

'Was it Clark's fault?' Victor said.

'Hell, no,' said Bruno.

'If the boy dies, there'll probably be an investigation. I guess that's all.'

'No, it ain't,' said Mrs. Tarantino. She cuddled Leander's head into her neck. He rolled his eyes and looked at her fearfully. 'I seen it all,' she said. 'If Frankie hadn't been skating, he wouldn't of bumped into the railing, and it broke, and he fell. If you want to know who's responsible, it was who gave him the skates, and I know who did it. Four years ago, Miss Leah Webster give Georgie Webster them roller-skates, but Mr. Webster was scared to let her use them because she ain't got such good balance, so Mrs. Webster passed 'em on to Mrs. Gomez. It was Miss Leah Webster's fault.'

'You're crazy,' said Bruno. 'The whole world is gone clean crazy.'

'Mind your own business!' said Mrs. Tarantino sharply.

LEANDER GOMEZ breathed on Mrs. Tarantino's neck. He had pushed Frankie against the balcony railing because it was his, Leander's, turn to wear the roller-skate. He hadn't meant to hurt Frankie, but he had thought he would be punished. Often he was punished for things he hadn't meant to do. But maybe he hadn't done it, after all. Mrs. Tarantino said that somebody else was to blame. He looked at Mrs. Tarantino trustfully. He thought about the chocolate cake and licked his lips. 'Can I have two pieces, huh?' he whispered.

VICTOR knocked on his mother's door. Receiving no answer, he concluded that she was taking her afternoon nap. He entered his own side of the house. 'Maudie?' he called. 'Oh, Maudie?'

She was asleep in the bedroom. Victor took off his wet clothes, and lay beside her.

'Stop it,' she muttered sleepily.

'Sweetheart.'

She opened her eyes. 'What on earth are you doing home this

time of day? Why aren't you at work? Is there any mail? Did you look in the box?'

'No.'

'D'you mean there wasn't any mail, or you didn't look?' Several weeks before, Maudie had bought a dress on Leah's charge account at a department store. She was trying to intercept the bill.

'I didn't look,' said Victor. 'I'm crazy about you.'

'In the daytime? . . . your mother might hear!'

'She's asleep.'

'For goodness' sake,' Maudie giggled. 'On WPA time?'

MRS. PERALTA couldn't find her door. She was ashamed to ask the way, and so she kept on walking. She turned one corner after another. Just before she turned a corner, she would be sure that this was the right one, and would be filled with pride and thanksgiving that she had not lost herself after all, but had gone straight home as Victor had told her—almost straight home. But it wouldn't be the right corner. It would be the wrong corner, the wrong block; and she had made a nuisance of herself by getting lost.

'Jesus, Mary, and Joseph,' she said, looking anxiously at strange houses. 'Where do I live?'

And so she would try another block. Halfway along this block, she would remember that she had not read the street sign on the corner, and that this might help her; but before she reached the next corner, she would again be so sure she had found the right corner at last, she would begin to hurry and forget to read. But it wouldn't be the right corner. It hadn't been the right corner for a long time.

To old Mrs. Peralta, sun was sun and rain was rain. Experiencing one, she forgot the other. She did not remember the sun.

For as long as she could remember, she had been walking in the rain in search of her house. All the houses resembled one another. They were all the same house, the wrong house, repeating itself forever in the rain.

AND THE RAIN KEPT ON FALLING. Children wondered aloud where so much water came from. Their curiosity was persistent. Mothers, padding across the floor to look at jello hardening in the icebox, pausing to swat a fly that worked its legs up and down on a spot of molasses spilled on the tablecloth at breakfast, could not answer, and swatted the children instead and told them to play with their toys. The fly escaped. Through faceted eyes it observed the ceiling at close range, disparate angles of mother and child from a distance, and returned to the molasses. Old men scratched ribs through heavy underwear and murmured about large rainfalls they had survived, but nobody listened; and wondered how many more they would live to see, but nobody cared; and got out the checkerboard, but nobody wanted to play. And so they dozed and dreamed of battles, while an army of beer bottles in single file sped along the conveyor in the Dixie Brewery and a metal arm descended and capped them—like little soldiers receiving their rifles or kings their crowns—and their brothers died in Gino's Bar, in Jake's Bar, in Louie's Bar, and were dumped in rattling boxes and carried to waiting trucks to be returned to the Dixie Brewery and refilled with life. One of the trucks drowned out on the streetcar tracks. A streetcar stopped on Canal Street.

On the stalled streetcar, Mrs. H. J. Johnson patted her wailing baby and read the advertisements of Wrigley's Chewing Gum and Linit Starch. Her eyes lingered for a long time on Helpful Hints. 'If you wish to keep your orchid fresh,' the sign said, 'place it overnight in champagne.' The car windows were down; the air was close. The motorman craned his head and gobbled under his breath. His name was John Potowski, and he was thirsty. But he was on the water wagon. Last night he had become a member of Alcoholics Anonymous. The rain fell. The baby cried. Mrs. Johnson bared her breast and pushed a serviceable nipple into the open mouth.

Jesse McPhail assisting the driver, the Dixie beer truck was finally pushed off the track, and the liberated streetcar moved up Baronne Street. As it passed the Jesuit Church, both Mrs. Johnson and John Potowski bowed their heads and crossed themselves. A block farther on, the car stopped to take on passengers. Through the streaming window, Mrs. Johnson's eyes met the eyes of Leah Webster under an awning.

Time had pressed Leah; she had grown tired of waiting for the rain to stop. Dodging under awnings and balconies, she had progressed a block on her way toward the Crescent Beauty Shop. Her hair was wet and out of curl and must be attended to before she went to work. Where would she find time to look any longer for Joe? She had not even eaten her lunch.

She looked into Mrs. Johnson's inscrutable eyes without really seeing them. A seed is dropped in a gutter, a seed is blown over a mountain, and nobody knows where it falls. So Leah was aware of the woman glimpsed through the foggy membrane of the car window, as part of the car itself; and of the streetcar—gray in the rain, its bell irritably clanging as it warned the public it was about to move—as moving time.

The hour was growing late. The car was beginning to move. Behind Leah a newspaper rustled. She turned her head. An old man with a pockmarked face crouched over a newspaper spread open on pale gold crates of pears and grapes and strawberries. Evidently he had been selling fruit on the sidewalk and had moved his wares back into his hole of a shop when the rain began. Leah saw the black name of Hitler in the newsprint and smelled, beneath it, the ripe sweet smell of strawberries. The man looked up.

'Nice strawberries?' he said. 'Two boxes for thirty cents.'

'No, thanks,' said Leah.

The morning had been clear, she thought, but a cloud had come over the sun, and the strawberry pickers stopped talking and worked faster. The field became gray and silent. Birds fled into the underbrush. And the august and shadowless shape of time moved over the pine trees; moved up the stairways; moved down the alleyways, touching a fern; moved up the street as the car gathered speed and plummeted along its shining tracks. An automobile cut into its wake; another followed. A new traffic lane formed. The streetcar tracks disappeared. The area of space briefly inhabited by Mrs. Johnson's eyes was empty now, was blind. The eyes were gone.

Pray for me, sister.

What private and unaccountable sorrow, Leah wondered, had forced the blind woman to beg for more than bread? Why could she not have helped her? The silver dollar, more than she could really spare, had been an insult. But there were the limitations of one's own timidity and a lifetime lived without ever having spoken what lay deepest in one's heart. And so, Leah thought, we are mute.

Trailing invisible streamers of racked faith, beleaguered hope, bewildered charity, and steered by John Potowski, the streetcar lumbered on its way through the rain. The baby was asleep now. Mrs. Johnson smiled at its small mouth still buttoned to her breast, and no longer wondered why she had had to conceive it with four much like it already up in the trees, and under the porch, and everywhere they shouldn't be. It was better to have too many children than none at all. She felt sorry for the woman under the Baronne Street awning, with nothing in her arms but a purse.

'What a beautiful baby!' exclaimed the woman who shared the seat.

'Thank you,' said Mrs. Johnson complacently.

The car swung around Lee Circle as a long rumble of thunder

rolled through the sky. Across the street, at a table near a window in the Public Library, Placide Giraud, copying a recipe for Beef Stroganoff from *Cookery of Many Lands* (he had the title carefully concealed, for he was a little ashamed of what he considered an unmanly preoccupation), looked up and saw the statue of General Robert E. Lee standing with folded arms against the gray sky. His mind filled with dim, brave images of tossing flags and tired men on galloping horses charging a hill against cannon fire. But the flags slanted, fell with the falling men and horses. The ground struggled, then received them softly. Thunder faded across the sky. Appomattox came and passed. The cause was lost—but the streetcar might still be caught. No, it was even too late for that. The streetcar had not stopped at the Public Library, but had gone galloping out St. Charles Avenue. Reseating himself, Placide Giraud penciled a neat reminder to buy a pint of sour cream for the Beef Stroganoff. He could catch the next car.

The car bearing Mrs. Johnson blustered by columned mansions which concealed, or so thought Mrs. Johnson, life's dearest hope of six white linen tablecloths with napkins to match, and a matched set of Rogers's Sterling Silver, the Bride's Pattern nobody had thought she deserved. But when she saw a couple, obviously just married, dash through the door of the Holy Name of Jesus Church and leap into a waiting Packard not hired for the occasion, she did not begrudge the Bride's Pattern; and even wished the bride good luck in babies. Tonight, she thought, would be a good night for making babies, if the rain kept up. No doubt the bride would keep her orchid fresh by placing it overnight in champagne. Ah, well.

Somewhere near Audubon Park, Mrs. Johnson pulled the bell cord. John Potowski stopped the car and allowed her to descend. She opened her umbrella. Folding the blanket over the baby's face, still attached to her nipple, she disappeared down a leafy side street—a little world, a microcosm of warm milk.

The lions in the Audubon Park Zoo knew nothing about Mrs. Johnson's disappearance. The lightning made them restless. Majestic heads with kingly manes swung back and forth along the bars, passing the same guttural question from cage to cage. The elephants were restless, too, and couldn't keep their feet still. They kneaded the sticky ground like flies on molasses, but in grave slow motion, a ponderous vertigo. The monkeys on Monkey Island clasped one another and hid their faces on the nearest shoulder when the lightning came, and chattered excitedly after each crash of thunder; and would have grown as pale, had they been capable of it, as stockbrokers after the market crash. Water was climbing in their caves.

Water was climbing all over the city, set in a shallow saucer between the Mississippi River and Lake Pontchartrain. On some streets in the old section of the city, wooden paving blocks rose from their beds and traveled back and forth in the wash of passing cars. The city drainage pumps throbbed; and the imprecations and importunings of day before yesterday's newsprint, along with candy wrappers and orange peel, bobby pins and old bones, and tattered scraps of letters bearing, perhaps, the words, 'Meet me in front of the Saenger Theatre at 2 p.m. tomorrow'; and the day passed as all tomorrows, and contact established or failed, swam through the gutters down the drains, and swirled under the streets along the covered canals past churches where candles fluttered, each lit with a special prayer, and the stern, still faces of the saints, remote in some beatitude beyond sun or rain, looked down from walls. Past unseasonal displays of fur coats and perennial cures for that tired feeling. Past shelves of books on how to build biceps and how to avoid foreign entanglements; how to lift up your heart to God and your income toward the higher brackets; how to approach the problem of overproduction of can-openers; and how to approach the opposite sex pleasantly and produce babies; how to sell alarm clocks, since time is of the essence; and how to be patient and wait and see what tomorrow brings, for the heart may lie dead under last year's leaves, but the life of the animal is only a fragment of the total life of the universe, and time, an illusion, marches on with Chrysler Corporations, and spring will come again. Past books on how to comfort the ego; and how to fool those other people politely, in pure English; how to love your neighbor; and how to aim straight, and shoot only when you see the whites of his eyes; how to keep America safe for Americans and gardens safe from the menace of cutworms and borers from within; how to determine the sex of a spider; and how to keep peace in our time. Past Placide Giraud, still quietly copying from *Cookery of Many Lands* at his table near the window in the Public Library—for he had missed the next car after all—and long ago had conquered by sheer will power (that particular book had been a revelation, the turning-point in his life) the wild impotent fury which constricts the heart of the sensitive in Public Libraries at sight of such rich wealth of knowledge, and life not long enough to glean it all, and so had ceased reading all books except cook books, where what one learns may be put to immediate and practical test, with something concrete to show for one's labor—now turning a page to lose himself in Hungarian Goulash, and keep his small share of peace in a world he suspected, on waking alone at two o'clock in the morning, to be quite mad. Past old Mrs. Peralta, lost somewhere in the French Quarter, whose eyes had just now lit upon a limp doll weeping in a shoe-box on the sidewalk. Nobody wanted it, or it would be safe inside. It must not be left alone. She picked it up and warmed it in her bosom. Farther on, she saved a jackstone abandoned by its small owner on the sidewalk, and as lost as herself. She comforted it in her hand.

Where she picked up the jackstone, she tried to read the smudged lettering of the street sign on the curb; but one of the blue tiles lay in the gutter under four inches of rainwater; and one of those which remained had been worn by passing feet until its face was undecipherable. The sign on the iron pole was too far above her to be read through the gray sheets of rain.

Mrs. Peralta had been a small woman in her youth, and her bones sometimes grew weary of supporting the vast weight she had put on in later years. Her feet suffered most. The delicately adjusted bones of the metatarsal arch in both feet had given way. With every step she trod on bruised and burning flesh and could have cried out with pain. But she did nothing of the sort. She kept on looking for her house.

Thunder and lightning still came at intervals; the rain still poured. Flowers in gardens and limp weeds in vacant lots were beginning to lift their heads, but Mrs. Peralta's head trembled on her neck. Her shoelaces dragged behind her. Rainwater poured through the cuffs of Victor's seersucker coat which she still wore like a shawl, clutched together in front by one brown, mottled hand. Inside the coat the brown, bewildered eyes peered anxiously, and the lips moved. If she could only remember her prayers, she knew she would find her way home. But she couldn't remember them straight. They kept getting mixed up with lottery numbers.

'Oh, Lord, I am heartily sorry for all my misdoings . . . ten . . . seventeen . . . nineteen . . . Hail, Mary, full of grace . . . twenty-nine . . . thirty-seven . . . sixty-three . . . and all the saints,' she said. 'Where do I live?'

SHE LIVED ABOUT EIGHT BLOCKS AWAY. Under the pillow in her empty room her lottery tickets waited to be honored by chance, and her dresses waited to be picked up from the floor. Something, perhaps the thunder, had shaken them from their nail. . . . Behind her room, in Leah's bedroom, a gray tomcat with battle-scarred ears was watching a mousehole. He had leaped through the open alley door to escape the rain. The nibbling mouse in the fireplace had fled to safety, but he might come out. A small piece of plaster fell from the ceiling. The cat flattened himself on the floor and looked over his shoulder. But no more plaster fell. Undisturbed by much louder sounds from Victor Peralta's room, the cat crouched on guard.

Next door, Mrs. Tarantino was holding open house. Half a dozen women had come to hear her retell the story of Frankie's fall. She had been too busy to bake Leander the cake she had promised; instead, she had stuffed him with sugar cookies and put him to sleep. He had a bad dream and woke up crying; and was consoled with more cookies. In his workshop, in an unaccustomed medley of women's voices that seeped across the courtyard, Bruno Tarantino sandpapered the gunwale of a skiff and tried at the same time to smooth away his troubled thoughts. If Frankie Gomez died, would Dan Clark be held responsible?

The front door of Merlin Webster's house was ajar. Orena, rushing out at the time of the Gomez accident, had left it so. She had not yet returned. Anybody who wished to do so might enter the courtyard and see that Georgie's windmill had stopped whirling when its blades faced southeast; and that the bud of the scarlet hibiscus, just beginning to uncurl in the morning, was wide open now and bright with rain. Everything seemed to be waiting for something, or somebody. At the foot of the hibiscus, hidden under a leaf, a newly hatched moth hung quivering. Its broad black wings were wet from birth and rain; they waited for the sun. The key to the Tuttle apartment waited in the lock. Sheets waited on the fourposter bed; towels waited in the bathroom. Over a masculine chest of drawers in the dressing-room, two prize-fighters belabored each other behind glass. Their zeal seemed to have tipped the picture sideways; it hung askew from its hook and waited to be straightened on the wall. Only falling lines of rain were reflected in the bedroom mirror—rain, and a few green leaves.

In the rain a ferry crossed the river safely and swung against the piling at the foot of Canal Street. The passengers disembarked. The scraping shuffle of feet trod up the ramp. Nobody thought the crossing had been perilous. Why should they? They crossed the river every day. A train that had traversed two thousand miles of city and country without losing its way came safely into a trainshed.

And Leah Webster came safely into the Crescent Beauty Shop and sat down to have her hair washed. She was very lucky that the operator could take her at once, without an appointment.

Fingers massaged Leah's scalp. The hands of the wall clock moved on toward three. If she intended to go to work at four o'clock, she thought, there was no more time to look for Joe. The sound of the water faucet turned off and on reminded her of the sound made by the creaking shutter early in the morning —a sound thinned through unimaginable distance as if it were, indeed, the plaintive whining of heavenly machinery in labor to produce another day. Well, the better part of the day was past; and so far, certainly, she had accomplished nothing worthy of such cosmic travail. She lifted her hand. 'Soap in my eye,' she said apologetically.

The operator wrenched a dry towel from a drawer.

'Could you order me a sandwich and a malted milk?' Leah said. 'I haven't had my lunch yet.'

DAN AND IRIS CLARK sat at the table in the Clark kitchen with Orena Robideaux. Dan was finishing his interrupted meal, but Iris could not eat. She picked at a thread on the checkered tablecloth. Orena stood up to make a fresh pot of coffee.

Rain pounded the courtyard bricks; water hissed on the bottom of the kettle Orena had filled and set on the stove; Dan's knife clattered against his plate. Nobody spoke, but the room spoke for them. It was as clean as Iris could keep it; but soap and scouring powder could not erase memories of black sweat and weatherbeaten walls and greasy meals scooped up in haste; beds sought in haste, anywhere, to ease the ache of limbs and heart and loins; beds left in haste to begin the endless work of endless mornings they were made to love, and so could not help but love in spite of knowing that the day's work would lead them nowhere except to bed again in a land which was theirs and not theirs, in a house they did not own. And yet, Iris thought, this was her kitchen.

'Ah had a feelin dis mawnin,' Iris said.

Dan shifted the wad of oiled cotton in his ear. Orena brought the coffee to the table. Iris began to rock herself back and forth.

'Eat yo dinnah,' Dan said gently.

Orena poured the coffee and placed a cup before her friend. 'Wheah-at's de cream, honey?'

'En dat lil cupboard.'

Orena found the can of condensed milk and set it on the checkered tablecloth. She looked at Iris pityingly. Iris and Dan had lost a child in a street accident years before and Iris had never got over it. The sight of Frankie Gomez lying on the pavement must be reminding her.

'Oh, Gawd,' said Iris, 'Ah had a feelin dis mawnin.'

Dan looked through the window. He, too, was thinking of Frankie Gomez, and of his own child, crushed by another car. He wanted to get at his work again, but the rain was falling too hard.

'Honey, drink yo cawfee,' Orena said.

Iris began to cry. Orena helped her to bed in the small room off the kitchen and returned.

'You finish eatin, Dan? Ah'll wosh up.'

'Ah'm finish.'

'She taken it hard.'

'Yeah,' said Dan. 'She taken it hard.'

'Po lil boy.'

'Yeah,' said Dan. 'Orena, how long you wuk fo Mrs. Webster?'

'Fi yeahs.'

'A long time.'

'A long, long time. Too long.'

'She pay you raight?'

Orena slapped the dishcloth against the sink.

'You said enough,' said Dan.

'Dat chinchy beetle-bug! Dat white trash!'

'Revilin won git you nowheah, Orena. Revilin don do no good.'

'Ah know, but seem lak hit sweeten out de blood . . . Mrs. Webster no wuss dan de yuthers.'

'Trouble,' said Dan. 'Trouble . . . Dat gallery rail oughta been fix. When ah sign de lease, ah tol Mr. Webster bout dat gallery rail, an he promus he fix it . . . ah oughta gone ahaid an fix it mahseff, oney ah nevah had no time, no money . . .'

'Dat's de way hit go,' said Orena.

'Dat's de way hit go.'

THE RAIN WAS FALLING not only in the city, but outside the city as well. The tin markers of U.S. Highway 90 gleamed wetly in the gray afternoon light. Beside one of these highway markers decorated with the State insignia of the pelican, some twenty or thirty miles from New Orleans, a black Ford sedan was pulled up under the Hi-line. The rain had drowned out the engine. The car bore a New Jersey license plate. Three persons were in it. One of them, Roger Tuttle, five months old, slept on the back seat undisturbed by the rain, the vivid lightning and the thunder, and the fact that Thomas Hardy's *Collected Poems* had worked its way off a stack of books in the corner of the seat, and was now sharing his blanket. The other two persons, his parents, were talking. Both were tired and cross.

'I loathe pelicans,' said Katherine Tuttle.

'Do you?' said her husband.

'I do. You never know what might drop out if one opened his mouth.'

'Pelicans have enough sense to keep their mouths shut when they travel—otherwise, they'd be an extinct species.'

'So would the Tuttles if our brakes had slipped when you tried to pass that moving van around a curve.'

'I would have made it if you hadn't yelled. When you drive, I keep quiet. When I drive, I expect the same courtesy of you.'

'All right,' she said. 'Go ahead and kill us. I won't say a word . . . but do you want me to stop talking now and just sit here in the rain?'

'Not necessarily,' he said. 'But this morning you loved pelicans. You thought those white ones flapping along the beach outside of Pensacola were too beautiful for words. Remember?'

'Did I?' she said. 'Oh, dear.'

'What gets me, Kathy, is that if you don't love something you have to loathe it. Why can't you take things moderately, without wasting so much emotion?'

Willis took a cigarette from his shirt pocket and leaned forward to jerk the lighter from the dashboard. Since the motor had been stopped for only a minute, the lighter would still be hot. As he touched the lighter, a forked streak of lightning struck a fence post some fifty yards distant. Simultaneously, the dashboard crackled with blue light, Willis put his hand to his mouth and cursed, Kathy screamed, and Roger woke on the back seat and wailed.

With one movement both Tuttles reached for their son. Willis handed him to Kathy. She felt him over carefully, extracted Thomas Hardy's poems, blotted them on a corner of the blanket, and tucked the book under her leg. 'Just wet again,' she said.

'Darling, find me that zipper bag in the back seat, will you?'

Willis kneeled on the front seat, crowding his long legs awkwardly against the steering wheel, and pawed around among the suitcases, manuscripts, and miscellaneous articles on the floor of the car.

'Imagine,' said Kathy. 'We might have been struck by lightning. Let's push the car in the road again.'

Willis had located the zipper bag which held Roger's dry diapers, and was trying to jerk it from under a suitcase. 'If we had sent these books by express,' he said, 'we'd have a lot more room. Why do you have to lug this poetry around with us? You know it all by heart.' He handed her the zipper bag. Reestablishing himself on the seat, he lit a cigarette with a match.

'It's just like Thomas Hardy says,' said Kathy, busy with a clean diaper and safety-pins. 'Everything is chance. That lightning could just as well have struck us as a fence post. Let's push the car in the road again. Why did we have to park under this Hi-line?'

'It's the safest place in a thunderstorm,' said Willis. 'Wires are conductors. Lightning couldn't possibly hit anybody under a Hi-line. . . . Look at it rain.'

'Rain and pelicans,' sighed Kathy. 'Pelicans and rain.'

They sat quietly for a while. Roger, his diapers changed, had fallen asleep again. Rain beat on the car roof.

'How long d'you think this is going on?' said Kathy presently.

'No telling.'

'Will you be able to start the car again?'

'Wipe off the spark-plug, and she'll probably go all right.'

'I wonder what our apartment will be like. I hope we like the garden.'

'You'll have to like it. We don't rent the garden from the Websters, just the house.'

'I hope we like the Websters. I mean, I hope they like us. I mean, we look like tramps, and Roger acts like a piece of fungus. Sometimes, I almost wish he didn't sleep so much. I wonder if he's all there. Do you think he's all there, Willis?'

'You wouldn't be happy if you couldn't worry about something.' Willis turned her face to look at it. 'The kid looks like you,' he said. 'You look pretty good to me, as long as you keep your mouth shut.'

They kissed each other for a while, and then Willis held Roger while Kathy rebraided her hair. 'What shall we do now?' she said, when she had finished. 'I could read you some more poetry.'

'No,' said Willis. 'Please.'

'All right. Do we have enough money to eat tonight or do we have to cash another check?'

'We have enough to eat hamburgers.'

'Maybe the Websters will ask us to dinner.'

'Maybe.'

Again, they sat in silence except for the beating rain. But presently, Kathy stirred. 'Oh, dear,' she said.

'What's the trouble now?'

'Roger's trouble.'

'Why didn't you go in that filling station down the road, when I asked you?'

'I didn't have to, then.'

'You certainly do pick the most inconvenient times and places anybody possibly could. About the only thing we don't have in the back of this car is a chamber pot.'

'Isn't your raincoat in one of those bags?'

'Dammit, no. I shipped it down. I'll have better sense next time we come to Louisiana.'

'What shall I do?'

'That's up to you.'

'Oh, dear.'

Rain slashed the green fields on either side of the highway and hammered the steel roof of the car.

IN NEW ORLEANS, however, the thunder and lightning had stopped; and in Gino's Barroom on Decatur Street, Pagliacci on the juke-box drowned out the lessening patter of the rain.

'What some people wouldn't do for an extra nickel!' said Joe Onion. 'I never could figure it out.'

He and his two companions had moved from the bar to a table. Joe sat with his back to the door and his feet propped on a chair seat. Behind him the swing door opened and closed.

She didn't even wear a brassière, Joe thought. She hung on the wall above a bunch of dusty pampas grass—a very pink, very clean and shining, very naked lady, urging you with all she had to drink Bella Campo wines. The pampas grass tickled her bottom. She didn't even wear a veil. She was too good to be true. Like unreality, she was boring.

The clumsiness of human encounters, Joe thought. The crass clumsiness of flesh meeting flesh, and nothing to show for it but a headache—and he had given the shoe-shine boy his box of Bayer's Aspirin. Outside, rain was falling and grass was doing its work; but Gino's Barroom had lain under water, completely submerged, for the past half-hour. Men swam through the splashy gloom like sad-eyed fish, with a slow waving of fins and tails that barely disturbed the sand—no, it was sawdust—on the bottom. They breathed through their gills. And each one longed to be loved. For we are not really so clumsy, Joe thought. Each one of us floats through the water with delicate feelers extended, so eager to be friendly, so easily bruised by a clumsy touch, so quick to shrink and hide; or else, from sheer fright, to spit a screen of protective fluid in each other's faces, and behind this screen turn hard and swagger off.

No doubt the grass skirt still dangled from its nail in the Mexican Shop; and the fat little girl in the blue playsuit, wherever she might be, was probably thinking of it. She would never own it now. Such a mother as the one in the green turban would never buy her daughter a grass skirt. The child would remember the skirt as something she had wanted desperately, and had not possessed. And he, Joe Onion, would not be remembered from this morning's encounter as a kindly man, but as an evil man. Most likely, he would not be remembered at all.

Joe had just finished his fourth boilermaker. A quarter-inch of beer remained in the bottle. He drained it, and requested another from the bartender finning slowly past him with a saucer of milk for the cat in the corner.

At an adjoining table, four Italians sucked their cigarettes over a game of Pedro. The five of spades fluttered languidly to the table-top. 'Pedro,' said the lucky one, and drank his glass of wine. The three losers joined him philosophically. All four had been seduced by the lady on the wall. All four were drinking Bella Campo wine. They began another game.

But he had been speaking of man's love for nickels, Joe remembered. He elaborated. 'They'll gouge your eyes out,' he said. 'They'll kick your teeth in. They'll screw your neck till you're looking backwards. They'll unravel your grandmother's knitting, roll it in a ball, and sell it to the hockshop. I never could figure it out.'

Whitey, across the table, took a quick drag on his cigarette and leaned forward. ' "Lissen, chum," I said. "I happen to know there's a flat taxi rate in this town, and nobody's gonna charge me four bucks for a fifteen-minute ride. Besides," I said, "I never asked you to carry me to this clip-joint nohow, you pimp." ' Whitey was nineteen, a messman on the same ship as Joe. His hair was a sun-bleached blond. His teeth were bad.

'For the luvva mud!' said Aleck. He crossed his legs, and looked at his companion with a contemptuous smile. Aleck was short and swarthy, with thick black eyebrows that met above his nose. At the age of fourteen, he had swung onto a freight train in his home town in Texas; and, after many transfers and stopovers, sometimes forcibly detained in jails and again forcibly propelled on his way, had arrived at this table garlanded with ashes and empty bottles. He did not know why. He was still quite young, and he had a bitter taste in his mouth. He was a wiper on the ship. 'You damfool,' he said to Whitey. 'The guy was only tending to business. What was that address?'

'I fergit,' said Whitey indignantly. 'Business in a pig's eye! It's a nasty racket. "Lissen, chum," I said. "One more word outa you, and I wrap this taxi around your neck." '

'Did you?' said Aleck.

'Hell, he started yelling for the cop on the corner. I had to leave. But I didn't pay.'

'That was right,' said Joe. 'Never argue with a cop.'

'Business or rackets,' said Aleck, 'I don't see no difference. It's human nature for a man to grab all he can get.'

'No,' said Joe. 'It's bad upbringing.'

'Aw, Joe,' said Aleck. 'Stop handing me that kiddy-car stuff.' The Pagliacci record had stopped playing. Aleck sauntered to the juke-box, and punched 'South of the Border.'

'He talks tough,' said Whitey, 'but he's just a crooner at heart.'

Joe moved his feet on the chair seat. The chair danced solemnly with the nostalgic music. From this day on earth, Joe thought, he would not be remembered at all, for there was nobody to remember him.

Aleck returned to the table and sat with his lower lip hanging, his lids lowered dreamily over his eyes. Whitey fidgeted and cleared his throat. The swing door squeaked. The newcomer, a woman, presently leaned against the bar. From behind, she looked like Leah, Joe thought. Maybe Leah would remember him. But the woman turned, and was a stranger. She was too unattractively drunk to bother about. Even Aleck looked bored. He and Whitey resumed their wrangling.

Joe looked at a rip in the shoulder of Aleck's blue shirt, and thought that he was a little tired of trying to educate the young. That WPA kid yesterday had taken up three hours of his time, and today he was wasting time on two more much like him. He should have accepted Coffee's invitation to luncheon with the Port Captain, he thought, except that both Coffee and the Port Captain, once you penetrated the layers of good cloth and fat, had about the same ideas as the boys. It was too late for the men to learn anything, but maybe not too late for the boys. Poor kids, they hadn't had much of a chance to get things straight. For years, they hadn't had much to look forward to but the roads and the rackets, or CCC camps, or WPA. And now there was going to be a war.

'Sure, there's going to be another war,' Whitey said. 'Whadda you think Japan is gonna do with all that scrap iron we been hauling over there?'

'Fight Roosia,' said Aleck. 'Let 'em fight.'

'Let 'em fight, hell! How you know they won't use it on us?'

'Japan fight us? You're crazy. They're scared of us. Nobody ain't gonna fight nobody but the Roosians.'

'Yeah? What about the Wops and Ethiopia? What about that? What about Mussolini?'

The Italians at the next table had stopped playing Pedro to listen. A significant look passed between them. They lifted pained eyebrows. The bartender came from behind the bar, tapped Whitey on the shoulder, and pointed to a fly-specked sign on the wall. 'Please, boys,' he said. 'We don't discussa da politics, please.'

'I'll be damned,' said Whitey. The Pedro players resumed their game with more energy, slapping their cards down smartly on the table-top. Whitey continued in a subdued voice. 'I bet if there's another war, we'll be in it. My dad was in the last one.'

'It's all a buncha graft,' said Aleck. 'It's all a racket.'

'A guy don't hardly know what to think, does he?' said Whitey. 'Joe, whadda you think?'

'Well—' began Joe. But he was interrupted by a voice at his elbow.

'Hey, Mista, wanna buy a comic book?'

The speaker was a small, coffee-colored boy with gray eyes and curly hair. He held up a second-hand magazine on a level with Joe's eyes. His dirty shirt, the tails tied together in front, sagged with the weight of more second-hand comic books. His brown toes worked industriously in the wet sawdust.

'Wanna buy a comic book, Mista?'

'What you got?' said Joe.

'Ah got *Supahman*, an *Terry an de Pirates*, an—'

'I'll take *Superman*,' said Joe. He accepted the grimy book, and put a nickel in the boy's hand. The boy grinned up at him ingratiatingly.

'Wanna buy *Terry an de Pirates*, suh? It almost bran-new. Oney a couple guys read it ahaida you. Wuth a dime.'

'You're a little coon, ain't you?' said Aleck.

'Nawsa.'

Joe put his hand on the boy's shoulder. 'If I buy *Terry and the Pirates* and give you a quarter for it instead of a dime, will you buy a toothbrush?'

'Sho, Mista, sho!'

'If you ain't a little coon, what are you? You look like a little coon to me,' Aleck said.

'Ah ain no coon!'

'Shut up,' said Joe to Aleck. Maybe this generation is already crazy, he thought, but maybe the next generation will have a better chance if they brush their teeth. Anyhow, they'll have better teeth. 'You got to promise me you'll brush your teeth,' he said. 'And you've got to keep your promise. I have ways of finding out, if you don't.'

'Sho, Mista, ah'll git a toothbrush. Wheah-at's de two-bits?'

'Remember, now. Once you get that toothbrush, you have to use it!'

'Sho, Mista. Ah'll brush 'em fi times a day. Wheah-at's de two-bits?'

'Here,' said Joe, dropping the coin in his shirt pocket. 'Once or twice a day would be sufficient.'

The boy lingered. Joe and Whitey talked. Aleck stared at the boy. 'Sure, you're a little coon,' he said. 'Here's what we do to little coons where I come from.' He made an exaggerated gesture of choking himself. His tongue protruded; his eyeballs bulged.

The boy shrank against Joe's leg, and looked up at him with sly, wistful eyes. 'Ah gotta brudda,' he said, attempting to join the conversation. 'He stuck a cop in de laig wid a knife. Mah brudda's a swell fighta. Gee, a cop!'

'Run along and buy that toothbrush.' Joe spanked the boy on the seat of his pants and went on talking to Whitey. Aleck turned the pages of *Superman*. Dismissed, the boy wandered over to the cat asleep in her corner. He squatted beside her and stroked her back.

'Ah ain no coon,' he whispered. 'Ah'm Eye-talian. Ef'n ah wuks hard, ah'll git rich. Mah brudda's a coon, but ah'm Eye-talian.'

The bartender saw him and banged his fist on the bar. 'Git outa here!' he yelled. 'I tella da cop, I catcha you comin' in here one more time, you hear me? Little black bastard, stealin' my Coca-Cola bottles an sellin' 'em back, I show you!'

The boy leaped to his feet. His eyes blazed. 'Ah ain no nigger!'

'Git outa my way, git outa my way! I catch him, I show him!'

The boy bolted through the door. The bartender chuckled. 'I teacha him a lesson, eh?' he said. 'I guess he don't come in here again pretty soon, eh? Stealin' Coca-Cola bottles, tryin' to pass as white, I show him!'

'Pedro!' yelled a card-player, slamming down his card.

'Fresh little nigger,' said the drunken woman. 'He's got a nerve.'

The cat stretched and lay down again with her tail curled

over her nose. Aleck looked up from his comic book. 'I told you he was a coon, didn't I?' he said in a smug voice.

Joe stood up angrily. The incident had happened so swiftly, he had had no time to interfere. He slapped his pockets. 'So long,' he said to Whitey and Aleck. 'See you later.'

'What's the hurry, Joe? Where you going?'

'There's a bad smell in here. I'm getting out before I get in another fight.'

The two boys looked at each other; Aleck threw the comic book under the table; they followed Joe through the door. 'Gawd,' said Whitey, 'it's still raining.'

'Yeah. Whatsa matter with Joe. He mad at something?'

'He spent the night in the jug.'

'I seen he got his face cut. What happened?'

'Dunno,' said Whitey. 'I just heard a guy say he spent the night in the jug. Before I come ashore this morning, I heard somebody say he spent the night in the jug. A cop busted him with a gun-butt, or something. The cops is tough in this town.'

'He's pretty high, an you know he can't hold much. What you think we better do?'

'We better stick around,' said Whitey. Joe was standing a short distance away, with his hat on the side of his head. Obviously, he was trying to decide which way to go. Whitey approached him. 'That's a sharp hat you got on, Joe,' he said. 'New, ain't it?'

Joe removed the hat and looked at it curiously. 'Too new,' he said. 'I just bought it this morning.'

'It looks swell,' said Aleck.

'I don't know,' said Joe. 'A hat never feels comfortable till you get drunk in it.'

'That's a fact,' said Aleck. 'Say, Joe, you been in this town before. Got any good addresses?'

'No,' said Joe shortly. 'Find your own. It's no trouble.'

'Hell! You're tellin me. Come on, Whitey, let's go.'

Joe punched the crease out of his hat, creased it again, and set it carefully on the back of his head. 'In a way, a man ought to get drunk and make a fool of himself at least twice a month, I guess,' he said reflectively.

'Why?' said Whitey. 'Sure, I agree with you. But why?'

'Gives him a little humility,' said Joe.

'What's he talking about?' said Aleck. 'What's eatin him?'

'A little humility makes a hat fit better,' said Joe.

'In other words,' said Whitey, 'it keeps you from getting a swell-head. Keeps you reminded you ain't so hot. Is that it?'

'No,' said Joe. 'Keeps you reminded that people are human beings, and so are you.'

'I don't get this guy,' said Aleck. 'He's too deep for me.'

'He just means everybody's in the same boat, and don't be a heel,' said Whitey.

'Hell with that stuff,' said Aleck. 'I want a dame.'

'That's what he means,' said Whitey. 'Gimme a light, Joe.'

Joe held a match and looked over his cupped hands down the street. He thought he saw Leah Webster. He wanted to tell her something if he could remember what it was he wanted to say. He dropped the match to the sidewalk. 'Run along, boys,' he said. 'Go suck your own eggs.'

He swung away down the street. Whitey and Aleck looked at each other, shrugged their shoulders, and fell into step behind him.

4

'MISS,' SAID THE OPERATOR, 'will you hold these hair-pins? I can get at them quicker if you do. . . . Just a little higher, please, Miss. I hope you don't mind.'

'Not at all,' said Leah, in a remote voice.

Enveloped in a white apron, she sat before a mirror in a booth of the Crescent Beauty Shop. The operator was setting waves in her wet hair. The booth curtains were green, the walls ivory. The top of the dressing-table was littered with spilled powder and stray hairpins. A circulating fan on the floor swept the hot air into a corner of the booth, paused, and returned the same air. The green curtains stirred. Around her Leah heard women's voices, the sound of splashing water, the hum of other fans, and the hot buzz of electric dryers. She was hot and tired. Her eyes felt strained from going so long without her glasses, and the back of her neck ached. As she did not want to look at herself in the mirror and had already examined the objects on the dressing-table past the point of boredom, she looked through the parted curtains at the street.

The sky was lighter; the clouds were passing over. Rain still pattered on the sidewalk, but the sun was trying to shine. A Western Union boy in a black slicker came coasting along the

166

street behind a laundry truck. The truck stopped abruptly. The messenger braked his bicycle. His tires skidded on the wet car rail. Leah caught her breath and craned her head. The bicycle curved in toward the bumper of a parked car. The boy dragged his feet.

'Miss, please hold your head straight. Otherwise, I can't do a good job.' The operator leaned across Leah's shoulder and twitched the curtains shut.

Leah sat up straight. If the boy had been hurt, she thought, there would have been a crash. She had heard no crash; still, she would like to have seen the end of the incident: the boy righting his bicycle and continuing on his way with his message. Somebody was probably waiting for that message. Leah felt cheated, and also a little angry at the reprimand. The operator moved her head firmly into position facing the mirror. 'If you'll just look straight ahead,' she said.

But Leah did not want to look at herself. She closed her eyes.

'Do your eyes hurt?' said the operator. 'Maybe you ought to wear glasses. . . . My, you have a lot of gray in your hair! I could give you a rinse and you'd look ten years younger. How about it?' She paused with the comb in midair, her bosom brushing Leah's shoulder.

'No, thanks,' said Leah, moving slightly. 'I haven't time.'

'Just as you say, Miss,' said the operator resentfully. The comb moved, the bosom moved, the fingers plucked another hairpin from the batch in Leah's hand. The operator had not missed Leah's slight movement away from her. She felt repulsed. She, too, was hot and tired. 'It's your hair,' she said.

Sure enough, thought Leah, surprised into opening her eyes. Sure enough, it is my hair. One side of it was now molded to her head in tight ripples; it looked like a hasty job of scalping. And once, she thought, she had liked to stick a feather in that hair and pretend herself Pocahontas. Was this tired, angular image what people saw when they looked at her? Where now were the

brave thoughts with which she had begun the day? They were
not visible in the face which looked back at her from the mirror.
What a face!

Leah had never liked her face and had always looked at it
from the corners of her eyes. But now, forced by the operator
and the day's events to face herself, she did so quite steadily,
with no attempt to evade what she saw.

The clock ticked. The comb dug into her scalp. The fan
hummed. The booth curtains swayed. Once, when she was a
child, she had seen the ribbed skeleton of a ship's small boat half-
buried in sand and twining peavines on a beach. She had never
forgotten it. Still, at eighteen, at twenty-five, at thirty-three,
hurrying past a florist shop, buying gloves at a department-store
counter, waiting for an order to be filled in a crowded restaurant,
she had seen the ribs of the small boat thrusting up through the
sand. The image had a way of coming to her at the oddest times.
Always before it had been a symbol of defeat; but now it did
not seem so. Battered by tons of green water, its cargo spilled,
it had come through shipwreck. She, too, had lost a cargo and
survived a shipwreck. She felt very battered, she had to admit.
Wrecked, you might say, and full of sand. But even sand was
something, she supposed. Peavines could live in it.

Leah looked straight into the mirror and knew that until now
she had been confused, knowing neither her friends nor her ene-
mies. Sometimes she had even been an evasive enemy of herself.
But one does not blame people, she thought; not even one's self.
One does not blame a strange woman on a streetcar because her
face is stupidly complacent; nor a beauty operator because she
appears to be lacking in the finer elements of consideration. One
blames forces which mold people into stupidity, complacency,
and rudeness. And one blames the weak, silly things in one's self.
It is very difficult to forgive one's self, Leah thought, but it must
be done.

The hardest things to forgive, she thought, are wasted time; prolonged indecision; years of timidity—of refraining when one wanted, and of doing when one loathed to do; and also blaming one's self for the fear of making a fool of one's self. What could be more foolish than the picture of herself, a conservative, middle-aged woman in frantic search of a drunken seaman whose last name she had not even known when she had started out? But was it any more foolish, actually, than what she had previously done? She had tried to shape her life to please others who were cautious, selfish, conceited, and narrow-minded; whose sense of living values, if they had ever possessed any, had been lost in the scramble of making money and impressing others like themselves. All the vague things which she herself had wanted in the past now boiled down to one thing; and she might as well admit it. For whatever it was worth, all she really wanted was a seaman who talked of commonplace things with a kind of magic and breathed poetry into the disreputable. She had come to the same conclusion this morning, but without knowing why. Now, she knew why. It was a relief to know herself at last.

Leah forgave the tired, foolish woman in the mirror, and knew that she could never have managed to do it if she hadn't met Joe. Somehow, even if she never saw him again, Joe had simplified things for her. He had cleared the air.

The act of self-forgiveness, she thought, is a greatly underrated service. It may be arrogant, but it is exhilarating. What did they matter now—the foolish acts, the wasted minutes, hours, days? To continue to carry them around with one was almost obscene—like traveling with a dismembered body in the rumble seat.

Until now, Leah had been trying to decide the problem of whether to go on looking for Joe or go to work. Now, the solution appeared simple. She should go to work. She would report as usual to her job in the ticket window of the neighborhood movie on Elysian Fields Avenue. And so, she thought, we renounce happiness to accept small change through a hole in a glass window and issue pink tickets leading to illusion and escape for small boys and romantic housewives. It was rather ridiculous, put that way; but the job was important. She would not be renouncing anything, really. Joe was no illusion; he was the realest thing that had ever happened to her; but the morning's belief that she would be able to find him, that happiness would result from finding him—that had been an illusion.

Maybe it was nothing but a good job of rationalization, she thought, but she felt quite calm and resigned, both to herself and to the clock, as she smiled at the face in the mirror.

The operator, who happened to be looking in the mirror at the same time, thought that Leah was smiling at her. The tired lines around her mouth relaxed, and she, too, smiled. 'Whew!' she said. 'Let's take that apron off. You must be burning up.'

Suddenly, Leah felt happy. How kind people are, she thought. How really kind. She thought of all the people she had seen today—this day with all its loose ends, its unfinished business that would never be finished. Having forgiven and hence, in a way, forgotten herself for the first time in her life, she became aware of others close to her; and, for an instant, caught a glimpse of the intricate, the infinite relatedness of human life on a small planet. How astonishing that anybody should feel himself alone!

'A person can't throw an eggshell out of the window,' she thought, 'but the whole planet heaves.'

She remembered the morning sound of the switch engine coupling onto the string of freight cars: how the crash had traveled from car to car down the line. Since early morning, she hadn't thought of the man on St. Philip Street who had backed through his doorway, buttoning his shirt. 'I'm going now!' he had shouted to his wife. 'Don't try to stop me!' . . . What had been his name? Firestone . . . Frisby . . . *Ferrabee*, his wife had called him. *Thomas Ferrabee*. What an odd name! Leah wondered about Thomas Ferrabee and wondered what would become of his wife and children if he didn't come home. Had the beggar woman, Mea Culpa, succeeded in finding any white hairpins? What had become of the Western Union messenger boy whose bicycle had skidded on the car track? Had he delivered his message? Somehow the blind woman's voice on the dark summer street a year ago had begun this train of thought in her mind. The blind woman, and then Joe. So few words had passed between herself and either one of them; they would never know how they had changed her.

The most profound debts remain unacknowledged because there is no way to pay them; and there is probably no help for this, nor ever will be, Leah thought. There are no words. But the spirit so burdened, as a tree bent down by snow, must find some way to rid itself of its beautiful and terrible accumulation or its branches break. There is probably no help for this, either, she thought.

The day was weighing too much on Leah. Her hand that held the hairpins began to sway.

'Just a minute, honey,' said the operator soothingly. 'I bet you're tired. We'll hurry. It's so hot, but I'll only be a minute more . . . only half a minute . . . Marjorie!' she bawled. 'Mar-jor-ie!'

A colored maid parted the green curtains.

'Has Mrs. Webster come yet? It's ten minutes past three, and her appointment was for three.'

'Yas'm,' said the girl. 'She waitin.'

'Tell her I'll take her in half a minute.' The operator stretched a net on Leah's pinned-down waves and thrust a dab of cotton over each ear. 'Now,' she said, 'we'll put you under the dryer.'

Leah wondered if this Mrs. Webster could be her sister-in-law, Marie. She didn't like Marie any more than Marie liked her; and if she could have escaped, she would have done so. But there was no escape. Nothing remained to do but to part the green curtains and step out.

THE WESTERN UNION messenger boy, whose name was Jerry Hammick, was now far along St. Charles Avenue. He was standing on his pedals, leaning forward over the handlebars, maneuvering his fleet bicycle in and out among the cars on the slippery street like a jockey bringing a horse into the home stretch. His zeal, as might have been expected, was not for the sake of duty, but for purely personal reasons. He was in love with a young clerk, named Miss Flowers, who worked in the Western Union office, and was in a hurry to resume his position in a direct line of vision with her haughty eyes, so that she could not avoid seeing him when she glanced up from her telephone. Miss Flowers had the most beautiful nose. He intended to marry her, and had already picked the house across whose threshold he meant to carry her one day, a bride.

As he passed the house, he looked up at it with urgent, dreamy eyes. It was not really worthy of Miss Flowers; but with its tall white columns and its great sparkling fanlight over the front door, it was certainly a beautiful house. Like Miss Flowers, it had class. He knew it intimately from the outside, but he had never delivered a message here, and so was unacquainted with its interior. As he passed, he wondered briefly what sort of people now occupied the magnificence which would one day belong to Miss Flowers and himself.

INSIDE THE HOUSE, a few minutes before, old Mrs. Laurent had laid aside her book, leaned back in her wheel chair, and shut her eyes. Her hands wandered on her lap. They were beau-

tiful hands with short, straight fingers and well-articulated
thumbs. Time had not marked them as it had marked her face
—but they were a little dirty. Before picking up Shakespeare's
Sonnets she had been reading the morning newspaper and ink
had come off on her hands. The paper, with its scandal headlines, lay on the floor where it had fallen beside her wheel chair.
But Shakespeare had erased for the time being any fear of mun-
dane retribution which might have been aroused in her by the
name of Federal Agent O. John Rogge (in town to investigate
the machinations of the late Huey Long's corrupt political
organization); and her thoughts, as they always did when she
read Shakespeare, moved from sunlit peak to ocean to shadowed
valley, and again to sunlit peak in sonorous blank verse. Life and
love and death occupied Mrs. Laurent; spring with its hidden
violets; summer with its full-leafed trees and dusty roads; and
autumn with its mold and yellow leaves.

Mrs. Laurent was something of a problem to her daughter,
Genevieve, and her nephew, Preston Dillon, who lived with her.
Both were unmarried, and were likely to remain so while their
aunt was alive. From their childhood, she had possessed their
thoughts and services. Genevieve resented the old lady, but
could not disengage herself; Preston was devoted to her, and
had no real desire to make any plans which did not include his
aunt. As a matter of fact, Mrs. Laurent was largely responsible
for any plan, business or otherwise, which Preston conceived or
put into action. He had not pursued his tentative courtship of
Leah Webster, because his aunt had refused to take her seriously.

Since the illness which had confined Mrs. Laurent, she had
become even more of a problem. She flatly refused to remain in
bed, as the doctor ordered, or even to suffer the presence of a
trained nurse. As she neared the end of her life, instead of de-
clining in a manner befitting one of her social position and background, she had grown obstreperous. Never what might be
called a religious woman, she had now become distressingly ir-

reverent; and her language, always rather free and easy, had become so piquantly colored that Genevieve lived in a continual state of embarrassment. Mrs. Laurent gathered her phrases from Shakespeare, from a full memory, from daily newspapers, and from snatches of servants' conversation she overheard. Neither her daughter nor her nephew was capable of understanding that her linguistic revolt was a delayed rebellion against the general stuffiness of her surroundings; a pathetic attempt to ally herself with the richness of a world she hated so much to leave; a last abortive attempt at blooming—as an injured fruit tree, knowing its end, invariably puts out an unseasonal crop of buds. Since speaking was the only social activity which remained to Mrs. Laurent, it was her speech which flowered.

At the moment of closing her book, Shakespeare and the rain had filled Mrs. Laurent too full. The house was quiet; the only sounds came from outside. The air was full of a sound of dripping, a musical tinkle and splash of falling water, a farewell echo of the passing storm. Mrs. Laurent felt that she could not bear another word, another drop without bursting—but the drainpipes continued to empty themselves in her hearing. Hastily, as if she were opening the safety-valve of a small reservoir which threatened to overflow, Mrs. Laurent opened her eyes. The window was open. She wheeled her chair close to the window and looked across the sweep of lawn to the palm-lined avenue.

The sun was trying to come out. A silent battle was taking place in the sky between the sun and clouds. Light and shadow shifted on St. Charles Avenue like the lifting and dropping of great wings upon the earth. The abrupt shadow of a magnolia tree lay black on the wet ground ivy and abruptly disappeared. It was disconcerting. Mrs. Laurent frowned.

'Father Vela is coming to have a talk with you,' Genevieve had said that morning.

'Tell him not to come,' Mrs. Laurent answered. 'If he comes, I won't see him.'

'Don't you think it's time you thought about a few things?'

'About God, you mean?' said Mrs. Laurent bluntly.

'Well, yes.'

'I think about Him all the time, and I've concluded I simply haven't the capacity to understand Him. Shakespeare could have written a better play than the one He gave me to act out.'

'Mama, that's blasphemy!'

'God has my address,' said Mrs. Laurent. 'If He wants to tell me anything, He can mail me a postcard any time. Or He can drop in and see me. My door is always open. Or He can telephone me. Nobody is more aware of the mystery of things than I am. I do the best I can.'

Genevieve began to cry. 'But the Church, mama!' she said. 'Father Vela can help you.'

'Father Vela is a nice old man who takes himself too seriously. He would have made a good gardener. His flowers are lovely.'

'But your soul!'

'My big toe,' said Mrs. Laurent.

'How can you be so blasphemous and arrogant!' Genevieve swallowed her anger with effort, and tried again. 'Death comes to all of us,' she said. 'We must accept it . . . we must be resigned.'

'Go and play Bingo,' said Mrs. Laurent, 'or bridge, or whatever it is you play these days, and let me have a little peace. Resigned?' she said melodramatically. 'Certainly not! They'll haul me off kicking and screaming. Good Heavens, girl, you're the one who's half dead already. Besides,' she added, with a malicious twist of her white eyebrows, 'resignation is nothing but a good investment for the family. I resign myself and confess my sins and you and Preston are relieved of the necessity for paying—excuse me—praying my soul out of damnation.'

'Mama, how can you?'

'Oh, run along.'

So now, Mrs. Laurent in her wheel chair at the open window,

spectator of the silent battle between shadow and light on the street, and for all her positive expressions of the morning a little troubled, a little fearful—her thoughts still running in blank verse —made up a line:

> Let me not be persuaded by the shadow . . .

Shadow of what? of death? But Mrs. Laurent was not afraid of death. As much as she disliked the idea of not living, she was not afraid of death. When the time came, in spite of what she had told Genevieve, she felt she could manage to be fairly cheerful about death. Then shadow of what? she wondered.

Bright and dark angels were battling in the sky. The flapping shadow of their wings raced down the street. Mrs. Laurent had never trusted angels; in fact, knowing so little about them, she was a bit afraid of them. Silly, sexless things, she thought, flaunting their immaculate feathers across every human crisis, in the anguished face of every human woe! The promises of such creatures would surely end with the same result as if the cook merely promised to put baking powder in the cake instead of actually putting it there. The cake wouldn't rise, and that was that. Angels, forsooth! she thought. Shameless converts, preening renegades!

> Let me not be persuaded by the shadow
> Of convert angels!

Down the avenue like a swerving arrow, came a Western Union boy on a bicycle. What message could demand such speed, such grim, tight-lipped frenzy of effort, which surely could never be paid for? No less than life, thought Mrs. Laurent; no more than death. For her? But she was not ready. Oh, send no messenger!

> Let me not be persuaded by the shadow
> Of convert angels! Send no messenger . . .

She closed her eyes, and held her breath. Just as the sun came from behind a cloud and shone on the messenger boy's wet black slicker in a flash of blinding radiance, she opened her eyes and peeked.

> Let me not be persuaded by the shadow
> Of convert angels! Send no messenger
> To blind me with his radiance. I know . . .

Mrs. Laurent squeezed her eyes tight shut again, and waited for the doorbell to thrill through the house. 'I know . . . I know . . .' she thought helplessly. 'I know so many things, and I don't know a damned thing. Maybe somebody peached, and Rogge shook salt on Preston's tail after all. Maybe he's going to be investigated. Maybe he has already killed himself, like some of the others.' Life could certainly be a mess. Of a sudden, Mrs. Laurent felt hopeless about everything.

But the doorbell did not ring. Mrs. Laurent released her breath and opened her eyes. The messenger boy had gone clean out of sight; but while her eyes had been closed, somebody else had come. At the car stop in the middle of the avenue, a man was waiting for a streetcar. There was nothing remarkable about his appearance; he was merely a man clothed in one of those sloppy, hot-weather slack-suits with shirt-tails dangling outside the belt; but Mrs. Laurent was so happy to see him instead of the messenger boy, so relieved to observe another human being waiting for nothing more disturbing than a streetcar, so altogether grateful at what she considered a remanded sentence, that she thrust her arms over the windowsill, and called, 'Hello!' The man had given her hope. She waved at him.

At her voice, the man turned. He was Placide Giraud, who had finished copying recipes from *Cookery of Many Lands* in the Public Library, and having failed to establish contact with half a dozen streetcars, had decided to walk beside the track and, so to speak, ambush one of the beasts along its traveled path.

When he heard the voice and saw the waving hand at the window, he was thrown into confusion. He did not know the people who lived in that house; but, unknown to himself, perhaps he was known by the woman at the window. He looked from the approaching streetcar to the waving hand, and attempted to lift his hat in salutation. But he was not wearing a hat this afternoon; he was bareheaded. He jerked his handkerchief from his pocket and waved it in circles. The streetcar stopped abruptly. Placide swung aboard and paid his fare, feeling somewhat embarrassed by the curious regard of the conductor, but very warm inside at the unexpected greeting from the window. The streetcar started with a jerk.

'What a delightful man!' thought Mrs. Laurent, laughing to herself at the man's confusion. She tried to finish the sonnet she had dropped while waiting for the doorbell to ring; but there was a considerable gap between where her thoughts had dropped it and where they now tried to pick it up. She attempted to weave the interim, but the influence of Shakespeare was fading. Her brain wasn't up to such nonsense. There wasn't enough time to fill one-tenth of the gaps she had left in her own life, much less a gap in a sonnet. Since Genevieve and Father Vela knew all there was to know about everything, she thought, let them finish her sonnet. Recalling the man's confusion at her unexpected greeting, she began to laugh again.

PLACIDE GIRAUD made his way along the swaying aisle of the streetcar in search of a vacant seat. The car was the same one in which Mrs. H. J. Johnson had suckled her baby a short while before; and the motorman, John Potowski, was very thirsty now and sincerely regretting his pledge to himself and the other members of Alcoholics Anonymous.

The only vacant seat happened to be beside a woman accompanied by a small boy wearing a red leather harness strapped over his shoulders. Placide sat down. The woman edged the boy between her knees. Since her arms were full of packages, Placide noted, she had evidently been shopping; and one could not remain unaware of the fact that the little boy wore new shoes, for they were making him uncomfortable in a very lively way. They were burning his feet, he said. He shifted his weight from one foot to the other; he squirmed and attempted to slide down and remove the shoes. But he could not reach them; the space was too cramped. He only bumped his head.

'Don't cry,' his mother sighed. 'Wait a little while longer. We'll be home pretty soon. Can't you wait just a little while longer?'

The boy pounded her knees with his fists, buried his face in her lap, and wept, 'No, no, no!'

Placide Giraud was a certified public accountant taking his vacation. Since he had recently come into enough money to ensure a comfortable sustenance, and had, over a period of years, been coming closer and closer to the dangerous conclusion that business consisted chiefly of men checking and rechecking other men's figures to ascertain how much everybody had been stealing from everybody else, he was not sure but that he might prolong his vacation into lifelong retirement from the business world. The only thing which gave him real pleasure, anyhow, was cooking. He was still a bit ashamed of what he could not help considering an unmanly preoccupation; but he looked forward to a time when he should have overcome this foolish hindrance to his enjoyment, and then he intended to provide fine dinners for all his friends. As a matter of fact, it would give him great pleasure to provide a fine meal, excellently cooked, for anybody who looked hungry. He didn't like to think of people being hungry. Hunger caused wars. A bachelor like himself, however, a World War veteran who had studied battle maps and generals' lives as well as hundreds of miscellaneous volumes in the Public Library before forswearing all literature except cook books—a man like himself might have an idea that the cause and remedy of wars was a simple matter of enough food for everybody; but distribution of the world's food was in other hands than his own, and there was little he could do beyond the small circle of himself and his friends.

He did not like children. The presence of the small boy beside him in the streetcar filled him with discomfort. But it had always been his way to make himself as helpful to others as possible; and it was not necessary for the mother to speak her thoughts aloud in order for him to know what she was thinking. Placide Giraud had intuition; in fact, he might be said to suffer from intuition. He was a very sensitive man.

'Go ahead and take off the child's shoes,' he said. 'I'll hold your packages.'

'I wanted to ask you, but I didn't have the nerve,' the woman said gratefully.

She transferred the packages to Placide's arms, took the child on her lap, wiped his nose, and then removed the new shoes and socks and stowed them in her shopping bag. The child looked at his bare feet, and laughed. On both feet the big toe curled outward in an energetic, enterprising way, like a thumb on a hand. The mother stroked the small feet.

'He never could stand to wear shoes,' she said worriedly. 'He learned to walk without them. The doctor said his toes would gradually get in line if he'd wear shoes. But he won't wear them. You see what he did, just now.'

'Yes,' said Placide.

The child looked at the man, his face grown suddenly solemn. He reached across his mother's arm, took hold of a shirt button, and stared up into the face above him. Placide Giraud looked down and felt a renewal of the warm feeling which had possessed him at sight of the hand waving from the window. Why, the child appeared to like him! Placide twisted his long face into a caricature of alarm. The boy laughed delightedly. What a bright little fellow he was! But what was probably in store for him, Placide Giraud hated to contemplate. The world would know another great war, he was sure. Isolation of any country seemed improbable now. A wind was coming, a wind of change. Windows were being pulled down, sandbagged, boarded up, blacked out. The child would grow up in a world at war; he might even be hungry. Placide winced as he thought of the hunger that not only causes wars but follows them. He had seen it with his own eyes. He had seen hungry old men pushing perambulators across mountains; hungry old horses pulling sewing-machines and rocking-chairs down long roads; hungry old women leading tired, hungry children and goats under the open sky.

He looked again at the child. It was looking through the window with its thumb in its mouth—a perilous, forbidden pleasure to be enjoyed to the utmost before its mother observed. No doubt, it had been slapped for this.

We teach them not to suck their thumbs, he thought. We buy them new shoes and put braces on their teeth and nurse them through whooping-cough and measles so that they may grow up and go to war.

'Take your thumb out of your mouth!' said the mother. She slapped the small hand. The thumb was withdrawn.

'I got new shoes,' the little boy said to Placide Giraud.

'I know you have,' answered Placide.

But new shoes and all, the boy would go to war some day, if people didn't learn not to grab. When would men learn to share an abundant world without grabbing? There was no excuse for some to grab and others to go hungry. It caused wars.

Placide Giraud looked through the car window at the bright, rain-washed street. How clean and beautiful the world looked! The rain, still showering down, had washed the dust from grass and leaves and street signs. All signs were clear. In such a clear world, it seemed impossible that men could not read that they were going to war, and turn around in time. Surely, they would see.

JOHN POTOWSKI, the motorman, was just now reading a sign in front of a drugstore. 'Drink Dr. Pepper at 10—2—4.' The rhythm of the words was hypnotic. The sign itself was already half a block behind him, but the sound of the car wheels reiterated the hypnotic suggestion.

> Drink Dr. Pepper at 10—2—4
> Drink Dr. Pepper at 10—2—4

John Potowski drew a long, quivering breath.

PLACIDE GIRAUD reached across the woman and managed to get a window open. With the rush of clean, sweet air, he felt enormously exhilarated. Maybe there wouldn't be a war, after all. The boy laughed and wriggled off his mother's lap to the floor. She relieved Placide of the packages he had been holding. Placide rested a hand on the boy's shoulder. How warm and rich with living the small body moved beneath his hand. Perhaps, he thought, the woman who had waved from the window had been enjoying the same feeling of richness as he now felt, a richness too great to be borne alone and time so short, and one must share it in any possible way, if only through a hand waving from a window, a hand placed on a shoulder in passing. All at once, Placide Giraud wanted more of the boy's company; he would have liked to take him to the Audubon Park Zoo, which was now but a few blocks distant. The idea was absurd; still, he would like to do it. But the woman was trying to get into the aisle.

'Good-bye,' she said. 'We get off here.'

'Good-bye,' said Placide to the woman, and 'good-bye' to the child who would like to ride forever; but looked over his shoulder with his thumb in his mouth as his mother dragged him by the strap of his red leather harness toward the door.

The streetcar, halted briefly, moved again; and between one block and the next, thought Placide Giraud, is time for the heart to know despair and to hope again—to burst wide open with laughter. He had just decided to visit the Zoo alone. He hadn't been there for years. In such a fresh, bright world, anything might happen. He might even meet a pretty girl and tempt her to his apartment with Beef Stroganoff. He mustn't forget to buy that pint of sour cream.

And between one block and the next was time for a message to arrive at its destination, Placide saw, for the car was passing a house where a Western Union messenger boy waited while a woman signed a form: time to see a gray silk dress before a heavy door closed and the messenger boy ran down the walk toward his bicycle that leaned at the curb.

IT WAS NOT A TELEGRAM, but a cablegram. Now that she had it in her hand, Mrs. Haimovitz walked steadily through the house to the kitchen. It was not her own kitchen; it belonged to the cousin who had brought her and her son's wife from Germany and guaranteed their support to the Government of this strange country, the United States. But strange as the room was, it was the one room in the house bolted to reality, the room Mrs. Haimovitz always sought when some change threatened her. Before opening the envelope, she stood at the window and looked into the back yard. The orange trees were loaded with green fruit. There would be a heavy crop this year.

She opened the envelope and read the message. Her son, Karl, was dead. The Nazis had killed him because he was a Jew.

Mrs. Haimovitz felt behind her for a chair and sat at the window. For a while she saw and heard nothing; and then she became aware of the scene before her in minute detail.

So the rain comes again, she thought, a slow, gentle patter from the gray sky; and the bumblebee only a minute ago looking for honey in the snapdragon has disappeared. The rain is a whisper, a brushing of fingers or garments, a thing which cannot be told. The neighbor's kitten has gone under the house again. He lifts a skinny leg to scratch an ear. The heavy heads of the roses would drench you if you touched them. They are fat with rain. The rain is falling in a soft, slow shower that stops for a while, and you think it is done. You hear it again on the roof, a gentle pattering. Now the sun comes again, shining through the rain. A mockingbird rises straight from the grass and settles on a telephone wire. His feet grip the wire and his lifted wings come down. His weight sets the wire to undulating. He bobs up and down on the wire, balancing with his wings. All over this continent (and beyond this continent, she thought), clouds are forming and fading: the towering, sun-shot shapes, the fish scales, the hoofprints, the flowers, the faces, the columns and castles in the sky. People walk under the clouds. They walk in and out of their houses. They hurry along the streets. They stand beside their machines with concentrated eyes. They drive on the roads. They follow their animals across the fields. But you will not walk again. From seeds that were planted this spring, melons are ripening; and corn is hardening in its husks. And you are dead, she thought.

Mrs. Haimovitz stood before the map of Germany pinned to the kitchen wall and put her finger on the place where her son's death had probably happened. She stroked the map softly and touched it with her lips. She sat at the window again. The mockingbird flung himself from the wire to a rosebush. The wire swayed for a while and grew still. Karl was dead—a man, with a man's weight of flesh and bone, a man's dark weight of unfinished dreams and plans for the future. Sitting by the kitchen window, watching the mockingbird (he had left the rose-bush, and was back on the telephone wire with a dragonfly in his beak), Mrs. Haimovitz felt her son's weight in her arms as if she really held him; and the weight in her heart, she did not think she could bear.

The telephone rang in the still house. Mrs. Haimovitz stood up to answer it. 'No,' she said gravely to the persistent instrument in the hall. 'No. Nobody named Jerry Colonna lives here. You have the wrong number. Nobody named Colonna lives in this house.' . . . The telephone had rung three times in the past hour, and each time with the same bewildering request in a childish voice. Mrs. Haimovitz did not understand.

Karl's young wife would have to be told soon, she thought, seating herself again at the kitchen window, looking again into the yard. But the girl was asleep now, taking an afternoon nap. Let her sleep while she can, Mrs. Haimovitz thought. After she hears, she will not sleep well for quite a while. Then she will sleep well again, for she is young, and the young heal quickly. Having borne no child, she would not understand about the weight.

So the rain comes again, she thought, but softer now, only a mist, a dream. The kitten has come from under the house to rake its claws on an orange tree. It chases a dragonfly across the yard. The trees are loaded with fruit.

Mrs. Haimovitz straightened her back, and sat very still at the window. There will be a heavy crop this year, she thought.

A DOZEN BLOCKS back along the avenue, Mrs. Laurent wheeled herself to her bedside and pressed a buzzer. Composing three lines of a sonnet and being scared half out of her wits by a Western Union messenger boy seemed cause enough for a drink. Presently, knuckles rapped on the door panel, and the door opened on a colored man in a white coat.

'Julius,' said Mrs. Laurent, 'did Mr. Preston and his friends do away with all the Scotch last night?'

'They drunk it, ma'am.'

'Is there any Bourbon?'

'Yes, ma'am.' Julius fidgeted. 'But Miss Claudie,' he said. 'De doctor say—'

'Never mind what he says. Bring me a Bourbon and soda, Julius, and for Heaven's sake, order another case of Scotch right away.'

When Julius, looking rather frightened, returned with the highball on a tray, Mrs. Laurent took the glass in her hand and studied it thoughtfully for a minute. She knew that she was not supposed to drink it; but she also knew that while yesterday it might have hurt her, and tomorrow would more than likely finish her, today it could not possibly hurt her. Today, nothing could hurt her. She felt too happy.

'Well,' she said, lifting the glass, 'here's mud in your eye, Julius.'

Julius bowed in acknowledgment of the toast.

'Have one for yourself—if you haven't already. If Miss Genevieve catches you, tell her I said the drinks were on me.'

'Yas'm, Miss Claudie. Yo heart is in de right place.'

'What's left of it is doing all right,' said Mrs. Laurent complacently.

Julius tiptoed from the room. Hardly had his careful footsteps died out on the stairs when Genevieve entered, fresh from her nap. At sight of the highball, she swooped forward. Mrs. Laurent gulped hastily, and almost succeeded in finishing the contents of the glass before it was snatched from her hand.

'Mama, how can you disobey the doctor's orders like this? He said absolutely no stimulants except as prescribed!'

'Oh, well.' Mrs. Laurent licked her lips, and patted her breast-bone delicately.

The telephone rang beside the bed. Genevieve answered it. She turned to her mother. 'It's Preston,' she said. 'He's worried about you. He thought the storm might have made you nervous. I told him you were all right, but he wants to talk to you.'

'Is he in jail?' said Mrs. Laurent calmly.

Genevieve put her hand over the receiver. 'How can you make such disgusting jokes!' she said fiercely.

'Preston always was afraid of lightning,' mused Mrs. Laurent. 'I can't imagine where he got it. He certainly didn't get it from me . . . the way that child used to come howling for protection when a little storm blew up . . . but I never encouraged him . . . I always spanked him.'

'You dominated him!' Genevieve hissed, with her hand over the receiver.

'Piffle,' said Mrs. Laurent. 'The idea of a grown man ringing up a sick old woman because he's afraid of lightning. Anyhow, the storm is over. But I'd spank him again, if he were here . . . the idea!'

'Mama, he's waiting. What shall I say?'

Mrs. Laurent did not answer. She was snoring softly. There was a little silence in the room. With superb control, Genevieve recovered herself and spoke into the telephone. 'She can't talk to you right now, Preston. She's almost asleep, and I hate to wake her . . . All right. Good-bye.'

Genevieve looked again at her mother. The beautiful, ink-stained hands gripped Shakespeare protectingly. Mrs. Laurent was indeed sound asleep.

'HELLO, MARIE,' said Leah Webster, parting the green booth curtains in the Crescent Beauty Shop.

Marie looked up from her magazine and held out her hand. 'Why, hello, dear,' she said. 'I didn't know you came to this place.' Her eyes took in Leah's wrinkled linen suit. 'You must have got caught in the rain,' she said. 'Georgie, kiss your Aunt Leah.'

Georgie did as she was told. Leah settled herself under the dryer. The operator readjusted the cotton pads over her ears, snapped on the heat, and followed Marie into the booth which Leah had just vacated.

A roar of hot air descended on Leah's head. The forefinger of her right hand began to prickle, a sensation she frequently experienced on meeting her sister-in-law. One Sunday, while walking in the Park with Marie and Georgie, Leah had noticed an iridescent spot of color in the grass, and had stooped down and picked up a beetle on her finger. It was a beautiful thing, she thought, with a lacquered back that burned with metallic colors, bronze and blue and green in the sunlight. Its head was small and its body broad and boxlike; its thorny legs bracketed her finger with a dry, tickling sensation. Marie's reaction had been instantaneous. 'How odious!' she said, and struck the beetle from Leah's finger. It fell to the ground where, for the next half-hour, Leah, her anger disproportionate to the triviality of the incident, had imagined it scuttling among the grass roots emitting a thin, high squeal of rage before it returned to its secret munching and squirming and burrowing. Marie, rustling the pages of the Sunday Society Supplement under the oak trees while Georgie gathered acorns, had the same small head and boxlike body as the beetle; she, too, was metallically girdled and lacquered; she, too, plundered with gigantic concentration among droppings.

When Marie emerged from the curtained booth and was settled under an adjoining dryer, Leah occupied herself with the sandwich and malted milk which had arrived from the drugstore. She felt her sister-in-law watching her curiously, and guessed that her mind was busy with probable details of the Saturday night adventure.

As it happened, Leah was correct. Marie was thinking that a change had taken place in Leah, and wondering if the sailor could be responsible. And why was Leah not wearing her glasses?

'What happened to your glasses, dear?' Marie said. 'Did you break them?'

'I forgot them this morning.'

'So inconvenient.' Marie was sure that the sailor had broken them, and she shuddered inwardly at thought of such a violent encounter. This was a good time to give Leah the book she had bought for her. The recipient of an unexpected gift from an enemy, she thought, is always placed in an uncomfortable position. Leah looked entirely too smug; she should be made to feel uncomfortable.

'Georgie,' said Marie, 'hand Aunt Leah that little package there on the divan.'

'What is it?' said Leah.

'A little present I bought you. A book I thought you'd enjoy.'

Surprised, Leah accepted the book from Georgie and smiled her thanks.

'Aren't you going to unwrap it?'

'Later,' said Leah.

Marie bit her lip. The book had cost nearly three dollars, she thought indignantly, and Leah hadn't even looked at it. Only this morning, she had felt sorry for Leah; had refused to judge her; had honestly believed her more to be pitied than blamed for her peculiar actions. How wrong she had been!

Marie Webster did not like to be ignored. She looked about her, and discovered an acquaintance of whose presence she had been elaborately unaware until this minute, although the woman, anchored under another dryer, had been making friendly motions with her hands ever since she had come into the shop.

Since both women raised their voices, Leah could not help overhearing their conversation. It was mostly a monologue. Marie was speaking of Clara Bilbo; explaining how Clara was such a quaint old darky; how she had served some of the best families of the state in her youth; how she, Marie Webster, had been so glad to be able to help Clara get the job selling pralines in the Cabildo porch.

Leah swallowed a rising disgust. Marie's charities were always well publicized; and the subjects paid for what they got by furnishing her with small chat. Association with Clara Bilbo was really a social asset to Marie Webster. To be the benefactor of one who had once served the great was a duty which paid dividends—tying one in as it did, by implication, with the old life of the South; with the devoted Mammy who had raised one's children and was practically a member of one's family. The impressionable no doubt found these implications very impressive. Any day now, Leah thought, Marie was likely to allow somebody to believe that the duty of benefacting Clara Bilbo had been handed down to her from her grandmother; and that Clara had not only been her own nurse, but had even had a hand in rearing Georgie.

'I heard a delicious story about Clara the other day,' Marie was saying. 'Some Northern tourist bought pralines from Clara and was quite impressed with her. "What a magnificent carriage you have," she said. Clara didn't know what she meant. "Carriage, ma'am?" she said. "Ah ain got no carriage." The woman tried to explain. "I mean the way you walk," she said, "with your back so straight, and your head so level, and the way you swing your hips. That's what I mean by carriage. You walk magnificently." . . . Well, Clara never could catch on what she meant, and the woman kept on trying to explain to her, until Clara finally got insulted. "You makin fun a me," she said. "Ah ain got no carriage. Wheah ah goes, ah walks!"'

The listener laughed appreciatively. Leah dropped the malted milk carton in the wastebasket and brushed the crumbs from her lap. She felt of her hair. It was dry enough.

AFTER HANDING LEAH THE BOOK, Georgie had wandered toward the telephone booth. The purchase of Miss Decker's birthday present had left her with one nickel in her purse, but this was sufficient for her purpose. The Beauty Shop was tiresome. Why not ring up her friend, Lucille Budd?

She slipped into the booth and dialed Lucille's number. The line was busy. She retrieved her nickel, waited a minute, and dialed again. Lucille was on a party line, and sometimes was hard to reach. The nickel came back. Georgie waited patiently, and dialed again.

'Hello,' Lucille sang over the wire, 'hello, hello, *hell*-O!'

'Oh, *hell*-o,' answered Georgie. 'Is this the butler speaking? I was just wondering, James, if I could speak to Miss Lucille?'

'What is the name, please?' said Lucille, in what was intended to be a deep, masculine voice.

'This is Mr. Clark Gable,' replied Georgie, in what was also intended to be a deep, masculine voice.

'Commup an see me sometime!'

Across the city from each other, both little girls burst out laughing. They always went through this routine, or a similar one, before they got down to business.

Lucille Budd was a year older than Georgie—a thin, muscular child with a long waist and extremely well-developed calves. She was good at mimicry, and possessed a vivid imagination. Georgie, gentle and quiet when alone, was a different person when stimulated by Lucille. To pass the time this rainy afternoon, Lucille had been picking numbers at random from the telephone directory, dialing one after another, and announcing herself to the bewildered stranger at the other end of the line

as Jerry Colonna, as Franchot Tone, as Rochester, as Mrs. Roosevelt, as Walter Winchell, or as the caretaker of the Audubon
Zoo, to say that the lions had broken loose from their cages
and were prowling all over the Garden District. Her industry
had resulted in emotions of fear, rage, pain, bewilderment, and
amusement all over the city. Some of those reacting most strongly
had been honored by repeated calls, until they felt like tearing
their telephones out by the roots and hurling them into the street.
Dial calls could not be traced, as Lucille well knew, and she
had the public at her mercy. She had been engaged on her happy
enterprise for nearly an hour when Georgie had first called.
While pausing to look up the number of another victim, her
own telephone had rung.

'What you doing?' Georgie asked.

'Nothing,' said Lucille. 'Just calling numbers. What you
doing?'

'Nothing,' said Georgie. 'I'm in the Crescent Beauty Shop with
my mama and Aunt Leah getting their hair washed.'

'My mama is reviewing a book at the Jung Hotel.'

'Why?' said Georgie.

'Oh, she reads a book and tells the other ladies what's in it.'

'Can't they read?'

'They haven't got time.'

'Does your mama have more time than other ladies?'

'She reads fast,' said Lucille. 'She reads awful fast.'

'The Tuttles are coming today,' Georgie said. 'I'm gonna help
take care of Roger.'

'Who's Roger?'

'The Tuttles' baby!'

'My mama's buying me a cocker spaniel puppy,' said Lucille.
'With a license, and everything.'

'A man walked up to me today in the French Market,' said
Georgie, 'and I bet you'd never guess what happened.'

'What?' said Lucille.

'He wanted to buy me a grass skirt!'

'He did?' said Lucille. 'Did he? Gee!'

'He was a stranger,' said Georgie in a dignified voice. 'I never saw him before in my life, until he just walked up to me and said—he just said—'

'Gosh!'

'I never was so insulted in my life!' Georgie brought out breathlessly.

'Did you get the grass skirt?'

'I never accept presents from strange men,' said Georgie. 'My mama says it isn't nice.'

'Your mama is funny, don't you think?'

'Yeah, I guess so,' said Georgie. 'Lucille, you remember that time we went to St. Peter and Paul's Catholic Church with Lizzie Cansino?'

'Sure. I remember. Your mama was mad.'

'Yeah. I was just wondering, Lucille, did you happen to notice who rang the bell?'

'What's that got to do with a grass skirt. Is this a gag?'

'Nothing,' said Georgie. 'No gag. I was just wondering who rang Catholic bells? It just occurred to me. I just wondered, that's all.'

'No,' said Lucille, 'I never noticed.'

'I thought you might.'

'Well, I didn't. I guess a man pulls a rope, like other bells.'

'I guess that's right.'

'Yeah,' said Lucille, 'I guess a man just pulls a rope, or something.'

'I guess so.'

'A man would have to pull a rope or something, wouldn't he? A bell couldn't ring unless a man pulled a rope, would it?' said Lucille in a vexed voice. 'Why?'

'I was just wondering.'

'Oh.'

The conversation was languishing. Lucille's end of the line was pregnant with impending farewell. Georgie didn't want to hang up. She tried to think of something more to say.

'Ladies look awfully funny in a beauty parlor,' she said. 'They all got their hair stuck down, and nets on, and cotton stuck in all their ears. They look awfully funny.'

Lucille laughed. 'I know,' she said. 'Under those dryers they look like they got football helmets on. They look exactly like big ole football helmets.' Suddenly, an idea occurred to her. 'This is the National Broadcasting Station,' she said. This is Station WROX. The big game is about to begin. The opposing teams are lined up on the field. The odds are heavy against Harvard. It is a beautiful day. We will now switch you to Walter Winchell in the stadium. The whistle blows.' Lucille put her finger in her mouth and vented a shrill, screeching whistle into the telephone. 'Come in, Walter Winchell,' she said.

'Uh,' said Georgie. 'Well . . . uh . . . wait a minute, Lucille, wait a minute!' She opened the door of the telephone booth a few inches, and surveyed the room.

'We will now switch you to Walter Winchell in the stadium,' Lucille said impatiently. 'Come in, Walter Winchell. Darn it, get off the ground!'

'HelloMr.andMrs.AmericathisisWalterWinchellbringingyou anotherjournalforJergen'sLotion,' said Georgie. 'They're all in a huddle and I can't see the tops of their heads but they're all showing their teeth at each other and the stands are roaring can't you hear them' (the noise of the dryers and electric fans did manage a creditable hum) 'and my mama is telling a joke and everybody is laughing except Aunt Leah and her hair is dry now and she is getting up and now she says never mind about combing it out to the lady that washed it and now she is putting on her hat and picking up her purse so Aunt Leah kicks the final goal and Harvard wins and the game is over.' She stopped, panting for breath and choking with laughter.

Lucille whistled again. 'It was too short,' she said.

'Aunt Leah left,' said Georgie. 'She forgot the present mama gave her.'

'What was it?'

'Just a ole book named *The Magnificent Obsession*. I guess she didn't want it.'

'Who wants a book?' said Lucille.

'My mama looks mad. I guess her feelings are hurt.'

'Lissen,' said Lucille hastily. 'I think I better hang up now. I hear my mama coming home. . . . This is Walter Winchell ending another broadcast for Jergen's Lotion.'

'This is Station WROX on the Blue Network signing off,' said Georgie.

IN THE FRENCH QUARTER below Canal Street, the rain-splashed sides of St. Louis Cathedral were drying in dark streaks; and the water in Pirate's Alley, which had run a foot deep during the heaviest part of the rain, had now subsided. A few old men had already returned with their checkerboards to sit under the pink crêpe-myrtles in Jackson Square. It was even hotter than before the rain. Pavements smoked in the sun, and shrubbery seemed to have grown an inch since morning. People moved slowly through the damp heat. Out-of-doors life in the French Quarter, interrupted by the downpour, was getting under way again.

Across Pirate's Alley from the Cathedral, in the flagged porch of the Cabildo, an old Negress sat on a camp stool and smoked a clay pipe. She wore a red bandana on her gray head, a white kerchief around her neck, and a starched white apron over her calico dress. She was Clara Bilbo. On a bridge table near at hand was a basket of pralines, round brown sugar candies wrapped in cellophane, and half a dozen black cloth Mammy dolls with roguish, shoe-button eyes. Squatting against the Cabildo wall were two WPA white boys: Victor Peralta and Lucien Taylor. They were discussing art; but Clara was not listening.

She was thinking of her grandson, Edward, called 'Cooter' by his friends, who had been jailed the day before as a suspect in a series of petty thefts from grocery stores along Dauphine Street. She knew that Cooter was no thief. He was a good boy, just turned seventeen; a quiet boy who liked books, and wanted some day to be a doctor. He had never been half the trouble his young half-brother, Ronnie, had been. Ronnie was ashamed of being a Negro; and this worried Clara a great deal. Because Ronnie had bright skin and gray eyes, he sometimes tried to pass as white. He was always on the streets. But Cooter was in jail; and even if they turned him loose, harm had been done. She had seen what happened to young Negro boys who went to jail. They came out ugly and hating, and were lost. Clara's reason told her that the same thing happened to white boys under the same circumstances, but now she was so old she found it hard to reason. Love and hate were all she could feel—and she had to reason; she had to keep on trying to reason how, if she couldn't get Cooter out of jail, she could help him when he did get out. Somehow, she had to keep his pride alive. A Negro could lose everything but his pride in his race, and still manage to live; but he had to have his pride, for this was what kept him able to take what he had to take all his life: what made her able to sell Mammy dolls, these insulting replicas of herself, to earn a living.

Clara looked at the two white boys, Victor and Lucien, free to come and go as they pleased, and felt hate gathering inside her. White boys could lie around in the free sunlight with pencils and paint brushes and get paid for it. They didn't even know Cooter Bilbo, in jail. But hate was an old acquaintance, sometimes not too hard to get rid of, and Clara's reason managed to edge it temporarily from her mind and close the door. They were just boys, she thought, still wet behind the ears. She couldn't help liking boys. What were they saying?

'Yes, sir,' Victor Peralta was saying. 'I think I'll take a correspondence course in short-story writing, or maybe I'll sign up for a night class at Tulane.' Victor had left Maudie about an hour ago. His eyes were soft; his head was full of plans.

Lucien Taylor looked at his friend with some amusement and envy. He was pretty sure he knew how Victor had spent his time since noon; all Victor's friends knew how he felt about his wife. Lucien had been sketching in the Alley until the rain had driven him to shelter in the Cabildo porch. He felt lazy, and found it hard to get started again. 'Aren't you already a writer?' he said sarcastically to Victor. 'You write, don't you?'

'Certainly, I'm a writer,' said Victor, 'but I want to write something besides anonymous sections of a City Guide Book. You sign your pictures, don't you? Well, I want to sign my stories. I got an idea for a story. I got ideas for all kinds of stories. Look, Lucien!'

'Look at what?'

'Why, people,' said Victor naïvely. 'Look at all the people. They're interesting. I never really noticed them before.'

A newsboy passed, calling the late edition of the *Item*. Lucien bought a paper. 'Record Rainfall,' he read aloud. 'Even the headlines got washed . . . well, what about people?' he said, answering Victor's ejaculation.

'Whadda you mean, "what about them?" You always tell me I ought to look at people instead of buildings, and now I look at them, and you ask me why!'

'Don't get so worked up,' said Lucien. 'It's too hot.'

But Victor was too excited to remain quiet. He told Lucien of the accident he had seen in the rain. He remembered everything about that walk home in the rain: the black hand wielding the pressing iron; the black lovers under their slanting roof; the white bone on the sidewalk; the faces of Dan and Iris Clark, of

Mrs. Gomez and Mrs. Tarantino; the wheels of Frankie Gomez' roller-skate slowly spinning and stopping. Words tumbled from his mouth. There was a story in it somewhere, he told Lucien. He already had a title for the story: *A Sparrow Falls*. He thought it a very good title, and told Lucien as much.

'You won't write it,' said Lucien.

'Yes, I will.'

'On WPA time?'

'I'll find time.'

'An honest artist has about as much future in this country as a bus-driver in the Himalayas,' Lucien said. 'We ought to organize,' he added gloomily, 'or something.'

'How, organize?' said Victor, regarding his friend with soft, alarmed eyes.

'Oh, I don't know. Take those fellas on ships. I met one yesterday, and he was tellin me about the seaman's union. Before they got organized they had low wages, lousy bunks, bum food. The union changed all that. Sounds like it might be a good thing.'

'Union?' said Victor, frowning. 'Aren't they full of revolutionaries trying to overthrow the Government?'

'I don't believe it,' said Lucien. 'This fella I was talking to yesterday seemed all right. Joe Onion, his name was.'

'WPA gave me my start,' said Victor. 'WPA's all right with me.'

'Sure, WPA's all right. But how long will it last? Besides, I don't want to stay on WPA all my life, even if it does last.'

'I couldn't even of married Maudie if it hadn't of been for WPA.'

'Yeah,' said Lucien, 'that's right. . . . Gimme a praline, Clara.' He tossed a nickel on her lap.

'Dem guls burnt de sugar dis mawnin,' said Clara. 'Ain tellin de tourisses, but ah'll tell y'all. Dem guls burnt de sugar dis mawnin. Dey ain no good today.'

'Gimme one anyhow.'

'I'll take one, too,' said Victor.

Clara handed over two of the sugar candies crusted with pecans. 'Y'all owes me a nickel apiece mo,' she said. 'Y'all knows dese pla-rines wuth a dime. Mah eyes ain too bad ah cain tell de lil uns fum de big uns. Scratch yo pockets, white boys. Y'all ain dat po.'

They laughed, and produced another pair of nickels. 'What's the matter with you Mammies,' said Lucien, nibbling his praline, 'is you ought to organize. Hot dog, Victor, I got an idea there! What you say, Clara? Organize all the Mammies in the Quarter, and you be President, or Secretary, or Kingfish, or whatever officer they have. Then you strike for higher wages and a feather cushion to sit on, and Kentucky Burley tobacco and briar pipes, and no more burned sugar. Don't you get tired sittin on that stool all day long, Clara? Wouldn't you like a nice, soft feather cushion to sit on? Well, strike, darn it! Strike! Make it a closed guild, or whatever they call it. Nobody can be a Mammy till she serves six months' apprenticeship, or something like that. . . . "What you doin tonight, honeychile?" he drawled. "Oh, I'se studyin hard to become a Mammy!" . . . Hot dog!' Lucien slapped his knee.

Clara Bilbo dismissed him with a contemptuous look. Give white folks an inch, and they took a mile. A yellow tourist bus had just pulled up in front of the Cathedral and the tourists were piling out. Most of them were women in open-toed, high-heeled shoes; with elaborate, fragile hats on carefully curled hair. Most of them limped into the Cathedral, but two of them fluttered toward Clara. Clara smiled. It was her business. The women looked at her curiously.

'A real, old-fashioned Mammy,' said one, nudging her companion with her elbow. 'They say all the Negroes speak French in Louisiana. D'you suppose she can understand English?'

'Let's ask her something, and find out.'

The first woman addressed herself to Clara. 'Auntie,' she said, 'we were just wondering. D'you remember the slave days?'

'Yossum,' said Clara. As a matter of fact, she didn't, but she knew what she was supposed to say.

'How exciting! Weren't you thrilled at the Emancipation Proclamation?'

'Which?' said Clara, puffing on her pipe.

'When President Lincoln set your people free, weren't you thrilled and excited? It must have been a great day in your life.'

'Ah disremembah,' said Clara.

'Imagine that,' said the woman to her friend. 'She can't remember the day she got her freedom. . . . Well, auntie, how old are you? Do you remember that?'

'Ah'm ole, ole,' said Clara.

'How quaint! She says she's "ole, ole." I guess she means old. Let's buy a praline from her.'

The women bought pralines, exclaimed over the Mammy dolls, and walked into the Cathedral. Clara took her pipe out of her mouth, grinned sardonically to herself, and spat on the sidewalk.

IN THE MEANTIME, the driver of the tourist bus had walked up to Lucien and Victor. He was an elderly man with a long nose. He wore a yellow cap with a black visor. 'Hi, kids,' he said.

'Hiyah, Pop,' said Lucien. 'Why ain't I a bus-driver, carryin pretty girls around all day like you, huh, Pop? How's the tourist business?'

'You seen 'em,' said Pop, jerking his chin over his shoulder in the direction of the Cathedral. His shoulders drooped. He mopped his sweaty face with a large blue handkerchief.

'What's wrong with 'em?' said Lucien, grinning.

'I ain't seen a purty one yet,' Pop sighed. 'Dawggone. I cain't figure it out, boys, but I ain't seen a purty one yet. Seem like the purty ones all stay home. Seem like all I get is the crazy ones that I cain't hardly drag 'em outa the Old Absinthe House but they gotta hang onto the bartender an screech. But Tour Z calls for the Old Absinthe House, so I gotta take 'em there. Two hours we been there today. Caught in the rain. Ever' last one of them girls oughta be in bed sleepin it off. Dawggone. Maybe travel makes 'em act the way they do, or maybe it's because they act that way at home, they got to travel. I cain't figure it out.'

'That girl over there is beautiful,' said Victor dreamily. 'I wonder what's she crying about?'

Pop and Lucien looked at a blond girl in a blue raincoat who had evidently just come out of the Cathedral, and was now standing on the sidewalk. She was crying. The mascara from her eyelashes had run down her cheeks. In spite of the loose raincoat she wore, they could see that she was pregnant. She was so big, she looked as if she might have the baby any minute.

'She's no tourist,' said Lucien. 'I've been seeing that girl around the Quarter for a month, off and on. What's the matter with her?'

'Tourist or not,' said Pop, 'she's on my bus, an what's the matter with her is plain to see. I was worried she'd have it in the Old Absinthe House. She oughta be in bed.'

'What's she cryin about?'

'Absinthe, I reckon,' said Pop.

'No, something's wrong.'

'Could be,' said Pop. 'Come to think of it, she didn't drink with the other girls. She kep kinda off to herself, and just keppa chewin her fingernails an readin a letter. But shucks, with all of 'em behavin so crazy, I didn't take much notice. . . . There she goes, readin that letter again. Wonder what's in it.'

But the girl had no time to read the letter. Just as she took it from her purse, a band of small, ragged colored boys darted out of Pirate's Alley and surrounded her. The girl looked at them, terrified, and stuffed the letter back in her purse. Disjointing themselves into comical and outlandish postures, the boys began to tap-dance. 'Looka me, Miss, hey, hey! . . . Looka me . . . looka me, hey, hey! Gimme a dime, lady, ain dis un wuth a dime? . . . Watch dis un, lady! . . . hey, hey! . . . Gimme a dime, lady, gimme a dime!' The bottletops they had stuck on their bare toes made a tremendous racket on the sidewalk. The girl in the blue raincoat shrank away from them. She started to run for the bus; stopped; put her hand to her eyes; and then, on long legs rather wide apart to balance the heavy load she carried, walked as swiftly as she was able up Chartres Street.

'Hey, Miss!' Pop called. 'We ain't finished with Tour Z. Better stick with the crowd.'

The girl's tear-streaked face looked back once, blindly. She walked faster. Pop took off his cap and scratched his head. 'Maybe I oughta go ketch her,' he said, 'but heck, boys, I reckon she knows what she's doin.'

When the girl disappeared from sight, Victor Peralta felt for an instant as if the sun had gone down. What he had seen was not the distracted girl big with child under the raincoat, but Maudie, in the same condition. Although he had left Maudie not much more than an hour ago, he wanted to see her again, to see if anything had happened to her. But of course, he thought, even if it had happened, it wouldn't show for a long time. Since morning, life had grown so exciting for Victor that he had to do something about it. He felt in his pocket for a pencil. He was going to begin that story right away. He knew of a quiet place where no WPA inspector would ever locate him. Maybe he could work a pregnant girl into his story, somewhere. He, too, disappeared.

'Well, yeah,' Pop admitted to Lucien, 'that gal in the blue raincoat was the pick of the load for looks, if she hadn't of been in the way she was. Hope nothin happens to her. First one in her condition I ever knew to ride around on a tourist bus. You say she ain't a tourist?'

'I'd swear she wasn't,' said Lucien. 'I've been seeing her around the Quarter for at least a month.'

'No tellin,' said Pop. 'Women all get kinda crazy that far along with a baby. Back in Mis'ippi, my ole lady done the quarest things. One time, she clumb a thirty-foot ladder with a hammer an shingles an nails to patch a leak in the roof. Can you beat it? Another time, she shuck the feathers outa all the pillows to put new covers on 'em. Didn't aim to let loose all them feathers, but when I come home the house was floatin with feathers, an my ole lady circlin around in 'em like a ole biddy tromplin a nest. . . . No tellin what they'll do. Pore girls, it's a hard life. Yeah, boys, it's a hard life. I don't begrudge nobody no absinthe frappé. But dawggone.'

The tourists were leaving the Cathedral. Pop climbed wearily back in his bus. Lucien Taylor picked up his sketch block and crossed the street to Jackson Square.

CLARA BILBO sat quietly smoking her pipe. From Victor's story to Lucien, she knew that Dan and Iris Clark were in trouble. 'Gawd,' she thought. 'Hit seem lak nuthin but trouble in dis worl fo cullud folks.' That crying white girl in the blue raincoat didn't know what trouble was. If she was in trouble, it was her own fault. She felt sorry for the girl; but she had enough to do trying to keep track of her own.

At this minute, a small coffee-colored boy in a dirty shirt darted past Clara out of Pirate's Alley. He was one of her own— her grandson, Ronnie, whose father had been white. Clara snatched her pipe from her mouth. 'You, Ronnie!' she called sharply. 'Wheah you headin?'

The boy hesitated, and threw a quick glance over his shoulder. 'C'mere, you!' said Clara. 'Shame on sech a daity face! You wosh dat face!' But he didn't come to her; he ran. 'Stick dat shait-tail enside dem britches!' she called after him. 'An pull up dem britches, or you gon lose em!' Ronnie clawed at his belt with one brown hand. 'Gawdamighty!' said Clara, as he dodged perilously through the traffic on Chartres Street and vanished, still running, into Jackson Square.

Muttering to herself, Clara picked up her pipe and laid it down. She took a cigarette from her apron pocket, lit it, and swallowed the smoke. A pipe was no good in moments of stress. But she had no time for more than a couple of pulls on the cigarette, when she recognized through the open gates of the Square, through the foliage, an old woman in a black dress. 'Oh, good Gawdamighty, ef ah ain had too much dis day. Did ole Mis' Peralta belong en mah family, ah swedda Gawd, ah'd limit her wid a rope tied on her laigs. A mewlin kitten got mo sense which way is home. Somebody don ketch her, she gon crawl roun tell big-dark an de po-leece come.'

Clara half rose from her camp stool. It seemed to her that everybody but herself was a child, and needed a nurse. But another group of tourists, these on foot, came out of the alley at this instant, and stopped to buy pralines and Mammy dolls. Clara had to attend to business.

BUT MRS. PERALTA, sitting on a park bench in Jackson Square, smiling from her neatly tied shoelaces to the sparrows bathing in puddles on the concrete walk, was no longer lost. The doll she had found lay on the bench beside her; the jackstone was safe in her hand. She had come by devious ways to Jackson Square, but one look at the Cathedral and she knew where she was. She crossed herself, gave preliminary thanks to all the saints responsible for guiding her, and was enjoying the sun and resting her feet for a minute before she went into the Cathedral to give more appropriate thanks, when she caught sight of Ronnie Bilbo, the boy whom she had seen moving Mrs. Cansino's watermelons that morning.

He stood a few feet away from her, talking with a young colored girl in a nursemaid's white uniform. The girl's mouth drooped; her eyes looked as if she had been crying. One of her slender black hands gripped the low fence that enclosed General Jackson on his prancing horse; and the other shoved a perambulator back and forth on the puddled sidewalk.

'Ahmo tell yo grammaw on you,' she said. 'Come bothin me when you knows ah feels too mizzable bout Cooter en jail, thout you an yo crazy haid-dreams. How you gon gittim out, huhn? You crazy!'

'Cooter nevah rob no grocery sto.'

'Ah'm well aware Cooter nevah rob no grocery sto. Huccum he had dat knife is ah gin it to im fo his birfday. Dey beatin im up fo somepun he nevah done. But how *you* gon gittim out, you crazy lil chinchy-bug?'

'Neb' mine,' said Ronnie. 'All ah'm askin, is you got any change?'

'Why you come beggarin otha folks change? You makes plenny money.'

'Gimme it, please, Laurie. Ahmo git Cooter out.'

'Accounta you bein Cooter's brotha, ah loans you fi'teen sents tell t'morra. T'morra, ah gits it back. An you stay outa deb'ment or ahmo tell yo grammaw. Dey ketch you, an beat up on you lak dey done Cooter.'

'Nobody gon ketch me,' said Ronnie.

'You de crazies boy ah *evah* see. Whut goin on en yo haid ain rait. Whuffo you want at fi'teen cents?'

'Neb' mine,' Ronnie begged. 'Gimme it, please, Laurie.'

'Ah'm tellin you, you gon git in trouble wid dem crazy haid-dreams you alltime cookin up,' said the girl. But she took three nickels from the roll of her stocking, and dropped them in his outstretched hand.

'Ain scairta nobody,' said Ronnie. Superman was in his mind. In a flame-colored cloak he would zoom out of the sky, twist the jail bars to liberate his brother, and zoom up again into the sky. Cooter would be grateful, and the world would marvel. He, Ronnie, would be revenged on the bartender who had chased him out of Gino's Bar. He would be revenged on everybody. But it would be a good thing to have a knife, just in case. This was why he wanted the money from his brother's girl friend. He pocketed the fifteen cents, tightened his belt, and darted away.

'You gits en anymo deb'ment, ahmo tell yo grammaw!' the girl called after him.

MRS. PERALTA stood up and looked after the boy with piteous eyes. He was running away from her again. 'Victor!' she called. She hurried after him. The forgotten doll called to her from the bench where it lay. Mrs. Peralta returned, snatched up the doll, and followed Ronnie, whom she had again mistaken for her son, through the side gate of the Square.

LUCIEN TAYLOR snapped his charcoal stick between his fingers. 'Damn!' he said. He had been sketching Mrs. Peralta. Swiftly, surely, the old woman in the black dress, with the battered doll sprawled beside her, had been transferring herself to his sketch pad when, suddenly, she moved. He looked up, and she was gone. The doll still lay on the bench.

There was the old woman again; she had returned for the doll.

Now, both were gone.

Lucien picked up his charcoal from the sidewalk and slumped on a bench. Frowning, he studied the sketch from all angles. He became excited again. He had caught her, after all. He would work on her tonight. She looked like she might turn out to be the best thing he had ever done.

MRS. PERALTA walked after the boy as fast as she was able. He crossed St. Ann Street, ran along the sidewalk in front of the lower Pontalba Building, and turned the corner onto De-catur Street. Ages later, or so it seemed to Mrs. Peralta, she, too, turned the corner. There he was, dodging along ahead of her. 'Victor!' she called; but he did not hear her. She lost him in the crowd, and found him. He had stopped before the window of a hardware store. He was pressing his nose against the glass. He went inside. Mrs. Peralta panted after him. He came out of the store before she could reach it, and again hurried ahead of her. Mrs. Peralta looked in the hardware window as she passed. The boy had been looking at knives; she knew it. What did he want with another knife? His father had already given him a fine, sharp knife. 'Victor!' she scolded. But he had turned an-other corner. He was always disappearing, the naughty boy. Why must he always disappear? Why must she always be run-ning after him? Mrs. Peralta wondered. Always this fear that some harm might befall him; this hurry to prevent it. How good it would be to rest! Now she was lost again, but she did not know it. Victor was somewhere ahead; and as long as her legs could move, she would keep him in sight.

He stopped before the window of another store, and she gained on him. Again, before she could reach him, he ran away. Knives again! What could the boy want with a knife when he already had one? What mischief could he be planning? Now, he was going in another door. Mrs. Peralta hurried. A block . . . half a block . . . the distance narrowed between them. The boy did not appear. Panting and hobbling, Mrs. Peralta drew even with the doorway which had swallowed him.

She looked up at a stalk of bananas that swung from a hook under the awning. Why, this was the Cansino Fruit and Vegetable Stand! Across the street was her house. 'Victor?' she said to the little boy, who had come out of the door and stooped at her feet to pick up a watermelon. 'Victor?' But he did not look at her. He gave no sign of recognition as he moved a watermelon out of the sun and picked up another and moved it alongside the first, working with feverish haste.

'Where you been? Where you been all dis time? I like to know where you been?' came Mrs. Cansino's scolding voice from inside the shop.

RONNIE ground his teeth together and heaved at a watermelon. Mrs. Cansino would promise to pay him no more than a dime for moving the watermelons again. Counting the two-bits the man had given him to buy a toothbrush, he had made thirty-five cents selling second-hand comic books. Cooter's girl had given him fifteen cents. That made sixty cents. The cheapest knife he had priced in the hardware store cost a dollar and two-bits. Ronnie was good at figures. As he worked, he added and subtracted in his mind. Sixty cents from a dollar and two-bits left sixty-five cents he had to earn between now and tonight. He didn't know how he could earn so much money in such a short time. Maybe he'd have to steal a knife somewhere. Of course, cheaper knives could be bought at Kress's or Woolworth's, but Superman wouldn't want to carry such trash. If he couldn't buy a good knife, Ronnie thought, he would steal it; but first, he would try to be honest and buy it. His grandmother had thrashed him and Cooter too thoroughly for previous small indiscretions for either of them to have forgotten that a minimum of honesty makes for a less painful life. He hadn't stolen the Coca-Cola bottles from Gino's Barroom. Another boy had done that. Sometimes, he did take bananas; but taking bananas wasn't stealing.

Ronnie tugged and strained at the watermelons. The late afternoon heat was intense. Sweat rolled down Ronnie's face and chest. The watermelons were cool and slippery in his arms; their weight dragged at his back. But Superman stood at his elbow—closer than his elbow. Superman was himself. The weight of the melons was nothing to Superman.

'Pull up yo pants, boy,' came Mrs. Cansino's rollicking voice from inside the shop. 'Pull 'em up quick or you gonna lose 'em, an den where you be?'

Ronnie gritted his teeth. He could kill Mrs. Cansino with one flick of his finger. Little did she know!

ON HER OWN DOORSTEP, Mrs. Peralta spread her legs inside her skirt and let her feet drop over on their sides. It was good to be home. The sun felt good. She scarcely remembered her long walk in the rain. Then and now were the same time. Now was this morning, and the rich, warm colors of fruits and vegetables under the Cansino awning rippled and curled before Mrs. Peralta's old eyes like water, like the river passing—and the boy across the street was not her son.

But a car spattered with red clay was coming slowly along the street; and a man and a girl, shading their eyes from the sun, were leaning out to look at house numbers. The car passed Mrs. Peralta; stopped; and backed up.

'Can you tell us which is the Webster house?' the man said. 'We lost the number. Somebody told us this was it.'

Mrs. Peralta smiled, and put her hand to her ear. The man had a dark mustache, which reminded her of her husband. The girl was pretty and blond, with a baby in her arms. Mrs. Peralta smiled broadly. 'Webster?' she said.

'Merlin Webster!' the man shouted.

Mrs. Peralta directed them to the white house with green shutters, and watched while the man parked his car and rang the doorbell. He waited a minute, then rang again. Nobody opened the door. He tried the knob. 'It's open,' he called to the girl. 'They've probably just stepped out for a minute. Let's go in.'

'Wait for me!' The girl climbed out of the car with the baby and joined the man. On tiptoe, like burglars, they entered the house.

MRS. PERALTA went in her own door. She hid the jackstone with other things she had saved; and wrapped the doll in the flannel petticoat she had known she would find a use for if she waited long enough. Her lottery tickets were still safe under her pillow; but, in her absence, her dresses had fallen from the nail. She picked up the dresses, smoothed them, and replaced them on the same nail—all except one, into which she changed from the damp dress she was wearing. From Leah's room came a sound of scrambling and squeaking. Mrs. Peralta opened the connecting door in time to see a gray cat leap into the alley with a mouse in his teeth. 'Tchk, tchk, tchk,' she said, and closed the door.

Back in her own room she eased her feet out of her shoes and lay down on the bed. She had not really lost herself, she thought happily. She had not been a nuisance after all. In a few minutes, her gentle, apologetic snore echoed through the house.

WAKED by the death of the mouse, Maudie Peralta thought again of the mail box and of the dress she had bought on Leah's charge account. She looked in the box. Sure enough, the bill addressed to Leah had arrived in the afternoon mail. She tore it into bits and dropped it in the garbage can.

Beyond the shadow of the house, sun still dappled the courtyard. Maudie put a sofa cushion on the wet seat of the deck chair and stretched her legs luxuriously. Victor was a dope, she thought—but sweet. Spanish men made wonderful lovers. What lovely smooth skin he had, and what nice curly hair. She thought it would be fun to go swimming in the lake tonight. Somebody ought to sew up that hole in her bathing suit; but it was such a small hole; it wouldn't show.

WHEN WILLIS went to ring the Webster doorbell, Katherine Tuttle, still sitting in the car, looked curiously at the unfamiliar shapes of the houses. The street was like nothing she had seen before; and, for an instant, everything was so still she felt as if she were looking at a painted picture of a street. Through the clean, hot, rain-washed air, the weather-beaten colors of the houses glowed softly pink and yellow, and gray and blue-green. The old woman in the black dress, from whom Willis had asked directions, sat on her doorstep as if she had sat there forever. On an upstairs balcony across the street, a clothesline sagged with a weight of colored wash. A blond cat, which looked as if it might have Persian blood, stood frozen on the sidewalk with one paw lifted, ears pricked forward. For an instant, the street lay in absolute quiet under the sky.

To Katherine Tuttle, whose mind was still moving and humming with the motion and sound of the car on the long drive, the impact of this cessation of movement, this sudden intense quiet, threw her off at an angle, as if she had actually run into a wall and rebounded obliquely into a realm of consciousness at once strange to her and hauntingly familiar. She felt as if she had been here before.

Willis pressed the doorbell. A cool chime echoed in the depths of the Webster house. The cat bounded across the sidewalk and slunk under the shadow of a truck parked at the curb. Willis turned. 'They've probably stepped out for a minute,' he said. 'Let's go in.'

'Wait for me!'

On tiptoe, like two burglars, they entered the house. It was larger than it had appeared from the street, Kathy saw. The rooms were deep and cool. Behind the house, through a vista of open French doors, was a garden burning with color in the late afternoon sunlight. They passed through the house into the garden. The mellow bricks of the small two-story house at the side of the garden were covered with flowering vines.

'This must be where we live,' said Willis. 'Pretty little place. They left the key in the lock.'

'How still it is!' Kathy looked at a toy windmill on a low branch of the oleander tree. On one of the quiet blades, a large black moth was lifting and lowering its wings. As she watched, it floated out and up into the sunlight. Following its course with her eyes, she saw a dark, Italian woman hanging clothes on a shed roof that overlooked the courtyard. When the woman saw that she had been observed, she became very busy with clothespins; but she peeped from under her wide straw hat, and looked as if she would like to speak.

'Hello,' Kathy said.

'Hello,' answered Mrs. Tarantino.

'We're just moving in. D'you know where the Websters are?'

Mrs. Tarantino shook her head.

'There you go again,' said Willis, under his breath. 'Gossiping again.' He turned the key in the lock, and went inside their house.

Mrs. Tarantino passed under the clothesline and came close to the edge of the roof to look at Kathy from closer range. 'Such a pretty baby you got,' she said. 'Is something wrong with him, he's sleepin so sound? He ain't sick?'

'Oh, no. He's very healthy. He likes to sleep.'

'Babies, no trouble at all,' said Mrs. Tarantino. 'I had five. But you see, you gonna have plenty more, and you love 'em all. So young, and your man such a big, fine man, you see you gonna have plenty more babies.'

In spite of her weariness, Kathy felt a warm glow of importance.

'Darlin,' said Mrs. Tarantino, 'could I have soma dem white flowers for duh Blessed Mudda? She loves white flowers, an mine is pink.'

'These?' Kathy touched a weighted cluster of white oleander flowers that touched her sleeve. 'I don't know if I should.'

'Oh, sure. Mrs. Webster won't mind. She gives me plenty, plenty white flowers for duh Blessed Mudda.'

'I'll need a pair of scissors or a knife,' said Kathy. 'Wait a minute.'

'So much trouble.' Mrs. Tarantino folded her hands on her stomach and waited on the shed roof while Kathy went in the house, laid the baby on a studio couch, and came out with a paring knife she had found in the kitchen. When a bouquet had been cut, Kathy stood on tiptoe, and Mrs. Tarantino kneeled on the shed roof and reached down; but, even so, the two hands could not meet.

Mrs. Tarantino hurried away for a piece of string, and returned with a length of thick cord she used for the clothesline. Kathy knotted one end around the stems of the flowers and threw the other end to Mrs. Tarantino. The bouquet rose in the air.

'Duh Blessed Mudda be so glad,' said Mrs. Tarantino, accepting the flowers graciously.

Hot and tired, the Tuttles unloaded their car and went upstairs. Over a chest of drawers in the dressing-room, Kathy found
a picture of two boxers hanging slantwise on the wall. She began to giggle. 'Come and look,' she called. 'They've put a couple
of prize-fighters in here, and they've knocked each other
crooked.'

'Shove 'em back in the ring,' answered Willis from the bedroom. 'I think I'll take a nap.'

Kathy took the picture off the wall and hid it in a drawer.
Willis stretched himself on the fourposter bed, and sighed comfortably. Hastily, he sat upright. 'Where's Roger?' he said.

He was asleep on the studio couch. Kathy brought him upstairs, still asleep, and laid him beside Willis on the bed. 'If we
had named him Thomas Hardy's Collected Poems Tuttle, I'll bet
you wouldn't misplace him,' Willis said.

They heard a newsboy shouting on the street, and wrangled
amiably about who should go out and buy a paper. Finally,
Willis went for it. Lying on the bed, while Kathy burrowed in
one of the tumbled bags, he read the headline aloud. 'Record
Rainfall.'

'I'm glad to hear it broke a record. I'd hate to think it happened every day.'

'Two more indicted in university scandal,' Willis read, then
lapsed into silence broken only by the rustle of the newspaper
as he turned to the second page.

'Go on. What else?'

Willis dropped his eyes to the bottom of the page and picked
a brief notice at random. 'Edward Cooter Bilbo, seventeen-year-
old Negro youth apprehended by Officers Lichte and Arnold on
Burgandy Street Sunday afternoon, has confessed to a series of
petty thefts in grocery stores along Dauphine Street . . .'

'Look, darling,' said Kathy, who hadn't heard a word of what
he had been reading. 'We ought to do some telephoning. We
ought to call the Budds, and let them know we're here. And we

ought to call Mr. Webster at his office, and tell him we're here so he won't shoot us for burglars when he comes home.' She picked up her husband's limp, sunburned wrist, and looked at his watch. The newspaper had drifted to the bed. Willis was scowling at the ceiling. 'It's after four o'clock,' she said drowsily. 'Too late to cash a check, and we have exactly seventy-eight cents left. Please call the Budds, at least, and get a check cashed.' She tugged at his arm, but was unable to move him. Tired from the long drive, he had fallen asleep. She lay down beside him.

MRS. TARANTINO, descending from her shed roof to the courtyard, thought, 'What a day, what a day!' Not only had she been the first witness of the Gomez accident; she had also seen the Tuttles actually walking into the Webster courtyard. She had seen them before the Websters had seen them—a little triumph all her own. She had seen them even before Rocco.

As she paused at the bottom of the steps, Rocco came up to her and tried to sit on her feet. She pushed him away. 'Get along, ole dog,' she said. 'Go take you anudda nap. Your eyes is getting bad.' Smiling, she arranged her bouquet into a more compact mass. At last she had the white flowers for the Blessed Mother from Mrs. Webster's courtyard, another triumph none the less real for Mrs. Webster's ignorance of the donation. The Blessed Mother would know to what trouble she had gone, and would appreciate.

What a day it had been, indeed! Nearly every woman on the block had been in her house this day; and all of them had commiserated with her about the black eye Bruno had given her in the morning; all had commended her patience and forbearance with Bruno; all had praised her quick thinking in an emergency —for none of them, they admitted, would have thought to call both the priest and the ambulance when Frankie fell. They had praised her kindness in caring for Leander Gomez until his mother returned; and had agreed with her that if Miss Leah Webster had not given Georgie Webster the roller-skates in the first place, the accident would never have occurred.

'Che sara, sara,' they said. 'What must be, must be.'

They had eaten her cookies, drunk her coffee, and admired her lace curtains. They had not seemed to notice her facial blemish, the harelip. They had left her company only because it was time to begin preparing supper before their men came home.

Best of all the things that had happened today, Bruno had lost his authority. It had disappeared, so far as Mrs. Tarantino was concerned, with his isolation. For whatever reason—and Mrs. Tarantino did not now bother to examine reasons—Bruno had ceased to mind his own business. He had shown definite sympathy for Frankie and Mrs. Gomez; he had revealed a deep concern about Clark's troubles. In other words, he had shown himself to be quite human after all. Ever since the irreverent episode of the nuns on roller-skates in the hospital, Bruno had not seemed quite human to his wife; perhaps a little more than human, perhaps less; but certainly in league with the diabolic one. Now, instead of being pleased by the change in him, she felt that Bruno had been fooling her all along; and that she had found him out at last.

Ordinarily, she would have hesitated before going into Bruno's workshop when he was busy. The workshop was Bruno's private domain, invaded by scarcely anybody except Dan Clark and the iceman. But now she stood in the doorway, with the flowers held triumphantly in her hand, and scuffed the shavings with the toe of her shoe. 'Such a mess you make,' she scolded.

Bruno looked at the white flowers. His paint brush stopped in midair. 'Did the kid die?'

'I got 'em for duh Blessed Mudda,' replied Mrs. Tarantino with satisfaction.

Bruno looked at her from under lowered eyebrows, shrugged his shoulders, and went on painting.

'The Tuttles is here,' said Mrs. Tarantino. 'Mrs. Tuttle gimme duh flowers. Mrs. Webster's flowers.'

Bruno dipped the brush into a can of green paint, drained it neatly, and slapped it on the skiff.

'Mrs. Tuttle is a pretty little skinny blond,' she said, eyeing her husband closely. 'One baby. But pretty. Oh, yes. Real pretty.'

With slow, smooth strokes, Bruno worked the paint into the wood. Mrs. Tarantino came into the workshop and sat on an upturned keg.

'Real friendly, too,' she said.

'You sittin on a buncha tar,' said Bruno.

Mrs. Tarantino stood up hastily and examined her skirt. Stooping, she caught sight of Leander Gomez, playing quietly with a knife and blocks of wood on Bruno's side of the skiff. 'Bruno Tarantino,' she said, 'you let a sick child that was screamin with the cramps not a hour ago play on the floor where he might cut hisself with God knows what with a sharp edge, and you just stand there?'

'He don't bother me,' said Bruno. 'Let him play.'

'Nobody said nothing about bothering you . . . I'm thinkin of the child . . . Leander,' she said, bending over the boy and placing her hand on his forehead, 'you got a fever. We gotta take care of mama's little boy. Come inside with Mrs. Tarantino. She'll give you something nice, an make you feel so good.'

'I dowanna,' said Leander. His mother had never let him and Frankie play anywhere but on the balcony. He was having a wonderful time in Mr. Tarantino's workshop playing with real tools, making a real boat. When Mrs. Tarantino attempted to lift him, he grabbed Bruno's leg. 'I dowanna!' he screamed.

Bruno scratched his chest, and kicked his foot. 'Take him and get out,' he said. 'A man can't think in this noise.'

'I dowanna! I dowanna!' wept Leander, clinging like a leech to Bruno's leg.

Mrs. Tarantino could not dislodge him. She picked up her flowers and turned in the doorway for a parting shot. 'You an your nuns an your roller-skates!' she said caustically. 'That ain't a reason to not go to Mass!'

'Say no more to me about roller-skates!' Bruno thundered. Shaking Leander loose from his leg, he advanced on Mrs. Tarantino with uplifted paint brush. 'Woman, say no more!'

'Mr. Tarantino, heah yo pliers,' said Dan Clark from the courtyard. But seeing the Tarantinos in attitudes of attack and defense, he excused himself and started to walk away. Bruno's hand dropped. His face worked. Mrs. Tarantino looked at him astounded, and fled to the house. Leander crawled back to his blocks and shavings.

'Have a bottla beer?' Bruno called after Clark.

Clark returned, hung the pliers on their accustomed nail, and leaned against the unpainted side of the skiff. Bruno opened the icebox, uncapped two beers, and offered one to his neighbor. They drank in silence, looking into the courtyard now peopled with growing shadows of the afternoon. Clark wiped his forehead on the tail of his shirt. 'Hot,' he said.

'Yeah,' said Bruno.

'Dis beer go good.'

Bruno agreed by turning the bottom of his bottle toward the ceiling. The beer slid from bottle to mouth in a long, smooth amber stream. Bruno's throat worked. He set the bottle down empty.

'Once trouble start, seem lak hit nevah stop,' Clark said.

'You mighty dam right,' said Bruno.

'Ah wuddna hurt dat kid fo no money. Ah feels as bad bout dat acci-dent as de Gomezes, ah reckon. But Mr. Tarantino, hit weren't mah fault.'

'How is the kid?' said Bruno. 'Have you heard?'

Clark looked down at Leander, and shook his head. Bruno crossed himself, and opened two more bottles of beer.

'Gomez claim he gon sue me,' said Clark.

Bruno made a sound with his tongue against his teeth.

'Claim he gon sue me fo evah cent ah got. Ain got much, Mr. Tarantino. Look lak ah'm gon lose hit. Ah wuks hard, Mr. Tarantino. You knows ah ain a man dat cause trouble. Ah treats evahbody fair an square, Mr. Tarantino, cause dat's good bidness. Ah turns in a good joba wuk, an soona give a man a lil mo dan he pay fo, dan not as much. Agin, dat's good bidness. Us is quiet folks, me an Iris, tryin to git along in dis worl de bes way we knows how, widdout causin hurt to nobody. Mindin our own bidness.'

'Yeah,' said Bruno, 'but the world is fulla crazy people, and nobody got a chance to mind his own business.'

Clark looked at Bruno for a minute. 'Nawsa,' he said. 'Dat's rait, Mr. Tarantino. Dat is sho rait. De way ah view hit, we all gotta live. People in dis worl oughta hep each udda, de way ah view hit.'

'Webster's the one oughta pay damages,' said Bruno. 'Did you sign a lease with Webster?'

' 'Fraid so. Hit down on papah dat ah'm de one responsible fo injuries s'tained by tenants.'

'Dio maledetto, he got you where it hurts.'

'Mr. Tarantino, hit occur to me mebbe you could change Gomez' min bout dat suin bidness? Mebbe talkin to im do some good, Mr. Tarantino? You got influence, an mebbe he lissen to you. He so wukked up, ah cain git in one word edgeways. Claimin dis, an claimin dat. Callin me names.'

Bruno looked soberly at his fingers; and looked up to see Leander's father, the Filipino, entering the courtyard gate. Gomez had changed his work clothes for his Sunday suit of green gabardine coat and white flannel pants. He had come for Leander. When he saw Clark, he scowled. Looking very unhappy, and also very nervous and self-conscious, he entered the workshop, spoke to Bruno, took Leander's hand, and walked stiffly away.

When he was nearly to the sidewalk, he turned. 'Black bastard!' he spat at Clark. 'Killin' my son! I'm gonna sue you for every cent you got.'

Bruno caught Clark's arm. Beneath his fingers, he felt the heavy muscle jump and quiver. Then Clark shook his head, and looked down at his clenched fists. 'Ah bust dat man, an wheah hit git me?'

'Maybe I'll talk to Gomez,' said Bruno. 'Maybe.'

5

---

5 p.m.–9 p.m.

IN A CHARTRES STREET BARROOM, Joe Onion and the
two boys from his ship, Whitey and Aleck, were growing bored
with each other's company. Whitey was hungry, and Aleck was
restless. Joe had been talking about Leah Webster, altering facts
to amaze his companions. His descriptions were so convincing,
he had already convinced himself.

'Come on, Joe,' Whitey coaxed. 'Let's go somewhere and
eat.'

'As I was saying,' said Joe, 'she's beautiful. Blue eyes. Dark,
curly hair. And what legs! Beautiful legs! Knows when to keep
her mouth shut, too. Most women talk too much, but this one
doesn't. No clinging vine, either. Most extraordinary face I ever
saw.'

'If I knew a girl like that, I wouldn't be sitting here,' said
Aleck. 'What's her name? Where does she live?'

'I'll settle for crab gumbo,' said Whitey. 'I know just the place
to get it. Come on, let's eat.'

'I've been looking for this girl all my life,' said Joe, 'but the
first time I saw her was Saturday night. I'm sitting in this joint
when this girl walks in by herself. Why such a beautiful girl is
by herself I'll never know, but there she is.'

'How come you wasting valuable time?' said Aleck. 'Is she still by herself? What's wrong with her?'

'Don't interrupt. I'm trying to think up a way to meet her, because, take it from me, she isn't the kind anybody can walk up to and say, "How's about a drink, baby?" No, sir. This girl is different. But, as I was saying, I'm trying to think up a way I can meet her when she walks right up to me and introduces herself.'

'If you was looking for her so long, how come she got away?' said Aleck. 'Come on, what's her name?'

'I want crab gumbo,' said Whitey. 'I know just the place.'

'I was floored for a minute,' said Joe. 'Imagine Hedy Lamarr walking up to you like that. But it was simple enough. The girl liked my looks.'

'Now I know you're lyin,' said Whitey. 'I'm hungry, you guys, I'm hungry.'

'Gee,' said Aleck, dropping his lower lip and lowering his lids over his eyes. 'Hedy Lamarr. Gee!'

'I'm hungry.'

'All right,' said Joe suddenly. 'Let's eat.' He dropped his legs from the table to the floor, and stood up. He swayed a little, and righted himself with dignity. He was holding his liquor remarkably well, and he felt wonderful. He had just decided to call up Leah Webster and find out if she remembered him. But he would first get something to eat.

'How did you boys ever come to ship out?' Joe inquired, as the three walked toward the restaurant where Whitey declared they would find crab gumbo. 'If you'd stay on shore, you'd both get plenty of what you want. Whitey, crab gumbo. Aleck, girls.'

'How come you to ship out?' Whitey countered.

Joe thought for a minute. 'Electric light trouble,' he said.

'Aw,' said Aleck, 'you're crazy.'

'No,' said Joe, 'it's a fact. I wasn't always this young. Once, I was an old man, and when I was old, I had a little farm in the

San Joaquin Valley. Wonderful soil. Grow anything. But I had electric light trouble. Had quite a dairy herd at that time, and was selling milk and butter on the side. Only one thing was wrong. The lights kept going out.'

'What you want with electric lights on a farm?' said Whitey.

'I'd be milking the cows and the lights would go out. I'd be reading and the lights would go out. Once, they stayed off for three days. I bought new bulbs and checked all the wiring. Nothing was wrong, but the lights kept going out. I began to think the place was haunted.'

'Aw, g'wan,' said Aleck. 'I don't believe it.'

'Don't interrupt. This is a true story. One time, as I was saying, those lights stayed off for three days. It was winter then, and got dark early, and I couldn't see to milk the cows. For three nights those cows weren't milked. We all suffered.'

'I know,' said Whitey. 'I bet the cows ate the insulation off the wires, and that's why they gave so much butter and eggs, and . . .'

'No,' said Joe, 'you're wrong. I happened to owe the electric light company eleven dollars and ninety cents. They wrote me the damndest letters about it. "Give us eleven dollars and ninety cents," they said, "or we'll attack you with a meat cleaver. We'll sever your jugular vein. We'll sprinkle your brains on the ceiling. We'll hack you, maim you, dismember and dishonor you for eleven dollars and ninety cents. Pay or else!"'

'What happened?' said Aleck in a puzzled voice.

'Why, I went to sea,' said Joe.

IN PIRATE'S ALLEY, the ragged tap-dancers were taking a breather from business to shoot a game of craps on the side steps of St. Louis Cathedral. The spot was an excellent one for the purpose to which the boys put it. The alley lay in shadow now, and a cool draft swung through it. Wandering groups of tourists passed. If any of the small, dark gamesters found himself out of funds, he could, merely by leaping to his feet and going into his dance, charm enough from well-lined travelers' pockets to get into the game again. Best of all, since the alley at this point had three exits, escape from pursuing plain-clothes men or policemen summoned by indignant citizens to break up this profanation of the steps of God's house was a comparatively easy matter. The alley gave on both Royal and Chartres Streets; and, besides, through another short alley, called by legend 'The Alley of the Wicked Priest,' it gave also on St. Peter Street. Sometimes, however, it did happen that some of the boys were caught. If no responsible person could be found to whom they could be paroled, they would be sent to the Milne Municipal Home for delinquent boys. Released, they returned to their interrupted careers.

Almost as soon as these boys learned to walk, they learned to dance. Their parents or relatives were usually too submerged in the business of living to look after them. Some of the boys had never seen the inside of a schoolroom—both because some of them were too young and because no colored truancy law in the city forced their attendance. Some of them organized 'Spasm' bands, made of tin cans and pots and kettles and old boxes, upon which they beat in syncopated rhythm with a stick; some of them sang; but all of them could dance. Some of the older boys were racketeers, who forced a rake-off on the earnings and winnings of the smaller boys with their fists or at the point of their knives. Tough, sly, humorous, nimble as stray cats, and pursued as no stray cat was ever pursued, they prowled the narrow French Quarter streets. They were hilarious and colorful and indigenous to the city of New Orleans, the birthplace of hot jazz. They were a tourist attraction.

Clara Bilbo thought she had one thing for which to be thankful. Her grandson, Ronnie, had never joined any of these roving bands of street Arabs to tap-dance for tourists. Unknown to Clara, however, he sometimes joined them for a game of craps.

Having moved Mrs. Cansino's watermelons for the third time, Ronnie had again computed his earnings, and found the total still sixty cents, with sixty-five to earn before night if he intended to buy a knife instead of steal it. And so, like many a better man before him, he had decided to run up his ante with the help of Lady Luck. Entering Pirate's Alley from the Royal Street entrance, he had joined the players on the Cathedral steps without his grandmother's knowledge.

For the past twenty minutes, Ronnie had been rolling the dice and raking in the money. The racketeer of this particular group, a boy perhaps fourteen years old, wore a Boy Scout shirt he had bought at a Salvation Army store. He had never had any luck with the dice himself; he kept a sharp eye on the growing pile of pennies and nickels and dimes in front of Ronnie. Ronnie was only half his size. It would be an easy haul.

As Joe Onion, with Whitey and Aleck, turned into Pirate's Alley on their way to dinner, the Boy Scout put his foot on Ronnie's winnings and drew his knife. Ronnie, unaware of the knife, aware only of the big foot that had come down in front of him, kicked at the foot and attempted to dislodge it. Small change scattered. The other players dived after it. Ronnie looked up and saw the knife.

'Ahmo cut out yo livahs an feed em to de cats,' the Boy Scout announced.

Ronnie paled, but continued to tear desperately at the foot planted on what was left of his money. 'Go haid,' he panted. 'Go haid an stick me, you big ugly ole worm-hawg, you! Jes try!'

'Here, here!' said Joe Onion. 'What goes on here?'

The Boy Scout assumed an innocent, casual look. Ronnie bit his leg. The Boy Scout kicked Ronnie off the steps. He scrambled to his feet, spun about, and threw himself on the scattered coins. The other players, seeing adult interference, had already blown away like brown leaves through the alley's three exits. Aleck collared the Boy Scout, and bent his arm until the knife clattered on the pavement.

'Grab him!' said Aleck.

'Grab who?' said Joe.

'Grab that little coon! That's the little coon they chased out of Gino's Bar for stealin Coca-Cola bottles!'

'So it is,' said Joe, recognizing in Ronnie the recent salesman of *Superman*. 'Well, son, did you buy that toothbrush?' He put his hand on Ronnie's shoulder. Four hours ago the gesture would have meant much to Ronnie; but much had happened to him in four hours. The hand on his shoulder was the hand of an enemy. He bit it.

Angered by the unexpected pain, Joe caught him and shook him hard. 'You little wildcat,' he said. 'You little . . .'

'Damn you!' Ronnie spat at him. 'Lemme go!'

'Ah ain done a thang, suh,' begged the Boy Scout. 'Please, suh, lemme go.'

'Sherrup!' said Aleck, twisting his arm behind his back.

'Come on, you guys, quit stalling,' said Whitey, in a bored voice. 'Let's go eat.'

Joe Onion, sobered by the pain in his hand, and Ronnie Bilbo, gray eyes blazing, small brown body squirming with rage and terror, looked at each other. 'Take it easy, kid,' Joe said. 'What t'hell you want to bite me for? I didn't go to scare you. Whatsa matter, kid? Take it easy, take it easy, take it—'

'Hold onto 'em!' somebody shouted. A fat man came running through the Alley of the Wicked Priest, elbowing the tourists aside. 'Hold onto 'em! Hold those boys!' He was a plain-clothes man summoned some ten minutes before by a girl in an antique shop, who had seen the crap game on the church steps and did not approve of it. The badge under the fat man's coat lapel identified him as one L. G. Tooley of the New Orleans Police Force.

For two years, off and on, Tooley had been chasing small tap-dancers and he hadn't caught one yet. In the past two years he had run so much that his friends wondered pointedly why it hadn't taken some of the fat off him. Under this constant needling, Tooley dreamed at night of small, elusive black boys, and took out his long frustration on his own children. Now, he saw victory at last. 'Hold onto 'em!' he puffed. 'Hold those boys!'

'Lemme go!' wailed the Boy Scout to Aleck. 'Lemme go, white man! Ah ain done you nuttin!'

'Sherrup!' said Aleck, twisting his arm still tighter behind his back.

Joe sized up the situation instantly. 'Beat it, Superman!' he said, giving Ronnie a shove.

Ronnie sprawled on the pavement. He was up in a flash, and running like a fleet, terror-stricken animal toward the Royal Street entrance of the alley. In the instant he had sprawled on the pavement, he had seen his grandmother coming toward him from the Cabildo on Chartres Street, the dick coming toward him down the Alley of the Wicked Priest, and black-robed young Father Poole and old Father Vela bearing down on him through the Cathedral.

'Grab him!' shouted Tooley.

'Ronnie! You, Ronnie!' called Clara Bilbo in a voice that cracked and broke.

'He got away,' said Joe Onion, nursing his bitten hand.

'Oh damn, oh damn!' panted L. G. Tooley, and would have said more had not so many tourists been present. Panting and sweating, he rolled after Ronnie as fast as he was able.

Ronnie looked behind him. His face was contorted and streaked with tears. 'Ah hate you!' he sobbed. 'Damn you, ah hate you!' Running, he scooped up a loose piece of brick and hurled it at his pursuer. Tooley, well trained in these tactics, dodged. The missile sailed over his head and struck Joe Onion on the shin-bone. Joe swore, and sat down suddenly.

'Aw, quit stalling, you guys,' said Whitey. 'I'm hungry. Let's eat.'

'Grab him!' yelled Tooley, to a man just entering the alley from Royal Street. 'Grab that little coon! Hold onto him!'

But the man took no notice. He was Bruno Tarantino, on his way to church for the first time in over ten years. Two nuns walked ahead of him with black skirts swinging, beads clicking. The nuns swayed out of Ronnie's path. When Tooley reached Royal Street, the boy was nowhere in sight. Tooley returned for his one prisoner, whom Aleck still held firmly, in spite of his squirming and pleading.

'Lemme go, white man, please, suh. Lemme go, lemme go.'

'Aha!' puffed Tooley, taking charge of the prisoner. 'Haven't I seen your face somewheres before? Ain't you been up before Judge Wittipher, an he sent you to School?'

'Nawsa. Ah swedda Gawd. Ah'm a Boy Scouts of America. Ah nevah been nowheah.'

'What was you doin in the alley with these?' Tooley kicked the dice, and the few pennies still lying on the Cathedral steps. He bent laboriously and picked them up.

'Ah wuz goin en de Church when dem boys stop me. Dey wuz crowdin de do, an wudden lemmc pass.'

'That is a falsehood,' said young Father Poole from the doorway. 'This boy is telling a falsehood. I saw him draw a knife on the smaller boy. He's no Boy Scout, I assure you. I know all the Boy Scouts in the French Quarter. I'm a scout master. This is a disgraceful incident, and one I sincerely hope the police will see fit to do something about.'

Tooley touched his hat. 'Where-at's the knife?' he said to the masquerading Boy Scout.

'Ah nevah had no knife.'

'Yes, he did,' sighed Father Vela. 'I'm sorry to say he had a knife, and it didn't look like a Scout knife. I saw him draw it. I was afraid the smaller boy would be hurt.'

'This is a slum!' said Father Poole indignantly. 'Somebody might have been hurt!'

'You said it,' said Tooley, touching his hat again. 'Come on, you!' He marched the whimpering colored boy away on the first lap of another trip to the Milne Home.

Clara Bilbo, watching from the outskirts of the crowd, turned back to her pralines.

'Where-at's the knife?' demanded Aleck.

'Superman got it,' said Joe. 'I guess he earned something, but I wish it hadn't been a knife.'

'Come on, you guys,' said Whitey. 'If you finished the Wild West Show, let's eat.'

Father Vela turned back into the Cathedral. He swept his eyes over the scattered worshipers as if to reassure himself of something, and paused, transfixed. He touched young Father Poole's black arm. 'Bruno Tarantino,' he whispered. 'Thanks be to God who accomplishes miracles. Bruno Tarantino has come to church.'

'The old sinner,' said young Father Poole. 'It's about time he came.'

FAR BACK IN THE SHADOWS, Bruno kneeled. His hands were joined; his head was bowed; his eyes were closed. But his mind was busy. He had not been able to stop thinking about Frankie Gomez. The suddenness of the boy's death had filled him with dark and urgent contemplations which oppressed him and hampered his work. Since the boy's father had come into his workshop, since Dan Clark had appealed to him for help, he had not been able to work at all, but had sat on his tool chest with his head in his hands. Because his thoughts of death were compounded of sadness and mystery, his mind had been drawn to the Church. Laughter and bright sunlight had never worked thoughts of religion in Bruno; but death, the realm of shadows, had drawn him irresistibly toward the cool gloom which marked the boundaries of his childhood's faith—as hushed and inscrutable as the whisper of nun's skirts, as confused and compelling as his own small-boy imaginings as to what their black sibilance had cloaked. Death and the Church. He could not think of one without thinking of the other. In his mind he had no more been able to think of one parted from the other than of one nun parted from the company of her sister. He had never seen a nun alone. Nuns always came and went in pairs. All afternoon, like two black nuns, the twin mysteries, Death and the Church, had swayed through his mind with black-cloaked bodies and downcast eyes. He could not have explained why he had come to the Church after so long a time: whether to immerse himself in the mystery and stop trying to think or merely to rid himself of the oppressive sense of the swiftness of life's passing—as swift and silent, as abruptly absent, as the hospital sisters had once seemed to coast by him on roller-skates and disappear into blue ether through the window. Bruno was confused. But he had come to Church; and he was kneeling.

It was necessary that he recover the feeling which had possessed him at his First Communion. It was necessary that the Crucified Christ should open His eyes and lift His drooping head; that the tragic body should descend from its cross and come toward him, as it had done that other time. He needed to see these things happen now, much more than he had needed to see them then. He was tired. His way had proved no better than the ways of other men. Things happened. Why? Who was to blame? The ways of men were cruel and dark. He desired to know God's way. He breathed the air of his childhood's faith: the dim smells of the Church, the smell of incense, of guttering candles; and the heavy air, rich with memories of christenings and weddings and funerals, and Holy Days of feast and negation, entering his nostrils, his lungs, his blood, wove him a solid pattern of memory so vivid he was conveyed for a time to the actual land of his childhood. . . . But the child grew into a boy and came to America.

Uncle Arturo had been a boat-builder, like himself, but in Mussolini's Italy. Uncle Arturo had believed in God, but he had died horribly in prison because he desired to continue building boats and ignored the *fascisti* men who came to visit him. He had been a good man, and his boats had been good, honest boats. Why had he died? Cousin Luigi had also believed in God, but he had died at Guernica by a bomb dropped from an Italian plane. He had died fighting to uphold a democratic government fairly elected by the Spanish people. The voice of the people was said to be the voice of God. Why had Luigi died? Mussolini, who had sent those bombing planes, did not believe in God. Why had the Holy Pope in Rome, the head of the Church, not stopped Mussolini, who warred against God? Why didn't the Holy Pope in Rome stop Hitler's Nazis? Why didn't he stop those concentration camps, the slaughter of young students in Prague? Many of these were Catholics. They were his children; and he was their Father, the Pope, responsible for their lives to God. Why did he not act on so simple a thing? It was very difficult to understand why the Pope didn't do something. He, Bruno Tarantino, was not an educated man accustomed to thinking profound thoughts; but he could see where simple duty lay.

In America, in New Orleans, it had been easy to live. His trouble had never been great trouble, to shake the roots of his life. Little troubles, little sorrows, he saw them now—things a man expected to encounter in a lifetime and expected to handle in his own way if he were not a fool. In America, everybody took what he could get. Everybody expected a man to take what he could get. A scrupulous man could not be a success in America; and in America it was necessary for a man to be a success.

Bruno did not regret the money he had made selling skiffs to the Conservation Department. They had been good skiffs; and the amount he had received for them had been no more than they were worth. Huey Long had promised that every man should be a king—why not? It sounded good. But look what Huey Long had done. He had given things to the people with one hand and taken them away with the other; and he had taken away more than he had given. Again, why had the Church, so powerful in Louisiana, not lifted its voice to see the people robbed? It may have done so, but Bruno had not heard about it. Because the Church did not mix in politics? Because its kingdom was of the spirit and not of this world? Bruno was not an educated man, but he knew better than this. He had eyes.

Must a man forget he had eyes? Must a man become like a child in order to believe in God? But he was not a child. He was fifty-six years old. He had seen and done a few things in his life; and in the past ten years he had thought some thoughts. He did not think that a man must be as a child to believe in God, for he, Bruno Tarantino, considered himself a man in every way, and he believed in God. But one must perhaps be a little child to believe in what the Church had become.

Two nuns in their black robes rose, bowed, and left the Cathedral. Bruno felt them leave. He should never have laughed at nuns on roller-skates, he thought. Nobody skated into Heaven without touching the ground. That idea, which had come to his mind in the hospital, had been a fever dream. He had not laughed at it for a long time. Even remembering, he had not laughed. One should not laugh, but weep. Women were created by God to be loved by men and to bear children. The Blessed Mother herself was a mother. What better example to put babies in a woman's arms? Maybe there was something he didn't understand about women wanting to be loved by men, but he did not think so. Of course, he had only a man's mind with which to divine God's will—but what more had any man possessed who ever lived on earth but a man's mind groping after God? Was he not a man like the others? Was he not equal with them? The Constitution of the United States declared he was. He, Bruno Tarantino, was no saint; but neither did he feel himself a sinner. He was a man who had his faults, as other men, but did not think too ill of anybody, not even of himself. Men did not have to be alike to be equal in God's sight. God was God, but men's minds were different; and knowing this difference, and making allowance for it, God came to each man in a different way—showing to one man maybe an eyebrow, and to another maybe a cheek; but to no man alone, all of His face at once. All men looking together might see the whole face of God. But never one man alone. Who claimed to have done so lied or was mistaken. No man was large enough to see God's face alone.

But all men looking together—who knew? Maybe it could be done. If men believed in God, anything was possible.

A man was a child and drew comfort from pretty fables. A man was a boy and drew comfort from hills and rocks and running water and the growing strength of his body. A man became a man and he still drew comfort from all these things and more —from wine and the bodies of women; from the bright eyes of his sons and daughters; from the talk of his friends; from the good feel of wood and sharp tools. But to be a man was to live in the end uncomforted by anything except by his own kind. Whom else was there to love or serve?

Bruno Tarantino opened his eyes and looked at the glittering crucifix on the altar. He felt that he understood it better than he ever had before. He would have lingered in the Cathedral, for it was quiet here; but he looked down and saw something on the back of the pew which his sun-blinded eyes had missed when he had first kneeled.

With bold white chalk, somebody had scrawled a swastika on the back of the pew.

Bruno left the Cathedral and walked through the noisy, narrow streets, through the slanting sunlight to his house. He went into his workshop and sat beside the half-painted skiff. He did not feel like working at the moment. He did not hear his wife's voice calling him to early supper; nor hear her footsteps approach and retreat.

Father Vela waited to hear Bruno's confession. But Bruno did not come.

AFTER MR. GRABER had visited the Cathedral, he felt tired. The day had been long and trying, and not too successful, he feared. There was so much work to be done. How could one man contrive to do it alone, without friends or encouragement? But great leaders before him had labored in anonymous poverty and died in exile and alone. They, too, had suffered contumely.

Mr. Graber paused on Royal Street to examine his umbrella. He had bent it over the back of a Negro child who had lewdly importuned him for pennies. The entire band of dancing colored boys had then followed him for two blocks, yelling insulting epithets. But he had dispersed them. When the time came, they would not survive.

Mr. Graber wanted to rest, but rest was out of the question for the present; he had to buy himself another red bow tie to replace the one which the rain had faded. A sidewalk mirror had disclosed this tragedy to him. He must have a new tie before the stores closed.

He made his way along Royal to Canal Street, walked several blocks, and entered Grant's Five and Ten Cent Store. When he had bought the new tie and put it on, he thought he might as well eat his supper at once. He was hungry.

He seated himself at the soda fountain beside a small boy in a stiff new pair of denim pants and a bright red cotton shirt. The boy had large ears that winged from either side of his sullen, frightened face. He was sucking a chocolate soda through two straws, holding the glass with both hands against his chest, as if he were afraid it might be taken from him. When Mr. Graber sat down, he brushed the boy's arm. The boy looked up and quivered away from him. Terrified, he forgot to suck his soda.

Mr. Graber was pleased at this recognition of his presence. 'Hello, little man,' he said.

The boy shrank against his mother, who was seated on the other side of him with a dish of ice cream melting untouched before her.

'What's the matter, Corey?' The woman turned her face in Mr. Graber's direction. He looked at her contemptuously. She was blind.

'That man,' Corey whispered.

'What man?'

Gripped in the boy's small fist was a lettered card which Mr. Graber recognized unmistakably as one of his own: *Down with the Jews! They are the cause of all your troubles.* The discovery unnerved him. It was a miracle, a sign sent from Heaven to reassure him that his work was not ignored. Once he had sped them on their way, Mr. Graber had never encountered any of his anonymous calling cards. Sometimes he had actually been afraid that nobody saw them. But here, in this little boy's hand, was proof that they were read. It was clearly a sign from Heaven that the boy had been sent to be his disciple, to sit at his knees and learn his difficult work—a strong young lad to help him.

Mr. Graber was so moved he could not speak. He stuttered. He pointed to the card in Corey's hand. He smiled. He stuttered. He quite forgot himself.

'Mama!' Corey threw his arms around the blind woman's neck. It was the first time he had ever turned to her for anything. She hugged him close and moved her blind face belligerently from side to side, seeking to discover what had frightened him.

Mr. Graber attempted to stroke the boy's head with a large, trembling hand. 'My little man,' he said, 'you must come with me. You really must.'

'Mama!' Corey screamed.

'Get away!' said the blind woman roughly.

'Madam, you don't understand. The boy belongs with me.'

'He's my boy. You can't have him. I won't let him go.'

'But madam, the boy must go with me. There's work for him to do.'

The blind woman tightened her hold on her son. Once before, people with authoritative voices had tried to take her son away from her. They had wanted to put him in a Home; but she had hidden him. Now they were after him again. She would rather send him to her friends in Mississippi than put him in a Home. 'No,' she said. 'You can't have him. I won't let him go.'

'I insist!' said Mr. Graber.

'Good Heavens above!' gasped a saleswoman across the aisle. She was a friend of the blind woman's—at least, she always waited on her, or found somebody else to wait on her when she came into the store. She had just fitted Corey with new clothes for his trip to Mississippi. Touched by the blind woman's desire to outfit her son as well as she was able, she had counted change from the ten-dollar bill very carefully into the blind woman's hand, and had expressed herself as being happy that a little would be left over, even after purchase of the Greyhound Bus ticket. Now, seeing the disturbance at the soda fountain, she rushed to intervene. 'What on earth is the matter?' she called.

For some distance from the soda fountain, every saleswoman and customer had turned to watch. The beggar woman known as Mea Culpa around the French Market had been looking at combs and hairpins. But the saleswoman turned her back. Everybody's back was turned. Nobody was watching. A hand like a gray mouse crept out of Mea Culpa's shawl, nibbled among the hairpins, and crept back under shelter. Safe under her shawl.

Safe. She had a package of white hairpins for her white hair. Folding her arms across her chest so that nobody could detect the scared, triumphant bounding of her heart, she left the store.

'My little man, you must come with me,' Mr. Graber kept insisting.

'No, Mister. Please. He's my boy. You can't have him.'

A sodajerker came from behind the counter and took hold of Mr. Graber's arm. Mr. Graber started, looked wildly about him, and perceived what he had done. A Jewish floorwalker was approaching. Mr. Graber shuddered. His pursuers were closing in.

'Whadda ya mean, makin such a racket?' said the sodajerker.

'I merely wanted to buy the little boy a soda,' Mr. Graber squeaked.

'I know youse guys. You oughta be locked up.'

'Mama, mama,' whimpered Corey, clinging to his mother's neck.

'Mama's got a-holt of you. Mama won't let nothin hurt you.'

'It's all right, dearie,' said the saleswoman. 'Everything's all right.'

The Jewish floorwalker looked at Mr. Graber and waggled his little finger in his ear.

'I've been insulted,' said Mr. Graber, in desperate appeal. 'I've been grossly insulted. I demand an apology.'

'What happened?' asked the floorwalker of the saleswoman who had rushed to intervene.

'Well,' she said, looking confused, 'I saw this gentleman put his hand on the boy's head. His face looked funny . . . it all happened so quick . . . I don't know.'

'I got kids of my own,' said the sodajerker indignantly. 'Dis fella oughta be locked up.'

'I protest!' trembled Mr. Graber to the floorwalker. 'As you can see for yourself, sir, this woman is blind. She completely misunderstood my generous intention. I merely wanted to buy her little boy a soda.'

'Turn him loose,' said the floorwalker.

Reluctantly, the sodajerker did as he was told.

'Thank you,' said Mr. Graber, in a state of collapse.

'Beat it,' said the floorwalker.

Mr. Graber collected his umbrella and tottered toward the door.

'Mr. Feingold, you shouldna let him get away like that,' said the sodajerker. 'He's crazy.'

'Who isn't?' said the floorwalker sadly. 'Indoors or outdoors, my friend, where would you put him?'

Out on the street, Mr. Graber paused to get his breath and glared about him. He struck the pavement with his umbrella. He had outwitted them again. 'Dogs!' he said. 'Stupid dogs!' He walked rapidly away. 'Dogs of spies!' Everybody was a spy, he thought. The city was full of spies. He had outwitted them again, but it had been a narrow escape. No doubt they were following him. It would be better not to go home. He crossed the street and mingled with a crowd that waited at a car stop. When the car came, he boarded it without knowing or particularly caring where it took him. Some minutes later, however, seeing that nobody in the car appeared to be interested in his presence, Mr. Graber spoke to a man reading a newspaper beside him.

'What car is this?'

'St. Charles.'

'Thank you, my good man. Thank you.'

· The man snorted, and returned to his newspaper.

The car leaned around Lee Circle, passed the Public Library, and rocketed out St. Charles Avenue. John Potowski, the motorman, was now so thirsty he could scarcely stand it. He was talking to himself.

Drink Dr. Petter at 10—2—4
Pink Dr. Drepper at 10—2—4

The car emptied gradually. John Potowski grew thirstier. At the outer end of 'The Loop,' on Carrollton Avenue, was a small restaurant and bar. When he reached this point, his day would be over. His relief always met him here. He would cross the street, enter the small restaurant and bar, sling his leg over a stool, and say, 'Gimme a double . . .'

Prink Dr. Depper at 10—2—4
Drink Dr. Drepper at 10—2—4

At Tulane University, the car halted for a couple of students to get off; and Mr. Graber, looking through the window, saw Audubon Park across the street from the University buildings. Recalling how the cuckoo had lost itself among the cypresses in City Park that morning, he thought that he would lose his own pursuers in the trees. He left the car and entered the park.

At a distance he heard hungry sounds of various waterfowl, sounds of quacking and hissing and splashing. It must be feeding time at the Zoo. Mr. Graber remembered that he was hungry, and felt sorry for himself. A lion roared. A parrot squawked. Mr. Graber walked toward the Zoo. He wandered about for a while, watching the feeding, and presently found himself before the spider monkey cage. As he looked at the monkeys, such a pompous, self-congratulatory expression laved his features that a girl in a blue raincoat, who had also been watching the monkeys, began to laugh hysterically.

The girl was pregnant. As she laughed, the baby moved inside her; the unborn foot scraped down along her side. She caught her breath. It was too much. It was absolutely too much. She caught her breath again and tried to hold it; but she could not stop laughing. Holding a crumpled letter to her breast, she got up from the bench where she had been sitting and blundered away, looking for a quiet place where she might laugh alone, or cry alone, perhaps even die alone on the damp leaves.

All afternoon, she had wandered distractedly, trying to decide what to do. She had ridden around in a French Quarter tourist bus; she had gone into churches, and wandered out again. Finally, she had boarded a streetcar and found herself at the park. What was there left to do but die? Nobody would know till it was all over. But her husband would finally know. News of a pregnant girl found dead in Audubon Park would travel; it had already begun to travel in the blades of grass that started up and ran ahead of her in little ripples in the mournful breeze. A flock of parti-colored pigeons rose from the grass, changed direction in midair, and vanished over the roofs. They knew. They would carry the news across country, past sleeping houses, and the lighted windows of passenger trains; past yuccas in the desert in the moonlight to the Pacific Ocean. The news would travel. Her husband would hear of this desolation. Somebody must hear.

Somebody heard. Placide Giraud, who had stopped off at the park in a light-hearted mood, with plans to pick up some pretty woman who liked Beef Stroganoff, had been watching the distracted girl in the blue raincoat for some time. She bothered him. Something was wrong, or she wouldn't be behaving as she was. In her right mind she would have been pretty enough; but in her present condition, with mascara streaked all over her face, stringy hair, swollen eyes—not to mention the bulge under the raincoat—she was far from attractive. She was just about the farthest thing from light-hearted that Placide Giraud had ever seen—and he had wanted some fun. But it had always been Placide's way to worry about others; it was a curse on him, he thought. He picked up women, he thought, but only after the head had fallen in the basket. Some other man had got this girl in her present fix; and now he, Placide Giraud, was destined to come along and pick up the pieces. But somebody ought to do something about the girl. She seemed in real trouble. Since nobody else appeared to be particularly interested, he thought that he had better keep an eye on her for a while.

And so, with hands in his pockets, his long face half-troubled, half-amused, Placide Giraud strolled behind the girl. He could still glimpse her blue raincoat through the trees.

MET BY HIS RELIEF on Carrollton Avenue, John Potowski surrendered the streetcar and entered the small restaurant and bar upon which his thoughts had centered all afternoon. He would have one drink, and no more. No man in the city was in worse need of cheer. After serving the whims of a capricious public for eight hours, he owed himself one small indulgence.

He passed through the restaurant, and seated himself at the bar between a man wearing a white duck uniform, with the words Bruce's Juices written in red Spencerian script between his shoulder blades, and a man wearing horn-rimmed glasses and a panama hat. The two were talking; and when Potowski sat down between them, they leaned forward on either side of him to keep each other in view. The bartender was busy at the far end of the bar. John Potowski waited.

'So I give it to her straight.' The man in the Bruce's Juices uniform leaned across Potowski, excused himself volubly, and shook his finger in the other man's face. 'So I let her have it right between the eyes. "I'm fed up," I said to her, just like I'm saying it to you. "I'm fed up. I'm going, and don't you try to stop me. I'm getting out of this crazy-house," I said to her . . . and s'help me, I went!' He clapped John Potowski, a small man, on the shoulder. Potowski nearly fell off his stool.

The man in the panama hat lifted his eyebrows so high his hat slipped. He restored it to its proper angle. 'You just think you did, Ferrabee,' he said, 'but you didn't. Know why you didn't? Because it can't be done.'

Thomas Ferrabee looked in his glass, found it empty, and called loudly for the bartender. 'Fix these gentlemen up, buster,' he said. 'Same thing all around?'

'Sure,' said the man in the panama hat.

Presently John Potowski, engaged in a silent struggle with himself, found a Coca-Cola and whiskey highball shoved under his nose. Thomas Ferrabee clapped him on the shoulder, and told him to drink. He looked at the glass longingly, but did not touch it yet. Why not? he thought. In the morning, Mrs. Potowski had declared with tears in her eyes that kidney stew would be waiting on the table at six o'clock; and she *knew* he would arrive home sober enough to eat it before it got cold. She was praying for him. It would serve her right, he thought, if he didn't come. John Potowski looked from the glass to the clock. The argument was continuing on either side of him; he was aware of it through the haze of his own thoughts.

'No,' the man in the panama hat was saying, 'I tried it myself one time, Ferrabee, and it can't be done. You get married and have kids, and you're stuck with it. You just as well to not of told your wife anything, for all the good it'll do.'

It would take a real man to down that highball, spit in the spittoon, and walk out of the door, thought John Potowski. A real man, by God, and he would be that man! He reached out toward the glass in front of him. The ice was beginning to melt. Again, Thomas Ferrabee clapped him on the shoulder, and told him to drink.

'You don't know me, friend,' said Ferrabee boastfully to the man in the panama hat. 'You don't know me, and neither did she. I'm a man that when I make up my mind, it stays made up, and this time I made up my mind. This is my last delivery to-day. I'm gonna run that truck back uptown, get a shave, bath, manicure, haircut, the whole works, and step out. Gonna have me some fun tonight. Better come along.'

'I promised to take my wife to the picture show tonight,' said the man in the panama hat. 'She said she'd divorce me, if I ever stood her up on a date again.'

'What t'hell, she'll be there when you get home. Better come along with me. I ain't ever going home.'

'Oh yes, you are. You might of left this morning, but you'll go home tonight. Come bedtime, you'll go home.' The man in the panama hat shook his head from side to side. The hat was too large for him. It slipped again. He righted it, and peering sadly through his horn-rimmed glasses at the other, said, 'Take it from a man that tried it, Ferrabee. Come bedtime, you'll go home.'

John Potowski was still looking at the glass. Men drink for many reasons. John Potowski drank because of Mrs. Potowski. She wanted a baby, and he had never been able to impregnate her. A large, buxom, bubbling woman, technically faithful, she nevertheless managed to carry on discreet flirtations with a dozen different men of her acquaintance at the same time. She was innocently unaware of what this did to her husband. If the subject of any sort of infidelity on her part had been mentioned, she would have flown into a temper, protested her purity, and made the Stations of the Cross in every church in town to prove it. She constantly implored her husband to give up drinking; and this had been the chief reason he had not done so. It had been his one weapon against her. He had joined Alcoholics Anonymous only because his long periods of inebriety were about to make him lose his job.

Already in a state of great nervous tension, Thomas Ferrabee's boasting talk and his commands to down the unsolicited drink set before him began to counteract John Potowski's own desire. The public shoved him around all day, and Mrs. Potowski shoved him around all night. He'd be damned if he'd let a stranger with no claim on him tell him what to do. Before he'd drink that Coca-Cola and whiskey highball, thought John Potowski, he'd drink a Doctor Pepper. He considered the presence of Coca-Cola in whiskey an unspeakable pollution, anyhow. When he drank, he liked his whiskey neat.

John Potowski summoned the bartender, ordered a Doctor Pepper, drank it defiantly, and left the place with Thomas Ferrabee still arguing volubly behind him.

Just what he had accomplished, he hardly knew. This evening was the first time in several years that he had left a bar cold sober. Immediately upon leaving, he felt as if he had won a victory; he felt proud of himself. But the nearer he came toward home, the more he began to wonder. Of his own will he had surrendered his weapon against Mrs. Potowski. Had he won a victory or suffered a defeat? Time would tell. Time might work changes in Mrs. Potowski, as well as in himself. Time alone would tell.

Children were playing with a baseball in the street. A boy was batting flies for three others to catch. At the clean crack of the bat against the ball, John Potowski looked up into the golden sky and saw three white gulls. Looking farther, he saw a mosquito-hawk dropping downward from a great height. As he watched the black speck of its body in the clear immensity of sky, John Potowski delivered himself to the future. Time alone would tell whether or not, if he stopped drinking indefinitely, he would then be able to impregnate Mrs. Potowski, and she would then stop flirting. Just which one of them had been the first to err, he could not tell. Time alone could tell. . . . Remembering his dinner with a hunger almost savage, John Potowski walked faster.

ALL OVER THE CITY, hands were putting away the tools of the day. Hands of watchmakers, stenographers, clerks, pawnbrokers, carpenters, mechanics, teachers, were closing drawers, covering typewriters and adding machines, blotting the last entry, locking the safe, totaling the day's receipts, oiling the saw before closing the tool chest, marking the page in the book where tomorrow's lesson would begin. The gloved hands of a crane operator manipulated levers, lifting the last load of scrap iron off the flatcar, swinging it, dropping it neatly in the hold of a Japanese freighter. Brown hands closed the hatch cover. Below, other brown hands were nursing up steam in the boilers. Grocers' nimble hands clinked cash registers as late shoppers hurried to finish their marketing before the stores closed. Salesgirls' hands were beginning to cover their counters; and some, already anticipating the homeward journey through the streets, were applying powder and lipstick to faces that looked lined and weary in the harsh light. In bookie joints, hands were paying money into reaching hands. Hands were paying out change in parking lots, and turning keys in ignition locks. Tired hands were being folded for the last time; and new hands, newly issued from the womb, were curling and uncurling in the strange, new air. The hands of attorneys for plaintiff and defendant shoveled papers into briefcases. The court adjourned until tomorrow. The judge's hands lit a cigar. Soon, the janitor's hands would be cleaning spittoons and sweeping up the countless cigarette butts that littered the courtroom floor—but time alone could sweep up the scandal. In some office buildings, the worn hands of scrubwomen were already beginning to empty wastebaskets, wring mops, and pour Lysol down lavatory bowls. In one office building, one nameless scrubwoman, rustling through the day's accumulation of discarded paper, reached for a fluttering memo sheet that had escaped her canvas bag. Somebody had been drawing pictures on the memo sheet. She paused to examine them. The pictures were of small triangular birds with pert tail feathers hoisted, long necks stretched downward, heads hidden in the earth—a whole army of them cluttering the page. She got it. *Ostriches.* And what had the artist scrawled beneath in crooked print? Laboriously, she spelled out the words: 'Mrs. Imogene Jones can't pay her bill at the corner grocery. So the world goes to war. That's what it boils down to. God help us all.' . . . 'Amen,' said the scrubwoman, crossing herself. Her husband had been killed in the last war; her only son was twenty-two years old—the age for war. She didn't understand about Mrs. Imogene Jones causing a war; but she understood about wars. 'God help us all,' she sighed, as she pushed her dust mop across the hardwood floor.

WHEN PLACIDE GIRAUD caught up with the girl in the blue raincoat, he found her leaning against the column of an outdoors dance pavilion that adjoined a soft drink and hamburger stand. She had got over her hysterics, and was watching the dancers, a dozen or so high-school kids about her own age, who were jitter-bugging to a juke-box record playing inside the stand. Placide leaned against the column beside her, and lit a cigarette. As a seeming after-thought, he offered her the package. She shook her head. Placide smoked in silence for several minutes. On a smell of frying hamburger meat and onions, the music flowed around them; the dancing couples bobbed and twirled. Placide looked at the girl, and saw that she was biting her lips and doing things with her hands—playing with a letter, buttoning and unbuttoning her raincoat, twisting her fingers.

'Like to dance?' he said.

Her distracted eyes rested on him briefly. 'With *you?*' they seemed to say.

'I may look like the Tin Woodsman,' said Placide, 'but I'm not so bad. Like to try it and see?'

Involuntarily, she laid her hands on her stomach.

'No,' said Placide. 'I guess you'd better not dance.'

'Why not?' she said suddenly. 'Why not dance? What difference does it make?' She slipped the letter in the front of her dress and held out her hands.

Dancing was awkward business; they didn't get along very well. Whether from weariness or something else, the girl began to lean heavily on Placide. He looked down at her face, and saw her watching him with wide, mournful eyes. He steered her toward the door of the hamburger stand, and led her inside. 'Like a coke?'

'What?' she said. 'Oh. A coke.'

Taking this as acquiescence, he ordered two Coca-Colas, and pulled up a chair for her at a table in the corner. She pushed her hair out of her eyes, and leaned toward him across the table. 'Go on,' she said wearily, 'ask me questions. Ask me why I'm wandering around like this. Ask me why I was crying. Ask me what my name is, and how old I am, and if my mother knows where I am, and if I'm a bad girl, and if I'm sorry. Go on. Ask me!'

'I wasn't going to ask you anything,' said Placide.

'Yes, you were. Everybody asks me questions. I'm so sick of people asking me questions, I rode around on a tourist bus just to hear somebody else answer them for a while.'

'Did you?' said Placide.

'No, I didn't. I don't know. I just . . . I wanted . . .'

'I'm hungry,' said Placide. 'Let's eat a hamburger.' He wasn't hungry, but guessed that she was. He ordered the hamburgers, and then looked at her in a serious way. 'See here,' he said. 'Anybody can see you're in trouble.'

'Is that what a baby means to everybody—trouble?' she said.

'I won't ask you any questions,' said Placide, 'but I'll listen if you want to talk.'

'Talk to you? What for?'

'Then, if you want me to, I'll tell you what I think. There's nothing to lose.'

She looked at him for a minute, and then, without a word, took the letter from her dress and laid it on the table in front of him. He looked down at it, and looked up questioningly.

'Go on. Read it.'

When he had read it, he looked at her again. 'It's from your husband, I take it?'

'Yes.'

'He says he wants to come back, and try things over again.'

'Yes.'

'That sounds fine. What's the trouble? Let him come.'

'You fool.'

'Why?' said Placide.

'Look at me. I'm going to have a baby.'

'All the more reason for him to come. He ought to be with you.'

'It isn't his.'

'Oh,' said Placide. 'Oh, I see.'

Disjointed piece by piece, she told the story and he put it together. Her husband, not much older than herself, played a saxophone in a touring dance orchestra of no great renown. They had quarreled; and he had gone away and left her. She couldn't remember what they had quarreled about, but he had gone. To make him jealous, she had gone with another man for a while. Neither her husband nor the other man knew about the baby. She had supported herself by working in music stores up until two weeks ago, when the doctor had told her to stop working. She had no friends nor relatives in the city; her money was all gone; she hadn't paid her rent. The letter from her husband had come this morning. More than anything in the world, she wanted him back; but if he found out about the baby, she felt that any hope of reconciliation would be spoiled.

'Maybe not,' said Placide. 'Maybe he'd understand.'

'You don't know him.'

'If I were you, I'd write to him, anyhow. Tell him about the baby. Tell him everything. No man would let a woman down when she's in such a predicament as you are. Afterwards, you can talk things out.'

'I can't tell him. I don't want this baby. What'll I do?' The girl gasped, put her hand to her side, and lay back in her chair.

Placide mopped his face. He had certainly put his foot in it this time. He had wanted an evening of light romance with a companion who appreciated good food, and instead, he found himself trying to counsel an hysterical girl in a hamburger stand. This was what came from worrying about other people's troubles. Two emotional kids who should have been in school had got themselves tangled up in something they couldn't handle, and now he was supposed to offer advice. What was there to say? The father, who wasn't the father, didn't know about the baby; and the mother declared she didn't want it. The baby appeared to be out on a limb. Another recruit for a destinationless expedition, thought Placide Giraud.

'Well,' he said dryly, 'you're going to have a baby whether you want it or not. Stop thinking about yourself for a while, and think about the baby.'

'Meanwhile, what would I use for money?'

'I'll lend you money to pay your rent, but write your husband as soon as you get home. In the meantime, go wash your face, and I'll take you out to dinner.'

'I'm not hungry.'

'But you look hungry. You ought to have a good meal.'

The girl had been watching him with glazed eyes, her mouth slightly open. She gasped again, and began to whimper.

Placide Giraud jumped out of his chair. 'My God!' he said. 'When's this baby due?'

ALL OVER THE CITY, hands were sorting, smoothing out, clipping together, locking up the mysteries of economics behind steel doors and iron grillwork and concrete walls. Today was today—was finished. Some good had been done, and some undone. Some mischief had been woven, and some unraveled. Confusion had been cleared up, and more confusion created. Who but God Himself, wondered some thoughtful ones, could tell if mankind on this day had advanced or retreated? The Mississippi River, now striped with purple and gold in the mellow light, had carried thousands of tons of sediment past the city through the day. Some of it would be swept into the Gulf; some would be dropped in the Passes to impede shipping. But the United States engineers would dredge it out. Today was over, and tomorrow was another day. The city was going home to dinner.

THE HANDS of the beggar woman called Mea Culpa, who had stolen the package of hairpins from Grant's Store—hands like quiet, gray mice—were just now picking up a dime her quick eyes had discovered on the Royal Street sidewalk. She could buy a whole new loaf of soft white bread with this dime; but she must hurry before the stores closed. She hurried. In a near-by grocery she selected her loaf. It was wrapped in crackling cellophane which nobody but herself would remove. She joined the line before the cash register. When her turn came, she laid down her dime.

'One token, please,' said the busy grocer, pausing with his hands on the cash register.

'Sir?'

'One sales token for every purchase of ten cents.'

'Token?' Mea Culpa smiled ingratiatingly, pushed the dime toward the cash register, and attempted to step out of line with the loaf of bread.

'Come back here,' said the grocer. 'You owe me a token.'

'Ain't it a dime? I thought it was a dime. It said so, on the shelf. It said a dime.'

'You forgot the sales tax. You owe me a token for sales tax. That token is the city sales tax to help the poor.'

Her face was both bewildered and frightened. She juggled the loaf in her hands.

'Don't you read the newspapers?' said the grocer facetiously. A few customers tittered. The grocer attempted something really funny. 'I don't know where you've been doing your shopping all this time,' he said, smiling broadly at the beggar woman who got her food from garbage cans. 'Everybody charges tokens. It's a city law.'

'Sir?'

'Please, lady, you're holding up the line.' The grocer looked at the clock. 'You'll have to pay tokens like everybody else. I can't make any exceptions. I have to collect tokens from everybody. If I don't, I'll go to jail. You wouldn't want me to go to jail, would you?'

Everybody laughed at this. Confused by the laughter, thinking it directed at her, Mea Culpa laid the bread on the counter and stepped out of line. 'I dowanna go to jail,' she said.

'Lady, you forgot your dime.'

She accepted the dime, mumbled thanks and apologies, and left the store. Like many who have suffered much, she felt guilty a great part of the time. Tonight, her sense of guilt was overpowering. She did not understand about the tokens. All she knew was that the bread had been refused her because she had stolen hairpins. She had stolen them because she couldn't find white hairpins on the sidewalk, and she wanted white hairpins for her white hair. But women were always dropping black hairpins on the sidewalks, and she could have used these just as well. She was guilty of vanity. Vanity was a sin. True, it was only a venial sin; but there were other sins on her soul which she had not forgotten—terrible sins of the past for which God now punished her. God would not punish her so much if she had not deserved it.

Hiding her face and head in the black shawl, beating her wicked breast with her offending hand, she hurried toward the Cathedral for confession and absolution.

'*Mea culpa, mea culpa*,' she groaned. '*Mea maxima culpa* . . .'

A FEW BLOCKS DISTANT, on Bourbon Street, Joe Onion's hand was just now dropping a nickel in the slot of a restaurant's pay telephone. And now his hand was spinning the dial. An hour had passed since Joe had interrupted the crap game in Pirate's Alley. A druggist had poured iodine on his bitten hand; and he and Whitey and Aleck had had another drink. Now, the two boys were sitting at a table waiting to be served with crab gumbo; and he, Joe, had just got up to telephone Leah Webster. Maybe Leah would remember him, he thought. He wanted to be remembered. From this day on earth, he was afraid that he would not be remembered at all if he couldn't find Leah. No telephone number was listed under her name; and so he was calling all the Websters in the book. There were quite a few. Joe's hand continued to drop nickels and spin the dial. Whitey opened the door of the booth and said that dinner was ready. Joe waved him away.

IN MERLIN WEBSTER'S HOME, the telephone rang eight times. Orena the cook, just returned from the Clark house and hurrying the Webster dinner, refused to answer it. In Merlin's real estate office uptown, the telephone rang. But it was not answered. Merlin had left some ten minutes before; and Amelia Decker, his stenographer, was just now taking the elevator. Two minutes before, she had unlatched the safety-pin that had held the wilted sprig of sweet olive at the place on her blouse where the third button should have been, and dropped both safety-pin and sweet olive in the wastebasket. She looked for the pin, but couldn't find it. It had been an awful day. She felt completely unbuttoned. A minute before, she had slipped the catch on the Yale lock, tried the doorknob to be sure the door was properly secured, then pressed the elevator button in the hall. She did not hear the office telephone ring behind her. She was already on her way to the YWCA Cafeteria.

JOE ONION HUNG UP. He was out of nickels. He left the booth, changed a bill to get more nickels, and returned to the booth. He had just remembered hearing Leah say that she worked as cashier in a neighborhood movie; but he did not know which movie. He would have to call all the neighborhood movies in the city. Bracing himself against the wall of the booth, he began.

A great many of the lines were busy. People, he supposed, damning them all, were throwing themselves on their telephones to check the names of evening shows all over the city. As he continued to call, more and more numbers gave him the busy signal.

JOE DID NOT KNOW IT, but one of these busy lines actually belonged to the theater where Leah worked; and it was Leah's own hand which had dialed a number—Victor Peralta's number. At this moment, Leah was inquiring of Maudie, who answered the telephone, if any letters had come for her during the day. She had thought that Joe might have found her address and dropped her a note. No, replied Maudie, neglecting to mention the bill from the department store which she had destroyed

—no mail had come for Leah today. Had Merlin come home yet? Leah asked. Maudie did not know, but she didn't think so. Neither had Victor come home yet. Mrs. Peralta had just gone to the corner grocery to buy something for supper and to see if she had won anything on the lottery. Wasn't it a scream about old Mrs. Peralta and the numbers racket? Maudie wanted to talk; but Leah excused herself and hung up.

In spite of the decision she had reached in the Crescent Beauty Shop, she had not been able to resist this last attempt to establish contact with Joe. She wished that she had left her telephone number with Neeley at the rooming-house, in case Joe happened to come by and inquire—but in her hurry she had forgotten to do so. And Neeley had no telephone. If Joe had wanted to see her again, she thought, he could have found her address in the City Directory. He had not wanted to see her.

Leah tried to recapture her calm feeling of the afternoon, but did not succeed very well. Her bones ached, her eyes ached, and her heart would have ached also, if it had not felt so empty.

'Miss, what time duh serial comes on?'

'At seven-fifteen, and again at ten-fifteen,' Leah replied to the spokesman for a group of small boys.

'Shucks, kids, we dowanna see dat ole love-story. Less wait.'

'Okay. Man, dey's some shootin gonna happen tonight, eh? Looka me, I'm Two-Gun Fagan, an duh cops is right in behind me. I toins. I shoots fum duh hip. Like dis. *Ack-ack-ack-ack!*'

'Man, dat's mowin 'em down!'

'Skinnay says . . .'

The boys loafed away down the sidewalk. She would never see Joe again, Leah thought, but she could not help looking for him. A man was coming out of the corner bar . . . No . . . A man was crossing the street . . . No!

But he wanted a ticket. He was Mr. Papadakis, who had picked up a waitress in the vestibule of the Jesuit Church during the rain. Mr. Papadakis was one of those astonishing men who, even during a rainstorm, even on a hot summer evening, manage to look as if they have just come from the Opera. His person and his clothes exuded soothing waves of romantic well-being. The waitress, with whom he had enjoyed a profitable luncheon hour, thought him a sugar chemist from Cuba; the man who came for his laundry thought him a member of the Greek consulate; his landlady thought him a foreign banker in New Orleans for his health. Mr. Papadakis thought of himself as a lover and a philosopher. In reality, he was an artist. From a paper cone, he squeezed *Happy Birthday, Happy Confirmation Day, For My Mother*, and *For St. Joseph*, on bakery cakes. Mr. Papadakis had infinite patience and a delicate hand; and his pink and green flowers and chocolate spirals were the best that money could buy. Several weeks before, he had rented a studio on St. Philip Street for purposes of pleasant seduction; and, to his dismay and astonishment (for he understood women thoroughly), had discovered himself madly in love with Leah Webster, who lived across the street. He did not have the courage to approach her directly; but every night he sat on his doorstep and waited for her to come home from work. Although he was well aware that a man is an idiot to die of love, he was now seeing Charles Boyer and Danielle Darrieux in *Mayerling* and Two-Gun Fagan in *Two-Gun Fagan* for the fourth time, for no other reason than that Leah sold him the ticket. To maintain such an establishment and such a wardrobe as Mr. Papadakis', surely required more money than a man could make in a bakery; but where Mr. Papadakis got his money was his own secret. Possibly he gambled on the sugar-beet crop or on greyhounds, and was lucky. Leah was not at all curious about him. When she slid his ticket toward him, she forgot him. Mr. Papadakis accepted the ticket with reverent fingers, complimented the weather in a hopeless voice; and, holding the ticket at arm's length, disappeared inside the show.

Somebody rapped a coin on the glass cage. 'Hey, Miss!' A

boy's face grinned at Leah, a 'teen-age boy, with his arm wrapped around his girl. Both were chewing gum so fast their faces looked blurred. 'Hey, Miss. Two loges, please.'

Leah accepted the money, tore off pink tickets, made change. This was her job. She felt a little calmer.

IN THE FRENCH QUARTER RESTAURANT, Joe Onion had just remembered a less impetuous way to locate a person in a strange city. He called the City Directory; caught the clerk putting on her hat; and, in a few minutes, had Leah Webster's address. He decided not to call her at work. She would be home around midnight, and it would be fun to surprise her. Just in case she didn't remember him, he had better buy her a present. He hadn't been able to buy the grass skirt for the fat little girl in the blue playsuit, but by God, nobody could keep him from buying a present for Leah Webster! He thought he might be a little drunk . . . just a little.

When he finally emerged from the telephone booth dripping with sweat, but with Leah's address in his pocket, he found that Whitey and Aleck had finished their meal and gone.

IN THE SAZERAC BAR on Carondelet Street, Merlin Webster was lifting a Sazerac cocktail to his lips when he heard Preston Dillon's name. Keeping his back turned carefully, he listened. Two men were speaking in guarded voices.

'Too bad about Dillon's aunt.'

'She must have heard about him. I guess the shock killed her.'

'Rogge's claiming mail fraud. Those boys didn't even send a postcard through the mails.'

'He says they sent checks.'

'They didn't send 'em. The banks sent 'em. Rogge's stretching the law too far. It isn't fair.'

'Looks bad . . . glad I kept my hands clean . . .'

'My income tax . . . in black and white . . . tough on Dillon . . .'

Merlin finished his cocktail and left. The door closed behind him. More than a door had closed: a way of life had just swung shut behind him. Now he was out on the street, and going home.

He had traveled a long way from home during the day, and he found himself wondering almost wistfully if home would still be where he had left it in the morning; if the garden would be the same—his beautiful garden, safe behind its walls. He had escaped death beneath the wheels of a truck; he had survived a flood. He, alone, had survived. He felt lonely.

He walked in a white linen suit that was a little soiled and wrinkled now—an unremarkable man, with a face neither young nor old. The crisp outlines of his youth were smudged, but not quite gone; the flesh was withstanding pretty well the furrows with which time would one day dignify it as a reward for having survived so many days similar to this one, so many narrow escapes. It was neither a kind nor a cruel face; neither avaricious nor generous; neither thoughtful nor impulsive; neither intelligent nor stupid. An acquaintance who happened to see him at this minute from a passing car noted briefly that Webster's face was easy to pick out in a crowd for the same reason that the eye lights instantly upon a clearing in a woods, or upon a white handkerchief waving above the heads of a mob. Nothing was written on it. It was merely a pale vicinity adjacent to the collar of his shirt.

But Merlin Webster's unremarkable face concealed a feeling that approached anguish. A double team of mules in shining brass-decked harness had just trotted past him pulling a heavy express wagon. The clip-clop of mules' feet, the jingle of harness, the rolling thunder of wheels, waked memories in him—memories of cotton wagons, the long, low-slung trundlers of cotton bales through the streets of his boyhood. He had run behind the wagons and jumped on them for rides, he and his friends, on bright summer mornings when living was not a business but a positive pleasure, as positive as the crisp jingle of harness now fading down the streets . . . a bright vision renewed each morning, now fading so that he could scarcely hear it . . . now gone. . . . Another express wagon rolled past him, drawing behind it Carnival memories of action and excitement, of suspense and fulfillment at sight of the first parade. . . . The floats were passing: flowers and birds and beasts from fairy tales, towering glitter in the torchlight on narrow Royal Street, on the white expressionless faces of the maskers, the black faces of the Negro torch-bearers, the wagging ears of the mules through the lifted, waving hands, the lifted faces on sidewalk and balcony, beautiful, sad, unreal, unholy, quickly passing turning wheels in the hot red torchlight on man and beast and flower and grotto, dwarf and imp from beyond the past, rolling now into nowhere between the old buildings down narrow Royal Street, and passing, swaying, nodding, rocking past him into nowhere in the hot, red, fragrant torchlight.

The crowd flowed into the street.

It was June now, a June evening. He had put away his papers and locked his safe. He was going home to his wife and daughter. The parade passes, the day draws to an end, thought Merlin Webster, and somehow, out of memory, a man must find his way to his own street, his own house, his own wife.

Somebody honked a horn near-by. Merlin jumped and scowled at the disturber of his thoughts. Some fool woman. When was the city going to outlaw unnecessary honking of horns? He kept on walking. The horn honked again, almost in his ear. He turned angrily.

'Daddy!'

It was his own car; his own wife and daughter. Marie, driving close to the curb, had been trying to attract his attention. He opened the back door and climbed in.

'We're late,' Marie said. 'I wonder if the Tuttles have come yet. I hope they don't come till tomorrow. We bought a crib for the baby, and the store promised to send it out on the last delivery, but I don't know if they did. Then I had my hair set, and then we went to a picture show, and then I simply had to have a new hat. How do you like it, dear?'

'It's fine,' said Merlin. 'I like it fine.' No wonder he had not recognized her. Still, he should have recognized his own car. He was growing absent-minded. He must check this tendency before it affected his business. As he leaned back on the car cushions, however, his mind was already wandering. Money, money . . . relax, he thought. Money, money . . . relax.

The clear vision fades with the jingle of harness and the thunder of wheels on the summer street; and in its place are men dressing and undressing dummies in department-store windows; and signs telling you where to dine and dance; signs advertising relief from rupture, relief from head colds, relief from constipation. All needs of the flesh are recognized and alleviated; but the spirit must fare as best it can among Gent's Furnishings. But no. Here is a sign for the spirit as well. *Jesus Saves.* One must go more frequently to church. One must try everything. But one must not write love-letters to nonexistent persons, and drop them through the slots of one's mind; or letters of farewell, he thought—for one is always taking leave, and nobody notices.

'What are we having for dinner tonight?' Merlin Webster inquired of his wife, breaking into a description of the movie she had just seen. He had not heard her.

'We're having . . .'

But he did not hear. The car had turned onto St. Philip Street. Little girls were dancing in a ring on the sidewalk, playing 'Farmer in the Dell.' They were singing. Merlin heard them plainly as the car passed. The childish voices were not carrying the tune very well; but the tune was familiar to Merlin, and he knew the words. *The bone stands alone*, the children were singing. *The bone stands alone.*

Bow to the images along the road, thought Merlin Webster. Bow to them all and implore their protection. The northwest wind is roaring in the willows along the riverbank and dead leaves are flying over half an acre. Crouched in the duck blind, hands freezing on the gun-barrel—who can tell if it is dawn or twilight? Somewhere, a loon cries all alone on the wild, wide river. And the ducks are somewhere else.

'Looks like the Tuttles have come,' said Marie. 'They've taken our parking place.'

A clay-spattered car with a New Jersey license plate was parked by the lamp post in front of the Webster house. Marie jockeyed the Webster car to the curb behind it. She came too near the curb, and scraped the end of the bumper on the sidewalk. Merlin's spine crawled at the noise.

'Watch what you're doing!' he shouted. 'Cut the wheel the other way, the other way, I said! You'll scrape the fender, you'll scrape—you've done it! Marie, I thought I'd taught you how to park a car.'

'No harm done,' said Marie nervously, cutting the switch.

'Mama, look!' said Georgie, pointing. 'Here comes Mrs. Peralta, and I bet she won some money on the lottery.'

Old Mrs. Peralta was hobbling across the street with a brown-paper bag of groceries. She waved her hand excitedly at the Websters. Her face was wreathed in smiles.

'I'm lucky,' she said breathlessly. 'Good evening, I'm so lucky. I won a dollar and seventeen cents—see! I had a feeling I'd win today. When I woke up this morning, I had a lucky feeling!'

'That's wonderful,' Marie said. 'I'm so glad.' Merlin went into the house. With a stiff smile for Mrs. Peralta, Marie followed her husband. In her nervousness at the Tuttles' arrival, she did not notice that Georgie was not with her.

GEORGIE went with Mrs. Peralta. She had been looking forward all day to seeing the Tuttles; but now that the moment of meeting them had actually arrived, she felt shy. It would be better to wait until her mother and father had become acquainted with the newcomers, she told herself; and then, perhaps she could slip in unnoticed. Anyhow, Mrs. Peralta's pleasure in her company always made her feel important. Besides, she wanted to ask Mrs. Peralta a question.

'I've got a present for you,' the old woman said mysteriously.

'What is it?' said Georgie, walking beside her.

'You wait. You'll be surprised.'

'How long do I have to wait?'

'Not very long.'

'Will I know tonight?'

'Yes, dearie,' said Mrs. Peralta. 'You'll know as soon as I put Victor's supper on to cook.'

From the sounds that issued from the bathroom, Aunt Maudie was taking a bath. Georgie was just as well pleased not to see her. Aunt Maudie never noticed her except to say, 'Hi, Fatso. When you goin on a diet?'

When Mrs. Peralta had put the chops in the icebox, peeled the potatoes, and scraped the carrots, she led Georgie to her own room and uncovered the doll she had found on the sidewalk in the afternoon. The doll's dress had dried, but it wasn't a pretty doll. From its appearance, it had survived more crises than having been left in the rain. As she looked at it, Georgie's face fell. She didn't care very much about dolls. Both she and Lucille had outgrown dolls six months before, and had buried two large families with fitting ceremony in Lucille's back yard. But old Mrs. Peralta looked so pleased at having a present to give her. She was offering the doll as if she thought it the prettiest doll in the world. She was smiling in such a pleased way. Georgie felt embarrassed. Mrs. Peralta was very poor, and didn't have much money to spend on nice presents. Her feelings must not be hurt. Georgie took the doll in her arms.

'Thank you, Mrs. Peralta,' she said politely.

'And now,' said Mrs. Peralta, 'what have you been doing all day?'

'I went shopping. I went to a movie. I saw a grass skirt.'

'That was nice.'

'What you going to buy with your lottery money, Mrs. Peralta?'

'Why, I think I'll buy a candle,' said Mrs. Peralta, rubbing her finger alongside her nose. 'A candle for the Blessed Mother. A beautiful white candle. And you shall light it. Would you like that?'

While speaking, Mrs. Peralta had opened her front door and drawn Georgie down to sit with her on the doorstep. Georgie sat reluctantly, hiding the doll's face against her chest. She did not want to be seen holding it. 'Yes, ma'am,' she said primly. 'I'd love to light a candle for the Blessed Mother.'

'Bless you,' said Mrs. Peralta fondly.

The angelus bell began to ring. Georgie looked up quickly. She had remembered her question.

'Mrs. Peralta,' she said, 'who rings the Cathedral bell?'

But Mrs. Peralta did not hear. She was listening to the bell, to the many bells that had swung across her life. The sound of bells was the sound of her life. Sometimes they had been happy bells, and sometimes sad. It did not matter too much, now, what kind of bells they had been. The rain fell. The sun shone. It was no more than one expected. It was life. One took it as God willed. But tonight the bell was happy. Supper was cooking. Soon, Victor would be home to eat. The smooth, scrubbed planks of the doorstep were still warm from the sun. She had won a dollar and seventeen cents. It had been her lucky day. The bell was ringing.

'Who rings—?'

But old Mrs. Peralta had forgotten the little girl beside her. Her hands were busy on her beads. Her lips moved.

GEORGIE WENT HOME. She opened the front door softly, intending to sneak through the house, run upstairs, and dispose of the doll before anybody saw her; but, as she opened the door, she heard a baby crying. The living-room seemed full of people, a bright confusion of shapes and sounds. She stood dismayed, the unwelcome doll dangling by one leg behind her.

'This is our daughter, Georgiana,' she head a voice declaim from a distance. 'Shake hands with Mr. Tuttle, darling.'

Georgie felt her hand clasped by the hand of something tall and thin in a striped T-shirt, with a mustache, that passed her on to another hand. Georgie looked down at the floor and looked up at the most beautiful person she had ever seen. She would have died for Mrs. Tuttle on the living-room floor—but Mrs. Tuttle took away her hand.

'I can't imagine what's the matter with him,' she said. 'He's usually such a good baby. He slept all the way down here, and changing his formula didn't seem to bother him a bit. He can't be hungry again. It isn't time. He almost never cries, does he, Willis?'

'Only when you want to show him off,' said Mr. Tuttle in a deep voice.

Everybody laughed politely in a cocktail glass. The baby went on crying. Georgie remained frozen beside Mrs. Tuttle, the forgotten doll swinging behind her.

Mrs. Tuttle danced the baby up and down on her lap. 'Look, sweetheart,' she said. 'Look, Roger, here's such a nice little girl who wants to meet you . . . oh dear, do they always behave this way?'

'Invariably,' said Mr. Tuttle. 'Let me have him. He's raising the roof.'

The baby changed hands. Georgie's father advanced with the cocktail shaker.

'Yes, do,' said her mother. 'Do have another, Mr. Tuttle. The new surroundings have upset him. I'm so sorry we weren't at

home when you got here. Did you have a nice trip, Mrs. Tuttle?
Did the rain catch you on the road?'

'Lovely,' said Kathy. 'You must forgive the way we look.
We were so tired and sleepy and so glad to get here, we fell on
the bed and went to sleep. Except we almost got struck by
lightning, because Willis—'

'Good Heavens, Georgie, where did you get that doll?'

Georgie blushed, and attempted to hide the doll in a fold of
her dress. What would Mrs. Tuttle think of her for having such
a doll?

'Don't try to hide it, darling. Where did you find it?'

'This?' Georgie looked at the doll as if she had never seen it
before. 'Mrs. Peralta gave it to me.'

'I think you ought to give it back, and let Mrs. Peralta give
it to some poor little girl whose mama and papa can't afford to
buy her a doll. Don't you think that would be a nice thing to do?'

'I can't give it back,' said Georgie. 'Mrs. Peralta would feel
bad.'

'Well, you needn't keep it. Suppose you drop it in the garbage
can, and run wash your hands thoroughly before you come near
Roger. We don't want Roger to catch anything, do we?'

'No, ma'am.' Georgie backed through the French door and
fled toward the rear of the house. Her face burned. What would
Mrs. Tuttle think of her? 'Look, Orena,' she said, pausing at
the kitchen door. 'Look at the funny ole doll Mrs. Peralta gave
me. Orena, look!'

'Don bodda me,' said Orena.

'But, Orena . . .'

'Ah says it agin, an ah says it plain. Don bodda me!'

Repulsed, Georgie tiptoed to the garbage can that stood in
the alley at the corner of the house. She lifted the lid. There
were coffee grounds, a squashed half of a grapefruit, celery tops,
eggshells. . . . She closed the lid hurriedly. She couldn't bear
to put a doll in such a place. She hid it among the thick vines

that covered the alley wall, and tiptoed upstairs to wash her hands.

When she came down, she heard water splashing in her parents' bathroom. Daddy was taking a shower. The pipes croaked as the water was shut off abruptly. As abruptly, the water was turned on again. Daddy did the shower that way when he wasn't feeling so well, Georgie thought, as she wandered shyly into the courtyard. Orena was laying the marble-topped garden table. They were going to eat out-of-doors. Mama was showing her flowers to Mrs. Tuttle.

'Beautiful,' Mrs. Tuttle was saying. 'Your garden is beautiful. Such lovely martinis—I mean, petunias. I adore those double, frilly, purple ones. And isn't that a scarlet hibiscus? May I have it for my hair?' Mrs. Tuttle picked the flower and stuck it over her ear.

Georgie scuffed her sandals on the bricks. 'Orena,' she said, 'are we going to eat outside?'

'Look lak it,' said Orena, flapping the starched tablecloth in place.

'What we having for dinner, Orena?'

'Go chase you some snails.'

Upstairs, in the bathroom of the new apartment, Georgie heard other sounds of splashing water. Mr. Tuttle was also taking a bath. Roger was still crying. Suddenly, Mr. Tuttle's voice broke into song.

> I yam Jesus' littul lamb,
> Yes, by Jesus Christ, I yam!

Mrs. Tarantino's dog began to bark. Mrs. Webster straightened involuntarily, and threw a worried glance at the bathroom window.

'The sound does seem to carry,' said Mrs. Tuttle apologetically. 'He was so tired. He shouldn't have had that last cocktail. . . . Willis!' she called, cupping her hand to her mouth. 'Oh, W-i-l-l-i-s! Pipe down! You can be heard for a block!'

The singing stopped, but the Tarantino dog continued to bark furiously. Roger cried. Mr. Webster croaked the pipes in the shower. Georgie saw her mother bite her lip.

'Mrs. Tuttle,' she said shyly, 'I washed my hands. Can I go look at Roger now?'

'Help yourself,' said Kathy gaily, readjusting the scarlet flower above her ear. 'Maybe you can make him stop crying.'

Georgie entered the living-room of the Tuttle apartment, and bent over the new crib. Nobody had yet taken time to move it upstairs. The baby lay on his back, flailing the mattress with angry arms and legs. His eyes were squeezed shut, and his mouth was wide open. 'Hey,' said Georgie conversationally. 'Hey, Roger.' The baby opened his eyes and looked at her. Georgie swung the ends of her long braids over his face. 'Hey, Roger, I bet I know something you don't know.' He stopped, astonished, in the middle of a sob, and rolled his eyes. 'Who rings the Cathedral bell?' He poked a finger in the general direction of the strange objects that swung above him. Georgie waved the braids back and forth above his face. 'I know . . . I know . . . bong, bong . . . bong, bong,' she chanted soothingly. Roger's face broke into a wide, slow, toothless smile. He grabbed for the braids.

By the time Georgie was called to dinner, Roger was asleep. Mr. Tuttle came downstairs looking like a different person with his hair combed. He put his arm around Georgie's shoulder and pulled out her chair at the table.

She sat primly minding her manners, very conscious of company. The talk was grown-up talk. For ten minutes it flowed over her head unheeded. When she had got something in her stomach, however, she began to listen; and, as was her custom, to record the puzzling sounds for later pondering. This was a little difficult, for the two men and the two women were conducting two entirely separate conversations. What she heard went something like this:

'How many outstanding men has the Negro race produced? A few, I grant, but nothing in proportion to their population. Not more than half a dozen, Mr. Tuttle. They're children, Mr. Tuttle, and they expect . . .'

'Ssh-h-h, here comes Orena. Yes, we often eat in the garden in the summer, Mrs. Tuttle. You'll find it so pleasant . . .'

'. . . to tie weights on a man's legs, ask him to compete with an unhampered man in a race, and call him inferior because he loses. Take the weights off the colored man, Mr. Webster, give him an equal chance, and then judge if he's inferior. You . . .'

'. . . find the mosquitoes not nearly so bothersome if you . . .'

'. . . indulge the Southern darkie like . . .'

'. . . Orena? Yes, she's a splendid cook, but not up to scratch tonight. Sullen about something. She's usually sullen on rainy days when . . .'

'. . . something must be done about this situation of . . .'

'. . . the servant problem in the South is quite simple. They'll work for almost nothing. Of course, you give them clothes, and let them take home food from the kitchen, and you . . .'

'. . . live in a highly industrialized, interdependent civilization, Mr. Webster, and you can't turn back the clock to the village blacksmith shop. I wonder . . .'

'. . . how anybody could live anywhere but in the French Quarter, Mrs. Tuttle. Why, this is the real New Orleans, the old New Orleans! Of course, you're bound to have curious neighbors, and you must . . .'

'. . . accept the fact, Mr. Tuttle, that you can't change human nature. Human nature has been the same since Adam. The old ways are the best. I think . . .'

'. . . I'll have another helping of that lovely—what is it?' Shrimp Creole? You must give me the recipe . . .'

'. . . for what the old ways have proved? That twelve million or more unemployed are inevitable? That periodic depressions are inevitable? That wars are inevitable? That . . .'

'. . . you must fertilize well, because the soil in these old gardens is pretty well run down, and you must remember . . .'

'. . . that our founding fathers warned against foreign entanglements, and Roosevelt should be careful how . . .'

'. . . tropical vines grow . . .'

'. . . in complete isolation. There's no excuse for this country to pull Europe's chestnuts out of the fire again! No excuse for . . .'

'. . . large chain stores like the A & P, but the French Market is so colorful, and there's no reason . . .'

'. . . for the laws of growth and change in living organisms, Mr. Webster. My wife can't look at my son's feet now, and tell what size shoe will fit his foot when's he forty. Neither could our founding fathers foresee . . .'

'*I wear size six in a lady's shoe!*' said Georgie.

'Ssh-h, darling, don't interrupt Mr. Tuttle. Now the Vieux Carré Commission is . . .'

'. . . government interfering with States' Rights, Mr. Tuttle! The Sovereign State of Louisiana is entirely capable of conducting its own inquiries on . . .'

'. . . preserving these fine old buildings for posterity, and . . .'

'. . . highly unorthodox proceedings when the Federal Government must . . .'

'. . . go to the Vieux Carré Commission before you can even paint your house to get their permission, but speaking of neighbors . . .'

'. . . every man in this country has an equal opportunity to rise to the top. If a man has it in him, Mr. Tuttle, he'll come out on top. There's always room at the top for people . . .'

'. . . like the Bruno Tarantinos, who live next door. They . . .'

'. . . can never hope to reach the top, Mr. Webster. There aren't enough bosses' daughters for every man in this country to marry. Ninety per cent of the people in this country are wage-workers, and can never hope to be anything else. It takes about one hundred wage-workers to support one big businessman, as you can see if you examine . . .'

'. . . Bruno, who is only an Italian laborer, you understand, but . . .'

'. . . the trend is away from free private enterprise in this country, Mr. Webster, and toward larger and larger monopolies, which preclude any sort of free enterprise. Cartels are a form of international gangsterism. The hoboes in this country have a simple way of putting it. They say, "You work one side of the street, and I'll work the other." Now . . .'

'. . . Bruno is quite a character in his own way, Mrs. Tuttle. He builds boats, quite good ones, I hear. He's a strikingly handsome man. But poor Mrs. Tarantino. So pathetic. I've often wondered why such a handsome man as Bruno Tarantino happened to choose such a homely wife. No doubt their families arranged it, in the Italian way. Lucky for Mrs. Tarantino. But Bruno doesn't seem to pay much attention to her. Apparently she consoles herself by playing hill-billy songs on her juke-box. So noisy. Such a nuisance. Thank goodness, she isn't doing it this evening.'

'A real juke-box?' said Kathy, who had noticed that Willis was arguing too heatedly on his favorite subject, and had just kicked him under the table. 'A real barroom juke-box in a private residence?'

'Yes,' said Mrs. Webster. 'A real barroom juke-box. He gave it to her for an anniversary present, I hear. Isn't it quaint?'

UP ON THE SHED ROOF behind the clothesline, where Rocco's frantic barking had brought her some time ago, Mrs. Tarantino hid her face in one of Bruno's damp shirts and quivered with anger and hurt pride. Her eavesdropping had finally boomeranged. 'Protason' bastards!' she wept. 'Protason' bastards!'

BELOW IN THE GARDEN, as Orena cleared the table for dessert, the conversation became more general. Orena brought candles to the table and lit them. They burned without flickering in the still air. Beyond the candles hovered Orena's white cap and apron. Her black dress, her black face and arms, were almost invisible in the gathering dusk.

Orena wasn't talking tonight. Let the white folks talk. Gabble-gabble-gabble. Just over the courtyard wall, Frankie Gomez had fell and broke his head because white folks was too stingy to fix a balcony rail; and Iris Clark was crying her eyes out; and Dan Clark couldn't do nothin about nothin but wait and see if he would be sued. White folks didn't see what happened right under their noses. Sure, she hadn't told them about the accident. She hadn't had a chance. But even if she had of had a chance, she wouldn't have told them. She was mad. Colored folks couldn't be mad when they talked to white folks. Colored folks had to keep they mouths shut. Gabble-gabble-gabble. Jes lissen at em talk. Them Tuttles comin all the way from New Jersey to make more trouble with their baby crib deliveries when she was bustin a gut to get dinner on time. Gabble-gabble-gabble about colored people's rights. It didn't take them Tuttles to come all the way from New Jersey to talk about colored people's rights. Plenty white folks right here in N'Awlins talked the same way at dinner tables. But nobody did nothin about nothin. Sweet Jesus, she wished they'd quit gobblin and gabblin, and let her go home.

MRS. TARANTINO crept down the stairs from the shed roof, and looked at the door of Bruno's workshop. It was closed. She crouched on the bottom step with her face in her hands. When Rocco came up to her and tried to sit on her feet, she pushed him away and went in the house. Rocco tried to follow her; and

From the shed roof, Mrs. Tarantino could look into . . .

she slammed the door on his nose. His grief subsided gradually. Grief had possessed Mrs. Tarantino up until this time; but as Rocco's yelping died out and she was again aware of cruel voices talking in the Webster garden, her anger flared. So her juke-box was funny, was it? So it bothered Mrs. Webster, did it? Very well.

Mrs. Tarantino slipped a nickel in her juke-box and pressed a key. The lights came on; the record dropped into place. Mrs. Tarantino hugged herself and waited. She had punched the first key her hand had encountered, without looking to see which record would play. She had acted from a terrible need to make her anger heard by those other people, those cruel people who had hurt her so. She had not known that the record which would drop into place under the needle would be 'Eleven Years With the Wrong Woman.' . . . *Mother of God!* Mrs. Tarantino tried to jerk out the wall plug and stop the music; but the plug was behind the juke-box, and the box was too heavy for her to move. She couldn't stop it. . . . Over the singer's lament, she heard a whoop of laughter from the Webster courtyard. That nasty Mr. Tuttle from New Jersey was laughing at her. She had made a laughing-stock of herself.

Mrs. Tarantino bowed her head on her arms. Mother of God, why had she been born so ugly? Why had Bruno Tarantino married her and begotten on her body five daughters who had grown up and left the city instead of remaining near their mother like good Italian girls to console her when she needed consoling? Why could she not have brought into the world one son to protect his mother from insult in her lonely old age? Bruno didn't care what happened to her. What was a woman to do with a man like Bruno? He hadn't even come to the house to eat his supper. He was still in his workshop. . . . *Was* he still there?

Mrs. Tarantino went to the window and peeped through the curtains. She did not hear Bruno enter the kitchen behind her.

He looked at her for a minute, and put his arm around her shoulders.

'Cara sposa,' he said, 'don't play the music tonight, eh?'

At the unexpected gentleness of his voice, Mrs. Tarantino hid her face on her husband's broad chest and cried in earnest. He stroked her hair. The music finally stopped. The colored lights went out.

'Why do you cry?' said Bruno.

'Why did you ever marry me, Bruno Tarantino?'

Bruno thought for a minute. 'I loved you,' he said.

'A woman like me, with the face I got on me, and you could have had so many pretty girls?' Mrs. Tarantino looked up at her husband. 'Look at me, Bruno,' she said. 'Tell me you could love a face like I got.'

'It is a face I love,' he said.

'Why did you hit me this morning?'

'I'm ashamed . . . things trouble a man.'

'What troubles you, Bruno, that it wouldn't help if you confessed the sins on your soul to Father Vela, and promise to not read bad books that ain't on the Index, and love God, and go to Mass?'

Bruno shook his head. Mrs. Tarantino sighed and drew away from him. 'Your supper is waiting,' she said.

When he had finished eating, Bruno returned to his workshop. Mrs. Tarantino saw that he did not put on the light. Then he wasn't reading, and he wasn't working. He must be thinking. Rocco barked, but Mrs. Tarantino paid no attention. She was no longer interested in what she could see or hear from the shed roof. Sooner than hang up clothes on that shed roof, she thought, the clothes could rot.

She wandered through the house and opened the front door. As she opened the door, the street lights blinked on. But there was nothing to see. The street was almost empty at this hour. Mrs. Tarantino closed her door against the lights. She had ironing to do. She might as well do it.

'Holy Mary, Mother of God,' said Mrs. Tarantino, as she worked the hot iron, 'pray for us now . . . pray for us . . . pray for us . . . an make Bruno Tarantino stop thinking.'

JOE ONION was midway along Pirate's Alley when, directly ahead of him, a street lamp came alive and incandescent in the dusk.

After leaving the restaurant, he had buzzed the bell of Neeley's Royal Street rooming-house for five minutes before one of the roomers had thrust her head through an upstairs window and informed him that Neeley had gone across the river to visit a friend in Algiers, and was not expected home until late. Joe took his thumb off the buzzer and stood for a minute undecided what to do. He had several hours before Leah came home. He had better buy her that present. But the uptown stores were closed now; and the antique shops along Royal Street were also closed. He could buy candy or cosmetics in a drugstore; but he didn't want to make Leah a drugstore present; a man would not be remembered very long as the donor of such gifts as these. Somewhere, he must find Leah such a gift as she would never forget; a gift which would make her remember him always from this day on earth. Perhaps, because the idea of gift-buying was associated in his mind with the morning's episode at the French Market, he had remembered the Mexican Shop, retraced his way down Royal Street, and was taking the short cut through Pirate's Alley when the lights came on.

Joe was always aware of the blooming of a city's lights at evening. In every port he had ever visited, no matter what outlandish tongue the people spoke, the lights spoke with the same tongue, one he understood. A hand pressed a button at a power station. As swiftly as the released spark flashed along the cables into the hair-fine filaments of a city's myriad light globes, Joe's thoughts traced the impulse back along the way it had come; down the heavy insulated wiring inside the lamp post; through the underground or aerial cables, as the case might be, to some central power station; and from there to the dynamos. Sometimes, the power came from a natural source: from some great river roaring through the spillways of a dam. He liked to think that men had given a river a voice of light.

And so, when the lights came on, he stopped to hear the brief ejaculation flung into the evening sky.

HELP! the lights cried for the city to the darkening sky.

IN THE SOFT DRINK AND HAMBURGER STAND in Audubon Park, Placide Giraud had been spending the most frantic hour of his life since the war. When the girl in the blue raincoat had come out of her first swoon, she had said that she often had pains; that the doctor had told her not to be alarmed; that the baby was not due for two weeks yet. Now that she had found somebody to look after her, she had assumed an air of stoic fortitude which Placide, a bachelor, found maddening. She was hungry. She wanted another hamburger. He bought her another hamburger, and sat on the edge of her chair while she ate it. He felt in the predicament of a man in a crowd who has stumbled across, and innocently picked up, a hand grenade with the pin pulled out. There was nowhere to throw it, and any instant it might go off. There was always a chance that a stray hand grenade might be a dud; but this girl was no dud; she was primed and potent with trouble.

By the time she had finished the second hamburger, the proprietor wanted to close his shop. He did so, and drove away.

Once out-of-doors, the girl promptly had another pain. Placide looked about him for a telephone or a taxicab, but none was in sight. Recovering, the girl had suggested that he take her to his apartment, where she could wash up. He replied that he lived miles away, and the plan would not be feasible.

It was growing dark. He was walking her toward the St. Charles entrance of the park when a third pain knocked her off her feet. Placide held her hand, and looked about him frantically. Not a human being, not a car was in sight. He strained his eyes through the gathering dusk.

Suddenly, the city lights came on.

Perhaps he had called for help. Perhaps the sound he heard when the lights came on was the echo of his own voice. Anyhow, the call for help brought results. Nearly a quarter of a mile away, a park lamp flashed on a yellow taxicab just passing beneath it. The cab was rolling very slowly—to Placide's distracted eyes, as if the dusk had bemused it—a great, kindly, varnished animal lumbering eyeless on the winding driveway, sniffing at flowers in the flower-beds. Placide called again. The taxi heard. It stopped, rolled backwards toward them, and stopped again. A man in a yellow cap jumped out.

A WANDERING BEETLE dived into the lamp in Pirate's Alley, and fell to the pavement at Joe Onion's feet. Joe contemplated the beetle.

'Young man!' called a voice through the fence of St. Anthony's garden.

Joe went on contemplating the beetle.

'Young man!'

'Now listen, Father,' said Joe to the black-garbed figure regarding him through the iron fence at the corner of the garden. 'Bacon says there are many degrees of strength and weakness in flame and ignited bodies, but no diligent inquiry has been made in this respect, and we must therefore pass it over hastily.'

'Young man, I believe you're intoxicated, but would you mind handing me that rubber bone my dog just tossed through the fence behind you?'

'Of all flames, that of spirits of wine appears to be the most gentle. But motion increases heat. The harder metals are not dissolved or melted by steady, quiet fire, without the aid of the bellows or the blowpipe. I am of the harder metals, Father. Ever read Bacon?'

'Be that as it may,' said Father Vela, 'if you would be so kind as to hand me that rubber bone, you'd save me a trip clear around the block. There's no gate on this side of the garden. . . . Be still, Tony,' he said to the young police dog that was trying to squirm through the fence to retrieve his toy.

'Heat with regard to the human senses and touch is various and relative, so that lukewarm water appears hot if the hand be cold, and cold if the hand be hot. My hand must be cold, for the water appears hot . . . pardon me, Father, what were you saying?'

'My dog's bone,' said Father Vela. 'His rubber bone. He threw it through the fence. It's right behind you. Would you be so kind as to pick it up and hand it to me?'

'I appear to be in love, Father,' said Joe. 'What do you think about love?'

'Love is the divine law of God, my son. Will you kindly hand me my dog's rubber bone?'

'Certainly, Father. Glad to oblige.' Joe searched for the toy, found it, and returned it through the fence. 'I believe I'm in love,' he said. 'At least, I appear to be in that state of emotional ignition.'

'Something else seems to have ignited you, my son,' said Father Vela, smiling in spite of himself. 'You'd better go home and sleep it off before you get in trouble.'

They parted, and walked in opposite directions—Father Vela toward the far end of the garden and Joe Onion toward the French Market.

The Mexican shopkeeper was just closing up when Joe arrived. He remembered Joe from the morning, and offered him a cigarette.

'Present for a lady,' said Joe.

'A reeng, no? A leetle box, no? Some deeshes, maybe? A grass skirt, no? Wat you want?'

Joe pointed. Hanging on the back wall of the shop, he saw what he wanted. Except for the serapes and the straw mats, it was the biggest, brightest thing in the shop. It would make Leah Webster laugh.

FATHER VELA snapped the leash on Tony's collar. The garden was too muddy to let him run free any longer. The heavy rain had washed soil from around the roots of the flowers; some of them lay over on the grass. They would have to be staked, thought Father Vela, bending above his favorites, the heavy-headed dahlias. Tony tugged at the leash and begged for his bone, but Father Vela kept it safe in his pocket. He had been teaching the dog to retrieve; but lessons were over for today. This was the hour for meditation.

Priest and dog paced up and down the garden. Several bucketfuls of soil had washed from the garden into the alley, Father Vela noted with worried eyes. Pirate's Alley was marked down the middle with a fan-shaped, earthy streak where the subsiding water had deposited sediment. Embroidered in the sediment under the lamp post, like traces left by some prehistoric animal, lay the footprints of the irreverent, intoxicated young man plainly pointing in the wrong direction for the salvation of his soul.

In the live oaks and the magnolia, sparrows were settling down for the night. The leaves rustled. Tony began to jump and bark. Father Vela pulled hard on the leash. It was a shame not to be able to turn the dog loose, for his powerful young body needed exercise; and it was also a shame that he himself could not be allowed to meditate in peace. It was difficult to meditate with sixty pounds of unprincipled flesh and bone tugging you along at a trot and tangling its leash around your legs; but he was very fond of Tony, and somehow—he still didn't know quite how it had come about—the task of training and exercising the dog had fallen entirely upon his shoulders. Young Father Poole had no patience with dogs. In any case, it was difficult to meditate in St. Anthony's Garden. The spiked fence might keep out the bodies of intruders; but it could not keep out their voices and the sight of them—angry, intoxicated, dawdling in doorways to make love, drawing knives, being chased by policemen, making lewd jokes and gestures with their hands—laughing, quarreling, weeping. On both sides of the garden where he walked to meditate, the world streamed past him morning and evening. This morning and again this evening, his meditations had been interrupted. A quiet place, a garden enclosed by thick, high walls, was what he wanted. Even the poorest of his parishioners owned this blessing, but not he . . . God's will be done.

Plop!

Tony, barking loudly at the last of the settling sparrows, had dragged Father Vela under the oak trees. The sparrows had dirtied his hat again, the dirty things. He moved hastily into the open, wiped his hat with his handkerchief, and put it on his head again. Through the open doors of the Cathedral, the thunder of young Father Poole's fine voice pronouncing benediction rolled out into the warm dusk. *Dominus vobiscum . . . et cum spiritu tuo . . .* Father Vela crossed himself. It was over now. The day was over. Along the alleys on both sides of the garden walked the faithful toward supper and bed.

His black clothes invisible to his parishioners in the gathering dusk, Father Vela watched sharply from under his hat brim . . . Mrs. Gallagher . . . Iris Clark . . . Mrs. Luchesi . . . Mrs. Balducci . . . Mrs. Duperrier . . . Mrs. Zupp . . . Mrs. Gelatti, and her old mother . . . the five Gemmill sisters, still unmarried, poor things . . . Mr. and Mrs. Anthony Donati. A fine man, Anthony Donati, a fine upstanding Catholic.

The dusk was growing so deep he had trouble recognizing them, but still he could hear their voices and footsteps in the alleyways. Tony whined softly, and grew quiet. How quiet the world was! For a brief minute, how perfect, how still! How friendly, with lights burning in the windows, and the smells of good food floating on the air! . . . *Dominus vobiscum . . . et cum spiritu tuo.* . . . May the deep waters of peaceful sleep roll over the souls of men. . . . But here came another, the last of all to leave the Cathedral, the woman known as Mea Culpa around the French Market. She flapped under the lamp in Pirate's Alley like a rusty moth. She had confessed her theft of hairpins from Grant's Store, and the priest had given her a light penance, only an Our Father and five Hail Marys, admonishing her not to appear in public with her head uncovered for a month. But he had made this stipulation before, and she had not obeyed him. She was sinfully proud of her hair. Poor woman, she could not seem to shake off this vanity of her dreadful past. She longed to make a Perfect Act of Contrition, but he doubted that she ever would. Her fear of hell was much greater than her love of God. . . . Yes, she had taken her shawl off her head. . . . Now she was gone. . . . But what of those who had not come? Frankie Gomez had died in the Church; but old Mrs. Laurent had died this afternoon with no help but the earthly counsel of Shakespeare. She was said to have gripped the book so tightly they had scarcely been able to get it out of her hands. And what of Bruno Tarantino?

Tony pulled on his leash. 'Heel, Tony,' said Father Vela in

a tired voice. He let himself out of the garden and crossed St. Anthony's Alley to the Parish House. Now, he would eat supper.

IT WAS DARK in Bruno Tarantino's workshop. The door was closed. Bruno had been sitting for a long while on his tool chest, thinking. For a man to perceive where duty lay, and for a man to do this duty he perceived, were two entirely different matters.

Ay Dio, if it were only a simple matter of going to see Gomez. But it was not so simple. He, Bruno Tarantino, had beaten up some good friends in defense of the right to mind his own business. Minding his own business had become a veritable dedication. If he got up off this tool chest and went around the block to try to persuade Gomez not to sue Dan Clark, he would be changing his way of life. What was a man to do?

The little blue books of Mr. Haldeman-Julius, hidden in the tool chest on which he sat, were no good in this emergency. Inside the tool chest, inside the blue covers with which Mr. Haldeman-Julius had provided them, Plato, Spinoza, Bergson, Nietzsche, Confucius, Schopenhauer, Darwin, St. Francis of Assisi, and others were making a terrific clamor. To Bruno Tarantino at this moment they sounded like old women on the sidewalk in their black coats, all arguing at once about the best cut of beef. Everybody contradicted everybody else in as loud a voice as possible. All philosophers talked about truth and duty and reality, but none of them could agree on what it was. Bruno couldn't stand it any longer.

He jumped to his feet and stretched his hand above his head in search of the hanging-light globe. He could not find it. He felt for it in the dark. The globe swung from a cord in the center of the room, a little to one side of the skiff on its trestles. He believed himself to be beneath it, but he could not find it with his hand. He moved, stumbling in the dark, both hands lifted and groping. One of his hands in motion grazed the globe and set it swinging. Angrily, with both hands, he sought to capture it, but it evaded him like a live thing, alert and malicious. He lunged after it, hit it, and set it swinging in a different direction. His foot slipped on the drifted oleander petals on the damp bricks, and he kicked over the bucket of green paint with which he had been painting the skiff. Cursing, sweating, treading on his own feet, lifted hands fighting the dark, he trod a circle beside the skiff. The globe in passing kissed one of his fingers; and he stood still, breathing heavily, knowing that if he remained quiet, it would complete its crazy arc and come to him of its own accord. With hands lifted above his head in an attitude of supplication, he waited. He felt the globe swing past him, and moved his hands a little to the left. The globe swung gently toward him, and nestled in the cage of his fingers. He turned on the light.

The bottoms of his pants, his shoes, his hands, were spattered with green paint. The floor was a sticky mess. Dio maledetto, what a lot of trouble a man made for himself when he thought too much about truth and duty and reality! If he had had a quarter of his wits about him, turning on the light would have been a simple matter. He would have stepped to the door, opened it, stepped back, and seen the light globe silhouetted against the gray dusk of the courtyard. Or he would have struck a match.

Bruno looked down at his shoes. Green paint on a man's shoes was real enough. He would have to clean it off before he went to see Gomez. What a lot of books had been written in order to tell a man to clean his shoes and visit Gomez in the next block.

With a rag and a can of turpentine, Bruno set to work.

DAYLIGHT fled through the streets, across the parks and the pale green marshes. The cuckoo in City Park was well lost now in the inky blackness of the cypresses. Dew was beginning to fall on the old cannon and bronze statues that guarded the city: on General Beauregard at City Park entrance; on Henry Clay and Benjamin Franklin in Lafayette Square; on General Andrew Jackson in Jackson Square; on General Robert E. Lee in Lee Circle, with his folded arms and far-off gazing eyes; on Jefferson Davis, and the plaque to the Confederate dead; on the World War Memorial in Audubon Park; on John James Audubon, standing quietly on his pedestal among the trees, watching and listening with pencil and notebook in his hands.

All around John James Audubon, now that the people had gone away and the park was quiet, things were happening which could not be heard through the day. A soft rustle, a sigh as trampled grass blades straightened themselves, and thirsty roots gripped the ground with new fervor. A sound of flowing sap and breathing leaves. The infinitesimal footprints of insect wanderers through grass roots and up and down the bark of trees. A twig snapped. A gray squirrel ran along a branch. A beetle embraced a piece of popcorn, and sought to carry it away. The moon rose. A tunneling rat broke through the earth's wet crust and shied at his shadow. Wings beat. A mockingbird coasted from a treetop to Audubon's head, dropped his wings, swelled his throat, and began to sing. The moon climbed higher, sparkling on the river, slanting on the dewy roofs of the flat city in the bright bend of the river, pricking the park into black-and-silver shadow. Another mockingbird answered the first; and they sang together.

6

MOONLIGHT glittered on the blank windowpanes of office buildings, and shone in Ronnie Bilbo's eyes as he glanced up briefly from the canyon of the street. Ronnie was on his way to the Parish Jail to free his half-brother, Cooter, revenge injustice, and confound the world. Wrapped in the invisible cloak of Superman, he swaggered through the crowds and slunk fearfully through the open places where he could see his shadow.

The knife he had picked up in Pirate's Alley was in his belt. He kept his hand on the hilt of the knife, and looked frequently over his shoulder. Every time he looked, he saw only his own familiar shadow, very small, and blacker than himself; but any minute it might change. The invisible cloak of Superman was a loose fit as yet, but any minute Ronnie expected to find himself filling it. He was still young enough to believe in magic when he saw a grub pop its gray jacket and emerge a white butterfly; and he felt such a strange bursting tension inside himself, as if his brown skin could scarcely hold him, such a deepening sense of portentous change in his person and his entire life, that he could not help believing a similar magic might occur in himself.

The pretty little seven-year-old mulatto boy who had moved Mrs. Cansino's watermelons, who knew how to dodge through traffic, and how to speak softly and persuasively to dice, knew that he was a fool to be going where he was going, with the plan he had in mind. But there was another Ronnie whom even his grandmother, Clara Bilbo, as much as she loved him, did not know. This was a boy who needed to believe that his own inarticulate need for something mighty and beneficent to believe in would be fulfilled. In spite of his terror, this need was great enough to be propelling him toward that dread place, the Parish Jail. And all the time he did not believe in magic; he was merely desperately willing to believe.

He stood across from the jail, and looked up and down the street; he sweated and shivered, and wriggled his toes, and wished that he could talk to somebody. 'Ain scairt,' he told himself. 'Whut de ole debbils kin do me, nohow? Dey gotta ketch me fust.' The sound of his own voice gave him more courage. He scowled. With diligent effort, he collected enough saliva in his dry mouth to spit. He hitched up his belt, and put his hand on his knife. Reconnoitering carefully, he slid across the street behind a passing streetcar, and crouched in the shadow of a car parked at the curb in front of the jail.

A man and a woman passed along the sidewalk, their heels clicking briskly. The man laid his hand on his stomach and belched . . . 'Ole rubbah guts,' said Ronnie. 'Bet e had im a good suppah.' . . . With a swish of tires and a wave of warm air, a colored delivery boy pedaled swiftly past . . . 'At ole boy got im a good wheel. Bet it ain hisn. Sho look scairt, passin de jailhouse.' . . . Four white schoolgirls passed with linked arms in a warm ripple of perfume . . . 'MM-m-m,' said Ronnie, 'dem chippies sho smells good.' . . . An old man stumbled by. He was talking to himself.

'Mama mia?' said the old man. 'Mama mia?'

Ronnie rolled his eyes. As far as he could see in both directions, the sidewalk was empty.

He slid from behind the parked car, stepped up on the sidewalk, and stared at the moon-blanched walls of the jail. 'Ain bothin nobody,' he reassured himself. 'Jes standin here. Ain . . .' He had not dreamed the jail was so big, so solid. Where was Cooter? Where was the body that had warmed him on chilly winter nights? The strong, black older brother of whom he had been half ashamed, half proud? Nothing around here looked or smelled like Cooter. He was utterly alone. Shrinking, he looked down at his shadow. It was still the same shadow that had followed him all the way. Dwarfed and crooked, it lay on the sidewalk—as black as Cooter, much blacker than himself. Ronnie clenched his hand on the hilt of his knife, and prayed. *In the sky a rush of wings, a flash of flame, he is coming, he is here!* SUPERMAN!

Behind him, a car door opened. Ronnie leaped into the air, his feet already running before he hit the ground. But a long arm reached for him. A large hand closed on the back of his neck.

'Whoa, bubba, whoa! Where you goin in such a hurry? What you got there? Knife, eh? I'm a sonofagun!'

The policeman began to laugh. Holding Ronnie by the scruff of the neck, he took the knife from his nerveless fingers and boosted him up the jailhouse steps into a bright room, where another policeman sat reading behind a desk.

'What you got there, Daugherty?' The man at the desk grinned at Ronnie over his spectacles.

'Dam if I know. I found it on the sidewalk with this.' Daugherty tossed the knife on the desk.

The man at the desk tested the blade with his thumb and made a few passes in the air. 'Good knife,' he said. 'What's your name, little nigger?'

Ronnie dangled from the large hand that held him like a limp twist of yarn. He could not speak nor move.

'Cat got your tongue, eh?'

The hand that held him, shook him. Ronnie licked his lips and made an unintelligible sound.

'Come on, little nigger, what's your name?'

'Hell, he ain't got no name. These niggers breedin like mosqui-toes all over the place, they ain't got no time to worry about names.' Daugherty shook with laughter. Ronnie quivered with the mirth of the thick body behind him.

'You got a mama and papa? You got a family? What you doin on the street with a knife? Don't you know niggers ain't allowed to carry knives this big? Where'd you get this knife?'

'Won it,' quavered Ronnie.

'Say *sir!*'

'How, won it?'

'Shootin craps—suh.'

Both men rocked with laughter. The man with the spectacles took them off, wiped his eyes, and put them back on. 'What you doin in fronta the jail with a knife, Half Pint?'

'Nuffin.'

The hand squeezed tighter on his neck. 'Say *sir* when you talk to a white man, you little black bastard. Go on! Say it!'

'Yassuh.'

'What was he doin, Daugherty?'

'Search me. There he was, spraddlin his legs an talkin to him-self with a murderous weapon in his hands. Creepin Jesus, he like to scared the pants off me. Big as a corncob pipe, an already carryin a knife! . . . Hey, bubba, what was you gonna do, eh? Tryin to slip somebody a knife, eh? Creepin Jesus, what we gonna do with him, Jim? He's dangerous!'

'Hmm-m,' said the man behind the desk.

'What we gonna do with the likes of you?' said Daugherty, giving Ronnie another shake. 'What we gonna do?'

'Say, bubba, can you dance?'

Ronnie rolled his eyes from one grinning face to the other. The face of the man who held him seemed enormous. The teeth glistened. The red jowls quivered and shook. The belly shook. The chest heaved. Ronnie struggled feebly.

'Sure, he can dance. I never seen a little nigger yet that couldn't dance. They come outa their mammy cuttin a rug. Git hot, bubba. Come on, git hot. Dance, an we'll turn you loose. Don't dance, an we'll take this knife an cut out your tongue an skin you alive. Dance, bubba, dance!'

Dangling from the large hand, Ronnie began to dance. His feet moved feebly. His face was ashen.

'Git hot, bubba, git hot! Put some pepper in it. We'll skin you alive!'

The man behind the desk clapped his hands. Daugherty began to clap, striking his hard hands together like washboards. Ronnie's feet shuffled faster and faster. His pants sagged. His face dripped sweat and silent tears. He snuffled the tears up his nose and into his throat, and tasted salt. He wiped his nose on the back of his hand and danced faster, faster to the quickening rhythm of clapping hands. Daugherty's red face swelled until it filled the room. Suddenly, a foot caught Ronnie in the seat of his pants, and he felt himself scrambling through the air and down the steps. He rolled on the sidewalk, bounded to his feet, and ran. The last thing he saw was the hilarious red face in the lighted doorway. His running feet beat a new rhythm on the sidewalk . . . *I hate you, I hate you, goddamn you, I hate you* . . . His knees and elbows were bruised. His breath whistled between his teeth. Holding up his too-big britches with one hand, weeping with fear and shame and gigantic hatred, he ran barefooted through the hot moonlight. A frowsy dog snarled at him. A garbage truck bouncing out of an alley nearly ran him down . . . *Little nigger . . . little nigger . . . that was all he was.*

DURING THE TIME Ronnie had been reconnoitering the front of the jail and dancing for the policemen, Cooter Bilbo had been lying in his cell trying to reconstruct what had happened to him. Yesterday afternoon he had been playing mumblety-peg, a silly kid's game, on the sidewalk with a friend of Ronnie's, when a squad car pulled up beside him with four policemen in it. Two of them had jumped out, said he was under arrest, and grabbed him. The knife with which he had been playing was in his hand. He cut at a man's arm. The man turned him loose, and he ran. They hollered at him, but he couldn't stop. They shot at his legs and missed him; but he stumbled and fell. He was scrambling to his feet when something hit him on the head.

Cooter felt of the place on his head that was still crusted with dried blood, and scowled at the shadows thrown by the hall light on the cell wall. Cooter was a tall, thin boy who had grown too fast. He seemed all bones under his black skin, and the bones ached. They had beaten him plenty. They hadn't stopped till he cried, and said a lot of things he couldn't remember now; and then they had carried him from the Precinct to the Parish Jail. He was scared, and lonesome for his grandmother. They said he was a thief, but he wasn't. He knew about other colored boys, and white boys, too, who swiped big things like tires, garage tools, second-hand clothes and ladies' purses; but he had never swiped anything in his life except bananas. Maybe a few snowballs off the snowball man's pushcart when he wasn't looking. Maybe some little chunks of ice off the iceman's truck when he went into a house. And one book. Taking that book was wrong, but he had wanted to read it, and couldn't get it any other way. He had made Ronnie, who could sometimes pass as white, go into the Public Library and swipe a book on deep-sea diving. Once he had taken the shoelaces out of a drunk man's shoes asleep in Pirate's Alley; and once he had taken a Mardi Gras mask off a drugstore counter; but all he had ever taken from any grocery store had been a package of powdered limeade one hot summer day when he was about Ronnie's age. What was going to happen to him now? When he got out of high school, he had wanted to go to Dillard, the colored University in New Orleans, and study to be a doctor. But nobody could learn to be a doctor when he was in jail.

Cooter turned over on his stomach, hid his face in his arms, and cried quietly to himself. He must have fallen asleep and dreamed, for suddenly he found himself sitting bolt upright, his throat taut from screaming.

'Fa Chrissake, boy,' said a disgusted voice. A body flopped heavily, sighed, and resumed its bubbling snore. Somewhere, a toilet flushed; a door closed. A streetcar passed, clanging its bell. Automobile horns babbled on the street. Out on the river, ships spoke to one another.

'What time is it?' Cooter said. He repeated the question several times, in growing panic.

The snore stopped. The snore said, 'Huhn?' in a sleepy voice.

'What time is it?'

'Ain no time fa worryin whut time is it,' said the disgusted voice. 'Hesh up dat big mouf, an let a man sleep dat know whut sleepin means.'

'I can't sleep. What they gonna do with me?' Cooter tried to keep his voice down, but it cracked in a scared falsetto.

'Huhn! you is sho a stupid boy. Wait an see, son, wait an see.'

Cooter Bilbo waited. A clock that seemed to be inside his head ticked off the minutes. *Tick-tock, tick-tock.* He shook his head bewilderedly. Where was the dam ole clock anyhow? Was it inside or outside? It ticked louder and faster, but failed to disclose its whereabouts. *Tick-tock, tick-tock, tick-tock.* He struck himself on the ears with the palms of his hands. The ticking accelerated until it became a buzzing whine; and he couldn't tell if it were outside in the city night or inside his own aching skull. Pictures slid across his eyeballs under the closed lids. His grandmother knelt before the fireplace on a winter morning, sifting clinkers from cold ashes to burn again. From the cold clinkers, the round shining face of his girl, Laurie, appeared black and rich as good coal above the starched white collar of her nurse-maid's uniform. Laurie's face disintegrated into a swirl of dark faces on South Rampart Street on a hot Saturday night; and these dark faces in turn faded, disintegrated, became a har-monica, a twenty-two rifle, an old stethoscope in a pawnshop window; a green slack suit; a pair of two-tone shoes he had wanted to buy. But he hadn't bought the green slack suit. He had gone on wearing the outgrown sweatshirt with the dim pic-ture of Mickey Mouse across the chest, which his grandmother couldn't boil out. He had had to wear it because it was the only shirt he owned. He had hated it. Mickey Mouse, symbol of hate and bewildered frustration, became the skeleton in the window of the Medical Supply Shop on Tulane Avenue. And this cold omen of mortality became, as his mind sought hastily to warm and reassure itself, the sun-heated walls and sidewalks of Bur-gundy Street; and the sight of his grandmother rocking quietly in her hide-bottomed rocking chair on hot summer evenings, stirring the air with a palmleaf fan.

The pictures moved faster and faster across Cooter's eyeballs. They were melting together, becoming confused and dreamy—pictures no longer, but a dim memory of childhood lost to him forever beyond the jailhouse walls. Sleep was finally overtaking Cooter Bilbo. The *Sipsey* tugboat, whose hoarse voice he could always recognize, moved away from the docks and out into the middle of the river. Her orange stack grew smaller and smaller in the distance. Yellow water washed over her deck. Heavier and heavier she grew; deeper and deeper she sank into the dark current that never stopped flowing; into the fear of unseen, un-known things.

OUTSIDE IN THE CITY, as well as in Cooter's head, the night was sliding in a faster tempo before the inevitable lull of sleep. The day had woven a pattern of threads between people, some of whom had not known each other's names or faces in the morning; and, although they lived in the same city for the rest of their lives, might never happen to cross each other's path again. But today, some had touched in passing; and because of the brief contact their lives were changed.

BLACK IN THE MOONLIGHT, a Japanese freighter loaded with scrap iron, aided by a tugboat with an orange stack, moved away from the wharf and out into the middle of the river. The tug backed away; the freighter continued alone down the river, headed for Yokohama. Its wake rocked the Algiers ferryboat on which Neeley, proprietor of the Royal Street rooming-house, was returning from a visit with a friend. Neeley stood at the ferry rail, angry clear through. Her friend's husband had tried to date her in the hall. His wife had overheard. There had been a scene. Neeley watched the disappearing lights of the freighter and wished she was on it, heading for a South Sea island where nobody expected you to have morals, not even your best friend —which thought sent her to wondering if that nice, funny little Leah Webster had ever found Joe Onion. She had certainly wanted him.

LEAH WEBSTER, in the ticket booth of a neighborhood movie on Elysian Fields Avenue, wanted nothing now but her glasses, left lying on her dresser that morning. Her eyes ached. So much for vanity. She knew that she had forgotten the glasses on purpose, because she had thought she would meet Joe. Attracted by the bright Neon lights that advertised Two-Gun Fagan in *Two-Gun Fagan*, and Charles Boyer and Danielle Dar-

rieux in *Mayerling*, insects and a few late customers for romance
rapped on the glass-enclosed booth. The sidewalk under the sign
was littered with crawling June bugs. The booth was very hot.
Leah kicked off her slippers, and ran her fingers through her
damp hair. The knowledge that had come to her while she
looked at her face in the beauty shop that afternoon lay in her
mind like an unwrapped package. It would still be there tomorrow, and tomorrow she would open and examine it. Tonight,
she felt too tired to fumble with the string. When somebody
rapped softly on the wall of the booth, Leah looked up, startled,
thinking it might be Joe. But it was only Mr. Papadakis, who
was leaving the show early tonight. Mr. Papadakis delivered
himself of another hopeless comment about the weather, and
took his leave. There was still a chance that Joe might come,
Leah thought, but it was almost too late.

FOR QUITE A DIFFERENT REASON, somebody else was
just voicing the words which lay unspoken in Leah's mind.

In a quiet garden on Prytania Street, Mrs. Budd, the mother
of Georgie Webster's friend, Lucille, was just saying, 'D'you
think it's too late to catch the last show? *Mayerling* is back in
town at that neighborhood movie on Elysian Fields Avenue. I
wouldn't mind seeing it again.'

Doctor Budd looked at his wrist watch in the moonlight. 'It's
ten o'clock,' he said. 'It would take us at least twenty minutes to
get there and park the car. I'm afraid it's too late.'

'Never mind,' said Mrs. Budd. 'It was just an idea to pass the
time for Sally. I don't think she wants to go, anyhow.'

'I'm too comfortable to move,' their hostess said.

In the quiet garden, all three of them were waiting. Early in
the evening, their host had been summoned from the dinner
table to deliver a baby arriving ahead of schedule. A short while

ago, a nurse had telephoned from the hospital to say that the girl was far along in labor and everything was going well. The Budds expected their host home in time to play a little bridge; and so they were waiting. They sipped highballs, and slapped at desultory mosquitoes. Lucille, said Doctor Budd, had managed to find herself a clump of poison ivy (Heaven knows where, but trust Lucille to find it), and now she would be in bed for several days, and the neighborhood could relax. And where, he wondered, were Willis and Katherine Tuttle? who were supposed to have arrived in town that afternoon, but who had not yet telephoned. Mrs. Budd suggested that Doctor Budd call the Webster house and find out what was what—but Doctor Budd was too comfortable to move. Instead, he remarked that Willis Tuttle was a fine young man; very progressive in his views; possibly a bit on the radical side; but he was awfully young. Mrs. Budd laughed, and replied that she had heard he had grown a large mustache in order to impress his colleagues in the Sociology Department; but, after all, he couldn't be more than twenty-three or twenty-four. Interested in the Negro problem, she had heard. Believed that racial chauvinism was to blame for the South's economic ills. This was certainly true, said Doctor Budd. Pay a large slice of your laboring class a less than living wage and the standard of living all over that particular section would be lowered—as the South had proved. But what, really, could be done about the Negro?

All three of the people in the garden wondered about this, and none of them knew. Give the Negro his equal rights in his present uneducated condition and he'd run hog-wild, and you'd have the same sort of situation the White Leaguers had had to break up during Reconstruction days. Gradual education was the only answer, said Doctor Budd. Education not only of the Negroes, but of the whites. It would take generations. How the Negro was to receive equal educational opportunities without equal political representation was hard to say. He believed that the Negro should be allowed his vote; but how was this possible in the poll-tax States? The whole problem was a mess. One never arrived anywhere in these discussions. Of course, said Mrs. Budd, the Negro was a human being and, as such, had rights. Lynching was an unforgivable outrage—but, on the other hand, how would you like for Lucille to have to sit beside a little colored boy in school? Doctor Budd replied that Lucille might learn manners from colored children; but there was nothing you could do for the present about Jim Crow in the South. The South remembered Reconstruction days too bitterly, he said. Fear and a sense of guilt lay deep in the blood. A purely economic basis? Well, it was hard to say. Education over a period of time seemed the only answer. How it was to be accomplished, he didn't know. The only thing he did know for certain was that the Negro was here, and here to stay. You couldn't forget him for a minute, and neither could you seem to do anything about him.

'Let's change the subject,' said the Budds' hostess, 'or I'll get in such a swivet I can't sleep.'

Mrs. Budd tactfully changed the subject. The Websters were nice people, she said. Their little girl, Georgie, was Lucille's best friend. Georgie was a funny kid, rather pathetic in a way. She resembled her mother. It would be interesting to see how the Websters and the Tuttles got along together. Doctor Budd interrupted to say that Merlin Webster was nobody's fool; he had a good business head on him; he'd make himself a pot of money some day.

The fountain splashed and sparkled in the moonlight. A clump of white butterfly lilies sent waves of sweetness across the garden. Crickets chirruped in the bamboo hedge. The Budds' hostess looked at the moon and thought about her husband delivering another woman's baby.

'Oh, by the way,' she said, aloud. 'Have you heard the rumor going around about Preston Dillon?'

'It's no rumor,' said Doctor Budd. 'It's the gospel truth. He's a dead duck—implicated beyond any possibility of clearing himself. It came out in court today. I heard on good authority that Rogge'll have Preston by the short hairs before the week is out.'

'Wasn't he interested in Leah Webster for a time?'

'I believe he was. But they couldn't make up their minds— or, rather, I imagine that Preston couldn't.'

'Old Mrs. Laurent always made up his mind for him, didn't she? What a shame!'

'Too bad she died . . . poor Preston . . . he did adore his aunt . . . I wonder what he's doing tonight?'

'Maybe you ought to give him a ring,' said Mrs. Budd to her husband.

But Doctor Budd had no idea what he could say to a man in such a predicament as Preston Dillon; and, besides, he felt too comfortable to move.

PRESTON DILLON wouldn't have come to the telephone, even if Doctor Budd had called him. Just now, in the old Laurent house on St. Charles Avenue, he was walking his bedroom floor with a pistol in one hand and his Aunt Claudie's volume of Shakespeare's Sonnets in the other. Aunt Claudie was dead. Without her, Preston wished that he, too, were dead. It would have been a good thing if he had never been born. He held the gun at his temple; but he couldn't pull the trigger. He went on pacing the floor. If only Aunt Claudie were here to tell him what to do, he thought . . . but maybe she had left him a last sharp word of advice concealed in Shakespeare's Sonnets. He ruffled the pages in an agony of haste. Like a child looking up prophecies in the Bible, he chose a page at random and stared at the lines until the print focused.

> But be contented: when that fell arrest
> Without all bail shall carry me away . . .

He groaned. Aunt Claudie had spoken. Nobody could save him now. Rogge would send him to jail.

Biting the inside of his cheek, Dillon walked to a window and looked out. Directly in front of his house, he saw a man standing under a street lamp, consulting a slip of white paper. Dillon drew back quickly, turned off the light, picked up the pistol with trembling fingers, and looked again. The man looked suspicious. Was he a detective, a stool-pigeon, an assassin hired by his business associates to do away with him before he could talk?

But the man put the paper in his pocket, and sauntered away. Dillon began to breathe again. As it had happened to his aunt that afternoon, when the Western Union messenger boy had failed to ring the doorbell, and she had opened her eyes to see a man merely waiting for a streetcar, he felt a renewal of hope. He was still a free man. Nobody had pinned anything on him yet. He went into the bathroom and washed his face with cold water.

THE MAN whom Dillon had seen from his window was Placide Giraud, again passing the old Laurent house—this time, on his way home from Touro Infirmary; and unaware of the fact that he had served as a symbol of hope to two persons in the same house, at different times that day. He had seen the girl in the blue raincoat safely in her doctor's hands; wired the girl's husband; remained for a while to see that things were going all right with her; and then had started home. He hoped to catch a streetcar somewhere along the way.

Placide could not help but wonder if he had done the right thing in wiring the girl's husband; but, in his experience, he had found that when everything he had learned seemed of no value and he couldn't see his way ahead, it was best to disregard all complications and tell the simple truth. Sometimes the hard and simple truth, and only that, could be trusted to scour away the miasmic sentimentalities which most young people believed they could not live without—and suddenly discovered themselves well rid of. He could not have told the girl in the blue raincoat how to pocket her losses with good grace and go on from where she was; she would have to discover it for herself through living. He hoped that she and her husband would discover it together.

The slip of paper which Placide had taken from his pocket to consult under the street lamp was the reminder he had written that afternoon in the Public Library to buy a pint of sour cream for his Beef Stroganoff.

There would be no Beef Stroganoff tonight, thought Placide Giraud. It was much too late; but never mind. He could buy the sour cream tomorrow. It was never too late for a person like himself to buy sour cream.

IN THE DELIVERY ROOM at Touro Infirmary, Doctor Budd's colleague was just assisting a child into the world; a healthy child with a good pair of lungs, he noted with professional satisfaction. The girl had had a remarkably short and easy time of it. Very soon now, he could go home to his wife and his dinner guests, and play bridge. He glanced at the girl's face, and saw her looking at the baby with a strange expression.

'Is that my baby?' she said. 'Let me see.'

Doctor Budd's colleague might have assured the girl till the sky fell that she had had an easy time of it—but she knew differently. She had worked for that baby harder than she had ever worked for anything in her life. She had earned it; and even if it did look like a monkey, she wanted it. She wanted it more than she had ever wanted anything in her life. She made a motion toward the baby in the nurse's arms, and began to laugh weakly. Neither Doctor Budd's colleague nor the nurse was aware of it, of course, but the girl, her exhausted mind playing tricks on her, was not in the delivery room at all; she was back in Audubon Park, watching Mr. Graber watch the monkeys. If Mr. Graber hadn't watched the monkeys, she wouldn't have had hysterics. If she hadn't had hysterics, Placide Giraud would never have followed her. If Placide Giraude had never followed her and taken care of her, the baby would probably not have been born.

IN AN ATTIC ROOM on Ursuline Street in the French Quarter, Mr. Graber, busy on the second volume of his autobiography, looked up for a minute to rest his eyes, and perceived that the moon was shining on him through his naked window. He rose to pull down the shade. The windowsills swarmed with cockroaches, waving their antennae in the moonlight. Mr. Graber killed them all and began Chapter Three, which dealt with infiltration. He jotted down a few swift notes, and paused to review his thoughts and polish his prose before committing it to posterity; but the boy in Grant's Store came between him and the paper. Mr. Graber nibbled his fountain-pen, and gazed fretfully at the cracked window shade. Spies had planted that boy at the soda fountain in order to catch him. The city was full of spies. What was that sound in the hall?

Mr. Graber tiptoed to the door and listened. A rat squeaked. The bumping noise had obviously been made by a rat dragging a bone down the stairs. The old houses near the docks were plagued with large rats. Mr. Graber was used to them. He returned to his observations on infiltration; but found that his work didn't go well tonight. He kept thinking of the boy in Grant's Store. What a pity he had been a spy.

THE BLIND WOMAN'S four-year-old son, Corey, now walking along Canal Street on his way home from the Greyhound Bus Station, kept a tight hold on his mother's hand. When she had tried to put him on the bus that would take him back to Mississippi, he had cried and refused to leave her. He hadn't forgotten Mr. Graber. He was less afraid of his mother than of the bad man he expected to jump on him any minute from the shadows. The blind woman was happy.

'Mama loves you,' she said. 'You won't run away from mama ever again, will you? You'll be a good boy, won't you, son?'

'Yessum.'

'Whose big boy are you?' she said, fondling one of the large ears that quivered on either side of his sullen, frightened face.

'Mama's,' said Corey.

'Mama'll sing you to sleep with her gee-tar tonight.'

'Yessum.'

Clutched tight in the small sweaty hand that had held Mr. Graber's anonymous calling card in the afternoon was a big, round, fifty-cent piece. It was the most money that Corey had ever held in his hand. He wasn't quite sure what it could be used for; but there it was. He separated his fingers and peeked at the shiny money.

It was part of the ten-dollar bill which had belonged to Merlin Webster that morning; but neither the blind woman nor her son knew where it had come from.

AND MERLIN WEBSTER, still sitting with the Tuttles in his courtyard on St. Philip Street, would never know what sorrow his gift had brought the blind woman through the day; or that the unpleasant person, Mr. Graber, whom he had seen accosting the postman that morning, had been the unwitting agent who had restored her peace of mind. It would probably have been

better for Corey if he had gone back to the pine woods; but
Merlin Webster knew nothing of this. He was unaware of
Corey's existence. Just now, he was recounting the story of
his generous mistake.

'I'd like to have seen that blind woman's face when she found
a ten-dollar bill in her box,' he concluded. 'Poor woman. She's
probably getting drunk tonight.'

For several hours, the Websters and the Tuttles had been
politely discovering that they hadn't one thought or impulse in
common. The Tuttles, by a well-worked-out system of signals,
were conveying to each other that they'd better take a walk
around the block; while the Websters, by an equally well-
worked-out system of signals, were telling each other that it was
time to get rid of the Tuttles and go to bed. Georgie had been
sent to bed hours ago. None of them had heard about the death
of Frankie Gomez that afternoon.

ACROSS THE COURTYARD WALL, in another world, Mr.
and Mrs. Gomez sat at the table in their combination kitchen
and living room with three guests. Leander was asleep in the
bedroom. Mrs. Gomez had lit a large white candle for Frankie.
She watched its slow burning with wide, dazed eyes. The room
was very hot.

One of the guests was Bruno Tarantino, who had arrived
some time ago with a jug of red wine. He had since been out
to refill the jug. The second guest was Mea Culpa, who had
heard of the accident, climbed the rickety stairs to the Gomez
apartment, and found herself welcome because in better days
she had given her washing to Mrs. Gomez' mother, a mulatto
woman, and had paid her well. Mrs. Gomez had not forgotten.
The other guest was an old man who had simply wandered in.
The Gomezes thought he had come with Mea Culpa; Mea Culpa

thought he had come with Bruno Tarantino; Bruno thought he belonged in the house. But he had come alone. There were many stairs in the city for lost feet to climb; but only one door that opened readily. A touch of a finger on the cloth-covered screen, and he was inside. There was a chair for him at the table and a glass of red wine. Perhaps there was nothing further to look for; but the old man was still not satisfied.

'Mama mia?' He looked questioningly at the friendly faces around him. 'Mama mia?' He was very drunk, and found it difficult to sit upright. He had pushed his chair a little way back from the table. Now he bowed toward the candle until his head was nearly on his knees. Mea Culpa paused with her wineglass halfway to her mouth, and watched to see if he would fall. But he did not fall. Bruno Tarantino caught him and eased him upright again.

'Be careful, old man,' said Bruno. 'You gonna fall.'

'Dey was two of em, Mr. Tarantino,' said Mrs. Gomez. She had changed her slacks for a tight black dress which made her dark face look darker still. 'Two of em, an could wear duh same clothes. Dey was a year apart.'

Bruno nodded his head. Mea Culpa went on slipping cheese out of the sandwiches Mrs. Gomez had made, and stacking the crusty bread, which her toothless gums could not manage, in a neat pile on the corner of the table. Her shawl was down around her shoulders; her uncovered hair was brilliant in the candlelight; her chin was stained with wine.

'Black bastard, dat Clark, I'm gonna kill him,' said Gomez. 'I'm gonna sue him for every cent he got.'

'Don't talk like dat, Refugio,' said Mrs. Gomez. 'God hears you.'

Bruno said nothing. He had talked very little all evening. He had merely listened to Gomez, who had talked as a man talks when he is starved for friends. Two hours ago, Gomez had spoken of a lawsuit with blazing eyes. Now, he spoke with less conviction. There would be no lawsuit, Bruno knew. When a lonely man loses a son as Frankie had been lost, his grief wants revenge. When he finds a friend, he talks away his hate. To Bruno it was simple. Clark and Gomez were both good men; they would get along.

'Mama mia?' said the old man, and bowed again toward the candle. Bruno caught him.

'Confess,' Mea Culpa coaxed the old man as he swayed upright. 'Confess to Father Vela. Then you can go home and sleep.'

'Two of em, so cute in new white sailor suits I made em, an new haircuts,' said Mrs. Gomez, 'an only yesterday I taken em bote to duh barbershop, an Frankie, he said—'

'Whose fault?' said Gomez. 'Whose fault that I sweat on the banana docks for my two sons, and now one son is gone? I am only Refugio Gomez, the Filipino, that doors is closed to in this country, but my son, Frankie, he coulda been anything. Who listens to Refugio Gomez, who comes if Refugio Gomez calls? Nobody listens. Nobody comes.'

'Don't talk like that, Refugio. God hears you.'

'But my son, Frankie, they woulda listened to him. My son, Frankie, coulda bossed ten men, twenty men maybe! He coulda made big money. Now he is gone. Who killed him?'

'Not Clark,' said Bruno. 'It wasn't Clark's fault.'

'We got Leander left,' said Mrs. Gomez sadly.

'Who comes?' said Mea Culpa dreamily, as she mumbled cheese between her toothless gums. 'Who comes when you call in the night?' She looked at Bruno Tarantino for an answer.

'Sometime people come,' Bruno offered.

Mea Culpa nodded her head in agreement. 'The patrol wagon comes,' she said, and slipped another piece of cheese out of a sandwich, and laid the crust carefully with other crusts on the corner of the table.

'Mama mia?' said the old man.

'He means his wife,' said Mea Culpa. 'He's too old to remember his mama.' She leaned toward the old man and poked him in the ribs. 'Huhn? huhn?' she said. 'Was you ever in jail, old man? Was you ever in jail?'

The old man looked at her weakly, and held out his glass for more wine. Mrs. Gomez gave it to him. The glass fell on the floor. Bruno picked it up.

'You shouldn't give him the wine till he confesses,' said Mea Culpa. 'Then he can go home and sleep.'

'My son, Frankie . . .'

'Don't cry, Refugio,' said Mrs. Gomez. 'I taken good care of em, Refugio, an never let em outa my sight on duh gallery all day long playin, playin, such a racket sometimes I cudden take my nap, Refugio, and spittin on duh cars, but I keppa hollerin keep offa dat rotten ironwork, botha youse, or you gonna fall! Oh, Mother of God, Refugio! Father Vela, he say—'

'An Our Father an Five Hail Marys, and keep your head covered,' said Mea Culpa, winking at her wineglass. 'But a shawl is so hot on your head, Mr. Tarantino. Do you like my hair?'

'Very pretty,' said Bruno, embarrassed.

'I'm a wicked woman, Mr. Tarantino, but I always confess it to Father Vela.'

'Mother of Infinite Mercies,' said Mrs. Gomez.

'White hairpins is so hard to find,' said Mea Culpa.

The old man toppled again toward the candle. His arms hung at his sides; his head lay on his knees. He almost fell out of his chair. But Bruno caught him and braced him upright again. The old man looked at Bruno strangely. He shook off the hand that held him, and sat very straight in his chair. He looked with piercing eyes around the room. But he did not see what he looked for. His chin fell on his chest. 'Mama mia?' he said, like a lost child. 'Mama mia?'

'I am only Refugio Gomez. Nobody comes when I call. But my son, Frankie . . .'

'God hears you, Refugio.'

'People come sometime,' said Bruno Tarantino, as he straightened the old man in his chair again, and poured the last of the wine for Gomez. . . . 'Sometime, people come.'

Mea Culpa listened to the guttural pounding of near and distant music, the sound of laughter on the street, the striking of a clock. She prodded the old man in his ribs again. 'Confess it all,' she coaxed. 'Then you can go home and sleep.'

IN A NEAR–BY BARROOM, somebody was playing the same juke-box record over and over again. The sound had become the undersong of the night itself, a throbbing of drums in the slow, hot blood.

Dan and Iris Clark had gone to bed, where they lay listening to the music and the murmur of voices in the Gomez apartment above them.

'Whut Mr. Tarantino kin do?' said Iris.

'Gawd knows,' said Clark. There was nothing to do but wait, and he was used to waiting. Tired out, he fell asleep.

But Iris could not sleep. She lay and watched the moonlight on the floor. She, too, was used to waiting. Waiting for a garden, waiting for good days, waiting for morning. Just waiting.

A FEW BLOCKS down the street, Clara Bilbo was also waiting. She was waiting for Ronnie to come home to supper. She had taken off her calico dress and white apron, her head handkerchief and her shoes, and was sitting in a nameless undergarment, with bare feet planted flat on the cool cypress planks of the floor. She had read in the paper about Cooter's confession. But she couldn't go to him tonight. She had heard about the Clarks' trouble. But she couldn't go to them, either. Ronnie might come in her absence. She had to be at home when Ronnie came. The last she had seen of him, he had been running down Pirate's Alley with the plain-clothes man behind him. Had Ronnie as well as Cooter been caught? Where was the little boy? Why didn't he come home? Long ago, Clara Bilbo had wept all her tears. She was dry now—dry and hard; polished purple-black by the lamplight; contracted to endure. For all her hate and love she could do nothing; and so she waited, stirring the close air with a palmleaf fan. Mustard greens and salt pork were keeping hot on the back of the stove.

RONNIE, still running through the hot moonlight, stumbled against the wall of a burned-out building to catch his breath. High up on the charred rafters under the broken roof, an owl hooted. And Ronnie was running again, seeing the red face before him swollen with laughter, the great clicking jaws.

HA–HA–HA–HA! HA–HA–HA–HA!

On a pedestal before the House of Fun on Pontchartrain Beach stood a mechanical man, twice life-size, and wired with a loud-speaker. An electrical impulse tickled him at regular intervals. His laughter, when it came, was Gargantuan. The crowd that watched him could scarcely get its breath before the plaster head moved, the pudgy hands lifted to clasp the belly, the hinged jaws dropped, the sound came again—and the upturned faces wrinkled and gasped in small human mimicry of the laughter larger than themselves. Maudie and Victor Peralta were in the crowd.

Colored lights spun and whirled before Victor's eyes. The roller-coaster zoomed up and down its safely perilous track, scattering screams behind it. From a tower under the moon, a diver dropped like a white silk fly. The spotlight caught him briefly; he was safe too soon. Today, thought Victor, he had partaken of life. Tonight, he had treated Maudie to everything. It had cost a lot of money; and he didn't know how they would eat tomorrow unless he borrowed his mother's lottery winnings —but it didn't matter. Tonight had been a night to celebrate. This afternoon he had written his first short story. Some day, he would be rich and famous. Victor was tired of laughing at the mechanical man. He wanted to talk about himself.

'About my story!' he shouted in Maudie's ear.

'Ha-ha-ha-ha!' said the mechanical man.

'Ha-ha-ha!' gasped Maudie, in her pink bathing-suit. She and Victor had been swimming in the warm lake. They had not yet put on their clothes.

'It's a wonderful story!' shouted Victor.

But it was of no use. The mechanical man laughed, the crowd laughed, Maudie laughed. Victor tried not to laugh, and got the hiccups. But Maudie wouldn't move. She looked very beautiful tonight, thought Victor. She had the best sun-tan on the beach. Shivering a little in his wet bathing-suit, he pressed against her. 'Maudie,' he said. 'Let's go home.'

She shrugged impatiently. He wound an arm around her waist, and kissed her ear. His heart beat faster and his hiccups stopped. 'I'm crazy about you, Maudie,' he said. 'Let's go home.'

Maudie screamed, and looked indignantly behind her.

'What's the matter?' Victor said.

'Somebody pinched me! A man pinched me right here!' Maudie rubbed her assaulted rear. 'There he is!' she screamed, pointing. 'Look at him, the fresh thing! He thinks it's funny to insult a girl. Hit him, Victor!'

'Which man, which man? Who pinched you, Maudie, who pinched you?'

'Yes, he did, and now he's laughing at me. Hit him, Victor! He's trying to get away!'

'Maybe he knows you, Maudie. Maybe he's a friend of ours.' But Maudie's finger was indicating a complete stranger—a heavy-set young man with black eyebrows that met above his nose. Urged by a skinny blond boy, he was trying to slip away in the crowd.

'There he goes! Hit him, Victor!'

Propelled by Maudie, Victor grasped the disappearing shirt. The shirt was already torn, and Victor tore it further. The owner of the shirt glared over his shoulder.

'Did you pinch my wife?' said Victor tremulously.

'Turn aloose of me.'

'That's him!' screamed Maudie. 'Hit him, Victor!'

'She's crazy.'

'Did you insult my wife?'

'I never insulted nobody. Turn aloose of me, you sonofabitch!'

'What did you call me?' said Victor, blushing. Finding himself suddenly alone in a little clearing with what he had captured, he released it quickly.

'Aw, jeez, my friend didn't mean no harm,' said the blond boy. 'Come on, Aleck, you dumb monkey, you gotta be on watch at twelve. You gotta.'

'The sonofabitch tore my shirt,' said Aleck. 'He can't get away with that.'

'Stop callin my husband a sonofabitch!' said Maudie. 'Hit him, Victor!'

'Whoever pinched my wife is a—a sonofabitch!' said Victor, very red in the face. He had never used such a word before. Its pronunciation seemed to have a stimulating effect on him. 'You pinched my wife, you sonofabitch!' he said, doubling his fists. 'You better apologize.'

'Who you callin a sonofabitch, you sonofabitch? How'd I know she was your wife?'

'You dumb monkey, you gotta be on watch at twelve!' Whitey tried to drag his friend away. But Maudie wouldn't let them go. 'Hit him! Hit him!' she screamed, jumping up and down.

Victor pushed his fist in Aleck's direction. Aleck shook off Whitey's restraining hand. 'Callin me names, I'll beat his face in, callin me names!'

Victor had often imagined himself defending Maudie against hordes of ruffians, but he had never been in a fight in his life; he had never even wanted to be in a fight. But something happened to him. Before he knew what he was doing, he found himself landing all over his adversary. Surprised, and already shaky on his feet, Aleck went down. Victor was more surprised than Aleck; he didn't know what to do next. But nothing further was required of him. Whitey took charge of his friend, and hustled him protesting through the crowd.

Victor got to his feet and looked at his knuckles with astonishment. They were bleeding. He had vanquished a large enemy with one blow of his fist. Merlin Webster would never frighten him again. But Maudie was fondling the injured hand and cooing in his ear.

'It's nothing,' said Victor, swelling his chest. 'Nothing at all. A mere scratch.'

They left the House of Fun and sat on the sea-wall. Far out on the still lake a white launch floated at anchor like a white swan on black glass. Some day, thought Victor, he would buy Maudie a much bigger boat. He swelled his chest again, and flexed his arms. Maudie felt his muscles, and cuddled his hand under her chin.

'Guess what?' she said.

'What?' said Victor innocently.

'Let's go home.'

'But I don't want to go home!' said Victor. 'The evening's just begun!'

'Mm-m-m. I could just eat you up.'

'Could you, Maudie?'

'Mm-m-m.' She looked at him from between her eyelashes and nuzzled his arm invitingly.

'Golly,' said Victor. 'Let's go home.'

They caught the next bus. Old Mrs. Peralta was sitting on the doorstep when they reached their house. She smiled and spoke to them; but they hardly noticed her. The door closed behind them. They did not turn on the light.

A TRASH FIRE was burning in an oil drum in front of the Cansino Fruit and Vegetable Stand. Insects circled the white islands of the street lamps; and children called to one another, playing tag on the sidewalk. Old Mrs. Peralta plucked a June bug from her hair, waved at the children, and watched the flames, nodding and smiling to herself. This was the nicest time of the day. All up and down the street, people had come outside to cool off in sight of each other and the moon before they slept.

Mrs. Peralta plucked another June bug from her hair—perhaps the same one flown back to her; for she could not bear to kill any of the little things, and always set them free. Across the street that dark man was smoking a cigar on his doorstep again. What a beautiful mustache he had! He had been sitting in the same spot for so many evenings, Mrs. Peralta felt she knew him. She waved at him; but he did not see her.

He was Mr. Papadakis, lover and philosopher, who had found himself unable to sit through another showing of *Two-Gun Fagan* even for Leah; and had come home to wait for his nightly glimpse of her entering her door. Somebody was just asking Mr. Papadakis for a match.

'Got a match, Mister?'

'Sure,' said Mr. Papadakis.

'Thanks.'

'Keep the box.'

The lighted cigarette crossed the street and came toward Mrs. Peralta in the corner of a boy's mouth. Half an hour ago, the boy had been tempted by a voice behind a shutter on North Rampart Street. His legs were trembling; his pockets were empty; and God, fresh air was good! The air was warm and sweet and languorous. Passing old Mrs. Peralta, he drew the sweet air into his lungs and expelled it blue with smoke under the street lamp. Mrs. Peralta smiled at him benignly, and went on ruffling the night with her own breath, lost in the night.

Followed by Mrs. Peralta's placid eyes, the young legs went past gossiping women, past playing children, past a group of chattering girls on a doorstep. Here, Mrs. Peralta lost sight of him; but he was swaggering now. He was a man, and his shape was printed by the moon on the sidewalk and infinitely reflected in the eyes around him; the eyes on the doorsteps; the eyes that peeped through shutters. And also in the eyes of Mr. Gregory, who sat in a rocking chair on the sidewalk, bolstered with pillows, and afraid to move.

Six months ago, Mr. Gregory had fallen down an elevator shaft and broken nearly every bone in his body; and the skin between him and the world was very thin and tender. He was painfully aware of his bones, and dismayed and astonished at the casual way other men accepted the pliant framework which enabled them to walk upright in the moonlight, to make love to a woman, to walk ten steps to the bathroom alone. He was first aware of the young legs as they came toward him, then of the slender torso, then of the face. When he saw the face he said, 'Hello, Damien,' for this was the son of a friend.

The boy stopped, and looked at him uncomfortably. 'Hi, Mr. Gregory. When did you get home?'

'About an hour ago.'

'How you feel?'

'Still a little shaky, but okay. I'm lucky to be alive. How's your dad?'

'Okay.'

The boy looked so uncomfortable, Mr. Gregory released him, feeling hurt that a mere boy should take his living presence so much for granted when eminent doctors had given him up for dead. But his wife had not given him up. Mr. Gregory thought of his wife, busy with something in the house behind him. He thought of her hands, her fine swelling hips. She would come if he called. Mr. Gregory was all at once aware of a verdant growth pushing inside him against his fragile bones: thin delicate shoots, green plumes and whorls. He was still so weak that tears came easily. They rolled down his cheeks. He had just seen smoke coming out of a chimney. It bulged and wrinkled and climbed under the moon. It was incredible! But it was true. Incredible that a man should still be alive with so many traps to catch him. Mr. Gregory caught his breath, for Damien, almost out of sight now, had fallen. No, he had only stooped to tie his shoe. But Damien did not know, none of them knew that a man could be zipping his trousers and drop down the bottomless pit which few men ever survived. If they knew, they would be more careful.

So Damien, now in the next block, adjusted the crooked buttoning of his shirt and jumped when a child's high voice called, 'Damien, I been lookin for you, Damien! Why didn't you come?'

'Shut up!' said Damien sullenly.

'Rudy, you come in outa the street!' called Mrs. Ferrabee.

Rudy came in off the street where he had run to look after Damien, and stood beside his mother sitting on the doorstep with his two sisters. As usual, one of the little girls was crying, and the other had her finger in her mouth.

'Has papa come home yet?' said Rudy, worriedly.

'No.'

'When's papa comin home, huh, mama?'

'When he gets good and ready.'

'He's away on business, huh, mama? What kinda business?'

'Monkey business!' snapped Mrs. Ferrabee, and put all three children to bed in the cleaned and garnished house; and returned to sit alone on her doorstep and watch for her mate, provider of red beans and rice, partaker for ten years of the sweet wine and sour dregs of married life on eighty dollars a month, who had criticized her housekeeping and threatened her with the dishmop at four o'clock this morning, and whom she had told never to show his face again (and meant it, this morning), but whom she now wanted a sight of as she some day hoped to see God.

The inscrutable moon hung in the fathomless sky while Mrs. Ferrabee tiptoed into her house, pinned on her coral brooch for Thomas, touched her hair at the mirror, and tiptoed out to wait.

'Mama,' said Rudy from the doorway.

'I tole you, get in bed.'

'A kitty come in the back door. Can he sleep by me tonight?'

'Like we ain't got enough to dirty the house already. Give it here. I'll put it on the sidewalk. It'll find itself a home.'

But the kitten, placed on the pavement, looked up at her, appalled. It tried to climb her leg, and came back again and again. Finally, worn out, it crept into a paper bag somebody had dropped on the sidewalk, and fell asleep. Its mother had already done all she could for it, and had stopped bothering about it weeks before. She had provided it with a body that was a precise jewel of casual creation from delicate whiskers to striped, tapering tail; and now, in the next block, was investigating a squid dropped from somebody's supper basket or parcel, and lying forlorn on the sidewalk before Mr. Gregory's house.

She stepped haughtily, sniffed delicately, pounced and growled. But she was not really hungry. A beautiful part Persian, diplomatically playful, and inhabiting most of the houses on the block in turn, she had a dozen meals waiting for her whenever she wanted them, a dozen different names given her by people who were flattered by her acceptance of their hospitality, and were pleased and proud to say they owned her. Mr. Gregory, having been six months in the hospital, had not met her yet.

He watched her smiling, thinking how light, how swift she was, how sweetly she glistened, how like a small jungle tiger she prowled and pounced—how, of a body, the faster it moves the lighter it becomes until it has lost all corporal weight and leaves the solid ground as in dreams one sometimes lifts one's self above danger and maintains one's self by agony aloft till the body grows so heavy the mind can no longer sustain it; and it drops, falls, sprawls on the rocking chair—and the tiger springs.

She was rubbing against his leg. She was kneading her claws in his leg above the ankle. He could not reach her, for he could not move.

'Josephine!' Mr. Gregory called in terror.

His wife ran to the door.

'It's only Selina,' she said, and took the purring cat in her arms. 'Isn't she beautiful? I wonder why she didn't come home to eat her supper. I wonder where she's been.'

Mr. Gregory eased back on the pillows and looked at the moon. He was safe. Moonlight bound him to the level sidewalk. Moonlight smoothed over the sharp splinters, the rough edges; and bent around the hurt angles of memory in a tourniquet so closely woven of dream and reality that the two were one thing —no seam, no fracture visible. He was safe. He closed his eyes and drank in the strange, familiar street sounds. The rhythmic thumping of a piano in a colored barroom on the corner beat against his eardrums like waves pounding and sliding on a beach. Mr. Gregory felt himself lying on a beach, cast up from the ocean for the first time, a boneless jelly that must learn through millenniums of trial and error how to stand upright and walk. Mr. Gregory felt as limp as a squid. But he felt incredibly joyful, for here came a sound he had forgotten. Here it was. The squeaky

wheelbarrow trundled by the old man in the brown sweater—
for what purpose Mr. Gregory had never been able to determine,
since it was always empty, its enigmatic emptiness and the old
man's truculent britches followed by the old man's scolding wife.
What was she saying? Something about her daughter-in-law and
the disputed ownership of a mattress? It had been the same com-
plaint six months before. Mr. Gregory laughed.

BUT MRS. PERALTA had been listening. Who called for
Josephine? This was Mrs. Peralta's own name, and nobody had
called it for years. Whose voice had called her out of the long
years? The voice did not come again. Mrs. Peralta thought she
must have been mistaken. The sound must have been made by
the squeaky wheelbarrow trailed by the old woman who walked
with her bent knees far ahead of the rest of her body, as if her
feet were sore. But had nobody called for Josephine? Mrs. Peralta looked questioningly at Mr. Papadakis, across the street.
His mustache reminded her of her husband. But Mr. Papadakis
had not called. He was being accosted by a colored man with a
yellow suitcase, wearing the wrinkled coat of a traveler. The
traveler took off his hat.

'Which way Ursuline Street, Cap'n? Ah jes arrive in de city.'

'Half a block this way, one block down.' Mr. Papadakis
pointed the way with his cigar.

The traveler felt around in his hat, and extracted a white card
from the sweatband. 'Obleege to you, Cap'n, an heah's mah card.
Ah'm preachin on de tex dat says a Holycos is comin when de
worl goin up in flame on Saddy night in Temple Numbah Nine
a de Gospel Hereafter, an white folks is welcome . . . yassuh,
thanky, suh, Cap'n . . .' The traveler accepted a contribution
and turned the corner. But the trash fire still burned in front of
the Cansino stand.

The flames swayed in a faint stir of wind. They burned high and then low, flickering on the walls of the old buildings on either side of the narrow street. From the next block, Mrs. Ferrabee watched the trash fire like a beacon of hope. Mrs. Gregory was reminded of tomorrow's roast in the oven, and went inside to turn down the gas; but she was so happy to have heard Mr. Gregory laugh that she forgot what she was doing and turned on the radio instead. Mr. Gregory thought of life. Mr. Papadakis thought of creation: of the first fire and the last long burning. In the interval, thought Mr. Papadakis, women passed. The night shook women from its branches like bright, giddy leaves. They lodged on doorsteps and loitered in doorways, and rolled their glistening sides to the moon. They chewed gum, and said to each other, 'Aw, honey, you shouldna let 'im . . .' They wore flowers in their hair, and grew savage or mournful when they menstruated. And knew nothing. And were everything. And were all alike. Then why did he wait for a glimpse of one woman entering her door? Mr. Papadakis shrugged his shoulders. He shook the ash from his cigar, watched the burning trash fire, and knew himself a fool. He said 'Poddon?' to a stranger who had petitioned him for a match; and 'Poddon me' again, as he handed over the box. Ignited by Mr. Papadakis' generosity, the stranger went his way.

But Mrs. Peralta still watched Mr. Papadakis admiringly. He seemed to possess everything, know everything. What a good man.

Somebody pitched an apple crate on the trash fire. When the flames burned high, the walls advanced, their gray and ravaged dignity grown rosy and blushing. When the flames burned low, the walls retreated. It was like a dance, thought Mrs. Peralta. Just like a dance. She hummed the tune of an old polka, and shuffled her feet to keep time . . . advance, curtsey, clasp hands, whirl . . . advance, curtsey . . .

'Hello,' said a girl's voice.

'Good evening,' said a man.

'Good evening?' Mrs. Peralta peered at their faces. Why, she remembered them! They were the young couple with the baby who had asked directions of her that afternoon and then gone in Mr. Webster's house. There they went, with their arms around each other. How nice for young people to be walking together in the moonlight with their arms around each other. They must be in love. How young they were—the young man so very young to have such a large, beautiful mustache. Mrs. Peralta loved young people. She watched them until she could see them no longer, and looked again at the trash fire burning in the oil drum. She picked up the tune where she had dropped it and shuffled her feet to keep time . . . advance, curtsey, clasp hands, whirl . . .

'What is that strange thing lying on the sidewalk?' said Katherine Tuttle, pointing. The Websters had gone to bed. She and Willis had come out for a walk around the block before they slept. Willis could never sleep at night in a strange place until he had investigated his environs.

'It's a squid,' Willis said.

'Oh,' said Kathy. 'I wonder how it got here. It doesn't look at home.'

'It isn't,' said Willis, as he pushed the squid into the gutter with his foot.

'Think how far it traveled to get here,' said Kathy. She added, sorrowfully, 'Its mother would never know it now.'

Willis began to whistle softly. He had just picked a tune off the radio playing in Mr. Gregory's house, a thin ghost of a tune through the pulsing boogie-woogie from the barroom, but still recognizable; and inhabiting the street very appropriately to-night, he thought, because a man called Debussy had also been acquainted with moonlight, and had squiggled the sound on a piece of paper, and copies had drifted all over the world, and the hands and lips comprising a symphony orchestra had reproduced it for a record, and . . .

Mrs. Gregory came out of the house with another pillow for Mr. Gregory, and said, 'Where did Selina go?'

'Who?' said Mr. Gregory.

'Our cat.'

'She wandered off,' said Mr. Gregory.

'It's hot,' said Mrs. Gregory, sitting beside him.

'It's June,' said Mr. Gregory.

Heat hugged the city. It would be a long embrace, lasting well into October, most likely. Mr. Gregory looked to the south, and saw the stinging tail of the Scorpion reared high above the roofs, but pale because of the bright moon; and looked down to see the squid being carried away in the jaws of a gray tomcat with battle-scarred ears.

Katherine Tuttle, looking over her shoulders as she turned the corner, was also a witness to the tomcat's capture of the squid. She had been thinking how far the squid had journeyed from its birthplace. Its final disposal vaguely alarmed her. 'Everything is chance,' she said mournfully. 'Everything.'

'What brought up that subject?' her husband inquired.

'The squid.'

'Hmm-m.'

'No,' said Kathy. 'It's true. It scares me.'

'What scares you, puss?' said Willis absent-mindedly. Good solid barrel-house was shaking a swing door with a sign above it saying, 'For Colored Patrons Only.' Willis was concerned with the agile arithmetic of the music. He snapped his fingers in time.

Kathy drew away from him. 'You aren't listening to me,' she said, 'but whether you listen or not, it's all chance. I've been thinking and thinking, and I can't see how it was anything but chance.'

'Hmm-m?'

'The way we met each other.'

'Wait a minute. I'm sorry. I want to listen to this music. It's real stuff.'

'It's pure, blind chance.'

'For Heaven's sake, please shut up or grow up!'

'I'm a year older than you!'

Willis stopped snapping his fingers and turned on her hotly. The difference in their ages was a sore point with him. 'You didn't learn much in one year,' he said. 'If you did, you forgot it. You forget everything. One thing you've forgotten is that every time we move to a new place, you pick a quarrel with me. You never feel comfortably at home in a new house till we've had a fight and made up. I don't want to fight now. I want to listen.'

'We aren't in a house,' she said.

'Please!' Willis begged. 'You promised you wouldn't do this to me again.'

'I didn't start this argument.'

'The squid did.'

'If you'd only take me seriously,' she pleaded. 'If you'd only take me seriously once in a while.'

'I take you too seriously for my own peace of mind,' said Willis, trying to control his irritation. 'What's the matter with you? Aren't you happy?'

'I don't know. Maybe I'm not.'

'What's the trouble? D'you know?'

Kathy didn't know. By this time she was so confused she said the first thing that came into her mind. 'I don't like Mrs. Webster,' she said. 'I simply loathe her. Do you like her?'

'What if I don't? D'you want me to put an alligator in her bed?'

'Don't be silly.'

'Look,' said Willis. He took hold of her shoulders, breathing heavily.

'I'm looking,' she said miserably.

'Shut up! *Chance*, she says. Everything is chance, and it scares her half to death. My God, of course it's chance that we met! I remember standing on the corner that day I met you, and thinking if I walk to the left, my life will be one thing, and if I walk to the right, it'll be something completely different. I decided to drop in that drugstore for a soda and think it over, and happened to meet you buying a bottle of ink. All right. It was chance. Of course life is chance, up to a certain point. Or maybe it isn't—but that's none of my business. It suits me to ignore such speculations. I accept the fact that life is chance up to a certain point. After that, it's up to people. If Thomas Hardy's Collected Poems and their cousins want to pace off the end of a promontory into the sunset, it's their business. I wash my hands of it. I refuse to be sad. So long as men can do something about this world, I'll love it. I refuse to hunt a promontory and moan, even if it sounds beautiful. Shut up!'

'I don't know what you're talking about.'

'Shut up! Can you stand here and tell me that Roger is chance?'

'Well,' said Kathy, 'in a way.'

'Like hell he is! Roger was inevitable from the minute I saw you buying a bottle of ink. Chance? Don't make me laugh!'

'He might have been a girl,' said Kathy demurely.

'You little female dope!' said Willis. 'You—you bitch of a married woman!'

He stalked away on his long legs. Kathy trotted to keep even with him. Everything was all right now. If Willis wasn't afraid of chance, neither was she. How funny Willis looked when he was angry—his hair bristled. But he wouldn't be angry at her very long, because he loved her. He flew around the block, opened the Websters' alley door, and walked ahead of her toward their apartment in the garden. At the end of the alley, he stopped suddenly. She bumped against him. 'Ss-h, look!' he said.

The garden lay in full moonlight. The oleander tree hung heavy with bloom from top to lowest branch; its whiteness ached and dazzled. The short grass glittered with dew, and something moved on the grass. It was a blond, part Persian cat.

The cat careened across the grass, leaped high, and batted the air with her front paws—two lightning strokes before she touched the ground. She minced sideways and leaped again. She dropped flat on her belly and lay with twitching tail. She rose, slithered, stalked nothing that the Tuttles could see, and pounced again upon nothing, caught nothing. In and out of the light and shadow she curved and twisted. Around and around she spun in a circle on her hind legs, only to whip sideways in a half-somersault and fight the air again. Incredibly light and fleet, in complete silence, the strange dance went on.

The Tuttles exchanged a look of wonder and mirth and delight.

A black moth floated between them. Kathy shrank back. Willis darted his hand. But the moth swerved and eluded him, and disappeared in the shadows.

'She was chasing moths.'

But she had heard them. She ran away.

A leaf spun on its stem. The oleander heaved in a weighted swell, a scarcely perceptible movement, and was still again. The Tuttles went into their house.

The bright square of their bedroom window flashed on the Webster bedroom wall. In a little while, it went out. Marie Webster cleared her throat a time or two, and seemed to fall asleep; but she was not asleep; she was listening for Leah. It was nearly time for Leah to come home, if she were coming, the shameless thing. Maybe she wouldn't come—in which event one need never bother to think about her again, much less to spend nearly three dollars' worth of sympathy on a book which she had purposely forgotten to accept. . . . A rich dark plume of laughter trailed past the Webster house. It was Negro laughter.

What was so funny? Marie wet her lips. What was so funny about the Webster house that niggers laughed when they passed it? She never hurt any of them. How dare they laugh at her house?

They were laughing because one of them had pitched a sack of chicken feathers and entrails clear across the street into Mr. Cansino's trash fire. It was a bull's-eye. Holding their noses, they passed. An unpleasant odor drifted along the street.

Merlin Webster got out of bed to close the shutter against a smell of burning feathers that permeated the room. His face shone briefly at the window; the closing shutter sponged it out; in darkness, it moved toward the fourposter bed. He hoped that he had not waked Marie. Tonight of all nights in his life for Marie to want one of her heart-to-heart talks! Getting ready for bed, he had felt her pregnant silence and had sensed that a self-doubting mood was working up. But he had learned what to do. When thick fog rolls in off the river, a safe driver moves at minimum speed and sounds his horn loudly at all intersections.

Marie cleared her throat again. She was not asleep after all. Here it came.

'I saw Leah today,' Marie said.

'Please. I'm tired. I had a hard day at the office. I want to sleep.'

Marie turned on her side and listened to the ineffectual beating of her heart. It was ineffectual because she had almost everything a woman needed to make her happy, and she wasn't happy. She simply couldn't understand people like Leah Webster. If she could understand Leah, she felt that she would understand herself, and then she would be happy. . . . It was easy to understand women like Katherine Tuttle—pretty, vain, selfish, completely devoid of any instinct for motherhood. That poor little Roger would grow up like a weed.

'I only wanted to tell you something about Leah,' Marie said plaintively. 'This morning you wanted to talk about her. Tonight, you snap my head off when I so much as mention her name.'

But Merlin wouldn't answer. He lay on his back and breathed slowly, trying to relax. He, too, had seen Leah today. He had seen her face like a desperate swimmer sweep past him in the flood. He, alone, had survived. The fan hummed. The wave of warm air swept across his body, across Marie's body, and returned. Merlin tried to time his breathing with the slow sweep of the fan. 'Relax,' he told himself. 'Relax.' But he couldn't relax. With a man like Willis Tuttle living in his courtyard, he felt a need for wakeful vigilance, as if the enemy were really inside his gates.

Across the courtyard, Willis Tuttle said to his wife, 'We quarreled because of a squid.'

Kathy, standing at the window for a last look at the garden in the moonlight, smiled to herself without replying. She had just seen a small figure steal from the Webster house. Georgiana Webster in pink pajamas had just run to the alley wall, felt among the vines, and resurrected the doll her mother had told her to drop in the garbage can. Now, with the doll in her arms, she stood under the oleander and looked at her quiet windmill. She stood on tiptoe, and blew her breath on the windmill. It moved. She ran into the house.

'And made up because a cat chased a moth,' Willis Tuttle continued to his wife. 'You ought to be satisfied. Now come to bed.'

THE BLOND CAT was no longer chasing moths. She was being chased. A few minutes past, a familiar odor had come to her from under a back doorstep, and she had followed the trail of scent to the remains of the squid. Deep under the Tarantino house, the gray tomcat stopped polishing his whiskers, spoke

authoritatively, and glided forward. They struggled, but not for
the squid. Mrs. Tarantino's asthmatic old dog, Rocco, nearly
burst himself barking; but Mrs. Tarantino wasn't interested.
Rocco handled the situation unaided. He chased the cats. They
ran. They met under another back doorstep.

A FRAGMENT parted from a planet. A shooting star arched
in a pale, cool parabola across the sky, glowed red above the city,
and disappeared beyond the chimneys and the leaves.

It had slipped over the edge of the world's darkness and nothing could save it, thought Mr. Gregory, who, alone of all those
on the street, had happened to see it fall. The remote catastro-
phe chimed from cliff to cliff of space in Mr. Gregory's mind
with a sound like a fingernail struck on thin glass, fainter and
fainter. Mr. Gregory was still falling, and nothing supported
him in all the whirling firmament but Mrs. Gregory's hand.
Holding to it, he began the long climb back to the level of
the sidewalk. And down the street, Mrs. Tarantino opened her
front door.

She stood in the lighted doorway, fanning her hot face with
her apron. Her ironing was finished, folded, and laid away. The
afternoon visitors had spoiled her for solitude. With Bruno absent from the house, she had found her own company insuffi-
cient.

'Good evening,' said Mrs. Peralta to her neighbor. Never, in
her memory, had Mrs. Tarantino sat on her front doorstep in
the evening. But Mrs. Peralta was not surprised.

'Good evening,' answered Mrs. Tarantino formally, and sat
stiffly on her doorstep.

'Such a beautiful day,' said Mrs. Peralta.

'What a day!' said Mrs. Tarantino. 'Lucky for Mrs. Gomez,
she got her anudda boy.'

'My lucky day,' agreed Mrs. Peralta. Frankie Gomez had not fallen on the courtyard bricks; he had fallen into the placid reaches of Mrs. Peralta's mind, and vanished. The ripple caused by his falling had widened past memory. Mrs. Peralta had forgotten the accident. 'I won on the lottery,' she said.

'I had white flowers for duh Blessed Mudda keepin fresh,' said Mrs. Tarantino, 'but maybe I'll carry 'em by Mrs. Gomez tomorrow. Mr. Tarantino is sittin by duh Gomezes tonight. I woulda gone, only my ironing. Mr. Gomez was gonna sue Dan Clark, but Mr. Tarantino gonna talk to him, an maybe he won't. Mr. Tarantino can talk anybody outa anything. When he talks.'

'She'll be so glad,' said Mrs. Peralta, who had heard only the first part of Mrs. Tarantino's long speech.

Mrs. Tarantino sighed, and wiped her face with her apron. 'Hot, ain't it?' she said. 'What a rain! My washin got wet on the line.'

'Did it rain?' said Mrs. Peralta.

'Two hours it thundered and lightninged, and the paving blocks was floating on Bourbon Street, the paper says.' Mrs. Tarantino spoke with pride, as if she were responsible.

'I must have been asleep,' said Mrs. Peralta.

Mrs. Tarantino looked sharply at Mr. Papadakis, across the street. She suspected his intentions. She suspected him of larceny, or worse. Mrs. Peralta looked at the trash fire in front of the Cansino stand. It was dying down, but the walls on either side of the street still advanced and retreated. It was just like a dance. Mrs. Peralta had danced a great deal in her youth; but now she was old, and her feet hurt. Before she went to bed, she intended to soak her feet in hot water, and then trim her corns.

Somebody stepped on her corns.

Mrs. Peralta pulled her feet under her skirt, and looked up at a small colored boy in baggy knickers who was trotting along the sidewalk, dragging his shirt-sleeve under his nose. He seemed familiar to Mrs. Peralta, and she wondered where she had seen him before. He was quickly out of sight. His bare feet had not really hurt her.

Humming softly through her nose, Mrs. Peralta thought of the fine hot water, very hot, the steam rising about her, the heat creeping up her legs into her body, the fine drowsy feeling; and then, when the bunions and arches had stopped aching and the corns were softened, she would sit on the floor and cut away the hard flesh that hurt so much. And then she would sleep. *La la, la la la*, she hummed, anticipating this pleasure.

UNNOTICED by anybody, Ronnie Bilbo trotted along the sidewalk until he arrived at his grandmother's house. Here, he stuck his shirt inside his britches, tightened his belt, and opened the door.

He had come home. Clara stood up from her rocking chair, and turned up the lamp.

'You hongry?'

'Y'am, grammaw.'

She served him with fierce pride. She knew all about him. One look at his brooding, angry eyes and his hurt mouth, and she thought she knew everything that had happened to him. Perhaps she did. He had been chased; he was a Negro now. He had come home. Later, she would talk to him, but now she turned down his bed. As she bent over the cot by the window, she heard summer insects tapping outside on the screen. The sound filled her with memories of beauty and terror and unending vigilance. . . . Lightning bugs or lanterns in the woods . . . a hound bayed the moon . . . the gate chain clinked . . . a footstep hit the porch. They would all come home in the end. From the wide fields, from the railroads, from everywhere, her patient, enduring anger gathered them in. So summer tapped on her window again. Clara Bilbo turned back the gray bedspread, lit a cigarette, and rocked quietly in her hide-bottomed rocking chair while her grandson ate his turnip greens.

UP THE STREET, Mrs. Peralta released another June bug that had somehow got under her skirt and tangled itself in her garter, and said 'Ma'm?' to Mrs. Tarantino, for she had been asking the moon where she had seen that little colored boy before, and had not heard what Mrs. Tarantino had said.

'That man,' said Mrs. Tarantino, indicating Mr. Papadakis. 'He's too dressed up. He ain't up to no good.'

'He's waiting for somebody,' said Mrs. Peralta.

'Waiting to break in somebody's house if you ask me, if they leave their door open a minute,' said Mrs. Tarantino. 'The papers is full of such goings-on, with thiefs and rapes and such.'

Mr. Papadakis looked at the old women with sad, humorous eyes, and suspected that they were talking about him; but they could not harm him nor help him now; they had no milk in their bosoms. Neither their love nor their malice, poor dears, could make any difference to him now. Time ran between them. The street was a dark river of time. Would Leah never cross the river, climb the steep bank, and take him by the hand? It would be well worth her while. He was a rich man. The ages had given him jewels of wisdom and tenderness he could never exchange for commodities obtainable in Dufossat's bakery. . . . Dark girls passed him with flowers in their hair. Mr. Papadakis looked after them sadly, admiringly, wishing them well. He looked at his wrist watch. It was time for Leah to come home.

'Just look at him,' said Mrs. Tarantino. 'He ain't moved an inch.'

'He's a good man,' said Mrs. Peralta.

'You know him?'

'Oh, yes,' said Mrs. Peralta. 'But I forget his name.'

'He sits up late, don't he?'

'Everybody sits up late.'

'Seem like it don't cool off till after twelve.'

'He's enjoying the moon, like us,' said Mrs. Peralta.

Mrs. Tarantino appeared to accept this explanation of Mr. Papadakis' presence. 'Ain't it duh truth?' she said. But she had her doubts.

Mr. Papadakis had his own doubts; and truth was more elusive than the mosquito that had been puncturing his shoulder-blade at regular intervals for ten uncomfortable minutes. When he analyzed his predicament, he knew he was a fool to sit here and suffer. There were many more pleasant things to do of an evening than sit on a hard doorstep and suffer from love and mosquitoes. But here he sat. He thought he might be sitting up to give strange persons matches. Another stranger had just approached him with the familiar request. Mr. Papadakis had plenty of matches. One match can light a fire on an uninhabited island. Never be without a match.

'Keep the box,' said Mr. Papadakis wearily. He watched idly while the stranger crossed the street; wondered idly what was concealed in the awkward package he carried; and heard him, not so idly, inquire of Mrs. Peralta if Leah had come home yet. When he heard the stranger say that he would wait, Mr. Papadakis shed his weariness and leaned forward.

He, Spiros Papadakis, was the man who was waiting for Leah Webster to come home! He had been waiting for weeks—he, and no other! Who was this uncultured person with his crazy package? Mr. Papadakis consulted the lounging, disinterested shadows of his unknown neighbors along the block for some explanation. His eyes narrowed. His cigar glowed red. He had been fabulously cheated. He found the curtain rising, the stage set for a second act. What had gone before? Where had Leah met this comical person? Mr. Papadakis looked searchingly at the other man who waited for Leah, but got no explanation from his appearance.

JOE ONION declined an invitation to join Mrs. Peralta on her doorstep and leaned against the wall beside her, smoking a cigarette. With the prospect of seeing Leah any minute, he felt too nervous to sit down. Maybe Leah wouldn't remember him; maybe she wouldn't laugh when she saw what he had bought her—and the only reason for buying such a present had been to make her laugh. Joe laid his package on the sidewalk, and took off his hat. He punched out the crease, turned the hat around a few times, creased it again, and set it on the back of his head. A new hat never fit a man comfortably until he wore it on a binge. Although the hat fit him better than it had this morning, there was still room for improvement. With Whitey and Aleck tagging him, he hadn't had much of a day.

Having spent two hours in a steam bath and a swimming pool, Joe was sober now. The hand that Ronnie Bilbo had bitten had been properly treated against infection and swathed in a bandage; and the cut on his cheekbone was covered with a fresh square of medicinal gauze. But Joe grew more nervous by the minute. Suppose Leah didn't come directly home from work? Suppose, instead, she stopped off somewhere? Suppose another man brought her home. Realizing that he knew almost nothing about Leah's life or how she spent her time, he now wondered why he had not called her as soon as he found where she worked. He should not have left so much to chance.

Would he be able to recognize her, if he did see her? He thought he remembered quite well how she looked; but those glamorous descriptions he had given Whitey and Aleck—inspired by the picture in Gino's Barroom advertising Bella Campo wines —had somewhat confused his memory. He could not be sure.

Joe was released from his worried meditation by Leah's voice greeting the old woman on the doorstep. During the instant it took his startled scrutiny to ally the voice he remembered with the face he was not at all sure he remembered, Leah opened the front door.

'Wait a minute!' he called, stepping forward hastily.

Leah turned and looked at him. 'What is it?' she said. 'What do you want?'

'Don't you remember me?' Joe felt very foolish. Apparently, she had forgotten him. 'I met you Saturday night in the St. Regis,' he said. 'I was passing by, and thought I'd drop in for a minute and say hello.'

'Joe?' she said. 'Joe Onion.' She came down the steps and stood irresolutely looking up at him. Confronted by the man's actual presence, all the doubts and hesitations of the morning revived in her. His manner was so casual. If he ever suspected how she had gone looking for him, she felt as if she would die of shame.

'You keep late hours,' he said.

'Yes, don't I?' she replied. 'But I work pretty late.'

'So I hear,' said Joe. 'How are you?'

'Pretty well, thanks.' Leah was in a panic. He probably expected to be asked inside; but if she asked him in at such a late hour, after the way she had picked him up Saturday night, he would be sure to misunderstand. Besides, she had just remembered her unmade bed. She had known him such a short time, thought of him so intimately, searched for him so frantically, and given up so completely any hope of ever seeing him again, that his unexpected appearance left her with no knowledge of what to say or do. She fell back on the one topic of casual conversation she could think of. 'We had quite a rain today, didn't we?' she said.

'We certainly did. Does it often rain like it did today?'

'In the summer, yes. Nearly every day. But it's early this year. It doesn't usually begin until the middle of July.'

'I believe I read somewhere that the annual rainfall in New Orleans exceeds that of any large city in the United States except Miami and Mobile,' said Joe. His cigarette had gone out. He threw it away, and fumbled in his pocket for another. His face was burning. From the corner of his eye, he saw Mrs. Peralta making signs and motions toward the package he had left on the sidewalk. He couldn't possibly give such a present to a woman who looked as cool and dignified as Leah; and neither must Leah discover from the old woman how he had stood here waiting for her to come home. He must get her away before she found out about his package and himself. Joe lit another cigarette, shook the flame off the match, and flipped it with a great show of nonchalance. 'How about a cup of coffee at the French Market?' he said.

They walked along St. Philip Street toward Decatur, making polite conversation, a wall of icy reserve growing higher and thicker between them. Both wanted desperately to break through it; but each was afraid, before the seeming casualness of the other, to disclose how he felt.

They entered the coffee shop and sat down. The waiter, who had served Leah in the morning, came up to them in a clean apron. 'Hello, Miss,' he said to Leah. 'Ja ever find the red-headed guy you was lookin for this mawnin?'

'What?' said Leah, startled. Then, recognizing the waiter whose help she had sought when she had first started out to look for Joe, she tried hastily to cover up, to dismiss him as quickly as possible. 'Yes, thanks,' she said. 'I found him. Coffee and doughnuts, please.'

'Same here,' said Joe.

When the waiter had gone, Leah stole a covert glance at Joe. He was playing with the can of powdered sugar meant for the doughnuts, tapping it on the table, shaking it, tapping it again. Leah looked miserably away.

'Who were you looking for this morning?' Joe said thoughtfully.

'Nobody,' she replied. 'A friend . . .' She looked down at her hands. Joe was sprinkling them with powdered sugar.

'How did you know my last name?' he said.

'How did you find out where I lived?'

WHEN JOE AND LEAH walked away down St. Philip Street toward the French Market, Mr. Papadakis discarded the cold butt of his cigar. 'Pah!' he said. He lit a fresh one.

Mrs. Tarantino watched Leah and Joe out of sight before she turned to Mrs. Peralta. 'Well!' she said breathlessly. 'Well!'

'Oh, yes,' said Mrs. Peralta. She was not surprised. As she bent over to pick up the package Joe had left on the sidewalk, a woman screamed.

The shrill sound split the street wide open. The pavement cracked. Walls toppled. Doors popped open. Shutters bulged.

In the hush that followed, Mrs. Peralta straightened slowly and looked to both sides of her, and looked at the moon. Mrs. Tarantino put her hand to her throat. In the next block, Mrs. Ferrabee gave up hope that Thomas would ever come home and went inside her house. Mr. Gregory reached for his wife's hand; but Mrs. Gregory had just smelled her roast burning in the oven and had rushed to save it. Mr. Papadakis was coldly analytical. The scream had come from the barroom 'For Colored Patrons Only.' A colored woman had screamed. The cause? No doubt trivial. The result? The patrol wagon might or might not come —probably not. Such passionate outbursts were almost nightly occurrences. So, Mr. Papadakis summed up coldly, if a woman wishes to scream, let her scream. But he hoped she wouldn't do it again. His spine still tingled.

Twenty minutes later, the patrol wagon still had not come.

But Thomas Ferrabee was coming; and he was worried, and stone broke. Passing the open plaza before the St. Ann Street end of the French Market, he had seen a man and a woman sitting on a park bench with their arms around each other. They had been sitting very quietly, their heads resting on each other's shoulders—so relaxed they might have been asleep. Thomas Ferrabee did not know, of course, that their names happened to be Leah Webster and Joe Onion; he knew only that they seemed about the same age as his wife and himself. Now, what would middle-aged people like his wife and himself be doing on a park bench at such a late hour, in such an attitude? The attitude of mutual trust and relaxation troubled him. It made him remember himself and Mrs. Ferrabee in their courting days; and he was ashamed for what he had done.

His evening of pleasure had been expensive. He had meant to offer Mrs. Ferrabee no explanation whatsoever; but now, feeling sorry, he was trying to think of some plausible excuse for his late homecoming and his empty pockets when, a block from home, around a corner, he encountered an idea in the shape of a blond, part Persian cat.

The cat was stepping jauntily along the sidewalk with her nose and tail in the air when Mr. Ferrabee saw her. She looked expensive. He bent down and scrabbled his fingernails on his pants leg—an enticing sound. 'Kitty, kitty,' called Thomas Ferrabee. The cat paused and looked at him coyly. He cleared his throat and tried again. 'Pretty kitty, pretty kitty,' he said. 'D'you want a home?' She came to him and rubbed against his leg. He picked her up. She purred in his arms.

He turned the corner. His door was unlatched. He sidled in. 'Thomas!' said Mrs. Ferrabee.

'God bless me,' said Thomas Ferrabee, in a guilty voice. 'Here I am.'

Rudy sat up in bed. 'Mama,' he said, 'papa's got a kitty . . . papa, mama don't like kitties.'

'I tole you, go to sleep,' said his mother, gingerly touching the cat which Thomas placed on the bed.

'Guaranteed pure Persian,' said Thomas, stroking the soft fur. 'They come expensive.'

Rudy pounded the pillow with his fists. 'I h-had a little kitty,' he sobbed, 'an you w-wudden lemme keep 'im. I want my little kitty!'

'What's the matter with the boy?' said Thomas.

'He's been stepping on his lower lip all day,' said Mrs. Ferrabee. 'Damien promised to take him to a baseball game, and forgot.'

'Guaranteed pure Persian,' said Thomas, unlacing his shoes. 'She cost me twenty dollars.'

'So much?' Mrs. Ferrabee's heart sank as she thought of the rent. She knew the cat for the tramp she was. She didn't like night-prowling cats, or women who resembled them. Thomas had laid a cross on her tonight; and there was nothing for her to do but to accept the cross and carry it. How else would she eat?

'Mama hates kitties! Mama hates kitties!' Rudy cried in his pillow.

'You heard me,' said Mrs. Ferrabee in a dangerous voice. 'Go to sleep.'

Thomas Ferrabee turned off the light and got into bed. Mrs. Ferrabee kicked the cat to the floor; but a minute later it was coiled on her feet. Its loud purr filled the room.

ANOTHER FRAGMENT parted from another unknown planet; arched pale and cool in the broad circle of upper moonlight; glowed redder and hotter as it fell. Nobody heard it fall. Apparently nothing happened except that Mr. Gregory couldn't stand it any longer, and called *Josephine!*—and somebody, his face turned up to watch the star, stumbled over the paper bag in front of the Ferrabee house where the blond cat's abandoned kitten lay sleeping with its nose in its paws. Mewing and spitting, the kitten projected itself from the paper bag and fled, all furred in terror, through the gigantic shadows of the street.

Mrs. Peralta was bathing her face thoughtfully in the moonlight when somebody called her name. Who called for Josephine? Mrs. Peralta looked questioningly at Mr. Papadakis. But he had not called. Accompanied by a woman, he was just opening his front door.

'Well!' said Mrs. Tarantino breathlessly. 'Duh things you see from your own front doorstep, Mrs. Peralta!'

'All day long,' Mrs. Peralta agreed.

'To think what goes on right under your nose!'

'People pass,' said Mrs. Peralta comfortably.

They are all alike, thought Mr. Papadakis, climbing the stairs with a strange woman. He was still a little worried, for he was unable to reconcile his possession of such wisdom with the fact that he could have been such a fool about Leah Webster.

But all such irreconcilables were reconciled in Mrs. Peralta, who had forgotten Mr. Papadakis for the time being, but would know him for a good man when she saw him again.

Mrs. Peralta looked at the trash fire in front of the Cansino Fruit and Vegetable Stand. It was almost out. No, it was burning high again. Somebody had just thrown a newspaper on it from a passing car—the day's record of rainfall and scandal, of death and birth. The bright sparks climbed and drifted in a wide, slow spiral, and went out. The dancing walls steadied under the inextinguishable moonlight and the insect-circled lamps. The dance was over; but it had been sweet to be young and dance. Mrs. Peralta picked up Leah's forgotten present from the sidewalk. From the size and shape of the package, she thought it must be a beach hat with a brim probably four feet across. If Leah didn't want it, she knew exactly what it could be used for.

'Heigh-ho,' said Mrs. Peralta, and bade Mrs. Tarantino good night, and went inside.

When she had soaked her feet, she lit a kerosene lamp and placed it on the floor in a corner of the room. She liked lamplight much better than electric light. If Maudie hadn't been so afraid she would set the house on fire, she would have preferred to use it all the time. Unknown to Maudie, she still used a lamp for the ritual of trimming her corns. Lamplight was so cozy.

Scissors in hand, she sat down. The floor creaked. The lamp chimney shuddered. The breeze shouldered the lamp flame sideways, smoking the chimney. Mrs. Peralta adjusted the wick. Seated flat on the floor, she hoisted one knee, gathered her nightgown between her legs, and moved the lamp in a semicircle along the floor until its light shone directly on her bare foot.

'Tchk, tchk, tchk,' she said pityingly.

The foot did not seem to belong to her, but to be a separate, lonely live thing, gnarled and twisted by suffering. She felt sorry for it. She stroked it gently.

She picked up the scissors and pared the corns. Presently, she shifted her position and hoisted the other foot into the lamplight. The floor creaked again.

'Tchk, tchk, tchk,' said Mrs. Peralta, repeating the ritual.

The fleet shadow of a cat streaked past the alley door. The light went out in the Tarantinos' house. Mr. Tarantino must have come home. Over by the docks, a switch engine coupled onto a string of freight cars. The train made a lot of noise before it finally moved out of hearing. Mrs. Peralta yawned. It had been nice to ride on trains and dance; but now it pleased her to be quiet. For a minute, it was so quiet she heard a cricket singing under the house.

A moth blew against the lamp chimney and stuck there, blistering. Mrs. Peralta dropped her scissors and set it free, and paused to look over the lamp, over the sharp peak of the Tarantinos' roof, into the night sky. The moon was out of sight, but moonlight hung a luminous halo around the brick chimney. God was good. Where the lottery tickets had lain under her pillow this morning, now lay a dollar and seventeen cents—and more tickets. God was so good. It had been a lucky day.

Crouched in the small circle of smoky lamplight, Mrs. Peralta rocked drowsily backward and forward, rubbing her feet and praying for good luck tomorrow. Her shaggy shadow rocked with her on the wall. When she was so sleepy she could scarcely move, she blew out her lamp.

Profound, pacific, immense, the sky stretched over her life.

THE END